# DIABLO

## A NIGHT REBELS MC ROMANCE

## CHIAH WILDER

I love hearing from my readers. You can email me at chiahwilder@gmail.com.

Make sure you sign up for my newsletter so you can keep up with my new releases, special sales, free short stories, and other treats only available to newsletter readers. When you sign up, you will receive a FREE hot and steamy novella. Sign up at: http://eepurl.com/bACCL1.

Visit me on facebook at facebook.com/Chiah-Wilder-1625397261063989.

# Chapter One

THE LARGE ROOM was loud and noisy, and aggression hung in the air. There was an aura of restlessness as the spectators moved about as if trying to spend their excess energy. Faded brown spots dotted the checkerboard linoleum floor, metal walls and beams gave the room an industrial look, and a metallic scent of copper mixed with sweat permeated the room. A square ring was the centerpiece in the room; four parallel rows of rope enclosed it. The glittering stars blinked through hundreds of small square windows.

A man in his late forties stood in the middle of the ring, a microphone in his hands. Gray streaks at the temples colored his brown hair, and his toned body shone under the bright white lights above the platform. The crowd of about two hundred and fifty turned their eyes to the man.

"That's Bloody Knuckles," someone from the crowd said.

"Thank you all for coming out tonight. We have a great lineup of fighters for your entertainment." The man paused for a few dramatic seconds. "Let the fights begin." His deep voice echoed through the room.

The lights flashed three times, then blasting hard rock music shook the walls. An electric tension filled the air as the spectators stood waiting for the first set of fighters to step into the ring. The crowd, who would soon be cheering, cussing, and whistling as the two fighters connected their punches, enjoyed the adrenaline rush of seeing hardcore fights.

Diablo, sergeant-at-arms for the Night Rebels MC, stood behind the audience, his eyes constantly moving. He worked as a bouncer for underground fights to earn some extra money. He'd done many gigs at small warehouses such as this for the past two years. His reputation as a no-nonsense enforcer who kept his nose out of the promoters' business earned him a solid reputation on the illegal fighting circuits.

That night was the first time he'd worked with fights organized by Bloody Knuckles. Diablo had heard about him; he was known as the kingpin of underground fighting in southwestern Colorado. As Diablo scanned the crowd, he saw the tautness of excitement etched on their faces. He spotted Chains, Army, Skull, Brutus, and Sangre—some of his Night Rebels brothers—among the sea of faces.

Then the crowd went wild as two men, bare-knuckled, shirtless, barefoot, and wearing black boxer shorts, walked up to the ring. They had a no-holds-barred attitude as they stepped into the ring, ready to draw blood on their opponent. Underground fighting brought strangers together to pummel each other for the entertainment of the crowd.

"Are you fighting tonight?" a woman in a short spandex skirt and tight sleeveless top yelled in Diablo's ear.

He ran his eyes quickly over her body and laughed dryly; he'd lost count of how many times he'd been asked that question. He shook his head and averted his gaze to the two men with raised fists.

The woman lingered.

"I'm working here. You have to move on." Diablo gave her shoulder a soft push.

"When do you get off work?" she asked.

"No reason for you to know that." He shifted his body away from her. Slowly, she walked away and disappeared into the crowd.

Diablo was used to the attention he received from men and women alike. Men tended to either be intimidated by his six-foot-four size or see it as a challenge. He'd lost count of the number of times guys started shit with him, sure they were going to prove they could beat his ass. During those altercations, he left bloodied and broken assholes on the floors of bars as he walked away practically unscathed.

Women were another story. They flocked to him, loving his toned chest and arms, his dark beard, and his colorful tats. His shaved head, ear tunnels, and penetrating stare lent to the danger and excitement a lot of the women craved. But he wasn't interested.

He didn't like the way women threw themselves at him. If he was interested, he'd let them know, but the chicks never gave him a chance. They always wanted to touch his firm biceps, run their fingers over his tattoos, and tug gently at his beard. He knew they wanted to fuck him because he wore the Night Rebels patch; they didn't seem to give a damn about *him*. All they wanted was the thrill of screwing a bad boy because they saw his height, his toned chest and arms, and his dark beard.

He usually didn't give them the time of day. When he wanted carnal indulgence he always went with the club girls. He wasn't looking for a woman in his life; he'd gone down that path once, and that was more than enough for him.

"The testosterone is bouncing off the fucking walls!" Bloody Knuckles bellowed in his ear. Diablo gave a curt nod. "Damn, man, don't you *feel* it? I love this shit. It's raw and unfiltered. It's combat at its most honest and ruthless state."

Diablo stared straight ahead, surveying the two men punching it out in the ring. Sprinkles of blood fell around them like thin mist. The two guys didn't look tough. *Probably work in a bank or a law firm.* In the two years that Diablo had been bouncing for the underground fighting world, he'd learned that the fighters came together for a variety of reasons: to release their anger and stress, to find their masculinity, and to go against the grain of normalcy in their safe lives. Fighting made them gods for that twenty or thirty minutes in the ring.

The crowd yelled and screamed as one of the fighters unleashed several punches on his opponent. There was a savageness that appealed to the crowd as the fighters went head-to-head in the ring. The more blood spilled, the crazier the crowd cheered. Diablo figured the spectators' anger was unleashed on each punch and kick; they were out for blood, and the more there was the better time they had. Betting on the fighters was another thrill, and big money could be made depending on how large the crowd was and who was in the ring.

"Tonight's gonna bring in a lot of dough. I told the other bouncers to be on alert." Bloody Knuckles clapped Diablo's forearm.

Diablo took a step away from the promoter. "I'm always on alert, and don't fuckin' touch me again."

The promoter's eyes widened, and then he laughed as he smoothed his hair back. "You bikers are so fucking sensitive. I keep forgetting that." He glanced at Diablo's stoic face. "I'm gonna circulate. If you need something, come find me."

Diablo narrowed his eyes as he watched him walk away. There was something about the man that he didn't like. *He's trying too hard for me to like him. I don't trust him. He better fucking pay me or I'll split his head open.*

Half the crowd cheered while the other half booed. He snapped his gaze to the ring and saw the blond-haired fighter crumpled on the ground. A short man with wiry black hair and beady eyes entered the ring, bent over, then blew a whistle. The loud music shut off and an eerie silence fell over the room.

After a couple seconds, a man in the crowd yelled, "What the fuck? Is the fight over?"

The wiry-haired man raised his hands. "Striker is passed out. The fight is over. McKinnley is the winner." A burst of cheers, whistles, and claps moved through the room like a tidal wave.

The rules surrounding the fights were simple: the fighters could do just about anything to one another's unarmed bodies, no shirts or shoes, and if a fighter called it quits or lost consciousness, the fight was over. Striker had lost consciousness, and the ones who'd bet on McKinnley had just made a shitload of money.

A couple of men carted Striker out, and a couple others threw buckets of water on the platform to wash off the blood and ready the floor for the next fight. The overhead music filled the place again and four women in scanty outfits gyrated and shook their butts on small stages, entertaining the audience until the next fight began.

Diablo saw Army, Chains, and Sangre walking toward him. He knew they'd bet on the fight, and from their smiling faces, he guessed they'd placed their money on McKinnley.

"Hey, dude. That was a good fight. I could've whipped both their asses at the same time, but for what it was, it was good. Did you bet on this one?" Army said.

Diablo shook his head.

"Too bad. The odds were good."

Skull came over, a buxom brunette on his arm. "How many fights are on for tonight?"

"Four more." Diablo recognized the woman as one of the entertainers who worked for Bloody Knuckles. All the underground fights he'd worked had women who were stacked and willing to shake their bodies between fights. Most of the time, they'd turn tricks on the side. Knowing how greedy the promoter was, Diablo was pretty damn sure he took a percentage of anything they made outside of dancing.

The brunette smiled at Diablo. "Are you doing okay?" she said into his ear as she leaned against him.

Diablo nodded.

"You know each other?" Skull asked.

"He works for Bloody Knuckles, same as me." She ran her fingers down Skull's bare arm. "I like your muscles." She licked her lips.

"Aren't you gonna introduce us to your chick?" Army asked.

"Yeah. This is…. What did you say your name was, sugar?"

She pushed out her lower lip, her brows creasing. "You forgot already?" Skull gave a half shrug. "I don't think I should tell you."

"Her name's Emerald," Diablo said.

Skull and Army looked at him. "Damn, that's good, brother," Skull said.

Emerald smiled widely and pulled out of Skull's grasp. Wrapping her hands around Diablo's bicep, she squeezed it while saying, "Thanks for remembering. I told your friend my name at least four times and he still forgot it."

Diablo's jaw jutted out. "I'm good with names."

"Doesn't matter. I still think you're sweet." She placed a small kiss on his jawline. He stiffened and she dropped her hands to her side.

"Looks like you're tryin' to take my main squeeze from me, dude." Skull laughed and the other brothers joined in.

Diablo crossed his arms and jerked his head to the ring. "Another fight's ready to start."

The brothers turned their attention forefront, then lifted their chins at Diablo and went back into the crowd.

The next two men looked more buff than the last two, a fact that wasn't lost on the spectators as a palpable frenetic energy wrapped around the ring. "To my left is Freddie," the small man announced as a medium height, dark-haired guy smiled to the crowd. "And on my right is Toque." A husky man of the same height as Freddie bowed to the audience. Then the fight began.

As Diablo watched, he could feel the adrenaline pumping in the room, and he realized that was what kept the people coming back; the rush was addictive and they needed their fix. Several women dressed in short, spandex black skirts and tight, plunging tops strutted in their spiked heels in front of the ring, trying to garner attention from the fighters. They were fangirls. It reminded Diablo of the hang-arounds who'd line up for one of the Night Rebels' weekend parties, hoping to get picked to come inside and party with a dangerous biker.

Plastered against the wall, a slight and delicate-looking woman drew his attention. From under her unkempt brown hair peeked eyes of hazel and honey. They shone like polished stone in the sunshine and held a fair amount of distrust in them. The connection between him and the woman was only a fraction of a second, but in that brief snapshot of time, a cry for help had been sent. He kept his gaze fixed on her; she darted hers everywhere, but it kept coming back to his. Shouts, jeers, claps, and whistles bounced around him, but he was transfixed by the woman trying to make herself invisible.

"Fuck!"

Metal slamming against metal diverted his attention away from her. He tore through the crowd, shoving people out of his way. Two gangly twentysomethings had thrown some metal chairs at the ring and were trying to slip under the ropes. Freddie and Toque were locked in a grueling match.

Diablo grabbed each of the troublemakers by the back of the neck and dragged them away from the ring. The men, startled at first, thrashed and cussed as Diablo threw them on the floor. Before they could react, he gripped their shirts and raised them to their feet, then locked an arm around each of their necks as he hauled them away.

Another bouncer dashed over, offering assistance, but Diablo shook his head. "I've got this," he mouthed as he walked toward the exit. In a matter of seconds, he'd thrown the two men face down on the asphalt. "I don't wanna see you back in here. Ever." He kicked both of them in their sides. "You fuckin' got that?"

One of the men groaned while the other mumbled something under his breath.

Diablo went back inside, tilting his chin at the doorman. As he walked toward the crowd, his gaze went to the wall where he'd seen the woman. She was gone. A tinge of disappointment ran through him. *Where the hell is she?* He scanned the room, but she was nowhere to be found.

"We've got a winner here! Fuck, that was a surprise," the wiry-haired man boomed in the microphone.

Diablo looked at the ring. With his nose bleeding and his eyes swelling, Freddie's skin glistened as he lay on the floor defeated. Toque, mouth bloodied and brow swollen, hoisted his arms in the air. The crowd roared as they celebrated his win. Sweat mixed with blood poured down his back as he left the ring.

For the next few hours men pummeled each other, blood was washed away, and some people made a hell of a lot of money. Diablo kept his eye out for the woman from earlier, but for the rest of the night, he didn't see her. After the last fight, people poured out of the venue, some happy with their wins while others glowered and shoved their hands into their pockets. Army, Skull, Sangre, and Brutus each had a woman wrapped around them as they bumped fists with Diablo. Chains had a wad of cash in his hands and grinned broadly. "I made a ton of dough. Damn sweet. Watching all the fights pumped me the hell up. I wanna punch the shit outta someone."

Diablo laughed. "You should show up to be one of the fighters."

"Maybe I will. I'd love to take out some aggression on some punk. Show the eight-to-five fucks what it means to live it rough all the time." He chuckled.

"If you do, let me know 'cause my bet'll be on you," Army said before he slipped his hand onto the blonde woman's breast. She giggled and snuggled closer to him.

"Even though bouncers aren't allowed to gamble, I'd place money on you," Diablo said.

"I can't wait to party at your clubhouse," the busty redhead who was glued to Sangre's side said. The other women agreed.

"We're gonna have all kinds of fun," Brutus promised as he tugged the woman with him closer.

"We'll see you back at the clubhouse," Skull said as the brothers went out the door.

Out of the corner of his eye, Diablo saw Bloody Knuckles coming toward him, a curvy woman half his age hanging on his arm. "Damn good night," he said as he came up to Diablo. "You handled those two assholes real good. I got another fight planned for next Saturday. Can I count on you to be here?" He pulled out a load of cash.

Diablo nodded. "Same time?" He ignored the bleached blonde who kept pulling her top down and sighing loudly.

"Yep. Everything's the same." He counted out ten one-hundred-dollar bills in Diablo's hand.

"You promised to take me to Colorado Springs next weekend," the blonde whined.

The promoter turned to her and kissed her quickly on her shiny lips.

"The weekend after. For sure."

"That's what you said last weekend." She pushed away from him.

"Don't be like that, baby. You like all the fancy clothes and jewelry I get you, don't you? Well, if I don't make money, how am I gonna keep you in the lifestyle you love?" He nuzzled her neck. She stared at Diablo and smiled.

Diablo cleared his throat. "I'll see you next Saturday." He walked away knowing the busty blonde was staring at him still. She was wasting her time; she wasn't his type. He swung his leg over his blue metallic Harley and pushed the ignition button. The iron beast sprung to life, purring loudly.

Before he turned onto the old highway, he looked back. And *her* sparkling eyes watched him. He tipped his head to her. She didn't move. When he turned back toward the venue, she moved away from the window. Then the lights went off, blackness shrouding the small warehouse.

He circled around the parking lot; then, with a hopeful glance backward, he roared down the empty highway, the reflectors glowing eerily when his headlight hit them. The inky sky shimmered with thousands of stars as the warm air caressed him.

When he went to his room later and lay on his bed, he didn't doubt for a moment that the woman's shining hazel eyes would dance in his head. *They're already dancing around in my mind. Next week, I gotta find out who she is.* Since she was still in the place when he left, he knew she was part of the staff and not a spectator or crazed fangirl. He didn't know why, but he wanted to talk to her. Wanted to get to know her.

He breathed in deeply. He loved riding alone on quiet roads in the dark. It made it seem like he was the only person in the whole universe. The solitude wrapped around him like a comfortable blanket.

He craved quietness. A lot of people feared it, but he'd become best friends with it. That wasn't the case for most of his life. Before he came to Alina, he'd lived amid chaos, noise, and turmoil. His childhood was fraught with grief, fear, and anger.

He shook his head as the memories of a past he wanted to forget faded into each other. He concentrated on the road and relished in the silence the night brought as he headed to the clubhouse.

# Chapter Two

"**G**ET OUT OF the way, you stupid bitch!" Emerald pushed past Fallon, nearly knocking her over. She had a rag over her head as she rushed over to the bathroom.

"Don't you pay any attention to her," Sylvia said as she pulled tightly on the sash around her robe. "She's pretty hungover from partying with them bikers last night. Come with me and we can have a cup of coffee in the kitchen."

Fallon smiled. Sylvia was the only ring girl who was nice to her; the others treated her like she was either a piece of trash or a nobody. Sylvia usually told the women to stop picking on her if she heard them making fun of her. Fallon appreciated her efforts, but she'd learned to ignore the girls, and a lot of other people as well.

Emerald came out of the bathroom, her face white as a sheet, her hair disheveled. She groaned as she brought her hand to her head, then staggered to a room down the hall and disappeared into it. Sylvia laughed. "Serves her right. She'll be a raving bitch all day. You better stay outta her way. Let's get that coffee." She grabbed Fallon's hand and led her to the kitchen.

The kitchen was small but convenient, and the ring girls had full use of it. Each of the six women had their own room, but they had three bathrooms they had to share. There was a large family room adjacent to the kitchen where the girls could watch television. Most of the time, they'd start arguing if they were in the family room together for too long.

Fallon took the thick mug Sylvia handed her and wrapped her fingers around its heat. She took a sip, then padded into the family room and sank down on one of the cushy chairs. Ahead of her stood the expanse of the desert through the picture window. She loved staring at the desolation of the land on Sunday mornings. Most of the ring girls were still in bed, either hungover from too much partying or exhausted from too much screwing. Her dad and his wife—her step-bitch—stayed in bed until early afternoon, so she had a slice of the luxury that was solitude every Sunday for a few hours.

"You okay? I'm gonna go to my room, but if you want me to hang with you, I can."

"I'm good. Thanks, Sylvia." She took another sip of coffee, the black liquid warming her.

When Sylvia had gone, she breathed out, her body finally beginning to relax. She hated living at the warehouse, but she usually spent weekends there because Shanna, her father's wife, hated her being around. Her dad deferred to her as he always did, and he gave Fallon a bunch of chores to do at the warehouse every weekend. Shanna acted like Fallon was a child even though she was only six years younger than Shanna. During the week she lived with them, but she stayed in her room most of the time.

She tucked her legs under her and watched the dust swirl around in the morning wind. The night before had been the first time she'd seen someone who intrigued her. She wasn't sure who he was, but she'd been thinking about him ever since she spotted him among all those people. *It was a sign.* And she believed it because her eyes had gravitated to his. What were the chances of that? After all, there were so many people there, and everyone was transfixed on the fight but him and her.

Goose bumps carpeted her arms as his face flitted in her mind. It was a handsome face but anger and distrust painted it. His eyes were dark and shone like chips of black onyx, and he had a bent nose that could pass for a streetfighter's. Even though his gaze was tough, she swore it'd softened when he looked at her. *I'm probably imagining all this. He was probably trying to figure out if I belonged in there or not.* But she didn't really think so. She knew he felt the connection she'd felt, even if it had only lasted a blink of an eye.

There was no doubt about it—he was built. From where she stood, he had colorful tattoos all the way up both of his arms. She giggled, then looked around quickly. No one was around. She giggled louder. When she'd seen the tattoos, she had an overwhelming urge to go over to him and get a better look at them. She wanted to touch them… maybe even lick them.

Fallon sucked in her breath. *I have to stop thinking like that. He probably wanted to take me upstairs and fuck me, but he didn't have a chance since that ruckus started by the ring. He ran in to break it up.* Then her eyes widened and she swallowed. *I bet he was one of the bouncers. I've never seen him before, but I didn't see Roy last night either.* All of a sudden, her stomach flipped over when she thought about the upcoming fights on Saturday. A part of her, buried deep down inside, wanted him to be there again. Even though he looked like he could break someone's neck with one hand, she was curious about him.

The loud voices from the television made her jump and spill her coffee on her freshly laundered shirt. She craned her neck and saw Heidi shuffle in, a frown on her face. "Don't you have to hose down the ring and stages?" She plopped on the couch and stretched out, her eyes glued to the TV screen.

"I've got all afternoon to do that," Fallon said softly.

"Last time you did a shitty job, so you better take some time doing it. My stage was sticky. It was fuckin' gross."

Fallon pushed up from the chair and left the room, disappointment over her morning being ruined climbing up her spine and pricking her nerves. *One of these days I'm gonna tell all of them exactly what I think of them.*

She went back to her room—a closet her dad had converted—and changed into her work clothes. Pulling her hair into a high ponytail, she locked her door and made her way downstairs to the room where the fights took place. She hated seeing the dried blood, vomit, and spit, and when she took a hose to it, the mixture of scents was putrid. *I have to get out of here. I'm twenty-one years old and all I've ever known is living with my dad and his world. I can't fucking stand it anymore.*

She limped over to the utility room and pulled out the long hose. As the water dissolved evidence of the violence from the night before, her mind floated back to the man with the dark beard and penetrating gaze. She couldn't get him out of her mind, which surprised her since she didn't trust men and tried to stay away from them as much as possible.

"You finished in here?" Jose asked as he took a cigarette out.

"Yeah. Did I miss any spots?" She squinted against the sun's rays pouring through the window panes.

"It looks good. If I find something, I'll get it. A lady shouldn't be doing this shitty job. What's your dad thinking?"

She rubbed her neck. "At least it gets me away from everyone."

"You should be going out with friends and have a *novio*."

"Friends are fickle, and I don't want a boyfriend." She dragged the hose behind her.

"Then you haven't found the right amigos. And you get the right *novio* and you'll be so happy. A good man makes a woman feel like she's the best woman in the world." He smiled, the deep lines in his tanned face running into each other.

"I think those men only exist in fairy tales and movies." She yanked hard and the hose curled around her feet. "Oh!" She flung her arms out, grasping wildly to hold on to something so she wouldn't fall.

Jose rushed over and caught her under her arms as she was ready to hit the floor. "See? You need a man to make sure you don't have to do this shit. You okay?"

Smoothing down her T-shirt, she nodded. "I just lose my balance easier than normal people." Her cheeks burned.

"What's normal? Just because you got a limp you don't think you're normal? You're better than the *putas* who sleep all day and make fun of you. You're a good girl, Fallon."

She smiled. "Thanks, Jose." *I wonder what he'd say if he knew I was a whore too.* "I better get going. I have to wash all the towels and rags.

Thanks for helping me."

"I'll see you this weekend. Take it easy."

Jose was an okay guy. Sometimes he drank too much and would fight with Sam, the announcer with wiry hair, but he always protected her. He was better than her father. She wished she could say that her dad changed since he'd married Shanna, but it wouldn't be true; her dad was a mean sonofabitch way before Shanna ever entered the picture. And now he thought he was the big honcho because he ran illegal fights where men spilled each other's blood and other men bet on them. *Real respectable job, Dad. Fuck you! And Shanna too!*

She threw the towels into the washing machine and slammed down the lid. Sitting on a chair in the corner, she took out a book from her back pocket and opened it. The words blurred together, and she couldn't concentrate on what she was reading. The handsome face of the stranger from the night before kept bumping around in her mind. Whenever she thought about seeing him again, her insides lurched.

Sighing, she looked back down at her book. It was going to be a very long week until Saturday.

# Chapter Three

DIABLO CHOMPED ON his nachos as he watched the race cars zip around the track on the big-screen TV in the main room. He took a long drink of his Corona, then lifted his chin at Muerto and Goldie as they approached.

"Hey, big man, how're the nachos?" Goldie asked as he looped his foot under a chair and pulled it out.

"Awesome," he said as he picked up a chip loaded with cheese, beans, and ground beef.

"Heard the fights this past Saturday made a few of the brothers a lot of dough." Goldie motioned to the prospect to come over.

"Yeah. I was surprised you didn't go. It seemed like your kind of thing." He looked at Muerto. "And yours too. Maybe Raven is keeping you home all the time?"

"Bring me a Coors, then go to the kitchen and have Lena make me some nachos," Goldie said to the prospect before turning to Diablo. "I had two chicks occupying me on Saturday night." He wiggled his eyebrows.

"Raven's cool with me going out with the brothers, but I wanted to take her for a ride over to Cortez. We had dinner and played some pool."

"Did she hustle?" Army asked as he joined the group.

"Nah. She told the guys she was fucking good, but you know how it is." He looked fixedly at Army. "A dude always thinks he can beat a chick. It's the way we're wired. Anyway, a few played, lost, and she won a bunch of money. I had to beat the shit outta one of the guys who disrespected her before we rode back to Alina. It was a fuckin' good time." Muerto brought his beer bottle to his lips.

"When's the next fight?" Army asked.

"This Saturday." Diablo guzzled the rest of his beer.

"I'm in," Goldie said as he dove into his nachos.

"Count me in too," Muerto said.

"We should enter the fights. It'd be cool to bust someone's head open." Brutus joined the conversation.

"We do that all the time," Diablo replied, and the brothers laughed in agreement.

"The ring girls are hot pieces of ass. It's worth it just to see them. A few of them came back to the clubhouse with us and partied." Brutus looked at the food on the table. "Lena's making nachos?"

"Yeah. Tell Ruger to get you some." Goldie picked up a tortilla chip and shoved it in his mouth.

"They wear these bras that make their tits look big and up to their chins, these sexy panties, and lace stockings. They wiggle around between the fights. The ones I've been to in Silverado and Durango just had the fighters and that's it. This is more like a legit show but it isn't. The promoter does a good job." Army leaned back.

"Now for sure I'm in for Saturday night," Goldie said.

"Where do they hold the fights?" Muerto asked.

Diablo pushed his empty plate away from him. "About twenty miles east of Tula. The combats are in a small warehouse. From what I could see, Bloody Knuckles owns the building. I think the ring girls and some of the dudes working for him live there."

"Bloody Knuckles is his road name? Fuckin' awesome!" Goldie pounded the table with his fist.

"He's not a biker. It's his nickname. You know, something he uses for promotion. The guy's an asshole, but he pays me well."

"You're not making enough money from the club's businesses?" Brutus said as he picked up a tortilla chip.

"I need more." Diablo's jaw tightened.

"That's the fuckin' problem with money... you always need more."

Goldie pulled out a bag of weed and a pack of rolling paper. "Who wants a joint?"

"You finished your nachos already? Damn, dude, you must've been hungry. I'll take one for later." Brutus held out his hand.

While the brothers talked, Diablo's mind wandered to the honey-eyed woman he'd seen the previous Saturday. She'd been on his mind for the past several days. He looked forward to working the next show mainly for the hope of seeing her again. He'd decided if he did, he'd make it a point to go up to her. He wanted to hear her voice and find out how she fit into the gritty underworld of illegal fighting.

"You tuning us out, Diablo?" Goldie's voice sliced through his thoughts.

"Just thinking 'bout something. Were you asking me something?"

"Just asking if you want a joint."

Diablo nodded. Inhaling deeply, he diverted his attention to the TV screen. Around and around the track the colorful race cars sped. He stared at them and the face of his brother popped into his mind. Beau loved race cars. Diablo remembered the summer he turned twelve was when Beau decided he wanted to become a race car driver. Beau was a year and a half younger than Diablo, and they'd walk together to the local tracks in Salt Lake City. They'd pay the small entrance fee and scramble up the bleachers to watch a bunch of metal heaps drive around a track.

That summer they must've seen a couple races a week, and at each one of them Beau had told Diablo that he wanted to be a race car driver when he grew up. His dreams were spun out during that one summer where their lives almost mimicked a fucking Norman Rockwell painting. It was before the Department of Social Services took them away from their mother and Beau gave up his dreams for the prick of a needle.

"What the fuck's with you?" Goldie's voice cut through the memories.

Diablo shook his head. "Sorry, dude." He looked at Goldie.

"I was asking if you'd gambled on the last fights?"

"Nope. I can't do that since I work there."

"Do you have some insider info about the fighters for this weekend's match?"

"I know a few of them 'cause I've seen 'em when I was working the shows in other towns. Spider has a mean punch, so I'd go with him. Danny's good but it'll depend on who he's up against. I don't know who else will be fighting. That's usually determined the day of. It depends who shows up. It's really random."

"You gonna keep working with this Bloody fucking Knuckles?" Army said while the brothers chuckled.

Haunting hazel eyes from a delicate face flashed through Diablo's mind. "Yeah."

Muerto's chair scraped on the floor as he pushed it out. "I gotta get to the pool hall. Later."

"I'll walk out with you," Diablo said as he stood up.

Outside, Muerto bumped fists with him, then jumped on his Harley and took off. Diablo sat on his bike, images of the woman at the fights, Beau, and his mother strung out on crack blazing across his mind. He switched on the motor and his bike vibrated underneath him. He needed to take a long ride to clear away the images that kept running through his head. Ever since the previous Saturday, his head was a clusterfuck of shit from his past, and the chick he'd seen at the fights was front and center. Why a woman he'd only seen for a short moment should stay with him was beyond comprehension, but she did.

He veered his Harley onto the back road and increased his speed. Riding fast always cleared his mind, and he needed to think clearly. The sand-filled wind pricked his skin like a thousand needles. It was good; it made him feel alive.

Picking up speed, he flew down the roads that crisscrossed the desert. He kept going, harder and faster, until it was like he was flying higher than a bird. And it was at that point that he was able to push her out of his mind.

# Chapter Four

O N SATURDAY NIGHT, Diablo pulled his Harley behind the small warehouse outside of Tula. The setting sun made the building shimmer as it caught the rose-colored rays from the west. Jose was outside smoking a joint when Diablo came to the back door.

"Hey, bro. Ready for tonight?" Jose grinned.

"Yeah." Diablo grasped the doorknob.

"You don't talk much, do you? The other bouncer, Rocky, is the opposite of you. He's always bragging about how many heads he's cracked." Jose sucked in a long drag on his joint.

Diablo swung the door open and went into the darkened room. Sam stood off to the side crossing and uncrossing his arms as Bloody Knuckles talked to him, their voices inaudible. A few of the ring girls stood on the small stages stretching out their limbs. Emerald waved to him while she bent down real low, her breasts practically falling out of the tight push-up bra she wore. He walked by without a side glance.

His eyes darted around the room, seeing everyone but the one he'd been thinking about all week. He pressed his lips together when he saw Bloody Knuckles coming toward him.

"You're a bit early," the promoter said. Diablo just stared at him. "Should be a good fight. A couple of the guys battling it out tonight have an amateur rep in the neighboring counties. I've hired a few extra guys to help you, Rocky, and Moe out." He wiped the corners of his mouth. "Uh... I guess that's all. We got some chow upstairs in the kitchen if you want. Might as well relax for a few as we set things up."

"Does the kitchen have any beer?"

The promoter let out a nervous laugh. "It does. Help yourself, but don't tell the other dudes." He grasped Diablo's shoulder but then quickly withdrew his hand when he glared at him. "I'll see you in a bit." He rushed off.

Diablo went over to Jose who was tightening the ropes around the ring. "Where's the stairway?" he asked. Jose pointed to the far left corner, then resumed his task.

Diablo made his way to the far end of the room. He entered a hallway and saw the stairs, taking them two at a time until he ended up on the landing. To the left of him was a long hallway with a bunch of closed doors. To the right, he saw a large family room and moved in that direction. When he entered the room, he found several couches and chairs, a large television, some lamps, and a coffee table. Walking through, he saw a small kitchen in the back. He ambled over and opened the fridge, taking out a can of Coors. Curling his fingers around the cold can, he popped the tab and guzzled it down in one long drink. After tossing the crushed can in a trash can underneath the sink, he took out another beer and went into the family room. The room had a lived-in feel to it, and a large sliding door facing east opened to a balcony.

As he looked out at the brown terrain, the jagged peaks of the San Juan Mountains drew his gaze. White still capped the tallest peaks, and for a moment, Diablo was transported back to his childhood home with its breathtaking view of the Rocky Mountains. The house had been small for him, his three siblings, and his mom, but it had been enough. He and Beau bunked in one room and his older sister, Clarissa, bunked with their youngest sibling, Taya. For a few years things had been great, until his dad had decided he didn't want a family anymore.

Diablo's chest tightened as he brought the can to his lips. *I don't know why I'm thinking of all this shit from my past.* He turned around and went back into the room.

Grabbing the remote, he switched on the TV before sinking into the couch. As he stared blankly at the screen, he felt someone watching him. He nonchalantly shifted his position and looked behind him to catch *her* peeking at him from the hallway. She moved away quickly. Afraid he'd scare her away, he got up and walked quietly to the doorway. She gasped when she came in for another peek and saw him standing before her. She spun around and started to leave.

"Wait. I want to talk to you." Diablo's deep voice filled the space between them.

Slowly she pivoted back around and carefully walked by him; she had a pronounced limp. He glanced down at her feet and he noticed one of her shoes was higher than the other. His eyes flew up to her face but her head was bent down and her hair covered her features. She settled into one of the cushy chairs and tucked her legs under her.

Diablo sat back on the couch and watched her, a small smile tugging the corners of his mouth when she stole a few glimpses at him. He snapped off the television and they sat there in silence, him waiting for her to say something and her looking through her hair at him. Wiping his hands on his jean-clad thighs, he said, "Why don't you lift your hair so I can see you."

Her small shoulders rose up and down.

"I'm not gonna hurt you. I just want to see you," he said gently.

"Maybe I don't want you to see me," she whispered.

"Why not? I've already seen your beautiful eyes."

"Are you a bouncer?"

"Yeah. Who are you?"

She ran her hand up and down her sleeved arm. "Nobody," she said in a soft voice. Then she lifted her head slightly and said in a stronger voice, "I'm nobody at all."

Diablo leaned back against the cushions and stretched out his legs. "Everyone's someone. You a ring girl?" That got a laugh out of her and he joined in on it. "Then who?"

"Bloody Knuckles's—I *hate* that damn name—daughter."

*Fuck. I didn't expect that.* "No shit. He doesn't seem like the fatherly type," he said, more to himself than to her.

"He's not." She rubbed her arm again.

Silence engulfed them once again.

"You live up here?"

"Just on the weekends. During the week I live with my dad and Shanna." He heard the contempt in her voice when she said the name.

"Not too crazy 'bout your dad's wife?"

"And they say all muscle men are dumb."

Normally her attitude would start to piss him off, but he heard such bitterness and loneliness in her voice that he wanted to reach out to her. He knew very well how easily life could throw a multitude of shitty curves. "So are you gonna show me your face? I don't like talking to a head of hair." Her small chuckle touched him, but she didn't move the hair off her face.

He stood up and walked over to her, bending down as he gently moved her hair away. Cupping her chin, he tilted her head back and gazed into the most beautiful eyes he'd ever seen. They weren't enhanced with makeup, and they were even prettier up close.

Staring into their depths, he saw distrust and fear.

"No need to be scared of me. I'm not gonna hurt you," he whispered as he scanned her face. She didn't wear a stitch of makeup except for a swipe of gloss on her lips. He surmised that her flawless skin, high cheekbones, straight nose, and perfectly arched eyebrows would make her the envy of most women. "You're a beautiful woman," he muttered.

She jerked her head away. "Don't say that to me!"

Taken aback, he straightened up. "Why not?"

"Just don't." She turned her head and stared out the window.

"Sorry if I offended you. I didn't mean to." *I'm apologizing for calling her beautiful. That's pretty fucked.* "You got a name?"

"Fallon," she said softly. "You?" She darted her eyes at him, then away again.

"Diablo." He grinned when she looked at him for more than a millisecond.

"I didn't know anyone ever named their kid 'Devil.' That's pretty cool." She licked her lips and then looked down. "I like your tattoos."

*Fuck, she's cute. I can't remember the last time a girl was so shy around me.* "I'm glad you like 'em. I got more on my chest and back. Do you have any tats?"

Shaking her head, she glanced up. "No. All the ring girls have them. Some of them are real pretty. I don't like needles. I guess I'm chicken."

He laughed. "I'm not gonna lie to you and tell you they don't hurt, 'cause they do. It's worth it, though. They're a form of expression you wear on your skin. I'm gonna get a couple more."

Giving him a weak smile, she started rubbing her arm again. Then their time together ended when Shanna bustled in.

"There you are. Your dad's been looking all over for you. He's so pissed. You forgot to put out the towels and rags. You better get your ass movin'." While she spoke, she ran her gaze over Diablo, slowly walking toward him. "And my hubby's looking for you too." She ran her finger down his arm. "You're looking mighty fine, Diablo."

Diablo glanced at Fallon who'd jumped up, panic etching her face. Shanna looked from him to Fallon, then back to him. Redness covered her face as her eyes narrowed. "Get downstairs. Now. I'm gonna tell your dad *exactly* what you were doing when you should've been working."

Fallon rushed to the door. "Fallon," Diablo said. She stopped and turned around. "It was good talking to you." He threw her a warm smile, loving the way her cheeks colored before she smiled back and then disappeared out the door.

"Fucking unbelievable," Shanna fumed. He'd forgotten she there. He turned to her, his face hard. She tossed her hair over her shoulders, the anger dissipating from her face. Stepping closer to him, she smiled. "Fallon is such a pathetic girl. Her whole existence begs for pity. Thanks for being nice to her. I know it wasn't what you wanted to do on your break."

Diablo brushed away from her and walked out of the room, then dashed down the stairs and entered the fight room. He spotted the large punching bag hanging from the ceiling at the back of the room, near the back door. He went over and pummeled the bag over and over until sweat soaked his T-shirt.

"What's going on, amigo?" Jose asked as he came from behind him. "A few of the fighters are here so we gotta hustle. You practicing for hitting some people tonight?" His laugh was tight.

Breathing heavily, Diablo stepped away from the punching bag. He felt better. He figured it was better than rearranging the plastic bitch's face. Grabbing the towel Jose handed him, he wiped his face, neck, and arms. "Is there a shower around here?"

"In the back room. Be quick about it. You need another shirt?"

"I'm good. I carry spares in my saddlebags." As he walked to the back room, he looked around for Fallon, but she wasn't anywhere to be seen. She intrigued the hell out of him. He thought he'd talk to her and satisfy his curiosity, but he found that he wanted to see and speak with her more. He hoped he'd be able to see her again before the night ended.

Two hours later, the fights were in full swing and the place was more crowded than the week before. Goldie and Muerto had come along with the brothers who were there the previous week. They all had taken Diablo's tip seriously and placed their heavy bets on Spider, cheering when they won a load of money.

During the break, the ring girls took to their stages and wriggled their buttocks for the audience that was mostly men. Goldie and Chains came over to Diablo, waving their winnings at him.

"Fuckin' good fight. And I'm gonna give you a solid ten percent for the tip," Goldie said as he counted out two hundred dollars. "And these chicks shaking their asses are giving me a goddamn hard-on." He laughed as he put the bills into Diablo's hand.

"How the hell can you stand there and not be affected by these chicks?" Chains asked.

"When you see something a lot, it doesn't affect you. That's how people get used to the shitty stuff in their lives—it becomes routine."

"Damn. That's some heavy shit for a Saturday night," Chain said.

"The only thing missing is booze." Goldie leaned into Diablo. "You don't have some beer stashed somewhere, do you?"

Diablo chuckled. "No. You're gonna have to wait until you get back to the clubhouse. These fights usually go until midnight. Promoters don't want them to end too late because they don't want to attract the badges or anything."

Army and Muerto came over, bumping fists with Diablo. "Tonight's even better than last week," Army said. "The fighters are better." He jumped in the air, kicking out his leg. "This shit gets me all pumped up! It's like a goddamn drug. I swear I'm gonna sign up to do one of these fights. I'm ready to go now."

"I don't think Steel would like that. You better run it by him before you enter the ring," Muerto said. "But I know what you mean about the rush. My adrenaline's been pumping since the first round started. I'm itching to smash something too."

The lights blinked on and off three times. "Time to get back. Later, dude," Goldie said to Diablo as they all raised their fists in the air.

During the next session of combats, Diablo kept scanning the room like he'd done ever since the first fight started, but Fallon was gone. It was like she'd hidden herself away from him, but he knew she was somewhere close. He could feel her gaze on him.

On his second scan of the room, his gaze caught a flash of red with yellow and black lettering on the back of a tall guy's leather vest. Unfolding his arms, he walked in closer to the crowd until he could see what was on it. His muscles stiffened when he read "Satan's Pistons MC" in red and yellow colors. A few others with the same cuts and logo flocked around the tall guy, screaming and cussing at the combatants in the ring.

*They must've come in when I was out back helping Jose. Fuck. I gotta tell my brothers.*

As he made his way through the crowd, he heard a group of people screaming. He spun around and saw Army and Chains punching it out with two Satan's Pistons members.

*Guess they know they're here.*

Then all hell broke loose.

# Chapter Five

FISTS CRUNCHED CHEEKBONES, brows swelled, blood sprayed, and the two fighters in the ring stood watching the crowd as men with and without leather cuts duked it out. Diablo jumped into the melee, trying to pull the non-bikers apart. His fellow bouncers rushed in, screaming, cursing, and dragging men out by the collars. Diablo saw one of the Satan's Pistons take out a knife and come toward Muerto. Leaping over a couple of guys on the ground, he yelled out, "Muerto, to your right!"

Muerto turned and saw the biker inches from him. He swung around and knocked the knife out of his hand, then kicked him in the chest with the heel of his boot. The outlaw biker crumpled to the floor. Diablo kicked the knife out of anyone's reach and it went sliding across the floor toward the back of the room. Wanting to make sure no one picked it up, he sprinted after it, pausing when he saw Fallon bend down and pick it up.

Bloody Knuckles was waving his arms all around as he ran around like a chicken with its head cut off. If there wasn't such a ruckus, Diablo would've enjoyed the anxiety the asshole was feeling.

Diablo came up to Fallon and she handed him the knife.

"Thanks. You better go upstairs. It's a fucking mess in here right now. You don't want to get hurt."

She stared at him. Standing in the doorway leading to the staircase, she looked so vulnerable. He wanted to wrap her in his arms and keep her safe. She was a delicate-looking woman, but she seemed even more fragile among all the violence behind him.

"Go on now. Do like I told you." He reached out and slid his fingers over her skin. She flinched and backed away. He watched her go up the stairs, and then he turned back around. The crowd had thinned out and he didn't see any of his brothers or the Satan's Pistons members. He started to walk back to the center of the room when he heard a small voice call out his name. He whirled around and Fallon stood crouched on the steps, her eyes shining.

"Be careful," she said, then scrambled up the stairs. Her words energized him and he marched back into the thick of things.

"Where are the bikers?" he asked Rocky.

"They're beating the shit outta each other outside. Most of the other people took off. I told Bloody Knuckles we oughta call the police, but he doesn't want them here for obvious reasons. I get it, but someone's gonna get killed."

"I'll figure it out." Diablo hurried outside and saw Crow, leaping like a panther, land on one of the Pistons' backs. They crashed to the ground and his brother beat the fallen man about the head and neck with a savagery Diablo had never seen.

He went over and pulled Crow off the unconscious man.

"What the fuck?" Crow struggled to break free of Diablo's grip. "I'm gonna kill that sonofabitch. He's the one who cut me up in Arizona. I've been wanting to pay this fucker back. When this chickenshit sliced me, it was me against five of these fuckers. At least I'm giving him a fair chance."

"Steel won't want you killing one of these fuckers without reason. You beat his ass, but it's time to move on." Diablo nudged the biker who was lying face down on the ground. He groaned. "He's alive. Let's help the others."

As soon as Diablo surveyed the fight, it was obvious that the Night Rebels outnumbered the Satan's Pistons. The tall man, who Diablo had seen earlier inside, yelled out to his brothers to get their asses on their Harleys and leave. Several of the members were stained in blood, and several Night Rebels didn't look any better. A couple of Pistons picked up the member Crow had beaten and dragged him to a SUV, threw him in the back, and jumped in. The rest of the club hopped on their bikes.

"We don't wanna see your fuckin' asses in our territory again! You sonsofbitches." Spit sprayed out of Crow's mouth.

"Next time you won't be riding away," Army said while the other Night Rebels yelled in agreement.

The tall man glared at them. "This shit isn't finished." He and the other Pistons rode away.

"Fuck them!" Muerto screamed as he stomped his feet on the dirt.

Rocky came outside, his gaze avoiding those of the bikers. He went up to Diablo. "Everything calm now?" he asked in a low voice.

Diablo nodded. "It's all cool. Some fuckers from a rival club started shit with my brothers. We took care of it." He spat on the ground, his saliva mixing with the blood that heavily stained the sand and dirt.

In an even lower voice, Rocky said, "Bloody Knuckles is beyond pissed. He wants to talk to you."

"I'll be there in a minute." Diablo watched as Rocky walked back inside. "I fuckin' let you guys down. I should've seen the fuckers in there." *I was too damn busy looking for Fallon.* "What happened shouldn't have."

"What the fuck are you sayin'?" Goldie jerked his head back. "There were so many people in there and you were doing some shit outside for a while. I bet that's when the assholes came in."

"And they must have known bikers were in here because of our Harleys in the lot. They were looking for a fight," Muerto said.

"And we fucking gave them one!" Crow kicked up the sand with his boot.

"They know better than to be in our territory. We should've killed them." Army shook his head.

"Damn straight," Skull replied, Brutus and Chains nodding in agreement.

"I'd say the fights are over inside, right?" Sangre asked.

Diablo nodded. "Pretty sure they are. I'll let you know when the next one is. You guys heading back now?"

"Yeah. Raven's gonna be so pissed and scared." Muerto chuckled.

"That makes for a great fucking later on," Sangre said, and the others laughed.

They went to their bikes and gave Diablo several chin lifts. He watched them as they roared onto the old highway, their red taillights flickering in the dark until they were out of sight. He walked slowly to the entrance, reminding himself not to lose his temper when Bloody Asshole got in his face.

"You took your fucking sweet time," the promoter said when Diablo stepped inside. "What the fuck happened?"

"Someone let in a rival outlaw MC. They were in Night Rebels territory, so they got their asses kicked."

"Well that makes everything clearer. Are we in a bad rerun of Brando's *The Wild One*? That's bullshit and you know it."

Diablo gritted his teeth. "Are we done?"

Bloody Knuckles's eyes widened. "No, we're not fuckin' done. Rocky, bring the other bouncers. I want to talk to all of you."

Diablo crossed his arms over his chest. *I wonder how long this asshole's gonna act like I give a shit what he thinks.*

Rocky and the other two bouncers came over.

"What's up, boss?" Rocky asked.

"Which one of you let the bikers in?" The promoter glared at each one of them.

"Diablo let some in, and I guess I did too," Moe said.

The promoter fixed his eyes on Diablo. "Now I'm finding it was you and Moe who let them in."

He clenched and unclenched his fists. "I let my brothers in. I didn't let the fuckin' Satan's Pistons in."

Shaking his head, the promoter raised his hands in exaggerated exasperation. "Whatever. From now on, no bikers are allowed in this venue. I don't give a shit if it's a granny on a goddamn Harley—no one with a bike is allowed in here. Got it?" The three bouncers nodded but Diablo didn't move a muscle. Coming close to him, Bloody Knuckles said,

"You got a problem with that?"

"Yeah, I do. There's no fuckin' way I'm turning my brothers away."

Anger mottled the promoter's face. "I own this goddamn place. I put on the fights. I pay your fucking wages. I'm not asking you—I'm fucking telling you."

"Back away, old man, or you're not gonna like the way your face looks in the morning." Diablo uncrossed his arms and leaned closer to the promoter.

He stumbled backward. "If you want to keep your job, then you'll follow what I say. No bikers. Period."

"Give me my pay for tonight, then, and I'm fuckin' outta here."

"So you're quitting?" Bloody Knuckles looked frustrated at the way things were playing out.

"Seems that way." Diablo's jaw jutted out.

"Boss, some of the biker dudes were here last week and there wasn't no problem. Maybe it's because the other bikers were here," Rocky said.

"I saw the ones who had the devil on the back of their vests start the fight with the other bikers," Moe added.

Bloody Knuckles breathed out an audible sigh. "Can you promise me this won't happen again, Diablo? I mean, I lost a shitload of money tonight, and I don't want people to be scared to come here. When they come, they fucking expect the fights to be in the ring, not in the crowd. Work with me, man. I don't want to lose you, but you have to give me some assurance."

Diablo stood silent for a few seconds, loving the way beads of sweat ran down Bloody Asshole's face. "If no one disrespects them, then it'll be good. If there aren't any fuckin' rival bikers in here, then it'll be good. Pretty simple."

The promoter nodded slowly. "All right. I just want to forget this damn night happened. I'll try and put something together right away. I don't want people thinking we're closed for business." He ran his hand through his short hair. "What a fucking mess tonight was." He stared fixedly at Diablo and pointed his finger. "I'm counting on you to control shit before it happens."

Diablo resisted the urge to grab his finger and bend it backward until it broke. The sound of Bloody Asshole's bone snapping would be music to his ears. "I'm still waiting on my pay."

"Okay. Now that we all understand each other, let me settle with all of you. It's been a long night."

A few minutes later, Diablo went up to Sam who was packing up to leave. "Have you seen Fallon?" he asked.

Sam shook his head. "A couple of the ring chicks are interested in you. They keep asking me about you. I'd die to have just one hour with any of them, and you're asking me about Bloody's dowdy daughter?"

"I didn't ask for your fuckin' opinion, just if you've seen her."

"No, but then I really don't ever notice her. She's not very remarkable."

In less than a second, Diablo grabbed the wiry-haired man by the shirt and lifted him off his feet. "I don't ever want to hear you talking trash about her. You got that? If I hear you saying shit, I'll crush your pinhead until your fuckin' brains pour out." He threw the trembling man to the ground and kicked open the back door, letting it slam behind him. He revved up his Harley and peeled out of the lot, his back tire sliding in the dirt.

As he rode down the deserted highway, his anger began to lift. Fallon touched him in a way no other woman had. He didn't know what to make of it. There was strength in her amid all the chaos she had churning inside her; he supposed that's what appealed to him. He wasn't even sure what he wanted from her—friendship or something more. All he knew was he wanted to get to know her. She fascinated him in ways that confused him.

He threw his head back and let the late May air roll over him as he rode back to Alina.

# Chapter Six

D IABLO STOOD IN the back of the room with his feet apart and arms crossed as Steel hit the gavel against a wooden block. The brothers stopped talking and focused their gazes to the front of the table where Steel and Paco stood.

"Heard you had some trouble with the Pistons on Saturday. Paco filled me in on the details."

"Those fuckers know better than to be in our territory." Rooster Mike's comment set off the brothers and they began cussing and yelling death threats.

Paco put two fingers in his mouth and whistled loudly. "We know the fuckers shouldn't have been there, but we gotta figure out what the hell they're gonna do. From the way the brothers who were involved in the fight told it, the Pistons got their ass beat." The room was filled with cheers and hoots. "We can celebrate that in the main room after church, but we have to figure out what's our next step."

Crow stood from his chair. "Steel's right. I know these sonsofbitches from when I lived in Arizona. They're not gonna forget."

"And we know they're still pissed about us shutting down their strip bar last summer," Army said.

"Maybe they'll get the 39th Street punks to hit us," Chains said.

"No way they'd let inexperienced wannabes do their job. Anyway, there's no satisfaction in passing off the hit." Diablo pulled out a chair and sat down.

Steel nodded. "Diablo's right. For now, the club is on high alert. Check out every single chick before she walks into the club." Cue Ball, Eagle, and Jigger groaned. Steel gave them a hard look. "I know it's going to be a pain in the ass on the weekends, but the club's security and safety are number one. I'm going to have a couple brothers on Raven and Breanna. They'll trade off with the prospects, who'll be keeping their eyes on Shannon and Sam."

"I can watch my own woman," Tattoo Mike said.

"You'll go fuckin' crazy if you're with her twenty-four seven," Brutus replied. Chuckles circulated around the room.

"With her working in the ink shop, Sam and me spend a ton of time together. If I need the help, I'll let you know."

Steel nodded. "Okay. You gotta watch your kids too. Same goes for you." He glanced at Rooster Mike. "We're here to help. I don't want anyone getting hurt, especially the old ladies and kids."

"I wouldn't be surprised if the Piston shits knew some of our brothers were going to be there on Saturday. It just seems like something's off here," Paco said.

"I was thinking the same thing." Diablo leaned his chair back against the wall. "And they came after our brothers arrived."

"And when you were out back," Sangre added.

The members began talking amongst themselves, their voices and anger bouncing off the walls as the minutes slipped away.

"We gotta take them down before they come for us," Crow said.

Steel shook his head. "We're not ready to start a war, but this makes me think that we've been too lax in building up our arsenal. We've had it pretty quiet since we put an end to the Skull Crushers."

"Agreed." Paco looked at Diablo. "Who do you think would've told the motherfuckers that Night Rebels were at the fights?"

Diablo pressed his lips together and ran his hand over his smooth head. "It had to be someone who knew the brothers were going to be there. It could be someone at the fights because our guys were there the week before. Not sure who it could've been, but I'll look into it."

"Maybe the Insurgents can help with finding out what the Pistons are up to. Hawk's good at finding shit out about rival clubs."

"I'll talk to him. In the meantime, we're on high alert. I'm putting

Paco, Army, and Chains in charge of getting some arms deals. We gotta make sure we have the weapons if we end up going to war with the fuckers. I'll also give Banger a call and see if he can lend us a hand. The Insurgents may have some guns they want to unload. That seems to be all for now. Church is over." Steel brought the gavel down; the meeting was adjourned.

The brothers went to the big room, their low voices buzzing like a swarm of bees. They were all concerned about the unknown. The only thing that was certain was that the Satan's Pistons would strike.

"I wondered when the Pistons were gonna come calling. The chickenshits waited a long time to strike." Crow took the beer the prospect placed in front of him.

"And on Saturday, they ran off like the pussies they really are," Goldie said.

"I don't think they figured there were that many of us." Muerto lifted his Dos Equis to his lips.

"That's 'cause there were only five of us the Saturday before. Some fuck definitely tipped them off." Army pounded his fist on the bar.

"You're right. I'll look into it, and when I find out who it is, I'm gonna crush the fucker." Diablo slammed his empty beer bottle on the bar and it shattered.

Several of the club girls came over to the men. Maria, a cute woman with long dark brown hair, came over to Diablo. "Hiya," she said as she leaned next to him.

A smile spread over his face. Maria and Lucy were the only club girls he hung out with when he was in the mood. They provided conversation and fun when he needed it. Maria had a softness about her that he really liked, and Lucy, a redhead, had a temper that turned him on. He wasn't into threesomes, so when his sexual desires craved a release he'd either go to one or the other. If he was in a pissed-off mood, Maria's gentleness calmed him. If he was in his not-giving-a-shit mood, Lucy's fiery temperament charged him up.

"How're things going?" he asked her.

"Good. It looks like you guys had a serious powwow in there." Diablo pursed his lips and raised his eyebrows. "I know. You can't talk about it." She ran her hand up his arm. "You gonna get me a drink?"

"Whatcha drinking?"

"Surprise me. I'll meet you at the table."

He walked over to the table, a beer in one hand and a tequila sour in the other. Maria pulled out a chair for him. "You been keeping pretty busy with your second job." She wrapped her lips around the small straw and took a drink. "Yummy. Thanks."

"I only work on Saturday nights if they need me. The rest of the time I'm still working at the mechanic shop."

"I was downtown the other day and popped into Skid Marks to see you, but you weren't there."

"I must've been at the junkyard looking for parts."

She leaned over and kissed his cheek, then wiped her nose, giggling. "Your beard tickles. You know, I miss you. The last time we hooked up was a few weeks ago. Lucy said it's been about the same for her. Aren't you horny as hell about now?" She rested her hand on his thigh.

The warmth of her hand made his dick jerk, but his mind wasn't where his body was. He gently held her hand, moving it away from his thigh. "I'm just not feeling it right now. You know me. I can wait a long while before I need your lovin'." He winked at her as disappointment settled into the fine lines on her forehead. "Sangre's horny as all hell."

"Sangre's always horny." She laughed and he joined in.

He liked Maria's easy-going nature, and if he were interested in a girlfriend, he might even consider her. But then there was Lucy, who also made him feel good. The two women complemented each other nicely; sometimes he wished he could combine them to make one woman.

"Anyway, I like being with you. I never told you this before, but you're my favorite of the brothers, and not just for sex. Even though you're not much of a talker, I always feel so comfortable with you." Diablo's gaze fixed on her. "And it doesn't make me nervous when you do what you're doing right now. Some of the other girls are like, 'It makes me nervous when he just stares at you. It's like he's looking right into you,' but I don't see it that way. You're just a very intense and sensitive guy. I know you want everyone to think you're badass all the time, but I think there's a real softness about you. Lucky the woman who can dig beyond the surface and reach your hidden, dark corners. I bet she'll find a treasure trove." She took the straw out of the drink and took a big gulp.

"Maybe she'll find dark demons she won't be able to tame." He took another swig of his beer.

"Maybe. Hell, we all got shit we keep from other people. Most of the time it's easier to pretend that you don't have a past, that the present is the only thing that matters."

"I'll drink to that." He motioned for Patches to bring him another round.

"Since you never go with anyone but me and Lucy, I figure you must like us the best."

He nodded. "Wasn't too hard to figure that one out."

"You ever wanna try out one of the other club girls? I was just curious." She stirred her fresh tequila sour with her straw.

"Nope."

"Hey, Maria, you busy?" Sangre asked as he sat on the chair next to her.

"Can't you see Diablo and me are talking?" She sipped her drink.

"Sorry, dude. I didn't know you guys had something going right now." Sangre wiped the corners of his mouth. "I was just horny and Maria popped in my mind."

Maria looked at Diablo and laughed while Sangre looked confused. "You good if I entertain Sangre? You know you got first dibs." She placed her hand over his.

"Go on. Have a good time," Diablo said.

She finished her drink, then slowly rose from her chair. Sangre tugged her to him. Throwing a soft smile at Diablo, she walked away with Sangre.

Watching the tips of her long hair swaying just above her butt, a girl from his past pushed through the cobwebs in his mind. *Hannah. Fuck. I haven't thought about her in years.* She'd been the only one he gave his heart to, and she'd been the first to decimate it.

"Any news on when the next fights are gonna be?" Goldie's voice startled him. The past scampered to the dark recesses of his mind.

"Not yet. The asshole promoter's trying to set something up as soon as possible. I'll let you know."

"You don't like him?"

"Nah."

"Any reason why?"

Diablo shrugged. "He rubs me the wrong way. Let's just leave it at that."

"It's gonna fuckin' suck to check out each chick who wants to party with us. I bet they'll stop coming. Those asshole Pistons have fucked everything up," Jigger said as he sat at the table.

"They'll still come. Chicks can't resist a bad boy. And they're fuckin' crazy for biker cock." Army placed a bottle of Jack and five shot glasses on the table.

As Army, Goldie, Jigger, and Skull—who'd joined them—spoke, Diablo threw back the shot of Jack Army had given him and let his mind wander. It landed where it always did for the past two weeks—Fallon. When he first saw her, he was struck by how pretty her eyes were and how delicate-looking she was. The sprinkling of freckles that lay over the bridge of her nose made her look young—he put her at twenty, but he couldn't be sure—and she was slender with small breasts and hips.

It disturbed him that she got angry when he told her she was beautiful. *She's been hurt real bad by some jerk. I wonder how she got her limp.* She may have been born with a club foot, or had an accident. He'd been surprised by it, and he suspected it was one of the reasons she was so shy. He didn't want her to be afraid of him. He'd have to go slow with her.

After spending that little bit of time with her, she reminded him of a little bird who'd broken its wing.

And for some unknown reason, he wanted to fix her wing so she could be whole and fly.

# Chapter Seven

"**Y**OUR DAD AND me want to be alone. Why don't you go out and do something with your friends? Oh, that's right. You don't have *any* friends." Shanna blew on her neon orange nails.

Fallon switched off the television, anger curling around her spine. "Dad told me you guys were going into Durango to shop and have lunch today."

"So the fuck what? Plans change, but you wouldn't know that since you *never* have any plans. Why your dad keeps you around, I'll never know. When I was twenty-one, I didn't freeload off my mom. I fuckin' worked." She reached for the bottle of topcoat. "I 'spose he feels sorry for you because you're a cripple."

*You pumped-up fucking bitch!* "I'm outta here." Fallon threw the remote on the table, spilling the topcoat everywhere.

Shanna leapt up. "Fuck! Look what you've done, you stupid ingrate. Come over here and clean it up."

Fallon went out the front door, slamming it behind her. Anger strangled her trembling body. *No matter what Dad says, I'm getting a job and my own place. I'm sick of all this shit!* She walked away from the house, ignoring the shrill calls of her name behind her. *Shanna can rot in hell for all I care. And I* hate *her long, gaudy nails.*

A horn beeping stopped her in her tracks. *Did Shanna actually ruin her nails to come after me?* Another beep, then a friendly voice. *Sylvia.*

"Where're you headed?" Sylvia asked.

"Nowhere. I just had to get out of the house."

"You want to come with me to Alina? I want to check out this one drugstore. I heard they have a great selection of makeup and shampoos.

We can get something to eat, you know, make a day of it. It'll be fun, and I'd love the company."

Getting away for the day was just what she needed. "Sure." She went over to the car and slid in.

Alina was a bigger town than Tula and had more shops and restaurants. Fallon hated living in Tula; she wanted to move away to a bigger town, or maybe a city. The memories she'd built there were ones she tried to forget. It seemed to her that after her mom had left and run off with another man, she'd stopped living. Fallon had only been ten years old when her mother left without taking her. Even though eleven years had passed, she still couldn't believe her mother had done that and left her with her dad—a miserable excuse for a man.

"I love the drive to Alina. It's so pretty with the sagebrush and barren landscape, and then in the background the tall, proud mountains. It gives me shivers every time I make the drive. Have you been to Alina before?"

"A few times with my dad when I was a kid. Once I had my fall, he stopped taking me."

"How old were you when you fell off the roof?"

"Fourteen." An image of her begging her father to take her to Alina popped in her head. It was a year after her fall and she'd wanted to buy a new dress she'd seen on the website of one of the dress stores. Her father had refused to take her. *"If you think I'm going to have everyone staring at me and whispering that I have a freak for a daughter, you're crazy. All you think about is yourself. You're just like your trashy mother."* The words had pierced right through her, and as she remembered them, they hurt just as much as they did when he'd first said them.

"You like country music?" Sylvia asked.

Fallon didn't but she'd listen to anything that would block out the memories. "Yeah. Crank it up."

For the rest of the morning, Sylvia shopped like she'd never seen stores before. She kept saying, "It's like I've been deprived for years," then would giggle and put some more lipstick or eyeshadow or tiny panties in her shopping cart.

"Aren't you gonna buy something?" she asked Fallon as she placed a pack of fuzzy lime green socks in the cart.

"I don't think so. I don't really need anything." Fallon put a pair of patterned stockings back on the shelf.

"We didn't drive all the way to Alina to buy stuff we *need*. Every woman deserves to treat herself to something frivolous every now and then. Now, what do you *want*?"

Fallon shrugged as she scanned the shelves, her gaze landing on delicate bottles of perfume. She'd never worn any fragrances before. Once in a great while she'd sneak into her dad's master bath and spray on some of Shanna's perfumes, but she always ended up washing them off. They made her smell cheap, and she'd wondered why women wanted to smell like overpowering gardens.

"I think a nice, light fragrance is just what you need." Sylvia took a sample bottle filled with purple liquid off the shelf and pressed the top down. A fine mist sprayed out and in a second or two, the small space between her and Fallon held the aroma of lilacs. "That's nice. What do you think?"

Fallon shook her head. "I don't like smelling like flowers. Although, I'm surprised how light the scent is. Shanna's stuff is overpowering."

"Shanna wants to make sure everyone knows she's there. I sometimes have to hold my breath when I'm around her. I don't think she agrees with the saying that less is more." Sylvia chuckled as she reached for another sample filled with a very pale yellow liquid. Once again, she spritzed the fragrance in the air.

The scent of fresh lemons and sugar cookies enveloped Fallon and she inhaled deeply. The aroma reminded her of the summers she'd spent with her mother before she'd run away. She and her mother would spend lazy afternoons sitting on the back porch, sipping homemade lemonade and eating freshly baked sugar cookies. They'd pretend that their time together was forever because both of them had been afraid to think of how everything would change once her dad got home from work. If he was in a good mood, the casualness of summer would continue, but if he was in a bad mood, she'd run to her room and climb out the window to sit on the flat roof that was underneath it. The roof was her hiding place and refuge. It was there that she turned off the hollering, the crying, and the occasional hitting that came from the house.

"Do you like it?" Sylvia pumped the top again.

"It's very nice. It's not strong or too sweet," Fallon said.

"It's delicate like you are. You should buy it. Every girl needs a nice fragrance. It makes you feel pretty and special." She handed a cellophane-wrapped yellow box with gold lettering to Fallon. "You should buy this."

She grasped the box in her hand, excitement coursing through her. "I think I will." She walked over to the cashier and paid for her purchase.

As she waited for Sylvia to finish checking out, she carefully removed the cellophane paper and ran her finger over the raised words. She thought it was the prettiest box she'd ever seen. Slipping her finger under the top, she opened it and picked up the tall elegant-looking bottle. She took off the gold cap and misted the perfume on the sides of her neck, her wrists, and around her hair. A burst of sugary lemon filled her nostrils and a feeling of weightlessness made her giggle.

"You smell real nice, Fallon. That's a perfect scent for you," Sylvia said as she pushed the cart with her bags toward the store's exit. After she'd placed all her purchases into the trunk, she turned to Fallon. "I'm starving. Why don't we get something to eat?" Fallon nodded, a smile spreading on her face. "I heard Leroy's Diner has good food and it's cheap. After all the money I just spent, cheap sounds real good."

After finding parking a block away, Fallon and Sylvia settled into a booth by the window looking out to the street. The diner had a few open tables, but it was pretty much full. Every stool at the lunch counter was taken, and the waitresses, in sky blue dresses with white piping, hustled about. A woman with her hair wrapped in a tight bun, wire-rimmed glasses, and the brightest coral lipstick Fallon had ever seen came over with a pad in her hands.

"Whatcha want to drink?" Fallon guessed their waitress to be in her late thirties or maybe early forties.

"I'll have a lemon Coke with lots of chipped ice," Sylvia said, her attention on the menu.

"Is your lemonade homemade?" Fallon asked.

"Not now. Only in the summer."

"Oh. I guess I'll have to come back in a couple weeks," she joked. The waitress didn't crack a smile as she tapped her pencil against her pad. "I'll have iced tea, please." The woman spun around and dashed over to the counter.

"Everything looks so good. I don't know if I want breakfast or lunch," Sylvia said. "What're you going to have?"

"I think I'll have a turkey club. I wonder if they have cranberry sauce."

"I bet they do. I think I'm going to have the chicken fried steak and eggs. It comes with homemade biscuits. I told you I'm starving." Sylvia laughed and closed her menu.

After they placed their order, Fallon leaned back against the turquoise cushion and stared out the window. She exhaled, then glanced at Sylvia, who was looking in her shiny red compact mirror. Fallon cleared her throat. "I'm having a nice time. Thanks for asking me to come along." She picked up her iced tea and took a sip.

"You gotta get out more. Staying with your dad and Shanna all the time would drive me crazy. And when you're not with them, you're hanging around the warehouse. It's not good. Don't you have any friends in town? I mean, you're from Tula, right?"

Fallon nodded. "I wasn't popular in school. Actually, I got picked on a lot, and when I had my accident, I hated going to school. Everyone stared at me and I felt like a freak."

Sylvia shook her head. "I'll bet there were a lot of people who didn't pay any attention to your leg. You felt self-conscious about it so you probably thought everyone was staring. Sometimes we're our own worst enemy." Her eyes lit up when the waitress placed a large plate smothered in brown gravy in front of her.

Fallon laughed. "You look like a kid on Christmas morning." She pulled out a couple more napkins from the dispenser on the table and then picked up her thick sandwich.

As they ate, warmth spread through her. She couldn't remember the last time she'd had such a wonderful day. It was nice going out with another woman, talking about makeup and rock stars, eating lunch together, and being like everyone else. Even though Sylvia was a few years older than Shanna's twenty-seven years, Fallon had so much more in common with her than with her stepmom. When her dad had first started dating Shanna, Fallon had been excited about having a woman around her age as a friend. Shanna had been friendly in the beginning, but Fallon now knew it was all an act to hook her father. Once they got married, she turned into a mean bitch, and any hope Fallon had of being friends with her was crushed by her hurtful words. The worst part was that her dad always sided with Shanna. It was like he forgot she'd been his daughter longer than the bitch was his wife.

"How's your sandwich? It looks super yummy." Sylvia dunked her biscuit into the egg yolk on her plate.

"The best. The turkey and ham are roasted. They're definitely homemade. It's not like the pressed junk you usually get in club sandwiches." She popped a potato chip in her mouth.

As they talked, the window shook slightly. "What the hell is that?" Sylvia said. Before Fallon could answer, about ten or twelve motorcycles roared past the diner; the sound was deafening. "Oh wow. I've never seen so many bikers riding all at once. I mean, damn... all that testosterone kind of gets you wet, you know?" She wiped her forehead with a napkin.

"I guess. Last Saturday there were a bunch of bikers during the fights. Don't you remember? There was that big fight between them."

"I remember, but your dad made us go upstairs when shit hit the fan. I didn't really get to see any of them. I don't know what it is, but a man in tight jeans with a bunch of tattoos riding a motorcycle just turns me to putty."

"I think they're scary. But I've begun to like tattoos on men." Diablo popped into her head.

All of a sudden, a lot of stomping, talking, and laughing filled the diner. Sylvia's eyes widened. "The bikers just came in from the back. Now we get to have some eye candy with our dessert."

"Dessert? I couldn't eat another thing." Fallon pushed her half-eaten sandwich away from her. "I'm officially stuffed. How many bikers are there? Do they look scary?"

"I'd say there're about twelve of them, and they look delicious. Turn around and see for yourself. And I've got to try a scoop of homemade chocolate chip ice cream."

Fallon nonchalantly looked behind her at a large table filled with men dressed in denim and leather. All of them had tattoos and wore black vests with a lot of patches on them. Then her eyes landed on Diablo. *Oh my God! He's here.* Panic replaced casualness and she faced forward, slinking down in the booth.

"What's wrong? You're as white as a ghost."

"I'm not feeling so well. We should go."

"I just ordered my ice cream. Get yourself a 7-Up or a Coke. Whenever I was sick when I was a little girl, my mama always gave me something fizzy. It really helps an upset stomach, but if you really want to go, we can."

"No… that's okay. Just hurry and eat your ice cream so we can go."

"All right." The waitress came back with a bowl of ice cream and placed it in front of Sylvia. She picked up the dishes and walked away. "Mmmm… this is so good. Do you want to try a small taste?"

Fallon shook her head, her stomach twisting. *Why am I so bothered by him being here? He was nice to me. He made me feel some weird shit. I hope he doesn't see me. I don't want to talk to him.*

"Well, I'll be damned. You know that bouncer your dad hired? You know, the good-looking one who's built real nice with the beard and shaved head? He's over there with that table of bikers. Shit, I didn't know he was a biker. That awesome Harley that's parked behind the warehouse during the fights must be his. Well I'll be damned." Sylvia pushed away her ice cream and took out her compact again. She touched up her lipstick and blotted her face with a tissue. Pushing up her hair with her fingers, she ran her tongue over her teeth, then smiled. "Any lipstick on my teeth?"

"No. Are you going over there?" Fallon whispered.

"What's the matter with you? And sit up. Before you know it, your butt's gonna hit the floor."

"It looks like you're finished. Can we go?"

Shaking her head, Sylvia scooted out of the booth. "I have to go to the ladies' room. Ask the waitress for the check."

Fallon motioned for the waitress who ignored her. "Ma'am," she said in a loud voice. A few diners looked at her. The woman came over. "We'd like our check now." The waitress nodded and walked away. Fallon began to breathe more normally. *We'll be out of here in about ten minutes.*

"Hi, Fallon." The deep voice washed over her.

She glanced sideways, but she knew it was him before her gaze landed on his. A clean scent of soap and the breeze wafted around her. His blue jeans were tight around his corded legs, and his black muscle shirt molded against his ripped chest. The ink images were brighter in the sunlight and beckoned her to come in closer for a better look. Her head swirling, she propped her elbow on the table and cupped her face in her hand.

"I didn't expect to see you in Alina. It's a nice surprise." His jean-clad thigh leaned against the table. He was dangerously close.

"Sylvia asked me to come with her," she mumbled. *Can I be any lamer? I wish I could just disappear.*

"Hey there." Sylvia's cheerful voice was like an electric shock to Fallon's nerves. "Why don't you take a seat and join us for a bit? I was just ready to order a root beer." She patted the space next to her.

"I think I will." Diablo slid into the booth next to Fallon.

*What the fuck?* She scrambled to the far side of the booth, plastering herself against the wall.

Diablo chuckled. "I don't bite, sweet pea." Fallon glanced at Sylvia whose eyes were twinkling. "What're you ladies doing in Alina?"

"We came to do some shopping. I bought a lot of nice things and Fallon bought a nice fragrance. She's wearing it now. Do you like it?"

*Sylvia... I could fucking kill you right now.*

Diablo scooted closer to Fallon, then inhaled. "You smell real good." His breath warmed her shoulder. "And you look real pretty today," he whispered.

A shiver ran through her. She turned to him. "Thank you," she whispered.

"I didn't know you were a biker," Sylvia said.

Diablo nodded. "I'm with the Night Rebels." His eyes never left Fallon's.

"You got some good-looking members sitting over there." Sylvia picked up her root beer and took a sip.

"They come to the fights. Next time they're there, I'll introduce you. They like meeting new women." He still held Fallon's gaze.

"Did you want anything else?" the waitress asked. "I added in the root beer."

"Anything else, Fallon?" Sylvia asked.

"No. We have to be going. It's getting late."

"You got some big plans for tonight?" Diablo said.

"Not really." It was hard to concentrate with him being so close to her. She could feel his body heat emanating from him. It touched her and made her feel funny.

"Do you have a blue Harley?" Sylvia asked as she fished out an ice cube from her empty glass.

"Yeah."

"I've seen it parked behind the warehouse. It's an awesome bike. I bet it's got a lot of power." She licked her lips. Diablo laughed.

*She's flirting with him. And she's doing it so easily. I wish I could do that. I should say something clever or funny.* But she just sat tongue-tied beside him while Sylvia continued flirting with him. Then he touched her and her insides fell like she was free-falling. His hand was on her shoulder, scorching her.

"Do you wanna go for a quick spin on my Harley?" Once again his warm breath fell on her shoulder; it smelled of cinnamon.

"I've never been on a motorcycle. Maybe another time."

"Why not go for just a quick ride? I'd love to do it, but I think Diablo wants you behind him, don't you, sweetie?" She winked at him as he nodded. "Go on. Try something new. He knows what he's doing. There's nothing to be afraid of."

*I really want to go. He's so nice.* "I don't think I could get on very well."

"I'll help you on," Diablo said. "I know you'll love it. The first ride is the one that'll hook you."

She laughed. "I don't know about that. Okay… I'll do it." A rush of adrenaline surged through her.

"Fuckin' fantastic." His arm around her, he squeezed her close to him. "You're gonna love it," he whispered in her ear, his lips brushing her earlobe.

Tingling, she nodded in agreement.

"Here's your check. Pay at the cashier." The waitress placed their bill down on the table.

Before either woman could pick it up, Diablo grabbed it.

"What're you doing?" Fallon asked as she opened her purse.

"It's my treat, ladies." Diablo slid out of the booth.

"You don't have to pay for us," Fallon protested.

"Thank you very much," Sylvia said, and threw a keep-your-mouth-shut look.

As they walked over to the cashier, several diners looked at Fallon's pronounced limp. She turned to Diablo and asked, "Are you sure you still want to take me for a ride?"

A puzzled look crossed his face. "Yeah. Why the fuck wouldn't I?"

A smile spread over hers. "I don't know. Just checking."

He moved her hair out of her eyes. "For the record, if I ask you to do something, I don't change my mind." She pressed her lips together and nodded.

After Diablo paid the bill, he escorted the ladies out back where Fallon saw a huge metallic blue motorcycle gleaming in the sun. "That's yours? It's so big."

"Everything about me is big." He threw his head back when Fallon's cheeks reddened. "Come on over here and let me help you on." She went over and in one fluid movement he lifted her up. She cried out. "You're as light as bird. Did I hurt you?"

"No. I just didn't expect that," she replied as she settled on the black leather seat. He laughed and swung his leg over the seat. Instinctively, she curled her arms around his waist, surprised at how firm he was.

Looking behind her, he said, "Hold on, baby." He winked and started the engine.

The bike rumbled beneath her and she could feel the power of its engine. Holding him tighter, she said to Sylvia, "I'll meet you in front of the diner soon." Sylvia waved and the bike roared down the alley.

At first she was a nervous wreck, thinking for sure she was going to fall off the bike, but as she gave in to its rhythms, she began to enjoy the ride. The wind blew through her hair and felt like it was carrying her on its currents. Without thinking, she rested her head against his broad back, loving the smell of leather and oil that permeated his vest. As houses rushed by, a sense of freedom took hold of her, and a smattering of disappointment sprinkled inside her when the diner came in sight. She'd wanted to keep riding, pressed against him, the wind carrying her away from the life she was living.

Sylvia, beaming, waved at her as they pulled up to the curb. "How was it?"

Diablo helped Fallon off the bike. "It was so cool. I liked it a lot," she said.

"I can take you for a longer ride if you'd like. What're you doing this Sunday?" Diablo asked.

"Sundays I work at the warehouse doing a bunch of chores."

"But Jose can help you out so you get done faster. I can even pitch in so you'll have the afternoon free." Sylvia beamed.

Heat crept up her neck, spreading over her face and leaving red tracks in its wake. She looked down at the ground.

"Sounds like you'll be free." Diablo bent down low. "Do you want to get together this Sunday?"

"Yes," she whispered.

"I can swing by the warehouse. There're a lot of back roads that are great to ride on. I'll be by at one o'clock. Will that work?" She nodded. "Give me your phone." She handed it to him and he started tapping. "I put in my number. Call or text me anytime."

"Okay." She glanced at Sylvia. "We better head back. Thanks again for the ride."

As they drove away from the diner, Fallon craned her neck to look in the passenger mirror at him. He stood there until they turned off Main Street. She leaned back and folded her hands on her stomach. Her body was shimmering like a sparkler on the Fourth of July. *This is by far the best day I've ever had.*

"He likes you," Sylvia said.

"I think he's just being nice because he works for my dad." *But I hope I'm wrong. I want him to like me. I've never met someone like him.*

"No... that's not it. He's definitely into you. I could see it in his face. If any of the other girls find out, they'll scratch your eyes out. Especially Emerald and Heidi. They've got the hots for him but he acts like he doesn't know they exist. Don't tell anyone about our day, okay? Even your dad. I mean, you can tell them we went shopping and had lunch, but don't tell them about Diablo."

"Why not?"

"Because they'll spoil it."

And she knew Sylvia was right. It seemed that whenever there was a glimmer of something special and good in her life, her dad always pissed on it. And now that Shanna was around, she made sure Fallon's life was miserable. "I won't breathe a word."

Sylvia nodded and turned on the radio.

As the car rambled down the old highway, Fallon closed her eyes and relived the whole encounter with Diablo over and over in her mind. *This is my memory. No one will ever be able to take it away from me.*

A couple of miles from her house, her stomach started knotting up. She dreaded a confrontation with Shanna, and she didn't want to hear her father's words condemning her for her earlier behavior toward her step-bitch. She waved goodbye to Sylvia and slowly walked to her house. When she keyed in the code on the keypad outside the garage door, she breathed a sigh of relief as she walked into the empty garage. Her father and the bitch weren't home.

She went up to her room and locked the door, then searched her phone for Diablo's phone number. Looking at it made her smile. This was the first time she'd ever had a boy's phone number. She held the phone against her chest and closed her eyes, the cool breeze reminding her how wonderful the ride had been. And holding him had been the best part of it.

*I'll never forget today. And no matter how awful Shanna or my dad are, I'll always have today.*

As she clutched her phone, sleep descended upon her.

# Chapter Eight

DIABLO WIPED HIS greasy hands on a towel, a surge of satisfaction pumping through him as he surveyed the Harley Super Glide. When the owner brought it in, it'd been on its last mile, but now it was humming and shining. Diablo worked at the club's auto and bike repair shop, Skid Marks, four days a week. He'd learned the ins and outs of bike repair when he'd joined up with the Night Rebels. Shotgun had liked the way he knew his way inside a car's engine, so he'd taken him under his wing and showed him the ropes. Shotgun ran the shop; he'd been with the Night Rebels since Steel had started over a decade ago. In their mid-thirties, Shotgun, Rooster, and Tattoo Mike were the older members of the club.

Diablo went into the salesroom, walked over to the small refrigerator behind the counter, and took out a large bottle of water. After guzzling more than half of it, he placed it on the back table.

"Is the Super Glide ready to go?" Shotgun asked as he thumbed through the rolodex.

"Resurrected from the dead. I'm gonna wash up." Diablo went to the laundry sink in the utility room and scrubbed the grease and grime from his hands. As he rinsed them under the stream of warm water, his thoughts drifted to Fallon. She felt mighty fine pressed behind him when he took her for a spin the previous day. He couldn't wait to see her on Sunday and take her for a proper ride. He pushed the paper dispenser with his elbow and tore off a long sheet, then dried his hands vigorously.

When she'd agreed to go with him on his Harley, he'd been surprised. *She must be kinda interested in me.* He wasn't too sure about it because she was hard to read. Most women were obvious in letting him know they desired him, but Fallon spent most of their short time together averting his gaze.

"You've got a call. It's the dude who brought in his Sportster this morning," Chains said at the doorway.

"Coming." Diablo threw the wadded-up paper in the trash and went out front.

When he was finished with his conversation, he sat on the stool by the cash register. "Where's Shotgun?"

"He went out to grab lunch. We've gotta hold down the fort until he gets back. It'll be a nice break." Diablo nodded. "Who was that woman you were talking to at Leroy's yesterday afternoon?"

"Someone I know." Diablo took the credit card a customer handed him.

"How do you know her?"

Diablo finished the transaction and stared at Chains. "How the fuck is that your business?"

"I was just asking. We were just wondering, that's all. You rarely talk to any chick except for Lucy and Maria. Fuck, man."

Diablo pushed up from the stool. "I better get working on that Sportster." He grabbed his half-finished water bottle and headed to the bay. He figured the brothers were buzzing about Fallon. At times they really got on his nerves when they started the petty gossip shit; they were worse than a bunch of women at a social.

*They don't need to know shit about her.* He took out a wrench and unscrewed a bolt. *I don't even know what I'm doing. I just know I like her.* And he wasn't going to tell his brothers that. They would never get that a man could spend time with a woman without thinking about fucking her the whole time.

Fallon's small body blazed through his mind. *She does have some nice tits on her, and probably a lot of sexy curves hidden under her baggy clothes.* He wondered why she hid her body the way she did. She wore clothes that were shapeless and looked too big for her slight frame. He guessed her to be about five foot four, and he'd been surprised how light she was when he picked her up to put her on the seat of his Harley. The skin he'd touched was soft like down feathers, and the scent she was wearing made his cock move against his zipper. But what woke it totally up was her arms tight around his waist and her head against his shoulder. It was the fuel he'd used when he'd jerked off that night while in the shower. Maria would've been so disappointed to know that he'd used his hands instead of her to come.

Breathing out, he took the tire off the bike. A ping drew his attention to the phone on his work table. Placing the wrench on the floor, he went over and looked at it. An unknown number flashed on his screen. He opened the text, suspicion creasing his brow.

**Unknown:** *Hi. Thanks again for the ride.*

A big smile cracked his face. *Fallon.*

**Diablo:** *I'm glad u enjoyed it. Sunday will be even better.*

**Fallon:** *How are you?*

**Diablo:** *Good. U?*

**Fallon:** *Ok.*

**Diablo:** *U working today?*

**Fallon:** *Yes. In the house.*

**Diablo:** *What do u do?*

**Fallon:** *I have a lot of chores.*

**Diablo:** *Chores? Isn't that shit u do when ur a kid?*

A long pause. *Did I piss her off? Fuck.* He started to text, but then his phone vibrated.

**Fallon:** *I have to go.*

*Fuck!*

**Diablo:** *I didn't mean 2 offend u. Let's text some more.*

**Fallon:** *I really just wanted to say thanks. Bye.*

**Diablo:** *What did u like the best bout the ride?*

He waited for an answer but it never came. Breathing out through parted lips, he placed his phone on the table and went back to the Sportster. *At least I've got her number now.*

For the next two hours, he worked on the Sportster until he'd isolated and fixed the problem. The intensity of his concentration kept Fallon from coming to the forefront of his mind, but she hung around the edges of it. When his phone pinged, he wiped his hands, a smile threatening. He groaned when he saw the name—Taya, his younger sister. *What the hell does she want? Money. She always wants money.*

**Taya:** *How're u? Been a while.*

**Diablo:** *Like 6 months. U need money?*

**Taya:** *That's all ur gonna ask me? Just bout the money?*

**Diablo:** *Cause that's the only time I hear from u.*

**Taya:** *U never contact me. U don't care.*

**Diablo:** *I spent 3 fuckin' yrs in the pen 4 u!*

He breathed out and put the phone down, ignoring the ping. Closing his eyes, he was transported back to his youth. He'd spent four years in the foster care system, separated from his siblings. When he turned eighteen, he went looking for his younger brother and sister, having heard they were placed together with the same family. By the time he'd contacted them, Beau was already using and Taya was terrified to be alone with him. Diablo got closer to her, and one night when she was munching on a slice of pizza at Luigi's Pizza Joint in downtown Salt Lake City, she told him that her foster dad made her touch and suck him. When she'd told him that, all color disappeared from his life except red.

Two days after Taya's revelation, Diablo had waited for the dirtbag outside the factory, confronting him as he came into the parking lot.

The man told him Taya was a liar and a manipulator and needed therapy. He'd said her life revolved around her getting attention.

Diablo told his sister what her foster dad had said and she denied it vehemently. That night, Diablo hid in the closet in Taya's bedroom. Around one in the morning, the dirtbag came into the bedroom and started messing with Taya, who tried to push him away. Without thinking, Diablo had burst out of the closet and pounced on him, almost beating him to death.

Less than a year later, the jury came back with a guilty verdict for second degree assault. On his nineteenth birthday, the judge gave him five years at Utah State Prison. Three years later he'd been released for good behavior.

He shook his head and picked up the phone.

**Taya:** *I know. I don't know y I said u don't care.*

**Diablo:** *I'm busy. How much do u need?*

**Taya:** *A thousand would be good....*

**Diablo:** *R u gonna smoke it all?*

Taya was a crank addict and she turned tricks to get money to support her habit. From the underground grapevine, he'd heard she had a pimp and had hooked up with an internet porn site.

**Taya:** *No.*

He snorted. *She's such a fuckin' liar. There's no way she's gonna tell me the truth.* He rubbed the back of his neck and stared out at the mountains in the distance. Images swirled around his mind: Taya cuddling next to him for comfort when their mom had beaten her bottom, her small fingers using magic markers to color in the faded and worn hand-me-down dress when she was nine years old, large tears rolling down her face when the Department of Social Services came to their house to take them away from their mother.

He blew out a long breath.

**Diablo:** *I can wire u 800. Western Union. Same place as last time.*

**Taya:** *Luv u!!! Thx. ☺*

**Diablo:** *Ya. Have u heard from Clarissa?*

**Taya:** *No. U?*

**Diablo:** *No.*

**Taya:** *No matter. She's a bitch. Like Mom. Gotta go. When u gonna send the money?*

**Diablo:** *In 2 hrs. Will text u. Take care.*

He knew he wouldn't hear from her again for quite a while. If people knew what she did to him, they'd think he was crazy for still talking to her, but she was his sister… his blood. As the images of his past started to creep from the dark corners of his mind, he willed them back. He didn't want the memories at that moment. What he wanted was to have dinner with Fallon, but he knew she wasn't ready for that.

Glancing at the clock, he decided to cut out early so he could wire the money to Taya.

A couple of hours later, he was clicking the remote absentmindedly as he stretched out on his bed, a towel wrapped around his waist. He settled on a station showing an infomercial on power smoothies, a blender mixing a container of green liquid.

A knock on his door snapped him out of his lethargy. Pulling up from the bed, he shuffled to the door and opened it. Maria stood there, her eyelids puffy and red.

"Can I come in? I really need a friend," she said between sniffles.

Diablo nodded, stepping aside to let her in. Comfortable in his room, she went over to the bed and sat down, running her hands over the green blanket covering it. He went back to his spot on the bed, pushed up the pillows, and leaned back against the headboard.

"What's going on?" he asked as he scanned her mascara-streaked face.

"I just found out that my brother's got liver cancer real bad. He's had it for a while and no one even told me." She covered her face with her hands.

"That fucking sucks." Diablo tugged her to him and she clung to him. "I didn't know you had a brother." He really didn't know anything about her, Lucy, or any of the club girls. They never talked about family or their backstory with the brothers. He suspected the other women knew each other's business, but the club girls were always jovial, sexy, and playful around the men.

"Yeah. Him and me were real close when we were kids. He ran away from home when I was twelve. I didn't hear from him for years. Three years ago he found me, just like that, and we went back to being close. I can't believe I'm gonna lose him."

Wetness marked his chest as he lay there silently, listening to Maria's heart break in a thousand sobs. He didn't know what to say. It sucked that she was losing her brother, but he was a man of few words, so he just massaged her shoulder.

As the last orange and pink rays before twilight beckoned the stars, Maria pulled away and sat up straight. He handed her a box of tissues from the nightstand and she took several, blowing her nose and wiping her black-stained cheeks. "I'm sure I look a mess," she said. He smiled. "Sorry for invading your space. I know how you guys hate an emotional woman."

"No need to apologize. You needed a shoulder to lean on. We're friends."

"You can be so sweet. I wonder if your brothers know there's a big teddy bear behind the mean exterior." She giggled and poked him, then scooted closer to him. "You wanna fool around?"

Smiling, he shook his head. "Why don't you freshen up and go downstairs for a bit. Being with people sometimes helps."

"Are you coming down later?"

"Nah. I got some stuff on my mind."

"Did you want me to bring some dinner up to you?"

He shook his head. She stood up and went to his bathroom. When she came out, she went over to him and brushed his lips with hers. "You sure you want me to go?"

Pushing back a bit, he said, "You should go see your brother. Where does he live?"

"Wichita. I don't have the money."

"I'll pay for it."

"I couldn't ask you to do that."

"You're not. I'm offering."

"I'll think about it. I don't want to run into my mom or sisters. I didn't leave under the best circumstances. I got some shit going on with my family."

"We all do," he said in a low voice. "Just let me know."

"I will." She reached out and lightly tugged his beard. "You know, if things were different, like you were just a regular guy and I was a regular woman, would you be interested in me? I mean, would you date me… pursue me?"

He shrugged. "Probably. I'm not exactly the settling down type of guy."

"But if you were?"

"Then yeah."

She grinned and went to the door. "Thanks for that, even though you're lying through your teeth."

The door closed behind her and he stared at it for a long while. He picked up his phone and tapped in Fallon's number.

**Diablo:** *Fucking awesome sunset tonight. U see it?*

For the longest time, he waited for an answer, but his phone stayed silent.

The voices of his brothers filtered through his open window. *Fuck it.* He rose to his feet and pulled on a pair of blue jeans, then tugged a black T-shirt over his head. As he pulled on his boots, he glanced at the phone. Nothing. He shrugged on his cut, then tapped in a text.

**Diablo:** *U get the money?*

**Taya:** *Yea. Thx. Ur the best!*

**Diablo:** *Right.*

Sighing, he slipped the phone in his pocket and headed downstairs to join his brothers.

# Chapter Nine

FALLON OPENED THE refrigerator and took out the hazelnut creamer, pouring it into her freshly brewed cup of coffee. She stirred it three times, took a big sip, and padded over to the kitchen table. Hazelnut creamer—the extra creamy one—was her guilty indulgence; it made her feel like she was in a Paris café, away from all the bullshit in her life. Sometimes when things got to be too much, she'd come down in the middle of the night, fix a cup of coffee with her favorite creamer, and drink it in the silence and darkness of the kitchen. The quiet was her refuge, but her world was full of noise and meanness. *Why do people want to hurt others?* It was a question she'd been asking for as long as she could remember. Her father was mean and hurt her mother, driving her away from them, and then he turned his anger on her.

Fallon sighed, then took another sip of coffee. She looked again at the text Diablo had sent her the night before about the sunset. When she'd received it, she dashed upstairs to her room and climbed out the window, watching the fiery sun make its descent over the mountain peaks. Warmth spread through her as she watched the last wisps of daylight disappear, knowing *he* was watching it too.

Diablo looked so fierce, yet he was so nice to her. By the way he looked, she never would've imagined he'd be so kind. And he did something to her; he gave her a quiet confidence, made her want to trust him, made her insides quiver in a good way. She hadn't trusted a man since James Thornhill pushed himself on her, pretending to like her when they were juniors in high school. She'd lost her virginity to him, thinking they were a couple, only to overhear all the whispers circulating around the school after they'd done it under the full moon on a blanket spread over the grassy part of Chacon National Park. She'd been nervous the park ranger would find them and tell her dad, but she pretended to like it even though it hurt and was all over in less than fifteen minutes. She'd figured she'd get used to it, chalking it up to her nervousness about her dad finding out. James had told her it was good as he'd rolled off her, but when she'd tried to cuddle next to him, he'd pushed her off and told her he had to get back home. He hadn't called her for the rest of the weekend, and when he'd ignored her that Monday morning in the school halls, her stomach had twisted and lurched. He'd used her. And when he'd finally spoken to her a few weeks later, he'd basically told her that he'd figured she'd be easy because she was a cripple. That's what he called her—a cripple. The memory of his words still stung even though five years had passed.

Diablo didn't strike her as a guy who'd do that to a woman, but she couldn't be sure. A part of her wanted to get to know him better, but a larger part was terrified. For most of her life she'd been sheltered and invisible, and there was definitely comfort in that existence. A part of her wanted to break away and *live*, but fear of the unknown strangled and held her back. She wanted to text him back, but she couldn't.

"Did you finish ironing the napkins for Thursday's luncheon?" Shanna's nasally voice grated on her nerves.

Fallon nodded and finished her coffee. She rinsed the cup and placed it in the dishwasher.

"Did you take your time polishing the silver? Last time you didn't do such a good job."

Fallon gritted her teeth. "If you don't like the way I do it, maybe you should do it the way you want it."

"Quit giving me sass! You know that shit ruins my nails."

"Well, I'm allergic to it and that doesn't seem to matter." She walked out of the kitchen.

"I'm trying to be nice here, Fallon. Don't piss me off. I'm nervous enough about having them society ladies over on Thursday for lunch. I don't need your attitude on top of it."

"Are you giving Shanna a hard time?" her father's voice boomed from the living room.

"She's just being her same ol' selfish self, Charlie. Maybe you can remind her how important the day after tomorrow is for me." Shanna's heels clacked on the marble as she walked into the living room.

"Fallon, come in here," Charlie said.

She took a few deep breaths, then stood at the entrance of the room. "What?"

"You know this luncheon is very important to your stepmother. She's worked very hard to get into these ladies' social circle. She's helping them with their big fundraiser, and all she's asking is for you to be cooperative. You're acting like a selfish child right now."

Fallon stared at her father as he lectured her, despising the smug look spreading across Shanna's face as she practically sat on his lap. Her dad looked like he could be Shanna's father. *He looks ridiculous. I have to get away from them.*

"Are you listening to me?" Charlie's stern voice brought her back. She nodded.

"And remind her that I don't want her around on Thursday. I don't need the women focusing on *her*."

"And where am I supposed to go for the day?" Fallon placed her hands on her hips.

Shanna shrugged. "I don't know or care. Go to the warehouse or shopping. I'm sure Charlie will give you his credit card." She placed a kiss on his cheek and he smiled. "The point is I don't want you around."

Heat flushed through her body as she tensed. Lifting her chin up, she said, "You know, Shanna, I don't give a fuck what you want. But you don't have to worry about me hanging around for your kiss-ass fest because I always want to spend as little time as possible in your presence."

Shanna's jaw dropped and Charlie stared at Fallon. Satisfaction coursed through her.

Then anger mottled Shanna's face. "Are you gonna let the little bitch talk to me that way?" she asked Charlie.

"No. I'm not." Charlie's nostrils flared. "How dare you talk to my wife like that, you ungrateful shit. Apologize to her. Right the fuck now!"

Her stomach rolled over and she bit her lip; her father's anger always triggered her instinct to flee. Normally, she'd hang her head and mumble an apology to Shanna, then trudge up to her room, lock her door, and fling herself on her bed, or go out on the roof and cry. And even though she wanted to resort to her routine, something kept her mute and rooted.

Charlie gently slid Shanna off his lap. "If I have to come get you, I promise you'll be sorry."

Images of her father beating her with his belt flashed through her mind. It'd been a long time since he'd beaten her, but he hadn't given up the occasional slap across her face, punch to her arm, or yank of her hair. *I should just say I'm sorry and go upstairs.* "I do want to say something to Shanna."

Charlie leaned back against the cushion, his arm circling Shanna's waist as her eyes shone like a lion watching its prey. "Go ahead," he said.

Fallon moved closer to the front door. "Shanna, take your luncheon and shove it up your ass. Fuck you!" They'd take a few seconds to comprehend what she'd just said since it was out of character for her to talk back like that. By the time she heard her father and Shanna yelling, she was out the door and in her car. Her father rushed out, but she kept backing up, even when he pounded on her window and threatened all sorts of punishment for her "insolence."

Tears clouded her vision but she drove on, creating as much distance as she could between her and *them*. She drove aimlessly through the town she was born in, realizing she had nowhere to go or anyone to turn to. Of course, she could go to the warehouse and see if Sylvia was around, but she didn't want to deal with Emerald, Heidi, and Cassie. They always gave her a hard time, and whenever they did it in front of Shanna, she'd join in. Her dad would usually give them a stern look except when Shanna was in on it. Another one of the ring girls, Pippa, didn't pay attention to her one way or another, too busy turning tricks to make a lot of money so she could move to Los Angeles. Fallon had overheard her telling Cassie that she wanted to start a career in acting. Sylvia was the only ring girl she liked and considered a friend, but she couldn't burden her *again* with her problems.

She drove out of Tula and headed south on the old highway toward Alina. *Maybe I'll get some lunch or window-shop.* She held her breath. *Maybe I'll bump into Diablo.* She exhaled and gripped the steering wheel.

Tula was only thirty miles from Alina, so Fallon made it there in no time. She'd never driven through the town, so she wasn't sure how to get around, but she kept driving toward the seven-story buildings until she hit Main Street. She drove up and down the large street, loving the way the cherry blossoms framed it in a wave of pink and white colors. Spotting the familiar sign for Leroy's Diner, she pulled into a parking space and got out of the car. *Maybe Diablo will be in there with his friends.*

People's voices, plates on counters, ringing bells for orders, and Chuck Berry on the overhead speaker surrounded her as she entered the eatery. The place was packed. Her eyes drifted to the chalkboard that had the blue plate specials written in yellow lettering. The waitress who'd waited on her and Sylvia a few days before waved her over to a seat at the counter.

"You're busy," Fallon said as she took the menu from her. The waitress nodded, then rushed away. It was apparent she hadn't recognized Fallon. She looked at the menu, then placed it down on the counter. She wasn't very hungry; her stomach was still in knots from the earlier fight at home. Dread threatened to suffocate her as she thought about going back home later that day.

"What'll you have?" a woman in her fifties with thick red-framed glasses asked.

Fallon looked to her right and her left to see what the other diners were eating. Plates of mashed potatoes and chicken fried steak swimming in gravy were all around her, and nausea assaulted her. "A ginger ale with a lot of ice. What soups do you have that aren't cream-based?"

"Vegetable."

"I'll have a cup of that with extra crackers." She'd read that soda crackers and ginger ale were good for a queasy stomach.

As she sipped her drink, she looked around the busy diner, hoping to see a good-looking bearded man who had the most amazing tats she'd ever seen. To her, he was perfect. She noticed how many women checked him out, but she'd never seen him pay any attention to any woman at the warehouse except her. Funny tugs at her breasts and between her legs caused her to shift on her seat. *So he's nice to you. He probably feels sorry for you.* The thing Fallon hated worse than deliberate cruelty was pity. She'd take a slap to her face or a mean phrase over the look of sympathy and pity she'd sometimes see in strangers' eyes when she'd go out in public. But Diablo didn't look at her with pity; his gaze was kind and was all for her.

"Anything more?" the waitress asked as she held Fallon's bill in her hand. She shook her head and the woman slammed the bill face down on the counter before going over to another customer.

She glanced at the clock on the back wall, wondering what she was going to do. There was no way she was going back home. She figured she'd wait until Shanna and her dad were asleep, then sneak in and go to her room. *I could go to the library and read.* She loved libraries; she and her mother had gone often when she'd been young.

Taking out her wallet, she saw her phone. The truth was that she really didn't want to be alone at that moment. Without analyzing it, she sent a text to Diablo, then held her breath.

**Fallon:** *Hi.*

A ping! She tugged at the front of her shirt, licked her lips, then looked down at the screen.

**Diablo:** *Hey. Good to hear from u.*

She smiled.

**Fallon:** *Guess where I am.*

**Diablo:** *No idea, sweet pea.*

She grinned. *This is the second time he's called me that.* When he'd first said it, she'd thought she hadn't heard him right, but she liked it. She liked that he didn't say something common like "babe" or "baby" or "sweetie." It seemed like a lot of men threw those words out to women, but when he'd called her "sweet pea," it felt like he used it just for her. Some women may find it hokey, but she liked it.

**Diablo:** *U still there???*

**Fallon:** *Yeah. Sorry. I'm in Alina at the diner.*

**Diablo:** *Is that right? Gonna have to come by & see u.*

She inhaled and exhaled deeply, her pulse pounding in her ears. *Here goes nothing....*

**Fallon:** *I'd like that. It's super crowded in here.*

**Diablo:** *Give me 30 mins. Gotta wash the grease offa me.*

**Fallon:** *Ok. Should I just wait here?*

**Diablo:** *Ya. Order a piece of coconut cream pie. It's fuckin' delicious.*

**Fallon:** *Ok. I'm at the counter.*

**Diablo:** *See u soon.*

Fallon set her phone on the counter, nervous shivers shooting through her. *He's coming.* A couple of women in short dresses waltzed in and sat at the small table for two behind Fallon. She casually spun around on the stool and looked at them: long brown hair, impeccable makeup, and plenty of cleavage. She noticed how many of the men stared at them. Since she'd come into the diner, no one gave her a second look—not even a first look, actually. Normally, she'd be glad not to have any attention on her, but at that moment, it made her sad.

She took out her compact and glanced at her face: no makeup, a pimple on the side of her right temple, and dry lips. Looking down, she groaned—absolutely no cleavage.

"Did you want anything else?" the waitress asked as a frown formed between her eyebrows.

"No, thanks. I was just getting ready to leave." Fallon took the bill and went to the cashier.

"Did you enjoy your meal?" the young woman asked.

"Yeah. Is there a drugstore around here?" She handed her a ten-dollar bill.

"A block down, across the street." The cashier placed the change in Fallon's hand.

After going back to leave a tip, Fallon left the diner and headed to the drugstore. Once inside, she went to the makeup department and glanced over the multitude of products. Her father hadn't allowed her to wear makeup when she was a teenager, so she used to sneak it in her purse and put it on at school, washing it off before she returned home. After the incident with James, she'd felt so ashamed that she'd stopped going to school. Her dad had been fine with it, so she'd spent the rest of her teenage years around the house, cooking, cleaning, and taking care of her dad.

She picked up a tube of mauve lipstick, mascara, a powder foundation, and a pink-hued blush. After purchasing the items, she went into the restroom and took out the makeup. Looking in the mirror, she scraped a hand through her hair. Feeling dizzy, she gripped the edge of the sink to steady herself as her heart pounded. Coughing, she struggled to catch her breath. She sank to the floor, her head down, her short gulps of air bouncing off the tiled walls.

*What possessed me to contact him? I can't see him.*

The creak of the bathroom door behind her made her body tense. "Are you all right?" a woman asked, her heels clacking on the tiled floor. A strong floral scent wafted from her as she bent down.

Fallon looked at the woman's round face. "I'm okay. I was just feeling a bit dizzy." *I'm fucking freaking out, lady. Move on and leave me alone.*

"Do you need some help up?" The woman offered her hand.

*How fucking more pathetic can I get?* "No, but thanks for offering. I'll be okay."

"All right… if you're sure." The woman straightened up and went into one of the stalls.

The wave of terrifying fear passed and Fallon slowly pulled herself up, then splashed some cool water on her face. *I can't do this.*

Her phone pinged and she jumped as if a bomb had exploded next to her. She took it out.

**Diablo:** *I don't see u. Where u sitting?*

Fallon inhaled deeply, letting the breath out slowly. She did five repetitions, then tapped in her response.

**Fallon:** *Sorry. Wasn't feeling well so left.*

**Diablo:** *What the fuck? Where u at?*

*I don't know what to do. I want to see him but—*

**Diablo:** *Fallon? Don't shut down on me.*

**Fallon:** *Sorry. Just feeling shaky. I'm at the drugstore.*

**Diablo:** *The one a block from the diner?*

**Fallon:** *Yeah.*

**Diablo:** *I'm on my way. Don't fuckin' leave.*

**Fallon:** *I won't.*

The worst of it was over. *He's coming and it's going to be all right.* She broke the seal of the lipstick, quickly swiping the color over her lips. The shimmer brightened her face, and for a brief second, she wondered if he'd like it. She finger-combed her hair and jumped when she heard the ping.

**Diablo:** *I'm here. R u?*

**Fallon:** *Yeah. In the restroom. Will be out in a sec.*

Staring at her reflection, she brushed some blush on her cheeks, pleased that it gave her face some color. "You can do this," she muttered under her breath. "You told Shanna off and it felt fucking good, and now you're meeting a man who's gorgeous. You're on a roll. Don't fuckin' freak out. Just. Don't."

She thrust her shoulders back, secured her purse on her shoulder, and exited the bathroom.

# Chapter Ten

DIABLO STARED AT a woman who held her small boy's hand, turning his head toward her dress as though to shield his eyes from Diablo. She tapped her foot as the cashier took her time checking out the customer ahead of her. The fact that his mere presence caused her so much consternation delighted him.

"Where the hell are you, Fallon?" he muttered under his breath.

"He has pictures on his arms," the young boy said.

"I told you to look the other way." His mother tried to hide his view of Diablo, but the young boy peeked around his mother's dress.

"I like them," he said.

"They're not for us," she said in a hushed tone.

Diablo cracked a half smile. "You into Freddy Krueger, kid?" He walked over and showed the boy the menacing face inked on his upper arm. The boy nodded as he stared at the image.

"Do you mind?" his mother asked.

"The kid seemed to want to see my tats, lady."

"I don't want him exposed to that... sort of thing. Jacob, put your candy on the counter."

"He's gonna be exposed to a lot worse as he gets older." He winked at Jacob, then turned away, seeing Fallon coming toward him. Even though her long gray top and baggy jeans covered most of her body, he grew tight in his pants. Her brown hair fell softly around her shoulders, and when she smiled at him, her whole face lit up. He lifted his chin and waited for her to reach him.

"Hi. Sorry it took me so long," she breathed, her hands trembling slightly.

"That's cool. It was worth the wait." His eyes slowly traveled up her body until they landed on her reddened face. "Let's get outta here."

Outside, the bright sunlight made him squint, so he took out a pair of sunglasses from the inside pocket of his cut. "You wanna grab a beer?" She nodded. He stopped in front of his bike.

"I thought we were going to a bar around here," she said.

"There's a nice one about twenty minutes outta town. It's got a kickass view I think you're gonna love. Anyway, I like the feel of you on the back of my bike." He laughed hard when she turned even redder than she had when he'd checked her out.

With Fallon snug behind him, he revved the engine and made a U-turn down Main Street. She clung tightly to him, and he laughed into the wind when her hand slipped down over his bulge each time he hit a bump in the road. Pressed against his back, she felt warm and soft. Her lemony scent wafted around him, tantalizing him and keeping his dick awake.

Diablo occasionally took women for rides on his bike, especially Maria and Lucy. They seemed to like it, and he could understand why. There was nothing like blending in with the landscape and feeling the wind rush around him; it gave him a high each and every time. When he'd taken various women for bike rides, he didn't feel turned on like he was at that moment with Fallon pressed behind him. The other women were friends and it was no big deal, but Fallon was causing all sorts of havoc with him as they rode through the desert and began their ascent to Sequana Peak.

There was a pervasive smell of burning garbage coming from a cluster of homes about a mile upwind. In many small communities, burn barrels were a common, traditional practice, and most of the residents used them to save on the garbage pickup fees. Even though open burning of garbage was illegal, the county rarely enforced the law. In the distance they saw domes of smoke rising up from brown metal containers near adobe homes. Taking a sharp left, Diablo rode up Deer Creek Road.

As he rode farther up the mountain, the air became crisper and groups of evergreens, clusters of vibrant wildflowers, and rich green vegetation replaced the rocky brown sand of the desert. Taking another left, a wood log roadhouse appeared with a bunch of Harleys parked in the lot surrounding it. Tall blue spruce trees flocked around the establishment, and the sweet scent of pine floated on a gentle breeze, curling around Diablo and Fallon. A large metal sign had "Iron Rose Saloon" written on it, and it hung high above the place on tall, thick poles.

He looked behind him. "Here we are." He jumped off his bike and helped Fallon get off. "They have a great beer selection, kickass wings, and the best burgers in this part of the state." He grasped her hand and led her inside.

The bar had a decent crowd, mostly men in leather, and a big TV hung on the back wall that had images flickering on it that the men ignored. Pulsing beats from a Mötley Crüe song filled the room.

Diablo went up to the bar, a pretty redhead beaming when she saw him.

"Hey, handsome. It's been a long time. What's kept you away?" Her gaze shifted to Fallon and then back to him.

"You know, the usual bullshit life dishes out. Gimme a beer and a...." He looked at Fallon.

"Whiskey and Coke," she said to the bartender.

"Sure enough. How're Goldie, Chains, Army, and Paco? I haven't seen them in a while either. Have you guys found another drinking hole?" She handed him his drinks.

"Everyone's too damn busy. Thanks." He gave her a ten. "Keep the change."

"Thanks. Tell the guys I said hi, and don't be a stranger."

He led Fallon out back to a patio strewn with wrought iron tables and chairs. They sat down and she looked around. "You were right—the scenery is beautiful. It's like we're nestled against the mountain. And it's so much cooler up here." She took a sip of her drink. "Was the bartender someone you used to go out with?" She averted her eyes from his.

"Sissy? Nah, I just know her from coming here. She's a nice gal. Is your drink good?"

"Very."

"I'm glad you texted me. I thought maybe you were pissed at me." He took a drink and watched the birds flit about on the branches.

"I wasn't mad at you. I just didn't know what to say. You kinda scare me." She gulped her drink.

"By the way I look?"

"Oh no. You look real good." Her eyes widened and red streaks painted her cheeks. "I mean, it's not your looks. Well, you do have a penetrating stare, but it's not that either. I guess it's that you're a guy. I mean… I don't have any male friends, so this is new to me." She took another gulp.

"Are you always this nervous or is it just me?" He cocked his head, a smile tugging at his lips.

"I don't feel comfortable around people. It's not like I'm crazy or anything, it's just that I make people uncomfortable. I think it's because of my limp. People don't know what to say about it. Some are cruel and some pity me, but mostly they spend a lot of time trying to pretend they're not looking or wondering about it. Like you. You never asked me about it, but I know you noticed it." She swept the stray hairs from her face.

"I never asked about it because it isn't a big deal to me. Do you want me to ask about it?"

She tore at the cocktail napkin, piling small pieces of white paper in a pile. "No. I mean if you want to it'd be okay, but you don't have to."

"I'll keep that in mind. Why'd you come to Alina? I thought you'd come with the friend you were with a few days ago. I was happy to see that you were alone."

She leaned back and stared at him. "I got into a big fight with my dad and step-bitch. I had to get away. I just got in the car and drove and ended up in Alina."

"I'm glad you did." He placed his hand over hers and squeezed it. "How old are you?"

"Twenty-one, soon to be twenty-two. How old are you?"

"Just turned thirty. Have you ever thought of getting your own place?"

She nodded. "I think about it all the time, especially since my dad married Shanna. I really don't like her."

"I don't blame you. I can't stand her either."

Fallon smiled broadly. "Really?"

"Yeah. You got a boyfriend?"

She shook her head. "And I'm not looking for one," she said hastily.

"I'm surprised you don't have a line of men waiting for you. You're a natural beauty, and there's a softness about you that makes a man's blood boil. I like your freckles too." He brushed his finger across the bridge of her nose.

"Men and I don't mix all that well. I don't really trust them."

He squeezed her hand again. "Do you trust me?"

She nodded tentatively. "For now. I don't know… it just seems hard to trust anyone. You do and then they go and do something horrible and leave you all alone, and all along you thought they loved you." Her voice cracked and she cleared her throat. Shaking her head slightly, she said, "Anyway, like I said, the scenery is beautiful."

For several seconds Diablo was quiet, the rustling branches and chirping birds filling the silent gap between them. "Who hurt you?" he asked softly.

He watched her lips quiver and her eyes shimmer. "My mom," she whispered.

"Want to tell me about it?" He stroked the top of her hand.

Licking her lips, she focused on him. "I was always close to my mom. I adored her, and she was so kind and loving toward me. My dad was out of town a lot back then. He worked for a company and was in the sales department. Whenever he'd go on a sales trip, my mom was so relaxed and happy, but a day before he'd come home, we would both be filled with dread. My dad was… *is* a mean guy most of the time. He'd always accuse my mom of cheating on him while he was gone. They'd fight so much and he'd hit her…." She reached for a napkin and wiped her nose.

"Families do a lot of shit to fuck up their kids. If you don't wanna talk about it, we don't have to."

Shaking her head, she blew out a breath. "I want to. Anyway, a lot of times I'd find my mom crying when she didn't know I was in earshot. Then a nice man with dark hair and a funny-looking nose started coming over when my dad was out of town. His name was Rich and he worked with my mom at the library. My mom worked part-time, and I remember thinking it was the coolest thing that she was around books all day. I decided that I wanted to be a librarian when I grew up. Pretty soon Rich was staying at our house during the time my dad was gone." She picked up her empty glass and brought it to her lips.

"You need another drink. Hang on." Diablo rose from the table.

"I'd like a glass of water and a ginger ale."

Before he left the table, a buxom brunette came over and took their drink order. They watched the pine needles ruffling in the gentle wind as they waited. The waitress returned and placed their drinks down, winking at Diablo. He gave her a chin lift and turned to Fallon. She gulped her water, then gazed at him.

"One afternoon, after school, my mom told me to come sit on the couch next to her. She said she wanted to tell me something. I sat down and my mom told me that she and Rich were in love and wanted to be together. She said she couldn't live with my dad anymore. I remember being happy when she told me about Rich. He was so nice, and I loved the way he took an interest in me. She then told me that she and I were going to leave my dad. She said we were going to move with Rich to California. I was so excited."

"How old were you?"

"I was ten. She made me promise not to say a word to my dad. I never would've, but I promised her. A couple months later, she ran off with Rich and left me behind. For the longest time, I kept waiting for her to come get me, or send a message to me, but I never heard from her again. I used to go to her room and open the closet just to smell the lingering scent of her perfume. It stayed in the air for a long time. That surprised me. I still can't believe my mother left me. She was the bright light in my life, and since she's been gone, the light has never been any brighter than a candle. So there you have it."

Tenderness filled Diablo as he watched her tear up her third napkin. He leaned closer and circled his arm around her, tugging her to him. He kissed the side of her head. "What your mom did fuckin' sucks. You're a survivor, sweet pea."

Fallon didn't pull away, resting her head in the crook of his neck instead. "You're the first person I've ever told the story to. My dad told people that my mom was a slut and ran off with another man. He loved the sympathy he got and the accolades from the town. Everyone thought he deserved Father of the Year. They still do. What a fucking joke."

Holding her seemed so natural and comfortable, and it surprised him. He normally wasn't a touchy-feely type of guy, but she brought out a side of him he didn't know he had. An urge to chase away her bad memories, her sorrows, overwhelmed him. He'd never felt such a pull to a woman. It was magnetic and mind-boggling.

"Are your parents still together?" she murmured.

"Nope. They split up when my younger sister was only a baby. My mom's a meth freak and my old man's in prison."

"That's awful. I'm so sorry."

"No reason to be. That's just the way the cards were dealt. I figured it out."

"How many brothers and sisters do you have?"

"Three. A sister a couple years older than me. I haven't seen or heard from her in a few years. She's a fuckin' mess like our mom. A brother who was almost two years younger than me. He died of a drug overdose. And a sister who's five years younger. I hear from her when she needs money. A totally fucking dysfunctional family." He laughed dryly.

"You must've had a tough time growing up. Was your mom able to take care of you all?"

"Nope, but that's a story for another time, sweet pea. I don't know about you but I'm hungry as hell. I'm gonna order a burger. You want something?"

"Not really. Go ahead and order."

For the next two hours, they talked and laughed, and anyone seeing them would think they were a couple enjoying a pleasant afternoon. *No one would think how fucked up we both are.* He could see the great ache of desolation in the depths of her eyes. He recognized it because its persistent hammer clunked away, trying to break through the cage he'd put it in. But at that moment, he was content to indulge in conversation with her.

After glancing at her phone, she said in a soft voice, "We should head back."

Diablo nodded, then helped her up and escorted her out of the roadhouse. On the way back to town, Fallon held him tighter than she had earlier, and she rested her cheek against his back. Those small gestures warmed him more than he cared to admit, and he found himself very aware of her presence during the short trip back to Leroy's Diner where she'd parked her car.

"I had a wonderful time. Thank you." She swept her fingers across his forearm. "I'm sure my dad will be pissed when I get home." She giggled, but Diablo picked up a strain of fear running through it.

"You don't really want to go back right now, do you?" Her head dropped down, shaking. "Then why don't you spend the night?"

Her head jerked up. "Spend the night? I don't know anyone in town. I don't want to stay in a motel."

He fixed his gaze on her. "You know me. You can stay with me." He chuckled when her mouth flew open and a small gasp escaped from it.

"At your apartment? I don't think I could do that. I barely know you."

"I live at the clubhouse. It'd be my room, and I could crash in another one. There're about fifteen people who live at the club. It's up to you. I just thought you may not be ready to go home just yet." He shrugged and leaned back on his boot heels.

"I'm not ready. I guess I can go over and see what it's like."

"Sure. You can always change your mind. You can follow me."

She nodded slowly and unlocked her car door. Soon he was checking in his mirror to make sure she was still behind him. She was.

He had to be careful with her. He wanted to hold her close to him all night, but he knew it was too soon for that. Just thinking of her in his room—in his bed—made him stiffer than he'd been in a while. It'd been over a month since he'd banged Maria, and the way his dick was acting told him how bad he wanted it. But the only pussy he wanted to slide into was Fallon's. She was doing all sorts of crazy shit to him and she didn't even realize it.

*Keep it easy tonight. I don't want to scare her away.*

He pulled into the club's parking lot and went over to her, helping her out of the car. The late afternoon light cast a rose-gold glow over her. *She's stunning.* He smiled and pointed to the stucco house behind them.

"There's the club. Come on." He grabbed her hand.

"I'm scared," she said.

"Don't be. I'm with you."

He squeezed her hand and led her to the clubhouse.

# Chapter Eleven

FALLON BLINKED SEVERAL times to get her eyes accustomed to the dimness inside the club. Scanning the room, she recognized a few faces from the fighting events. Everyone stared at her, and she wanted to disappear in Diablo's cut. *Why did I agree to this?* Panic grabbed her nerves with its icy fingers as she walked toward the bar, her hand still in his. In her mind, each step sounded like a wooden block slamming down on the floor in an offbeat rhythm. Even though she stared straight ahead, she could feel all eyes on her.

"You want a ginger ale or something stronger?" Diablo asked as he lifted her and plopped her on the barstool.

"Whiskey and Coke." She turned away from the people and stared at the wall behind the bar.

"Hey, dude, what've you been up to? Shotgun said you cut out early today," one of the brothers said as he placed his elbow on the bar.

From the corner of her eye, she saw that he was looking at her. Her heart pounded.

"Yeah. I finished my work and had something to do."

"I can see that." Fallon turned to him and he smiled, staring at her chest. "I'm Army." He lifted a shot glass and threw its contents back.

"I'm Fallon." Turning away quickly, she knocked over her glass. "Damnit!" Before she could grab her napkin, the guy behind the bar wiped up the spill. "Thanks," she muttered.

"I've seen you before. I know I have." Army picked up his second shot glass.

"Lay off, will you?" Diablo's stern tone made her turn around.

"What the fuck's your problem? I was just saying that I've seen her before." Army straightened up.

She placed her hand on Diablo's arm. "It's okay, Diablo. You've seen me at the warehouse when you came to see the fights. Charlie's my dad."

Army snapped his fingers. "That's it. Who the fuck's Charlie?"

"Bloody Knuckles," Diablo said.

Army stared at her again, his gaze lingering on her chest. "I'll be damned. You don't look a thing like him, but that's good."

She chuckled. "I hate the nickname, Bloody Knuckles."

"Who's your lady?" another guy who'd come over asked.

Diablo groaned and looked around the room. "Are you all gonna be creeping over here asking me who the hell this pretty woman is?" He looped his arm around her waist.

Some of the men nodded while others yelled out "Fuck yeah." The women who wore clothes similar to the ones the ring girls wore stared at her, and she flicked her eyes away from them.

"Then fucking listen up 'cause I'm only gonna say this once. This is Fallon. Her dad is the promoter who puts on the fights in Tula." All eyes were on her, and she cast her gaze downward as she leaned closer to Diablo.

"Hi, Fallon." A man next to her smiled. Some of the other brothers started to come over.

Diablo gently raised her chin up with his fingers, locking his gaze with hers. "And these are my brothers." He named each one of them, but she noticed that the only people in the room he didn't name were the five women sitting on some of the men's laps. "No more questions or fuckin' comments or I'm gonna bust some balls." He turned his attention to her. "You wanna hang down here or go upstairs?"

"I'd like to go upstairs." In one movement, she was off the barstool, traipsing behind him as he guided her to his room.

The room in the middle of the long hallway was his. When she entered it, a beautiful vista of the mountains greeted her, as did a large bed that took up a good portion of the room. She glanced around and saw a nightstand, recliner, and tall dresser with a TV on top. The walls were ivory and bare except for a few hooks that held a couple pairs of jeans and some T-shirts. A cool wind blew in from the open windows.

"I like it." She crossed her arms and stood near the door.

"Make yourself comfortable." He gestured her to come over to the recliner. She smiled as she went over and sat in it. He sank down on the bed and leaned against the headboard.

Silence fell over them. *I'm going to tell him I've decided to go home. I don't think I can do this.* But the thought of facing her dad and Shanna made her nauseous, so she just sat there, pulling at a hangnail. *I wonder if he wants me to have sex with him. It wouldn't be so bad. At least he's good-looking. Not at all like the others.*

Her mind drifted back to the times when her dad had brought some men to her and told her to treat them right. She'd known what he'd meant, so she'd spread her legs and let them do what they wanted. In a perverse way, it made her feel pretty and wanted, but she'd felt like shit after the act was over and they left without even a goodbye. After the fourth time, she'd decided she wasn't going to do it anymore. So when her dad had asked her to do it again, she'd refused, not even caring how mad he'd become. After that, he never asked her again.

"What're you thinking about? You don't look too happy." Diablo's deep voice startled her.

"Oh… uh… I was just thinking about the fight I had at home this morning. Who were the women downstairs? Are they some of your friends' girlfriends?"

He quirked his lips and looked fixedly at her for several seconds before replying. "They belong to the club… to all the brothers. They wear the club's patch."

"Belong? What does that mean?"

He blew out. "You gotta be part of my world to get this. A lot of citizen women get super pissed about the club girls. They either hate them 'cause they're available to pleasure us whenever we want, or they fuckin' hate us and think we're barbaric in our treatment of them. I'm not sure which way you're gonna go on this."

"Why don't you just tell me about them and I'll let you know what I think. Are they like the ring girls? They dress like them."

"Sorta, except the club takes care of them. They live here and have our protection. We give them a monthly stipend. It helps them pay their bills and buy shit. If they need more, Steel, Paco, and Sangre decide whether it's justified."

"Why those guys and not all of you?"

"Steel's our prez, Paco the VP, and Sangre's the treasurer."

"Do the women work?"

"Only inside the club. They clean and help our cook, Lena, with the food. The important thing is that it's the club women's choice to live this lifestyle. No one's forced."

She sat still as what he said sank in. "They're sorta like the ring girls but then they aren't. The ring girls live at the warehouse, but I doubt my dad would protect any of them. They turn tricks, but my dad gets twenty percent. It's up to the woman if she wants to do it or not. Sylvia doesn't, but Emerald, Heidi, Pippa, and Cassie are totally into it. They don't screw the fighters unless they pay. So I guess it is different in a way, but you giving them money each month is really like paying for sex. I don't know...."

"We don't see it that way. We're just helping them out because we have the money. In most clubs, the women have jobs, or they're put to work at the strip bars and other businesses a club owns. We don't do that. The lifestyle's different, and the mindset."

"I guess. Do you have any favorites among them?"

"I don't go with any of them that often. You want something to drink?"

"No, thanks. You didn't answer my question."

"I don't wanna talk about them with you. They're a nice bunch of women—some nicer than others—and that's it. Nothing more to say about it. You wanna watch a movie? I bet you're hungry. Lena makes kickass burritos. I'll ask her to make us a couple." His face was earnest and his brown eyes were hopeful. Her insides fluttered with excitement and tenderness for him.

"I love burritos. I'm pretty open to most movies, but I hate the super-sappy love stories. I'm gonna bet you're not in to them either." She laughed.

"You'd be right. I can ask one of the women if they have something for you to sleep in that won't make me wild." He raised his eyebrows.

"Tell them a long T-shirt would be fine."

He chuckled. "I don't think they have that, but you could wear one of mine. I know it'd be long on you." He opened his dresser, took out a gray undershirt, and handed it to her. "I'll be back with the food in about twenty minutes or so. Lock the door." Then he was gone.

Bringing the shirt to her face, she breathed in deeply, loving the way his clean scent invaded her nostrils. She slipped off her jeans and top and tugged the T-shirt over her head. It fell just above her knees and felt soft against her skin.

After folding her clothes, she went over to the window and looked at the darkening sky. Excitement curled around her; this was the first time she'd ever been on her own. She was usually at home or the warehouse, but that night she was a free agent, and she loved it. Her phone kept flashing and she knew it was her dad trying to get a hold of her, but she ignored all the beeps and turned it off. *For just one night, I want to live in the moment.* She continued watching the encroaching ebony sky swallowing up the fading pink, orange, and purple streaks.

When the door clicked, she spun around, fear attacking her nerves. *What if it's Dad?* Her mind told her that was ridiculous, but her body responded as it had for years, telling her to hide so she wouldn't get a beating. Clamminess coated her pebbled skin, and when she saw Diablo come in holding an aluminum tin, threads of steam above it, she almost cried.

"You okay?"

She nodded. *I'm acting like an idiot. Why do I let Dad get to me all the time? He isn't even fucking here.* "It smells delicious. I didn't realize how hungry I was until now."

"Lena made enchiladas and tostadas too. I hope you like Mexican food." He placed the tin on the nightstand and took out two folding trays from his closet.

"I love Mexican food, especially enchiladas. Do you want me to help with something?"

"I'm good. The prospect's coming up with some beer, whiskey, ginger ale, Coke, and water. That should cover it." He threw her a warm smile.

Without thinking, she went over to him and hugged him tightly. His arms immediately hooked around her as he hugged her back.

"You smell real good, woman," he said thickly, then kissed the top of her head. "Your hair's so soft. You're making me feel all kinds of good shit."

A knock on the door brought her to her senses and she pulled away. "I just wanted to say thanks for being so good to me." With small steps, she walked back to the recliner as he padded to the door to get the drinks.

A few hours later, her eyelids drooped as the credits came up for the movie they'd watched. Yawning, she stretched, then pulled the soft blanket under her chin.

"I'll be going," Diablo said, standing up.

"Do you have to?" she asked softly.

When he didn't answer, she rolled on her back and sat up, the blanket falling down to her waist. She pulled in her knees and gazed at him, her stomach fluttering when she saw his heated look. "Do you want to have sex with me?" He took a few steps toward her and she sucked in her breath.

"Why're you asking me?" His voice was low with a sharp edge to it.

She shrugged. "I figured you did since you asked me to spend the night in your room. Men like that, and you've been paying a lot of attention to me."

"I'm not gonna lie and say that I don't wanna fuck you, but I like it when the woman wants it too."

"Maybe I do," she whispered.

He shook his head. "I think you're talking yourself into wanting it. I want you when you're quivering and dripping with desire, not when you feel obligated because we had a nice day together."

"Oh." She hung her head down.

Diablo sat next to her and cupped her chin, pushing her head up gently. "I've been fighting the urge to slam my cock inside you the whole time we've been together. I like you... a lot, and I don't say that shit to women. So don't think I don't desire you."

"All the guys I've known would already have me pinned down. You're different, and I like that." She raised her eyes and caught his gaze, smiling when she saw tenderness and lust reflected in it.

"I'm glad I'm different. You're not like any woman I've met."

She leaned in and brushed her lips against his. "Thanks for caring and being patient with me," she said against his mouth.

"I'm a very patient man when I think something's worth it. And you, sweet pea, are definitely worth it." He stroked her cheek, then stood up.

"I don't want to be alone. Can you stay with me?"

Breathing out, he wiped his hands on his jean-clad thighs. "There's no way I can stay in the same bed with you without fucking you, but I can sleep in the recliner."

Shaking her head, she said, "No, I'll sleep in the recliner. You take the bed."

As soon as she said it, she knew he'd never do that, so she slipped down under the blanket, covering her shoulders with it. His boots thudded against the floor as he kicked them off before settling into the recliner, pushing it back as far as it would go. He leaned over and switched off the floor lamp, flooding the room in darkness.

"Good night, Diablo," she said.

"'Night."

In a few minutes, she took comfort in his deep breathing that filled the room. Shards of moonlight seeped in through the slats in the blinds, casting an almost angelic glow on him.

*I can't believe he didn't fuck me. He's a good man. The first one I've ever met.*

Burrowing further into the mattress, she closed her eyes and fell asleep with thoughts of Diablo floating in her mind.

# Chapter Twelve

THE CLAP OF thunder and Fallon's blood-curdling scream brought Diablo to his feet. Flicking his gaze to the window, a flash of lightning sparked through the blinds, and then another boom shook the sky. Fallon moaned and tossed in her sleep. Diablo went over to her, sitting next to her as he ran his fingers through her damp hair.

"No. Don't. Stop. Get away from me," she moaned, thrashing her head from side to side. Diablo took his hand away but her distress only increased; then he realized she wasn't talking to him. Some bad things in the dark corners of her mind had snuck out while she slept to torment her.

"No. No!" she screamed again, and Diablo drew her close to him, pushing back the hair that stuck to her sweaty face. In sleep, she clung to him, trembling like a fragile reed. He leaned down and kissed her hair, holding her tightly.

After a few seconds, the demons that had come out to wreak havoc seemed to have scattered back to their shadowed parts of her memory.

Resting against the wooden headboard, he stared vacantly at the light show seeping in through the slats covering his window. *Something bad hurt her.* Sighing, he looked down at her, her face now peaceful; it seemed as though she'd weathered the internal storm.

"What's going on with you?" he muttered under his breath. His gaze flicked to the clock on the wall above the dresser; it was six thirty in the morning. He laid his head back against the wall. He couldn't believe he'd behaved the entire night. Several times he'd woken up and looked over at her soft form in his bed, and it'd taken all his strength to stay in the recliner. If it were any other woman, he would've been banging them without any thought, but with Fallon, he wanted her to come to him because she *desired* him, not because she felt *obligated*.

*What the fuck am I doing, anyway? I don't have any business fucking up her life. She's already got enough shit to deal with. I'm not looking for a relationship. Lucy and Maria suit me just fine. Easy without commitment is perfect for me.*

But he couldn't stop thinking about Fallon. There was something about her that drew him in. Maybe it was because they were both twisted and broken by all the shit that hurt them in their past. Maybe that was the tie that pulled them together. He wasn't sure, but he knew he wanted to spend a lot more time with Fallon.

The minutes passed into hours, and he didn't even know he'd fallen asleep until a knock on his door woke him up. Fallon was still curled around him. He smiled as he untangled her arms, then went to see who was knocking.

Sangre stood there, a smirk on his clean-shaven face. "Steel's called church in thirty minutes."

"Thanks. I'll be there." Diablo ran his hand over his face, suppressing a yawn. Sangre just stood there. "Is there something else?"

"No."

Diablo knew he wanted to ask him about Fallon. "Then I'll see you at church." He closed the door, chuckling at the disappointment on Sangre's face. He knew all the brothers would be dying to know what the deal with Fallon was. The brothers teased him about not fucking every club woman, hang-around, or citizen who shook her ass his way. He heard the hushed voices when he'd stand drinking at a party, then go up to his room alone. He never understood why they were all so interested in how many women he stuck his cock into, but they were.

The talk around the pool table and the bar always centered on Harleys, booze, and pussy—in that order. He was the only one who almost never talked about women. It wasn't his style. What he did with Lucy and Maria was between him and them. He knew he was an anomaly among the brothers, but he'd never been one to talk about the women he bedded.

"How long have you been up?" Fallon asked.

He turned around and took her in: sleep-filled eyes, mussed-up hair, glowing skin. *She's fuckin' beautiful.* "Not too long. I got church soon. I'm gonna take a shower."

"Church? On a Wednesday morning?"

He sniggered. "Church means a meeting in biker lingo."

"That's weird." She covered her mouth and yawned wide.

"I'll be out in fifteen minutes."

Freshly showered, he came out with a blue towel wrapped around his waist. Fallon was still in his T-shirt, standing by the window and looking out. He came behind her and wrapped his arm around her waist, kissing the top of her head. "It's a fuckin' deluge out there." Sheets of water and graphite-smudged skies made the desert landscape seem more desolate than usual. "You can go down to the kitchen if you're hungry. Just tell Lena you're with me and she'll treat you nice."

"How long's your meeting?"

He pulled away, took a pair of blue jeans off the wall hook, and put them on. "I don't know. It could be twenty minutes or several hours." He slid his belt through the loops.

"I'll freshen up. I should really go home."

"Not in this rainstorm you're not. Wait for it to pass and then see what you wanna do. I got some extra toothbrushes in the bottom drawer of the vanity."

"Thanks. Do you stock up for times when a strange woman ends up spending the night in your room?"

"Nope. I stock up 'cause I grew up never having enough of anything. Now I got toothbrushes, toothpaste, shampoo, and a ton of other shit stuffed in my drawers, closet, and a storage shed I have out back. See how a bad childhood can fuck you up?" He winked at her, then tugged his T-shirt over his head.

"I'm the queen of life fucking me up."

"It's the way you handle the shit that makes the difference." He pulled up his boots, then came over to her. "Promise you'll wait until I get back."

Nodding, she smiled. He gave her a quick kiss on her lips and rushed out of the room. If he stayed a second later, he'd have her in a heated embrace, his hands roaming over her body, exploring the curves she kept hidden.

When he entered the meeting room, all eyes were on him. Some of the brothers had smirks on their faces while others straightened up, preparing to question and rib him about Fallon. He pulled a metal chair out and plopped down, his eyes fixed forward.

"How was your night?" Goldie asked.

*Of course it'd be Goldie who'd start the grilling.*

"Good." He crossed his arms over his broad chest.

"How's Fallon? Did she have a good night too?" Goldie pushed his chair back against the wall, and some of the brothers snickered.

"She's good." *I'm not giving 'em shit.*

"Lucy and Maria were moping most of the night because you had her in your room," Army said.

"First time we've seen you with a non-club woman," Chains said.

Their words were beginning to wind him up as irritation jabbed at his gut. "So?" he gritted.

"It's just that we wanna know what's so special about this chick. Something is. Does she fuck better than Lucy or Maria?" Goldie laughed. Some of the brothers whistled while others guffawed.

To Diablo, their words and gestures were like acid—burning, slicing, potent. Anger hissed through his body as he sprang out of his chair and smashed his fist into Goldie's nose, splattering red drops on the white walls.

"What the fuck, you asshole!" Goldie clipped Diablo's jaw, and soon the two men were punching the shit out of each other.

*Bam! Bam! Bam!* The loud banging flooded Diablo's ears and pulled him out of his rage. He shoved Goldie away and turned his attention to the front of the room. Steel, holding the gavel, didn't look too pleased. Diablo wiped his mouth with the back of his hand, the coppery tang of blood overpowering his taste buds.

"What the fuck is going on here?" Steel demanded, his green eyes glaring.

"Nothing," Goldie said as he held a wad of tissue to his nose and tilted his head back.

"Bullshit! Muerto?"

Muerto shook his head. "Raven and I were texting, so I wasn't paying attention."

"Army? Crow?" The men just shook their heads or shrugged. Steel crossed his arms and glowered at the brothers. "Diablo, what the fuck happened?"

"Goldie said some shit that I didn't like. No big deal. He knows he was outta line."

"Fuck you," Goldie said.

"Does this have to do with Fallon?" Steel glanced at Paco, who nodded. "Next time take it outside. We don't do shit like this at church. What the fuck were you thinking, Diablo?"

He stared at his president without saying a word. *Steel's right. I fuckin' lost control.* He couldn't explain why, but when he heard Goldie disrespecting Fallon, it was like he'd thrown gasoline on the fire that had been burning inside Diablo since he'd seen Goldie's smirk as he walked into the room. He'd just exploded and his primal instinct took over. He didn't think he'd broken Goldie's nose—he hadn't heard the crackling sound he knew so well after years of fist fights—but it *was* swelling up pretty good.

"You good, Goldie?" Steel asked. Goldie nodded. "Then let's start. I called church because Hawk called me a couple of hours ago and said Satan's Pistons are planning retaliation for the shit that went down at the warehouse and what we did to their strip bar. He said they've been buying a bunch of arms from some of the gangs in Denver. How're we doing with adding to our artillery, Army?"

"Good. Banger hooked me up with this Irish dude, Liam. Seems the Insurgents have worked with him for many years. Banger said he's a good guy who can be trusted for the most part. Muerto, Chains, and I are meeting with him next week. He said he can get us whatever we need."

"Did Hawk say what the fuckers have in mind?"

Steel shook his head. "No, just that they're talking a lot of shit about us, and the way they're building up their stockpile makes him believe they're planning to strike. Paco's been in charge of installing security cameras at all our businesses."

The Night Rebels never needed the cameras because no sane citizen would dream of vandalizing, breaking in, or stealing from the outlaw club, but since the Pistons' acts of aggression, security cameras and alarms had to be installed.

"We need to strike them before they strike us," Crow said.

"That'll just escalate everything. We need to anticipate their movements," Paco countered.

Steel nodded. "Hawk's gonna keep monitoring the grapevine chatter, and we'll monitor stuff on our end. Chains, you're the IT guy, so you're in charge of monitoring as well. Give Hawk a call and coordinate with him."

*I gotta focus on the club and keep Fallon in the back of my mind. Some serious shit's going on here.* Diablo looked up when he heard the gavel hit the wooden block. The brothers left the room, but he hung back.

"Something on your mind?" Steel asked as he put some papers in a folder.

"I just want to let you know I'm on top of this. I'm gonna find out who tipped off the Pistons that our brothers would be at the warehouse. There's no way a group of these fuckers is gonna come into Alina in full colors and attack us. They know that would be suicide. We gotta keep our eyes open for anyone who acts like he doesn't belong. Do you think Jimmy Delarosa would be the Pistons' lackey?"

"No. Jimmy's a slime bag, but he's too much of a coward to get on our bad side. He's into scamming the vulnerable. This isn't his scene. But you're probably right about having someone else do their dirty work, just like they had the punk gang put their name on the strip bar.

Let me know if you find out anything at the warehouse."

"Sure thing." He turned to leave.

"Diablo? I know how a blinding rage can consume you when someone talks shit about your woman. I used to see red every time one of the brothers ribbed me about Breanna. I'm just saying, Goldie had it coming." Steel laughed.

Diablo nodded. "Later, brother." He bumped fists with his prez and left the room.

When he walked into the main room, Goldie came up to him and extended his hand. Diablo grasped and shook it. "Did I break your fuckin' nose?"

Goldie shook his head. "Just busted a blood vessel. You got a fuckin' hard punch."

"What're you drinking?"

"Double shot of tequila sounds damn good."

The two men went over to the bar and Diablo told Patches to bring them their drinks. Goldie picked his up and clinked it against Diablo's beer bottle. "I didn't know the chick meant something to you, bro."

His jaw jutted out and he raised the bottle to his lips. "Now you do." He took a long pull on his beer.

"How about a game of pool?" Brutus asked as he and Army came over to join Diablo and Goldie.

"I'm in," said Goldie.

"Me too, but first I gotta check on Fallon."

"Cool. We'll meet you at the pool table in thirty. I gotta get some chow," Army said.

Diablo finished his beer and made his way upstairs. When he went into his room, he saw Fallon dressed in the clothes she'd worn the previous day, sitting on the edge of the bed, her cell phone in her hand.

Looking over her shoulder, she smiled at him. "How'd your meeting go?"

"Good."

"Why's your bottom lip swollen?"

"Just roughhousing with another brother. It's no big deal. You wanna come down and get something to eat?"

"Not really. My stomach is sorta in knots. I have to get going. The downpour's over. I even saw a rainbow arching over the mountain peaks. It was so pretty. Let's see if it's still there." Diablo followed her over to the window and stood behind her. "There it is. See?"

Through the mist a brilliant band of color hung in the sky over the San Juan Mountains. The trees that dotted the mountains were a patchwork of vibrant greens while the desert ground in the forefront was dark brown from all the moisture.

"Isn't it awesome? I love the way the air smells after a rainstorm." He saw her shoulders rise as she breathed in deeply.

Grasping her shoulders, he pulled her back, crushing her against him. "You're awesome." He bent down and nuzzled his face against her neck, her sweet sugary-lemon scent swimming around him.

She twisted and threw her arms around his waist. "Thank you for everything." Light shimmered in her eyes as she looked up at him, her lips parted.

Bowing his head, he pressed his mouth to hers and kissed her gently while his hands moved down to her hips. Instead of pushing him away as he suspected she'd do, she squeezed him tighter and moaned. The small sound was his undoing and he hungrily thrust his tongue deep into her mouth, all the while gripping her nicely rounded hips. His lips left hers to nibble at her earlobe, and she cocked her head to the side to give him better access to her soft and delectable neck. He traced the elegant curve of her neck with his tongue, licking a path to her shoulder.

"You're so beautiful and sexy," he rasped against her skin as he nipped and kissed her tender flesh. He nipped his way back up, his lips recapturing hers, more demanding that time. As they kissed, his cock punched against his zipper, desperate to get out. He wanted her so bad. His fingers tugged at the hem of her top, slipping underneath it, inching their way up her satiny skin. When they reached her bra, he felt her stiffen under his touch.

"You don't like that?" he asked, his dick throbbing like mad.

"I do, but I don't know. I'm confused," she said as she began to pull away.

Disappointment clutched his cock. "You're so fuckin' sexy that I got carried away." He stepped away.

Looking down at the floor, she wrung her hands. "I'm sorry. I want to be with you but—"

"No reason to apologize. I told you last night that I'm a patient guy, but my cock isn't." He chuckled and smoothed down her hair. "It's cool. No worries."

Glancing upward, she pressed her lips together. "I really have to get going."

Nodding, he ambled toward the door. "I'll walk you to your car. Remember, we still got a date this Sunday for a long ride."

A wide smile lit up her face. "I can't wait." She followed him out of the room.

When they walked through the big room, he held her hand, his chin jutted out and a don't-say-a-fucking-thing look on his face. The brothers watched them leave the room.

Standing by her car, he gripped her hands and tugged her to him, kissing her lightly on the lips. "You gonna be okay at home?"

Taking a deep breath, she nodded, then exhaled. "It should be all right."

The skin around her mouth twitched, telling him she was scared. "If you need me, call me. I can get to you fast. No reason to put up with Shanna's or your dad's bullshit."

"I know. I'm sure everyone's cooled down by now." She opened the car door. "Thanks again." She kissed him quickly, then slid into the driver seat.

"Take care of yourself. I'll call you later to see how it's going."

She nodded, closed the door, and started the engine. Waving, she drove away.

When he couldn't see her anymore, he sucked in his breath and readjusted his jeans, then turned around and headed back to the clubhouse to play pool with his brothers.

# Chapter Thirteen

THE CRISP AIR rushed through the open windows of Fallon's car as she drove toward Tula, the hard beats of Warrant's "Cherry Pie" blasting on the radio. A sweet, fresh smell mingled with the musty scent of wet dirt that permeated the air. In the distance, a lightning bolt split the sky as a low rumble of thunder threatened another downpour. Fallon loved the rain, especially the smell of it before and after a good storm. When she was a child, she'd run outside and twirl around as the large drops fell on her face and hair. She loved the way the parched ground soaked up the water, the trees grew brighter, and the hot silver rays from the sun pierced the gray skies. To her, rain created life; it was life's blood.

As she drove down the old highway, she felt weightless, giddy, and happy all at once. She was bursting, and the most wonderful kiss she'd ever had still scorched her lips. *He's amazing.* The way he kissed her not only took her breath away, it was beyond awesome. No man had ever kissed her that way—not that she had a lot of men kissing her. James had been more interested in touching her, and when they did kiss, it was wet and uncontrolled. But Diablo made her toes curl, her heart pound, and her insides explode. His kisses seared her skin, and their intensity hit her right between her legs. *And he wants to see me again even though I didn't put out.* She giggled and turned the volume even higher. *I really like him, and I think he really likes me. He wants to be with* me.

After James Thornhill had humiliated her, she'd stayed away from men. She didn't trust them and, to be honest, she'd never known a nice man in her twenty-one years. The men her dad had asked her to fuck rarely kissed her. One of them, a man in his mid-forties, had kissed her, but she didn't feel anything. But she felt *everything* with Diablo, and she craved more.

It seemed like such a long time until Sunday. She stretched her arm out the window and let the cool wind caress it as tiny drops of water covered it. The time she'd spent with Diablo had been the best in her life since her mother had left.

When she entered Tula, her muscles began to stiffen. Turning the radio off, she willed the creeping anxiety in her to stop as she made her way to her home. When Fallon entered the house, it was quiet even though both Shanna's and her dad's cars were parked in the garage. Since it was early afternoon, she'd thought they both would've been gone. The carpeted stairs muted her footsteps, and she hoped she could make it to her room before either of them saw her.

As she walked to her room, Shanna's voice rang out.

"It's a lot of money. The little bitch's been a pain in the ass for a long time, so it's time we cashed in on her."

Her dad answered, but she couldn't hear what he was saying. He was always soft-spoken unless he was pissed; then the whole neighborhood could hear him. She figured Shanna must be right by the master bedroom door because Fallon could hear her clearly. Their master bedroom was larger than a lot of people's homes. *Dad must be on the other side of the room. I wonder who they're talking about.*

"I keep telling you she has no fucking clue about the money. I took the letter the minute I saw the law firm's return address. I figured it was important since it came from lawyers. They just assumed she knew her grandmother died."

More garbled responses from her dad. *I wish I could hear what Dad's saying. Maybe I can get a little closer.* But fear of detection rooted her to the spot. She tried to make sense of what Shanna was saying, and a suspicion niggled at the back of her mind that *she* may be the topic of the conversation.

"We have to make it look like an accident. You're good at creating accidents." Shanna's high-pitched laughter grated her nerves. "I'll pretend to actually like the freak. She's so desperate to have a friend, that won't be a problem. We have to make it look good, because I have no intention of spending the rest of my life locked up."

The color drained from Fallon's face as her pulse pounded in her ears. *They're talking about me. What're they saying about an accident? Are they planning to hurt me? I can't believe Dad would do that.* Then a memory long buried deep down inside began to take shape, reaching out to drag her back to a late afternoon in autumn when she was in high school. *No! I don't want to remember!* Shallow breaths in rapid succession indicated she was on the verge of a major panic attack. She cried out, then quickly placed her hand over her mouth to stop any more sound from coming out.

"Wait a sec. I heard something."

*I can't let her see me. I can't let her know I heard them.* She knew she couldn't make it to her bedroom fast enough because of her gait, so she slipped inside one of the guest bedrooms and hobbled over to the closet, closing the door just in time. Through the narrow wooden strips on the closet door, she saw Shanna pop her head through the doorway and look around the room. After a few seconds, she went away.

Fallon stayed in the closet until she heard the tires squeal as Shanna pulled out of the driveway. She waited to hear her father's car drive away but the sound never came. *He must still be in the bedroom.* Then she remembered her dad was having car trouble and the mechanic couldn't work on it until the end of the week.

Slowly she opened the closet door. The house was as quiet as a tomb. Relief flooded over her as she reached her bedroom, locked the door, and sank down on a chair. *Maybe I just imagined what I heard. I don't even know what they were talking about. A letter from a law firm? Why would they write to me? It must be someone else.* It just couldn't be her. Her paternal grandparents had died long before she was born, and her mother's parents disowned her mother when she'd married Fallon's dad. *Could they have been talking about Mom's mom? My grandmother? Why would a lawyer want to find me?* Just saying "grandmother" seemed awkward, but a shiver of anticipation ran through her. *Maybe they have some information on Mom. Maybe my grandmother found out where she is and doesn't want to contact me directly.* Excitement fluttered in her belly, and she made a mental note to do a search and see if she could locate her grandmother.

She went to her room and stared out the window, scanning the view that'd brought her comfort and heartache for so many years. She'd longed to be someone other than herself, so she'd pick out a house in the distance and pretend to live there with the life she always had inside her but no one would let her come out until Diablo. Looking at the houses dotting the landscape, she realized that she didn't want to be anywhere other than right where she was. Diablo was a part of her ordinary life, and she wouldn't trade that for the world. In that moment, as the crisp breeze blew through her hair, she decided she'd get a job and move away from the only life she'd ever known, away from her dad and step-bitch. And if fear threatened to hold her back, she'd just have to face it straight on and do it anyway.

Excitement coursing through her body, she took out her phone and tapped in Diablo's number.

**Fallon:** *I had a really good time. Just wanted you to know.*

She caught her breath when she heard the ping. It always thrilled her to hear it, knowing he was close to her.

**Diablo:** *Me 2. Everything good @ home?*

**Fallon:** *Not sure. They didn't hear me come home, but my car's parked on the street. Anyway, they're gone now. I'm looking forward to Sunday.*

**Diablo:** *Oh yea!*

**Fallon:** *I know you're at work. I'm thinking of you.*

**Diablo:** *Good 2 know. I think of u 2, & fantasizing bout doing some nasty stuff to u. ;)*

She swallowed and touched her warm cheeks. As she reread the text, desire unfurled deep in the pit of her stomach and she clenched her legs. Remembering how wonderfully he kissed, she brought her fingers to her lips and closed her eyes, replaying the way he held her while he crushed his mouth on hers. A ping brought her out of the moment.

**Diablo:** *U still there?*

She sucked in her breath.

**Fallon:** *Yeah. Just remembering how you kissed me. It was nice.*

Hurriedly, she sent the text before she chickened out.

**Diablo:** *I plan on kissing u a lot more. U felt good in my arms.*
**Fallon:** *I liked it. I better go. Talk to you later.*
**Diablo:** *K. If shit happens, call me. I'll come get u.*
**Fallon:** *Ok. Bye.*

She beamed while she reread their texts over and over, feeling like a schoolgirl. A low rumble in her stomach reminded her that she was hungry, so she went downstairs to the kitchen. Opening the refrigerator, she saw it was stocked full of platters of food: deviled eggs, canapés, sliced fruit, raw vegetables, and several quiches. *That's right. Shanna's having her kissing ass luncheon tomorrow.* She pulled out a couple of the trays, took out a mocha yogurt, and sat at the table.

As she ate, her phone rang, and dread filled her. She wasn't ready to talk to her dad; he'd ruin the good feeling that was humming through her. Relief spread over her when she saw Sylvia's number flashing instead of her dad's.

"Hi, Sylvia. I was just thinking about you."

"Hey, girl. Were you thinking good thoughts about me?" Fallon could hear the smile in Sylvia's voice.

"Of course. Actually, I wanted to know if you were up to hanging out tomorrow. Shanna's having some hoity-toity luncheon, and I want to be as far away from it as I can." She didn't share the fact that Shanna had ordered her not to be around because she thought she'd be an embarrassment.

"Sounds awful. I wish we could go shopping, but tomorrow won't work. I have to do some personal stuff. What're you doing now? I wanted to know if you're up to coming over here for a bit, and then we can go get something to eat. You know I'm dying to hear about your time away from your dad."

"How'd you hear about that?"

"Your dad was so pissed off that he was venting about it with us. He had no idea where you went and he was asking us if we did. I was pretty sure you were with that good-looking biker, but I didn't say a word. Were you with him?"

Fallon giggled. "Yeah."

"I knew it! You gotta tell me all about it. So, can you come over?"

"Yeah. I'll just freshen up and be there in twenty minutes. Where do you want to go eat? I feel like a burger."

"Big Daddy's has the best burgers in town. We can go there, but first you gotta tell me *everything*. Deal?"

"Deal. See you soon."

Less than thirty minutes later, Fallon pulled in behind the warehouse and took out her keys, letting herself in through the back door. The main room where they held the fights was empty and eerily quiet. The ring seemed smaller without the combatants in it and all the spectators crowded around it. She shuffled across the concrete floor and went upstairs. Entering the family room, her muscles stiffened when she saw Emerald and Heidi sitting on the couch. She took a few steps back, hoping they didn't notice her, but vultures always sense their prey.

Emerald looked over her shoulders and sneered. "Look who just came in. Your dad's gonna beat your sorry ass, bitch."

Heidi turned the volume on the television down and laughed. "Where you been hiding?"

"It's none of your business," Fallon said as she walked farther into the room.

Emerald stood up, an evil grin making her face look distorted. "You've forgotten your manners since you threw your little tantrum. Your dad said you're an ungrateful, spoiled brat. You know my mom and stepdad tossed me out when I turned sixteen. I didn't live in a fancy house and have a dad who paid for everything."

"Maybe she was with a man," Heidi said.

Emerald tilted her head back and laughed loudly. "A man? What man would touch *that*?" She pointed at Fallon, her nose crinkled in contempt.

"Never know. Some men are real desperate and will put their cock in any pussy." Heidi glared at Fallon.

"If anyone wanted her pussy, it'd only be for Charlie's money." Emerald fixed her stare on Fallon.

Fallon straightened her shoulders, looked at each of them, and said coolly, "Fuck you."

The room went quiet, the only sound the ticking of the wall clock. Then Emerald's face darkened and she leapt in front of Fallon, shoving her back so hard that she stumbled and fell backward. Emerald loomed above her. "Don't you ever say that to me again, bitch."

"What's going on here?" Sylvia's voice broke through the tension in the room.

Emerald waved her hand over Fallon. "She's got a real attitude and I don't like it."

"We were just chilling on the couch watching our program, and she comes in here like she owns the place, giving us shit," Heidi said as she leaned against the back of the couch.

"I highly doubt that," Sylvia said as she helped Fallon up. "What happened?" she asked Fallon.

"The same shit. It makes Heidi and Emerald feel better to pick on me because they're so damn insecure. And Emerald, you're so jealous of me it's pathetic." Fallon brushed off her backside.

"Me jealous of *you*? What a joke." Emerald took a few steps closer.

"Why would she be jealous of you? She's pretty. You're not. She can walk right. You can't. It's a no-brainer, stupid," Heidi said.

"Stop it! Both of you. If you keep this up, I'm going to tell Charlie. He's not going to like what happened here." Sylvia held Fallon by the arm. "Let's go grab that burger now," she whispered. Fallon nodded.

"Charlie doesn't give a shit about *her*." Emerald's words pierced Fallon's heart because, deep down, she knew the bitch was right. Emerald glared at Fallon. "I had your dad's cock way before he hitched up with Shanna. I can make him do whatever I want. You just remember that."

"She still does it with your daddy." Heidi snorted. Fallon's eyes widened. "That's right. When Shanna's being a bitch and won't let your dad near her pussy. Emerald takes care of it, and if she's not around, I step in."

Fallon wanted to smack the satisfied smirk off both Emerald's and Heidi's faces. *I have to get out of here.* "Let's go," she said to Sylvia as she walked away. Sylvia followed as the other two women laughed and said things to each other in hushed voices. Fallon turned around. "You need to stay away from me. I'm sick of your shit, and I won't put up with it anymore. And I don't give a damn what my dad does or who he fucks."

"You bitch!" Emerald rushed toward her, but Sylvia pushed her back. Then she and Fallon headed down the stairs and out the back door.

"Emerald is such a slut. I'm sorry she said all those things to you. Don't pay any attention to her." Sylvia slipped into the passenger seat.

Switching on the ignition, Fallon shook her head. "I don't. She means nothing to me. It makes her feel better to make people around her miserable. She's a bully. I had my fair share of them when I was in school. I meant what I said back there. I'm done with her, Heidi, and Cassie. And I don't give a shit what my dad does. I guess I'm done with it all."

Sylvia gently patted her shoulder. "You must've had a hell of a good time with Diablo. You came back with an attitude. I love seeing it."

"I've always had attitude inside me, but I felt alone and dependent on my dad. I was always so scared he'd make good on his promise to throw me out." She pulled into a parking space in front of the restaurant.

Seated at a table, a ginger ale in front of her and a beer in front of Sylvia, Fallon put the menu down and took a sip of her drink. "You know, a part of me is scared to death that Diablo is just being nice to me because he feels sorry for me. I'm afraid he'll leave me," she said softly.

"From what I saw when we were at the diner and he came up to you, he seemed really into you. And the way he looked at you at the warehouse afterward was intense. I've been with more men than I want to admit to, so I have more experience in reading them than you do. Diablo doesn't seem like he just wants to get in your pants and then move on. He doesn't seem jerky like a lot of guys. He strikes me as someone who plays it straight."

"I think the same thing, but you never know."

"If you want any hope at happiness, you need to take a chance with him. Love isn't foolproof. It can be wonderful and it can hurt, but never having it is worse. You gotta start living."

Fallon nodded. "I know. I've been thinking about that. I've been wanting to move out on my own for the last couple of years, but I've been too afraid to do it. The last few days I've been on my own felt fantastic. It made me think that I could really do it. If I needed something, I know Diablo would help and—"

"And you got me. You know I'll help you out as best I can. You can do this, girl."

Fallon smiled. "After all this time, I think I'm ready. I'm going to check to see what jobs are available in Alina and apply for them. Oh my God, I can't believe I'm going to do this." Heat flushed her face.

"You need to. You're going to be twenty-two this year. It's time to spread your wings. You need to start experiencing and interacting with life. I'm so excited for you."

"If it were up to my dad, he'd always have me with him, making sure my wings were clipped. I can't figure out why he wants me around when he's mean to me most of the time."

"It's probably a matter of control. Some people are like that. They never want family or friends to leave them until they decide they can go."

The waiter placed a cheeseburger in front of Fallon and a half-pound burger loaded with cheddar cheese, bacon, and barbecue sauce in front of Sylvia.

"No wonder you're so slender. You barely eat," Sylvia said as she picked up a fried onion ring and put it on her burger.

"It's just the way I'm built." Fallon squirted ketchup on her cheeseburger.

"You're lucky. I've been battling my weight since I was a kid. It's a pain in the ass. So Diablo must like slender women. I heard bikers like real curvy women with big boobs."

"Really? I'm not sure what he likes." She glanced down at her chest. "If he's looking for big breasts, mine are definitely not."

"He likes you, so he's good with your boobs. Anyway, you'd look ridiculous with big ones on your slender build."

Fallon giggled as she pictured herself with a huge bust. "I would look ridiculous."

"Have you seen him naked? I bet he's really hung. The big guys are." Fallon shoved a few fries in her mouth and shook her head. "He didn't have you suck him or anything?"

Putting her drink down, she laughed. "No. It's not that he didn't want to, but I'm not ready." She looked away.

"And he's good with that? Wow… he's a keeper. He definitely respects you, girl. You got this one." Sylvia opened her mouth wide and took a bite of her burger.

For the rest of the afternoon, they talked about Diablo, their dreams and hopes for the future, and their disappointments thus far in their short lives. As Fallon grabbed the bill, insisting on paying, happiness spread through her. *I'm going to do this. Tomorrow I'll go to the library and surf the net for jobs. I can't believe I'm actually going to do this.* She didn't dare stay home and use her computer. She wanted to be away from her dad and his wife. Besides, she always loved going to the library; it reminded her of her mother and all the times they'd spent roaming the aisles in search of books.

When she arrived back home, it was early evening. No one was home, and Fallon went to her room and locked the door. She opened her closet and looked at her oversized clothes, deciding that since she was on the road to change, she'd go through her clothes and choose which ones to leave behind. As she was moving the outfits she was going to take to one end of her closet, she heard Shanna's car pull into the driveway, followed by another one. Anxiety replaced the gaiety she'd been feeling.

A mix of light and heavy footsteps on the stairs made her stomach gurgle and her nerves fray. The footsteps should have gone away from her room, but they were heading toward it.

*Shit! I won't let them ruin my mood. I won't....*

A heavy knock on her door. "Fallon? Open up. I want to talk to you."

She held her breath, frozen in the middle of her walk-in closet.

Another heavy knock. "Did you hear me? Open the fuck up."

Fallon moved over to the window and opened it. She climbed out and sat down, hugging her knees as she rocked back and forth.

The knocks became pounds and she rocked hard, humming loudly to block out her father's voice.

Then it was quiet. She strained her ears to hear her father's retreating footsteps, but she heard Shanna's voice.

"Just let her be. You can talk to her in the morning. I have the luncheon tomorrow and I'm nervous as hell about it. I don't want a lot of drama right now. Anyway, she's old enough to spend some time away from the house. You need to lighten up."

"I'll speak to you in the morning," her father said, his hand slamming against her door, making her jump.

Then he went away. Shanna had cooled his ire. Shanna had *helped* her. *She's up to no good for sure.*

For the next few hours, she sat outside, even though her body shivered and was covered with goose bumps as the cool air blew over her. The roof, the night, the lights from houses twinkling like tiny fireflies in the distance were her refuge, and she wasn't ready to leave their comfort. Her phone vibrated against her thigh. She hoped it wasn't her father sending her hurtful, vindictive messages as he often did. She opened it.

**Diablo:** *Everything good?*

She smiled and brushed away the hair from her face. *It is now.*

**Fallon:** *Yeah. What are you doing?*

**Diablo:** *Thinking bout my sweet pea.*

**Fallon:** *That's nice. I wish I were with you.*

**Diablo:** *U will be. Soon.*

**Fallon:** *Nite.*

**Diablo:** *Nite.*

*He makes me feel so wonderful. Tomorrow I'll get up super early and be out before Dad or Shanna are even up.* She went back inside, washed up, and slid under her down comforter. Glancing out the window, she took comfort in knowing that Diablo saw the same sky from his window. Instead of thinking about her dad and how angry he was, Diablo was on her mind. She knew the dark shadows of her dreams would be replaced by bright colors and sunlight.

That night, she welcomed sleep.

# Chapter Fourteen

THE FOLLOWING MORNING, Fallon sat in the parking lot of a convenience store, blowing on a steaming cup of coffee as she watched the sun come up. The wipers cleared the damp morning dew from the windshield, letting in the first orange-hued rays. She set the coffee in the holder and unlocked her phone, tapping in the last name of her maternal grandmother—Odom. Instantly, numerous findings populated the screen. She scrolled down, finding an obituary for a Barbara Odom, age seventy.

Fallon clicked on the link and the window opened to the Horsham and Lowry Mortuary page, a full-page obituary with a photograph on the right side of an older, nice-looking woman with white hair. Fallon scanned the obituary and learned that Barbara Odom passed away after a short illness two months before. Her husband had predeceased her a few years before. Fallon read through the list of accomplishments she'd done for various charities and foundations in Denver, and then she stared at two names of the surviving relatives to Barbara Odom: Joanna Richardson and Fallon Richardson.

Fallon touched her parted lips, a flush of adrenaline tingling through her body. Her eyes went back to the smiling woman in the photograph. *That's my grandmother. I wonder if Mom knows she died. I wonder if Mom is in Denver.* Her heart beat rapidly and she struggled to breathe. For a long while, she gulped in air as her gaze stayed glued to her grandmother's picture. *Shanna was talking about me.*

Another car pulling in next to her in the lot made her jump. A young man in a suit dashed into the convenience store. Fallon glanced around and noticed several cars coming and going from the parking lot.

The sky had ripened from an orange color into a pale blue. Wisps of white clouds stood unmoving. She looked down at her phone and tapped in the words "law firm probate for Barbara Odom," and in a second, the Naylor Hastings Garber LLP law firm popped up. She leaned her head back on the rest, knowing time would pass at a snail's pace until the law firm would be open. There was a two-hour wait until nine o'clock, but it seemed like a lifetime.

Closing her eyes, images of her mother and the older woman in the photograph danced in her mind. From what she could make out, her mother had the same eyes as Barbara Odom. *She's my grandmother, and all this time we were only separated by four hundred miles.* A thread of sadness wove through her as she realized that she'd never get to know her grandmother. They were related, yet she never had the chance to decide whether she wanted a relationship with her or not; it had already been decided for her. Heaviness set in as she waited for the time to pass.

At nine fifteen, she dialed the law firm and told them who she was. The secretary put her on hold.

"Scott Garber," a pleasant voice said.

"Hi. Uh… my name's Fallon Richardson and I think you know… uh… knew… my grandmother. Her name was Barbara Odom."

A small laugh came through the phone. "Have you forgotten our last phone conversation?"

"I've never called you before. I just found out about my grandmother by doing an Internet search. I overheard my dad and his wife talking about a letter you sent about my grandmother's death."

A long silence ensued, and then she heard him clear his throat. "Can you please give me your social security number, date of birth, and driver's license number?" She complied. "There seems to be something strange going on here. I spoke to someone saying she was Fallon Richardson. The only thing she didn't know was the driver's license number, but she said she didn't have it on her and would call me back with it. I spoke with her a few days ago. I set up an appointment with her for next Thursday."

"It wasn't me. I never got any letters sent to me. I live with my dad and his wife."

Another pause. "Can you come to our office?"

"Yes. When?"

"Is tomorrow too soon? I would like to straighten this out. I can't tell you any particulars over the phone about your grandmother's estate. Can you drive to Denver?"

"Tomorrow's good. Can you do me a favor, Mr. Garber?"

"What is it?"

"If anyone calls pretending to be me, don't let them know I called and we have a meeting for tomorrow."

"I won't. Let's make this an afternoon appointment since you're coming in from the southwestern part of the state. What about four o'clock?"

"That'll work. Thank you."

"I look forward to meeting you."

Fallon's head spun as she put the phone down. *Someone's pretending to be me. I know it's Shanna, and Dad's helping her.* The betrayal crushed her chest, threatening to suffocate her. *How could Dad do this to me? I'm his fucking daughter!* Tears slipped from her eyes as she stared at the people in the store. *I have to find someone to drive with me to Denver. I don't even know how to get there.* She tapped in Sylvia's number.

"Hey, Fallon. Is anything wrong?"

"No. I just wondered if you want to get away and go to Denver with me tomorrow." She didn't want to tell her about the situation. Even though Sylvia had been a wonderful friend, she wasn't sure if she could keep a secret.

"*Denver?* Damn, girl. When you decide to start living you go all out." She laughed.

"Yeah. Well, I've never been there and thought it would be great to spend the weekend and shop."

"I'd love to, but your dad arranged another fight for Saturday night. I gotta stay around and help get things ready, and so do you."

"I didn't know Dad had set it up. Okay. We'll have to do it another time."

Disappointment curled around her as she strummed her fingers on the steering wheel. She'd go alone if she had to, but she really didn't want to do it since the farthest she'd ever driven was to Alina. Without thinking, she dialed Diablo's number.

"You in trouble?" his gruff voice crackled.

"No, nothing like that. I actually need a huge favor from you."

"Name it."

"I have a very important appointment in Denver tomorrow afternoon and I don't want to drive up there alone. I was wondering if you'd mind going with me."

"If you got an appointment, we need to leave today. That's about a seven-hour drive."

"So you'll go? I mean, just like that?"

"Fuck yeah. Did you think I'd say no?"

"I wasn't sure." She laughed, lightness replacing the heaviness she'd felt before she'd called him.

"You can always count on me. I told you I have your back. Can you leave at noon? I gotta finish up with this car, then clean up. I'll be ready to roll after that."

"Noon's fine. We can drive my car. Should I meet you at the club-house?"

"Yeah. See you then."

"Fuck yeah!" she yelled after ending the call, raising her fist as high as she could in her car. Not wanting to return home and face Shanna and the society ladies, she decided to buy a few things before she drove to Alina. She'd need toiletries, a nightgown, and maybe even a new dress. Giddy with excitement, she switched on the ignition and headed toward downtown. After she bought a few items, she went over to the diner to kill some time before she headed to Alina.

The diner was packed, the only place to sit was a two-seat table in the middle of the room. The hostess led her to the table and handed her a grease-stained menu. Fallon shrugged off her cardigan and glanced at the menu. Her stomach was sour from having only coffee in it; she hadn't eaten since she'd had the cheeseburger the day before.

"Ready to order?" the waitress asked as she looked around the room.

"A turkey swiss sandwich on light rye. And I'd like fruit instead of the potato chips." Fallon handed her the menu. The waitress rushed away.

Sitting in the middle of the restaurant made her feel conspicuous and, even though she knew it wasn't true, she felt like everyone was watching and talking about her. She pulled up a game of solitaire on her phone, glancing up when the waitress refilled her water. Before Fallon could thank her, she dashed off. Fallon looked back down at her phone. The scrape of the chair opposite her against the floor made her jerk her head up. A woman a little older than her stood next to the table with a shy smile tugging at the corners of her mouth.

"Do you mind if I share this table with you? I've spent ten minutes of my lunch break waiting for a table to open up. I have to get back in a half hour, and I'm so hungry."

The clatter of dishes and loud voices surrounded her, and she could barely hear what the woman was saying. "Are you asking to sit down?" she said loudly.

The young woman nodded, and Fallon reluctantly gestured for her to sit at the table. The woman slid onto the red vinyl seat and scooted the chair in toward the table. The waitress came over with Fallon's sandwich and did a double take at the woman who was now seated across from her customer. "You joining her?" she asked.

"I'm sharing a table," the woman answered.

"You got a menu?" The waitress handed her one before the woman had a chance to reply. "I'll be back in a second."

Fallon put down her phone and squeezed a small amount of mayonnaise on her sandwich. The woman watched her intently, making Fallon self-conscious. She hated when people watched her eat. If she were honest, she'd admit that she hated when any attention was focused on her. *Years of bullying and feeling like I don't belong are probably the reasons.*

"I'm Annie." The woman extended her hand.

Fallon wiped her hand on her napkin, then shook Annie's. "Fallon." She went back to concentrating on her sandwich.

"You from Tula?" Annie asked.

Fallon groaned inwardly. *She wants to chat.* She nodded, keeping her eyes on her plate.

"I'm new to the area. I just moved here a few months ago. I really like it so far."

Sighing, Fallon looked up. "Where were you living before?"

"New Mexico. A small town in the desert. It was so boring. My boyfriend's dragged me all over the west." She laughed.

"Where do you work?"

"For a guy. He has me logging in a ton of names and products into a database. He has an Internet business and he sells stuff on it. It's boring work, but it pays good. What about you?"

"I help in my dad's business."

For the next half hour they talked and laughed, and Fallon stayed way after she'd finished her sandwich. It seemed like they had a lot in common, and Fallon felt like she'd known Annie for a long time. It surprised her how easily she talked with the young woman.

Annie flicked her eyes to the chrome clock on the wall behind Fallon. "Shit! I gotta run. I'm five minutes late. Do you want to get together again? I don't know anyone in town, and I'd love to go out to dinner or maybe a movie."

"I'd like that too."

The two women exchanged phone numbers before Annie rushed out, waving as she went by the window. Fallon paid her bill and left the diner. Soon she was singing along with the radio as she blasted down the old highway to Alina. She couldn't wait to see Diablo. As she drove, she felt that her life was starting to take a turn for the better. Diablo seemed to care about her, and she'd met Annie, who had suggested exchanging phone numbers. The young woman with the shoulder-length plum-colored hair wanted to get together again... with *her*.

The drive to Alina had taken less time than she'd thought due to her speed, so she decided to go to the library, a couple bookstores, and a printing shop to turn in her application for part- and full-time work she'd found listed on a job database.

After she'd finished her task, she headed to the clubhouse, her damn nerves getting the best of her. *How crazy am I? I just spent the last couple of days and nights with him. I'm so fuckin' pathetic. Get a damn grip!* She popped an antacid to quell the heartburn from the turkey sandwich and her nerves, then gripped the steering wheel tightly as she drove down the road.

When she entered the clubhouse, a couple of men were playing pool and a few girls she recognized from before were watching television and talking. Tentatively, she walked over to the bar and sat on a stool. The man behind the bar put a ginger ale in front of her.

"Thanks. How did you know?" she asked.

"You're welcome," he said brusquely, then turned away.

From the couch, a woman with long brown hair kept staring at her while the woman next to her stood up and walked toward Fallon. The woman had red hair with neon purple tips. Fallon averted her gaze from the woman to the guys playing pool nearby.

"What's your deal with Diablo?" she said.

Fallon spun her stool around so she was facing the woman. "Excuse me?"

"I asked you what's up with you and Diablo?"

"We're friends," she replied. She poked at the ice cubes in the glass with her straw.

"Are you fucking him?" The woman crossed her arms and glowered at Fallon.

"I can't believe you just asked me that. It's really none of—"

"Back the fuck off," a good-looking man with blond hair and a ton of tattoos said.

"I'm not talking to you, Goldie, I'm talking to her." She pointed her finger at Fallon.

"You're tryin' to start up some shit. You know what a brother does and who he hangs with is his business. Go on. Maria's not shooting off her mouth." Goldie jerked his head toward the woman who'd been staring at Fallon since she'd come in.

"She's wondering too."

"I'm not gonna say it again, Lucy. You don't wanna piss me off."

Lucy glared at Goldie, then Fallon, then back to Goldie. "Don't sniff around me tonight 'cause you're not gettin' any." She whirled around and marched back to the sofa.

"Don't pay any attention to Lucy. She's very territorial. You're a new face around here, and she wants to let you know that she's already marked this territory." He picked up the beer the man behind the bar gave him.

"Was she Diablo's girlfriend?"

Goldie guffawed. "Hell no. She's a club girl and is for everyone. Don't worry your pretty head about it. You want another one?" He pointed to her empty glass. She shook her head. "You want me to tell Diablo you're here?"

"I already know she is," Diablo said as he came up to them, glaring at Goldie.

Fallon sucked in her breath as her gaze fell on Diablo. He was gorgeous in his white T-shirt that molded over his sculpted abs, and his jeans fit so snugly over his corded legs and crotch that she found herself transfixed by the big bulge against his zipper. A shiver slid up her spine as a sweet ache pulled between her legs.

A soft chuckle brought her eyes up to his dark ones, which smoldered with desire.

"I was just keeping the jackals away from your woman," Goldie said as he jerked his head to Lucy and Maria.

Diablo came over to Fallon and swept her hair over her shoulder. Bending down low, he whispered against her ear, "How's my woman doing?"

Desire burned through her from the tips of her nipples to her wet pussy. "Perfect, now."

He tugged her earlobe between his teeth and sucked gently on it, then trailed his mouth along her jawline until he captured her lips. Parting them slightly, his tongue dove in and tangled with hers. As they kissed, everything and everyone around her didn't exist. The only thing that was real was him, the kiss, and his blatantly raw maleness. His scent spun around her, his hard muscles pressed against her, and the smoky taste of him drove her wild.

He pulled away. "You ready to head out?"

"Where're you going?" Goldie asked as he munched on a handful of spicy peanuts.

"Denver for a few nights." Diablo helped Fallon off the stool. "I cleared it with Steel."

Fallon placed her small hand in his large one and walked outside. From the way everyone looked at them—the guys even stopped playing pool—she figured they'd be the topic of discussion that night. She giggled and handed him the car keys. Soon they were on the highway on their way to Denver.

As they approached the city, thousands of lights made the skyscrapers glitter. Threads of cars rushed past them on the freeway, and on the horizon, the setting sun took the last traces of daylight with it.

"It's so big," she said.

"Too big. I prefer the quiet of the Four Corners."

"It's exciting, though. I've seen cities in the movies but I've never been to one. It's awesome."

Diablo chuckled and took the exit heading into downtown. He pulled in front of a tall hotel and two men rushed over, one of them opening her door and helping her out. She and Diablo walked into the lobby where a wall of water with blue, green, and yellow lights on it greeted them.

"This is beautiful," she said as she spun around, taking it all in.

"Let's go check-in."

She followed him to a long wooden counter that had several men and women with computers behind it. On the back wall hung an exquisite bronze sculpture of cowboys rustling cattle.

"May I help you?" a woman in a brown jacket with the hotel's name on it asked.

Diablo looked at Fallon. "You want your own room?"

She shook her head. "I don't want to stay alone." She rose on her tiptoes and tugged at his leather jacket. He bent down. "I don't think I'm ready to have sex. Are you okay with that if we share a bed?"

He smiled. "I'm not gonna push you, but we'll have to get two beds. There's no fuckin' way I can have your body next to me all night without fucking you." Her face was heated and she knew her cheeks were flaming red. "You look real cute when you're fuckin' embarrassed." He kissed her quickly on the lips, then straightened up. "A room with two beds," he said to the receptionist.

When they went inside the room, the lights in the buildings shimmered and twinkled through the windows. Fallon went over and stared down: the cars looked like toys and the people like miniatures. "It's so beautiful," she murmured as the golden dome of the capitol building shimmered in the moonlight.

Diablo snagged her around the waist, pulling her back against him. "You're beautiful," he said, nuzzling her neck.

"I'm so happy right now. I can't remember being this happy. These past few days have been incredible."

He spun her around and kissed her deeply, and she wished she could freeze-frame the moment so it would never end. She loved being in his arms and kissing him with the sounds of the city below them. For as long as she lived, she'd never forget this moment.

*In the midst of darkness, brightness can come when it's least expected.*

Diablo was her light.

# Chapter Fifteen

THE SLIVERS OF bright light filtered through Fallon's thin eyelids, waking her up. Blinking against the sunlight that invaded their room through an opening in the curtains, something warm against her made a light sawing noise. Her arm was draped over a sculpted chest, and tilting her head, she saw Diablo's bushy beard. *What the hell?* She knew they'd each fallen asleep in their separate beds, but he'd made his way over to hers at some point during the night. *Did we do something? I didn't think I had that much to drink last night.* They'd gone to a happening area of downtown known as LoDo and had a delicious steak dinner. She'd drunk a couple of brandies, but they just make her giddy, not smashed.

Fallon tried to move away, but her legs were tangled in the sheets. *I bet we did do it. I don't even remember. That totally sucks.* Diablo's light snoring made her smile; she liked waking up next to him. As she ran her fingers over his chiseled chest, a tight pull between her legs made her shift positions. She moved her hand down until she hit his hardness, popping out of his boxers; it was alert and ready for action. Holding her breath, she lightly curled her fingers around it. It was warm and the skin was taut. Looking at it, the vein that ran through it pulsed, and she stroked the smooth head with her thumb. Licking her lips, she moved her hand away.

"Don't stop now."

Slowly she raised her head and gazed at him. His eyes were molten, burning with lust. The look sent a bolt of fire between her legs. Wrapping her fingers around his hardness again, she moved closer to his face and kissed his smooth lips. A low growl rumbled in his chest as he held her tightly, tugging at her nightshirt. She moaned when his hand skimmed over her rounded butt, past her hips, and landed on her breast, kneading it.

"Oh, Diablo," she whispered.

"Sweet pea," he murmured, his breath hot against her face. "You're so fuckin' sweet."

She sat up, slipped her panties off, and tugged her nightshirt over her head, licking her lips when he sucked in his breath, his gaze lingering on her tits. With a courage she didn't know she possessed, she climbed on top of him. She'd never done that before with a man, but she craved seeing his face as she slid him inside her, running her nails over his magnificent chest.

She held his hardness and began to put it in her slippery pussy when he said hoarsely, "Hang on." Tenderly he moved her off him and got up. Picking up his jeans, he took out a small packet, then came back to the bed. Shrugging off his boxers, his full erection mesmerized her. He slipped on the condom and lay back on the bed, drawing her to him. Once again, she climbed on top of him, took his now-sheathed dick in her hand, and slipped it into her wetness, loving the way he groaned and his face contorted. Pushing back from him, he went deeper inside her and she felt her walls enshroud him like his dick was made for her pussy.

"Fuck, Fallon. That feels real good." His callused hands ran up the sides of her body as goose bumps followed in their wake.

"I've never done this before. Tell me if I do something wrong."

"You're doing real good. Fuckin' good."

Leaning over, she kissed his mouth, her tits touching his chest. Her nipples hardened and she bent over more, dragging her hair over his eyes before her breasts brushed against his face. He grabbed them and sucked one hungrily, taking as much of it as he could into his mouth while he rolled the other nipple between his fingers. Everything inside her tingled, even her scalp, and she moaned and wiggled her ass. She pulled back and kissed his eyelids, then his mouth, trailing her lips past his chin to his Adam's apple, sprinkling feathery kisses over his damp skin.

"You're driving me fuckin' crazy," he rasped as he bucked, shoving deeper into her.

"That feels so good," she whispered as she pushed down.

He gripped her by the hips, their rhythm wild. The bed began creaking. He moved his hands from her hips to her ass, cupping her buttocks as his fingers dug into them. Her flesh shook and quivered under his touch and suddenly, she was nothing but her body, feeling each sensation as he thrust into her. Sweat formed on her hairline and under her breasts as she met his frantic movement. It was like a wave in a stormy sea, and she rode him hard and fast, their heated gaze locked onto one another's.

"Lean back a bit," he said as he gently guided her backward. "I want to see your pretty pussy." She arched her back, shivers cooling her damp skin as the air touched her glistening folds. "So beautiful," he murmured as he ran his finger between her puffy lips.

She jumped from the intensity of that one touch; her whole body was supercharged. "It's so good," she croaked. Her mouth was dry from panting.

Fallon watched in fascination as he took his finger, drenched with her juices, and slowly put it in his mouth, licking and sucking it. "So fuckin' tasty," he said thickly.

Without thinking, she leaned over and kissed him deeply, his thick beard tickling her skin. Their tongues swirled together and she tasted herself on his: salty and fresh like the sea. Then she pulled up and leaned back, guiding his hand to her aching clit. His dark eyes smoldered as he rubbed the side of her sweet spot. With her head thrown back, she reached around and touched his smooth, taut balls, gently stroking them. The even pressure on her stiff nub made her insides coil tighter and tighter until they exploded and a sweet spasm coursed through her. It seemed like she was rising into the air, and there was no more hurt, no more loneliness, just the incredible, the sweetness, the—

Diablo's panting and grunting brought her back and she looked down at him. His parted lips and scrunched face touched her deeply, and she moved in sync with him as a deep growl rumbled from his throat and he stiffened under her. She pressed hard against him and he hooked his arms around her as his chest heaved. They stayed like that for several minutes, the sweet glow of her orgasm still burning inside her.

"Come by my side. It's more comfortable," he said as he guided her off him. Instantly, he tugged her close to him, his fingers stroking her upper arm. "What the fuck was that?"

Insecurity pricked at her. "What do you mean?"

"That was fucking unbelievable." He squeezed her tighter as a smile broke out over her face.

"It was." She rubbed her hands over his chest and kissed it. Her body was still humming. That was the first orgasm she'd ever had with a man. She'd experimented with herself, but she never could relax enough with a man to let it happen. A couple of the men her dad had sent to her seemed to need her to come, so she'd fake it just to get it over with. But with Diablo, it was more than she'd ever imagined. A concoction of emotion swirled inside her: excitement, happiness, fear, and anxiety. Part of her was afraid and anxious that Diablo would leave her now that they'd had sex. Her past relationships with men had taught her that was what they did.

"You happy?" Diablo interrupted her concerns.

"Very. I didn't plan on this. It was awesome." She burrowed closer to him.

"The things we don't plan turn out better than the ones we do." He kissed her head.

They lay sated and tangled in each other's arms until she heard his deep breathing. Looking up, she saw his eyes were closed. She rested her head back on his shoulder and soon fell fast asleep.

When they woke a couple of hours later, Fallon sat up with a start. *The lawyers. What time is it?* Frantically, she grabbed her phone and opened it. Noon. A breath of relief escaped from her lips. *I have some time.*

Deciding to get ready, she unraveled herself from Diablo's hold and tiptoed to the bathroom. After she'd brushed her teeth and washed her face, she turned on the shower. Stepping inside, she welcomed the warm water as it cascaded over her. Closing her eyes, she let the water take her away.

A cool gust of air chilled her and her eyes flew open, landing on Diablo's desire-filled ones. He stepped into the shower and drew her to him, licking the drops off her face as his hands roamed her wet skin.

"I can't get enough of you," he whispered in her ear. With a bar of soap, he gently washed her from her shoulders down to her feet, then rinsed it away with a washcloth. Turning around, she took the soap from him and washed his body slowly, marveling in how wonderful his defined muscles felt against her wet fingers. When she was finished, he washed her hair, then, after rinsing, yanked her head back and kissed her deeply as the warm water pounded against her back. When she pressed closer to him, his hardness poked into her flesh and an instant rush of heat burn through her.

As they kissed and touched each other, her body danced in a million different ways: twirling, leaping, swaying. He turned her around, facing the white-tiled wall and, with an arm around her waist, guided her to a bent position. Her hands pressed against the cold tile, she heard extended activity behind her. Glancing over her shoulder, she saw him lean out of the shower and pick up a condom he must've brought into the bathroom with him. She stared at him and he winked as he slipped the sheath over his hardness. Bending over her, he cupped her breasts as he ground against her ass.

"I love that your tits fit in my hands. They're the perfect size for me." His breath warmed the nape of her neck.

After playing with her breasts for a while, he slipped his finger between her puffy folds, making her feel exquisite. As she was ready to go over the waterfall, he pushed into her, going so deep that she thought he'd come through her. He thrust in and out of her as his finger kept the pace on her sweet button until she couldn't hold it anymore. Waves of euphoria splashed through her, and she was taken higher and higher until she was both above the world and one with it at the same time.

Behind her, Diablo was scratching her back, grunting, and breathing quickly until he groaned, the sound echoing against the tiled wall. "Fuck," he muttered before pressing her hard and tight against him. He peppered her neck with gentle kisses. She wasn't sure if it was the way he'd washed her, the way he took her, or the way he kissed her, but the intensity of the moment threw her emotions into overdrive and tears streamed down her face. A surge of love shot through her. At least she thought it was love. It was so intense and pure that she guessed that's what it was, but she couldn't be sure since she'd never been in love before. She'd never felt that way for any man, and the fact that she'd only known him for a couple weeks scared the hell out of her. She wasn't even sure if what she was feeling was indeed love or just gratefulness. But there was no denying that she felt *something* intense for him.

He spun her around and a bright grin greeted her. She tugged playfully at his beard before he hugged her close. "Let's get some food before you go to your appointment."

"I'd love that. Thank you for everything. I mean coming here with me, the wonderful hotel, the delicious dinner last night... and this." Her cheeks warmed.

"No need to ever thank me. I'm happy you trusted me to share yourself with me. I've been fantasizing about you since I first saw you. The reality is way fuckin' better than the fantasy." He chuckled, then kissed her.

"I don't know what to say. This is all new to me."

"Don't need to say anything. Just get some clothes on so we can go eat." He swatted her butt playfully and she laughed. "Don't overthink this, sweet pea. Just go with it. Life's better that way." He stood aside and let her out of the shower.

Soon they were dressed and headed out the door.

"MY GRANDMOTHER WANTED me to have this money?" Fallon's hand flew to her neck. The sum of seven hundred thousand dollars seemed inconceivable to her, especially from a woman she'd never met.

"That's what she wanted. She made her will a few years ago and was adamant that the money went to you. I set the trust up for her. Our law office is the trustee. Once you turn twenty-two, the entire trust will go to you. She was specific about the age. She shared with me that her lucky number was twenty-two. In the meantime, your grandmother wanted you to have fifty thousand dollars. I'm prepared to write a check to you."

"But she never met me. She never even tried to get in contact with me all these years. She'd disowned my mom before I was born."

Scott Garber jerked his head back. "She tried many times to get a hold of you. Your dad wouldn't let her. Colorado doesn't have grandparents' rights, so her hands were tied. She sent you cards and presents for your birthday and Christmas. When you never answered, she figured your mom and dad had poisoned you against her and your grandfather. She stopped reaching out, but she always carried you in her heart. She used to come in here and cry about it. You know, you're her only grandchild. She desperately wanted a relationship with you."

"I never received anything. I can't believe my dad would've hidden all that from me. What would be the point in him doing that?"

The attorney shrugged. "There's a lot of emotion—good and bad—in families. I see it all the time in my practice."

"You know my grandma abandoned my mom. My mother was very upset about it."

He nodded. "I wasn't with the firm when all that went down, but Barbara told me she regretted what she'd done. A lot of times, it takes years to mellow someone and to forgive past hurts and indiscretions. Your grandmother came from a different mindset. She just couldn't accept that your mother was with a married man. As time went on, it didn't matter as much, but then your mom had run off. Barbara's biggest regret was not making amends with your mom, or having a relationship with you."

Fallon's head was swimming. "Wait. Are you telling me that my dad was married while my mom was going out with him? Was I responsible for breaking up his first marriage?"

Garber's face blanched. "You didn't know that? Damn," he muttered under his breath.

"I can't believe my dad was married. My parents gave the impression that it was their first marriage. I can't believe all this."

"Don't blame yourself. Your mom and dad were the ones responsible. I'm sorry if I upset you. I thought you knew."

She shook her head. "I didn't. Maybe that's why my dad kept my grandmother apart from me. Maybe he was afraid she'd tell me a bunch of stuff that would hurt me." *Although he never seemed to care about hurting me himself.*

"I don't know. All I know is that your grandmother wanted to make sure you were provided for. Her hope was that you invest the money and let it grow. She wanted to give you a head start." He smiled weakly.

"That was nice of her. I wish I had known her."

"Now I have to figure out who was impersonating you. The why is obvious—money."

"What would happen if I die before I'm twenty-two?"

The attorney's eyes widened. "Do you think you're in danger?" He paused for a second before continuing. "Well, if you did happen to pass away before the trust became effective, it would revert back to your grandmother's estate and be distributed to a charity."

"My dad wouldn't be able to inherit it?"

"No. It doesn't work that way with trusts. They revert back to the grantor's estate. Your grandmother designated Denver Food Bank as the charity to receive the funds if you were unable to."

*Maybe Shanna and Dad don't know that. Why were they saying they wanted to get me out of the way? If I die, they wouldn't get the money.* "What if I get the money and then die?"

Garber pressed his lips together. "In that case, if you don't have a will, it would go to your father. With this kind of money, you should really have a will in place by the time you reach twenty-two. Do you have any idea who knows about the money?"

Fallon blew out a breath, nodding. "My dad and his wife. I overheard them talking about the letters you sent and about my grandmother's death. If I hadn't, I wouldn't have had any idea that my grandmother had died."

He leaned back and folded his hands across his belly. "This is pretty serious. You should get the police involved in this."

"I don't know for sure it's Shanna. She's about six years older than me, so she could pretend to be me. I don't know. Maybe they were just talking."

"If she calls again, I won't tip her off that you came and saw me. I can tell her a long-lost relative is threatening to contest the will. When that happens, it ties up an estate for years in probate court. But you really do need to have a will in place before all the money goes to you."

"I plan to. I'd like you to do it. My grandmother trusted you and your firm, so I would like to work with you."

He nodded. "If you need any of the money in the trust, let me know. Barbara made provisions for distribution of necessary funds before you turn twenty-two."

"I should be good with the check you're giving me. I'm going to turn twenty-two in a few weeks." She laughed.

With the check in hand and promises of calling Mr. Garber soon, she and Diablo left the office. On the way back to Alina, her mind was spinning from what the lawyer had told her. She was pretty sure her dad and Shanna were planning to hurt her to get to the money, but her dad wasn't stupid; he'd definitely know whether he could get the money or not, so he was probably planning on pretending Shanna was her and she'd get the money. *With me out of the way, no one would really know. But once they find out Mr. Garber isn't going to give it to them, will they be so mad they'll kill me anyway?* She rubbed her temples. *I can't believe Dad would kill me. He's a mean sonofabitch most of the time, but* kill *me? No way. But I did hear them talking. I don't know what the fuck to think.*

She pounded her fist on her thigh.

"Something wrong?" Diablo said.

"No." *I don't want to burden him with this. Anyway, I don't even know if any of this is real.*

"You've been real quiet since we left the lawyer's. Did he tell you something about your grandmother to upset you?" He reached over and grasped her hand. "You can tell me."

She shook her head. "Not really. She was my mother's mother, but I never knew her. He said she told him she tried repeatedly to get in contact with me over the years, but my dad thwarted all her efforts."

"That's a bunch of bullshit."

"It is if it's true. I mean, I don't know if my dad did that or not. My grandmother may just have been an old woman who knew she was dying and was afraid, so she tried to make amends by leaving me an inheritance. I really don't know what to think."

She leaned her head back on the rest and stared out at the open expanse in front of them. Before she'd gone to the law firm, she'd told Diablo a bit about the trust, but she didn't tell him all the details or how much money she stood to inherit. Even though she trusted him more than she'd ever trusted anyone besides her mom, she was still wary; trust had been broken so many times in her young life that it was hard to give it one hundred percent.

"I know this sucks for you, but sometimes it's best to let things be. Digging around too much opens a bunch of fuckin' wounds it took years to heal." He glanced at her.

"You're right. I'm just going to forget all of it. I'm glad my grandmother thought about me before she died. Whatever did or didn't happen doesn't matter." *But I have to figure out what the fuck's going to happen.*

"You good now?" Diablo leaned over and gave the side of her head a quick kiss, his eyes fixed on the road.

She brought his hand to her mouth and kissed it. "Yeah. I'm good."

*Not.*

# Chapter Sixteen

THE FOLLOWING MORNING, Diablo watched as Fallon slept, loving the way she looked so peaceful when the demons that tormented her in her sleep lay dormant. The night before, they'd stayed away, not unlike the night at the hotel. That night, they were in full force, clawing and scratching at her mind as she'd cried and screamed out in her sleep. Her voice had been laced with fear as she pleaded with someone to not hurt her. She'd kept mumbling over and over that she was sorry, like an eerie mantra piercing the quiet of their dark room. Diablo had rushed over to her, calmed her thrashing body and held her close to him, wiping the sweat off her face with the sheet. Eventually, the storm had passed and she'd fiercely hung on to him. The minutes had ticked away, and he'd fallen asleep holding her.

That next morning, when she'd wanted to fuck him, he'd been both surprised and elated about it. When he'd slipped inside her, it'd felt so natural and comfortable, like they'd been made for each other. It'd seemed like she filled a part of him that had been missing for a long time.

Still looking at her, his heart tugged and he breathed out slowly as a shadow from his past snuck into his head, making him wonder if Fallon would break his heart the way Hannah had a long time before.

He'd been living at his foster home for two years when he'd meet Hannah in high school. They were both sixteen and she was the prettiest girl he'd ever seen. She belonged to the elite group at school, and when his teacher had asked him to tutor her in geometry, he'd jumped at the chance. Since he'd started high school, she was the main attraction in his wet dreams. He'd been with a few of the neighborhood girls, but no one compared to Hannah.

When she'd gone for him in a big way, he'd been over the moon. Soon they'd meet up after school all the time, kissing and screwing between hikes in the mountains and lazy afternoons at the lake.

She'd told him she loved him at the end of their junior year, right before the summer had begun. He'd told her the same.

She'd kept their relationship a secret from her parents and good friends, claiming they'd never understand since he was a foster kid. He hadn't given a shit if she wanted to keep it a secret; all he'd wanted was the scent of her baby powder perfume, her soft skin, and her tight pussy. He'd given her his heart.

That summer had burned into their teenage lives, and Hannah kept putting him off every time he'd call to get together. It'd seemed like she never had any time for him. So one hot June afternoon, he'd gone to her house and started up the front porch when he'd heard voices coming from the back. When he went to the backyard, he saw several girls in bikinis and men in trunks. Hannah reclined on a chaise lounge. The look of horror on her face when she saw him had chilled his heart. He nodded at her but she'd turned away.

An older man had asked her who he was and she shrugged. Her words from fourteen years ago echoed clearly in his head as though she'd just said them.

"I don't know. I think he's come for the gardener job."

A hot surge of anger zapped up his spine. After all this time, it still had an effect on him.

He shook his head as if to make the memory scamper away, but it wasn't ready to. The image of a guy a couple years older than he punched at his mind. He'd had his arm around Hannah, and Diablo had been so pissed that he'd been ready to beat the shit out of him. Hannah's dad had come over and told him that it was a party and he'd meet him in the front to discuss the job.

"I didn't come for no fuckin' job," he'd said.

"Why did you come?" Her father had looked puzzled.

"Hannah and I have been going together since last October."

A horrified look passed over her dad's face. "Is this true?" he'd asked his daughter.

"I don't know what he's talking about. Maybe he wished he could go out with me. I remember him now. He's the foster kid who goes to my school." Her cold, detached eyes had bored into him. Her words had been an icepick to his heart.

"You better leave," Hannah's dad had said.

He'd wanted to hurt and destroy everything in the backyard that summer afternoon, especially Hannah, but he'd clenched his fists, gritted his teeth, and stormed out, the snickers from the other teenagers blinding him with cold fury.

From that day on, he'd sworn that no woman would ever humiliate him or take his heart. And he'd never had to worry about it until now.

He stroked Fallon's cheek; it was as soft as cotton. *You're so sweet, and you're fuckin' doing something to me.* She was knocking on his heart, asking to be let in, but he wasn't sure he was ready to let another woman in again.

Fallon's eyes fluttered open and she stretched long and hard like a cat. He chuckled, then bent down and kissed her. "You slept real well," he said as his rough finger pad stroked her cheek.

"I feel great. I guess I was more tired than I thought."

He stood up and went toward the bathroom. "There's a fighting event set at the warehouse tonight. Did you want to go or stay at the club until I get back?"

She giggled. "I better go. My dad has been blowing up my phone. He's beyond pissed. I haven't spoken to him in the last several days and it's been wonderful. Believe it or not, it's the first time in my life that I've been on my own and I love it. I'm thinking of getting a job and moving out of the house."

He raised his eyebrows. "Yeah? It's time. You gotta learn to stand on your own feet. Why don't you move here?"

She smiled. "I was thinking about moving to Alina."

"That'd be cool. You could crash with me."

Her lips quirked. "I want my own place—a real apartment." She paused when his expression changed. "Don't frown at me. Please. I just need some time to figure out how to take care of myself. I've been sheltered my whole life. My dad has always taken care of me, and I don't want to go from being dependent on him to being dependent on you."

"It wouldn't be the same thing."

"In a sense, it would be. I need to learn how to make it on my own. I hope you understand."

He nodded. "I do. I can ask Muerto if he has any vacancies at his rentals. He owns several properties."

Her eyes sparkled and it made him smile. "That'd be great."

When Diablo was showered and dressed, he told Fallon he'd meet her downstairs. Taking the stairs two at a time, he walked into the main room. He spotted Muerto by the bar and moseyed up to him.

"How was your trip to Denver?" Muerto said.

"Good. How's Raven?"

"She's kicking ass. She just sold a few more paintings at that gallery she's at in Denver. Looks like we'll be making the trip to the big city soon."

"That's fuckin' awesome." He picked up the can of Coors the prospect placed on the bar.

Goldie came over and slapped Diablo's back. "Dude. How's Fallon? Shit, I still can't believe you got a woman. You were always the one who didn't seem much interested in pussy."

"I've always been interested in pussy, just not rabid like all of you."

Muerto and Goldie laughed. "I gotta admit I didn't see that coming. I mean, you seemed good with Lucy and Maria. I didn't know you were looking." Muerto picked up his shot of tequila.

"I wasn't. You got any vacancies in any of your rentals?" he asked.

"A couple. One's the front of the duplex where Raven lived and the other is an apartment. You planning on moving out?"

Goldie sniggered. "There's no way you're giving up Lena's cooking and the washing and cleaning the club girls do around here."

"It's not for me. It's for Fallon. She wants to get out on her own. It's about fuckin' time."

"Gotcha. Since it's for her, then I'd say the apartment is best. Raven loved the duplex, but Walter creeped her out. The next tenant I'm putting in there is gonna be a dude. I can arrange for her to see the apartment sometime next week."

"I'll let her know."

"Here comes your former playmate, and she looks pissed." Goldie chuckled.

Diablo turned around and saw Maria approaching him, a deep crease in her brow. "Later," he said to Goldie and Muerto. He went over to a table and sat down. She came up to him. "Sit down." He kicked out a chair.

She slipped in. "You have a woman." It was a fact. Her voice didn't hold any malice or accusation, just disappointment. He nodded. "That explains why you've been ignoring me and Lucy."

He nodded again.

"I…. We know the score. I just wish you would've told me. I guess I expected something different from you. You seem more mature than the other guys around here. It would've been nice to have known. Just out of respect, you know?" Her brown eyes fixed on his.

"I didn't think about it. What we had was some fun and fuckin', same as what you have with most of the brothers. Didn't seem like something I'd think to tell you."

She reached out and stroked his hand. "I get it. As I said, I know the score. I hope you're happy with her. If you ever need another woman, you let me know." She stood up and gave him a big hug.

The gasp thudded in his ears. He looked at the bar and saw Fallon staring at him, her face mottled with red blotches. He gently pushed Maria away, and she glanced at the bar and smiled. Before she walked away, she leaned down and whispered, "Sorry to have gotten you in trouble, honey." She walked away, her curvy hips swaying.

Fallon stormed up to him. "Couldn't you wait until I was gone, at least?"

He laughed and tried to draw her to him but she resisted. "You're not serious, are you?"

She jerked her hand out of his and marched outside. He quickly followed her as she struggled to walk fast.

"Fallon. This is fuckin' stupid. I was just talking to Maria."

She stopped by her car and turned around. "You're free to do whatever you want with whomever you want. We had a good time. Thanks for the mind-blowing orgasm. I have to go."

He narrowed his eyes. "You're beginning to piss me off. I told you nothing happened. I'm with you."

"Aren't the women supposed to be there for all of you whenever the mood strikes? How ridiculous is that? How fucking chauvinistic."

"Now you're dissing the brotherhood. You don't know what the fuck you're talking about."

"I can't believe I even started up with you and your world."

"You're fuckin' blowing things out of proportion. What the club girls do for the brothers, they do because they want to. I'm not gonna defend my club and its lifestyle to a woman who's acting like she's a child. I was talking to Maria. I didn't go off the deep end when you were talking to Goldie the other day. Calm the fuck down, will you?"

"I may be acting like a child, but you're acting like a typical man. None of you can be trusted. I'm out of here." She slid into the driver seat.

"Don't leave like this, Fallon. Let's talk about it."

She slammed the door and started the engine. Diablo pounded his fist on the trunk before she drove away. He breathed heavily, his nostrils flaring, as he watched her disappear around the curve.

*What the fuck just happened? Talk about fuckin' messed up.* "Fuck!" he yelled as he kicked the dirt. He went back inside, straight to the bar, and ordered a double Jack. The brothers were talking Harleys. None of them asked what happened; they knew if he wanted to talk about it, he would.

Maria sat on Sangre's lap, kissing him as he played with her big tits. Diablo threw back his whiskey. The burn from the booze down his throat was nothing compared to the way her accusation had scorched him.

*Fuck her.*

He ordered another double and joined in on his brothers' conversation about Harleys.

BY THE TIME he arrived at the warehouse that evening, he had cooled down. He knew Fallon wasn't like other women he'd been with; she was fragile and a bit backward. From what he could gather when they'd talked, she'd been getting the shit end of the stick most of her life. He figured that made her ultra-sensitive. It seemed like she was always looking for a reason not to get close or trust someone. He understood that. Trust was a hard one for him too, but when someone gained his trust, he was there for them to the end. Like the brotherhood. They were his brothers and he was theirs, and they'd each give their lives for one another. The club was what had saved him. If he hadn't joined the Night Rebels, he'd probably be doing a stint in the state pen.

He sighed. More than anything, he wanted Fallon to trust him implicitly, but he knew it was a very long and twisty road to get to that point. He'd thought she'd begun to open up, but then she went ballistic over something innocent. *But she's worth the trouble.* From the first time he saw her gorgeous eyes, she'd pulled him in. She was so sexy, pretty, and a genuinely good person, and she didn't even know it. *Bloody Knuckles did a fuckin' number on her.*

Diablo pulled into the dirt lot and saw Emerald and Cassie standing there, laughing with a couple of guys. Fallon was cleaning out the trash cans. She glanced at him, then averted her eyes. She looked miserable. His heart lurched.

Emerald said something to her and the others laughed. He got off his bike.

"Hey, handsome. Why don't you come over here and join us? I love your Harley," Emerald said.

Diablo saw Fallon stiffen and give him a sidelong glance. Ignoring Emerald, he strode up to Fallon, grasped her shoulder, and whirled her around. Before she could protest, he took her into his arms and kissed her deeply. From behind him, the guys yelled, "Way to go, dude."

"You should know that I'd never do shit behind your back," he whispered in her ear.

"I thought about it the whole drive here. You were right. I acted just like a kid. You're the only good and decent thing in my life, and I'm fucking it up."

"You're not fucking anything up. I just want you to trust me. If I'm gonna do some shit, I'll be straight with you. You'll see that as we get to know each other better."

"What's going on here?" Emerald's nasally voice asked.

"Looks like the biker man's taken pity on her," Cassie replied.

With gritted teeth, Diablo gave the women a steely look. "I'm giving you only one warning to stop disrespecting my woman. Your shit stops now. If I hear or see you disrespect her anymore, I'll make sure your dancing days are over."

Emerald put her hand on her hip and glared at him. "You must really be—"

Diablo leaned in close to her face. "You've been warned."

As they shouted their outrage, he ignored them, tugging Fallon close to him as they walked away.

"We'll see what your dad thinks about this," Cassie said.

He and Fallon went inside. "You good?" He kissed her again.

She pulled away, her eyes darting around the room. "Yeah. I have to help set up. I'll see you later."

He watched her as she walked away, warmth spreading through him.

As Diablo checked the windows and doors, Charlie came up to him. "Hey," the promoter said.

Diablo gave him a chin lift and continued checking the windows.

"I gotta talk with you."

Diablo stopped and turned to him, his face stoic.

Charlie cleared his throat. "I heard you're cozying up to my daughter."

Diablo stared straight ahead at the ring.

"I want you to leave Fallon alone."

"She's old enough to decide what she wants to do."

"Fallon's not like other girls her age. She's been sheltered most of her life."

"She seems fine to me."

Charlie audibly sighed. "But she's not. She's very shy and backward." Diablo fixed his stare on the man's sweaty face. Charlie laughed nervously. "I mean... you've seen her. She's got a bad limp."

"What the fuck does that have to do with her deciding who to go out with?"

"She's self-conscious about it—even obsessed. So when a rough-looking man gives her attention, she's obviously flattered. She may not understand that you're feeling sorry for her. I just don't want her to get hurt."

Diablo's nostrils flared. "I don't feel sorry for her. I like Fallon. She likes me. Fuckin' stay out of it. And the only reason I'm not smashing your face is because of her. This talk is over." He walked away, his fists clenching and unclenching.

A half hour later, Diablo was by the door, frisking the men as they came in for the fights. Emerald and Heidi pranced around on stage in push-up bras one size too small, bikini bottoms, and fishnet thigh-highs while Sam darted his eyes nervously around the room. Diablo watched the wiry-haired man as sweat dripped down his face, his gaze flicking to Diablo's several times. Diablo's muscles tensed. Something was up.

Then the ring girls exited the platform and Sam blew the whistle. Two tall and well-built men entered the ring and faced each other. The one with the red shorts looked a little bit frightened and unsure of himself. The fighter in the yellow shorts grinned, then attacked. His right hook was so hard that his opponent fell down immediately. The spectators went wild as the fighter on the floor struggled to rise.

"How long's it been going on?" Army asked, taking Diablo's gaze away from the ring.

"Hey." He raised his fist in front of him, greeting Army, Chains, Brutus, Cue Ball, Jigger, Goldie, and Paco. "The fights just started. The swaying dude in the red shorts went down with one punch. It was fuckin' awesome."

"I gotta see this," Paco said as he, Jigger, Brutus, and Cue Ball walked toward the crowd.

"Is that sexy ring girl still here? I think her name was Diamond," Goldie said.

"The ring girls are the same as always." Diablo scanned the crowd.

"Her name wasn't Diamond, it was Sapphire," said Chains.

"Nah, that doesn't sound right. I know it was the name of some fucking stone. Maybe Ruby." Goldie scrubbed his hand across his chin.

"There she is, with the hot blonde who partied with us last time," Army said.

"We'll catch you later, bro," Goldie said as the three brothers made a beeline for the two women who stood by the wall across from the ring.

Diablo jerked his chin and panned the room, looking for Sam. He spotted him behind the ring, watching the Night Rebels. There was something about the way he looked at Paco, Cue Ball, Jigger, and Brutus, then turned his attention to the other three brothers who were talking to the women. Sam then looked around the room again, his gaze briefly catching Diablo's. *It's like he's counting how many brothers are here. And he keeps looking to see if more are gonna come in.*

Diablo focused all his attention on Sam, careful not to make direct eye contact with him. After twenty minutes, Sam took out his phone and went outside. Diablo motioned Rocky over and told him he'd be back in a few. Diablo went outside and walked to the back of the warehouse. For being such a tall, built man, he could be surprisingly light on his feet; as he treaded carefully, the sand underneath his feet absorbed his steps.

"I only counted seven. Oh, and the stupid fuck who's the bouncer. I didn't even know he was in the Night Rebels until last week when all that shit went down."

Diablo saw Sam pacing back and forth as he spoke on the phone.

"I waited for a while. I'm sure that's all who's gonna show up from the club. Are you gonna bring the money when you and your boys get here? I'm a little short in paying some guys back and they're putting the squeeze on me." Sam wiped the corners of his mouth with his thumb and index finger.

"I just need the money tonight. We got a good crowd here. You'll make some good money tonight. Fuck!" Diablo's viselike grip clamped onto the back of Sam's neck. The man dropped his phone and clawed at Diablo's hand. "What the fuck are you doing?"

Diablo tossed Sam to the ground and kicked him hard in the stomach. The crumpled man groaned and curled into a tighter ball. Diablo picked up the phone and put it to his ear.

"What the fuck is going on? Sam?" a rough voice asked.

"The Night Rebels are ready for you fuckers." Diablo threw the phone on the ground and stomped on it, scattering plastic pieces every which way. He bent over and dragged Sam up by his shirt. "You better fuckin' tell me why you're talking to the fuckin' Satan's Pistons about the Night Rebels. And if you lie, I'm gonna kill you. It's pretty simple."

Sweat poured into Sam's eyes and he blinked repeatedly as he wiped his forehead. "I swear I didn't want to do any of this shit, but I needed the money. I was desperate. I got some fuckers on my ass and they're threatening to hurt me real bad," Sam spilled out.

Diablo tightened his hold on the front of Sam's shirt. "You got a real pissed-off fucker right in front of you, and I'm not threatening to kill you—I'm telling you I'm gonna do it. So give it to me straight. Why the fuck are the Pistons coming to the goddamn warehouse to see the fights?"

"If I tell it to you straight, you'll be cool with me, right?"

"I don't negotiate. All I can tell you is if you don't, it'll make it a lot more painful for you."

"Okay… okay. Satan's Pistons fund some of the money that brings in the fights. Bloody Knuckles does shows in Arizona and they approached him. They wanted in. They had a cash flow and Bloody Knuckles needed that to get his business going. They put in money to help him buy the warehouse. Now that he's doing good, he wants them out, but they don't wanna go. When he found out you were in a motorcycle gang, he shit his pants. When he found out your gang is a rival of Satan's Pistons, he told me to make sure not to have the Pistons around when the Night Rebels were at the fights."

"I see you take instructions real good, asshole. Why the fuck were you calling them and setting up my brothers?" Diablo shook Sam, his lips curling in a feral smile as Sam's teeth chattered and his bones creaked.

"I need the fucking money! They said they'd pay me if I let them know when the Night Rebels showed up. They said they had a score to settle with you guys. I didn't want to do it, but they threatened me."

"Yeah right, asshole!" Diablo punched him in the face and he bellowed.

"I needed the money," he sobbed. "I didn't want to do it."

"How the fuck did they even know my brothers were at the fights last week? Did you call them?"

"No. I swear I didn't. I think one of them is fucking one of the girls and he was there and saw the other guys from your club. That night, they called me and told me I had to let them know whenever the Night Rebels came to one of the fights."

"Who's the bitch they're fucking?"

"I don't know. I swear."

"Is Bloody fucking Knuckles involved in this shit with the motherfuckers?"

Sam shook his head. "He's trying to get rid of them. He's offered to pay them what they put in and then some, but they don't want it. He's stuck. You gotta believe me. I'm not involved with these guys. I just did it this once because of the money."

"When an outlaw club pays a citizen for information, it owns him all the way. You fuckin' belong to them." Diablo punched him in the face again and he groaned, his legs buckling. Diablo let go of his shirt and Sam fell to the ground. After a few kicks to the kidneys and ribs, he rummaged through Sam's pockets and found a set of keys.

He took out his phone, calling Paco.

"What's up, bro?" the brother said.

"I got some trash that needs to be taken out. I'm out back. I found the goddamn snitch. The fuckin' Pistons are on their way in full force."

In the few seconds it took Diablo to slip his phone in his jeans pocket, Paco, Army, and Brutus joined him. Army spit on Sam's unconscious body. Handing the key ring to Paco, Diablo pointed to a bronze SUV near the large trash bins. "That's the fucker's car."

Paco nodded. "We can strip it and sell the parts after we take care of him. I'll put my bike in the back and drive back."

Diablo nodded. "I gotta get back in." He went back inside and took over his position, adrenaline pumping through him. He knew the Satan's Pistons were a little over a hundred miles away, and with little to no traffic on Highway 491, they'd be pulling into Tula in just over an hour, unless they were staying somewhere within the Colorado borders.

Goldie, Chains, Cue Ball, and Jigger came over to him.

"We're gonna head out. I wanna stay and kill those sonsofbitches, but Steel's saying we're gonna be outnumbered," Goldie said.

"He's right," Diablo admitted.

"And there're too many damn witnesses. The Highway Patrol would be all over our asses on this," Chains added.

"Army said the arms deal's going down end of next week. Once we get the shit, we'll decimate them."

"Just like the fuckin' Demon Riders," Diablo said.

"We getting the Insurgents to help on this one?" Jigger asked.

"Steel will let us know," Diablo replied.

"You coming with us?" Chains opened the front door.

"Since I found out Pistons got their money in this shit, I decided to walk out. I'm gonna get Fallon, then get the fuck outta here."

"You need us to wait around until you leave?" Goldie said.

Diablo shook his head. "I'm good."

The four men walked out just as Charlie came over. "Have you seen Sam? I can't find him."

"Last time I saw him, he was heading out back."

"I already looked there. Where the fuck is he? I need him in the ring."

"Don't know. Ask Jose to announce the fights until Sam turns up."

"I'll have to. It's always one fucking thing after another." Charlie stomped away.

When Paco came in, Diablo knew Sam's announcing days at the warehouse were over. Paco clapped his hand on Diablo's shoulder. "We took care of the fucker. I'm heading out. You need to get the fuck outta here."

"Planning to. Just gonna get Fallon. See you at the clubhouse." They bumped fists, and then Paco slipped out into the darkness.

Diablo scanned the room looking for Fallon but she wasn't around. He hadn't seen her since the fights had started. He motioned Moe to watch the door, and then he went to find her. As he climbed the stairs, Charlie's yelling assaulted his ears.

"You've always been nothing but a dumb, ugly fuck! You've been nothing but a pain in my ass. You're the reason Joanna left. Your mother couldn't stand you. She'd tell me how having you ruined her life."

"That's not true! My mother loved me and hated you. You drove her away," Fallon's voice rang out.

Diablo rushed up the stairs and burst into the family room. White-hot rage surged through him when he saw Fallon cowering against the back wall and Charlie looming over her, his face red and bloated. Shanna sat on the couch, a smirk plastered on her face. *Crack!* Charlie slapped Fallon hard across the face and Diablo leapt forward, dragging

Charlie away from her before slamming his fist into the side of the fucker's face.

"Oh God!" Shanna screamed.

Charlie, stunned at first, staggered backward, then swung back at Diablo, yelling, "You're fucking fired!"

"I don't give a shit!" He punched Charlie again in the stomach and the man bowled over, gasping for breath. "No one fuckin' disrespects my woman. And no one fuckin' hits her. No. One." He struck the promoter again in the face and Charlie lost his balance, stumbling backward before falling to the floor. Diablo dropped to his knees and pummeled him over and over. Blood spurted everywhere and Charlie's body stopped trying to resist the attack.

"Stop, Diablo! You're going to kill him!" Fallon's tear-filled voice broke through his haze of hate and rage. Breathing heavily, his fists stopped in midair.

"You've got to admit that he's had it coming," Shanna said.

"Please, Diablo. For me." Fallon's hand on his shoulder melted some of the fury that had consumed him.

He stood up and she dropped to her knees, pressing her head against her father's chest. Diablo looked at Shanna. She met his look, her eyes darkened with lust. He shook his head and turned back to Fallon.

"He's still breathing," she said as she wiped some of the blood off his broken face. Charlie groaned. "He'll call the cops for sure. You better go." Her shimmering gaze locked onto Diablo's.

"I'm not going without you."

Shanna cleared her throat. "Go on, Fallon. I'll handle this. I mean, your dad attacked you and Diablo was only protecting you. Lie low for a couple days before you come back home. By then, I'll have your dad all calmed down."

Diablo stared at her, not believing a word she was saying. Something was going on with her that he couldn't pinpoint. "Come on. We've gotta go." He held out his hand and Fallon took it. He pulled her to him and they walked out of the room.

With her settled behind him, he revved his Harley and sped away from the warehouse. When they arrived at the clubhouse, he planned on having a talk with Fallon. *There's a lot of shit going on inside her, and I'm gonna find out what it is.*

It was a starless, moonless night as the gray clouds stretched over the sky. A single beam from Diablo's Harley was the only light bouncing off the black road and piercing the darkness. Fallon buried her head against him, her arms gripping him like a vise as they put distance between them and the fucked-up world they'd left behind.

# Chapter Seventeen

WHEN DIABLO HELPED Fallon off the bike, streaks of sand highlighted her tear-stained cheeks. Gently, he brushed his fingers across her face, the grains sticking to his skin. "It's going to be all right," he said in a low voice before he kissed her lightly. Her lips tasted of salt, and they were gritty from the blowing sand.

"I don't want to be around a bunch of people," she said.

"We'll go straight to my room. Come on." He pressed her close and wrapped his arm around her. She burrowed into his side and they walked slowly through the parking lot. Inside, the air was hazy and music filled the room. Women and men hung on to each other, and the tangy and sweet scent of sex, weed, and booze floated in the air. Over the hard beats of the music, the din of indistinct chatter rose.

Cue Ball and Sangre came over to Diablo as he pointed to a bottle of Jack. The prospect grabbed it and put it down in front of him. "Two glasses, a two-liter bottle of Coke, and a few bottled waters."

"Glad to see you got here okay, dude," Cue Ball said.

"Yeah. When I left the fuckers hadn't yet arrived. Paco and the others took care of things?"

Sangre nodded. "Tomorrow we'll pay a visit to Bud at the junk-yard."

Army, Chains, and Crow came over and Fallon pressed closer to Diablo, her face against his T-shirt. "Good to see you're back," Army said while Chains and Crow nodded in agreement.

"Yeah. I'm going to my room now. Later." He turned to grab the bottle of Jack but it wasn't there. None of the things he ordered were there. "What the fuck?" he said to the prospect.

Ruger smiled. "I already took them to your room. They're outside your door."

Diablo tilted his chin at him and walked out of the room.

In his room, Fallon pulled away from him and went over to the window. "There isn't a star in the sky. They're all hiding."

He yanked off his bloodstained T-shirt, kicked off his boots, and stretched out on the bed. "Get comfortable. We gotta talk."

Fallon turned away from the window and stared at him for a few seconds; then she took off her jacket, slipped off her shoes, and joined him on the bed. He poured her a glass of whiskey and pointed to the Coke. "You want me to add that?" She nodded and he poured it in her glass, then filled a large glass with Jack for him.

"I can't believe how things got so out of hand," she murmured.

"Sometimes life happens like that. That's why you always have to be ready for it."

"I don't think he's going to die." Her voice broke.

"The bastard will be fine. Does he always talk to you like that?" She nodded. "Fuck." He took a big gulp of whiskey, placed the glass on the counter, and grabbed her hands. "What's the bastard done to you? You can trust me."

Her eyes widened. "What do you mean? You were there. He just said some mean things to me and slapped me. I'm used to it."

"Does he always hit you?"

She shook her head. "Not like when I was young. He's only physical if he's really angry at me. I knew he'd be mad. I expected it. I mean, I didn't call him or anything. I just disappeared, and I had a lot of chores to do—"

"Stop." Diablo put his fingers over her mouth. "Don't even think this was your fuckin' fault. You didn't do shit. Is this the way it's been for you the whole time?"

Pausing for a few seconds, she stared down at the blanket. "Ever since my mom left. Before she left us, he basically ignored me unless he was really mad at her or drunk. He'd go out of town on sales trips, and when he came home he'd be real nice to my mom, but then Mr. Hyde would take over a few days later, and he'd yell at my mom a lot. Sometimes he'd beat her."

"Fuck. No wonder she left."

"But she didn't want me to tag along with her and Rich. She wanted to start over. My mom didn't love me. It's that simple. I need to grow up and accept it." She wiped at her eyes.

"I'm sure your dad's told you that a million times."

Her shoulders slumped. "Yeah. When she first left, he told me she didn't love me because I was stupid and ugly. He blamed me for making her go away. He really missed her. I'd sometimes hear him crying in their bedroom. I felt awful, and for a long time I wished I were better. I wished I wasn't ugly. I figured if I were prettier and smarter, then maybe my mom would've taken me with her. I know it broke my dad when she left, and it doesn't help when I do stupid things that make him mad. I should've called him and told him I needed a break from Shanna. I know he was worried about me."

*He's browbeaten her for so long that she believes his shit.* Diablo lifted her chin and wiped her damp cheeks. "I'm not gonna pretend like I know what your mom was thinking when she left you behind, but I can bet it wasn't for the reasons your dad's been telling you. You're a beautiful woman with a ton of shit going for you. You aren't stupid, and you're not responsible for the way your dad acts. He is. Fuck."

"I'm a cripple."

"What the fuck does that have to do with any of this?"

"My dad says that's why I'm the way I am."

"What does he say you are?"

"Mean, selfish, and lazy. He says I'm so mad about being a cripple that I take it out on people who aren't. He says I use it as an excuse to get out of chores."

"Fuckin' bullshit. I don't think you're mean or selfish."

She smiled weakly. "You're biased, although my dad's right about me being angry. I do have a lot of rage inside me because of this." She pointed to her leg.

Diablo watched her for a couple of seconds, then inhaled deeply. "Were you born that way?"

"No. I don't want to talk about it."

"Once you told me you'd tell me if I asked. I'm asking. What happened?"

She drew her knees up and wrapped her arms around them, resting her chin on the top of them. "I had an accident when I was fourteen."

"What type of accident?"

"Why does that matter?"

"Why don't you wanna tell me?" He rubbed her back.

"I fell off the roof. My dad had built an addition on the first floor and it was under my bedroom. The roof on the addition was flat and I could climb out my window and sit on it. I used to go out there when the yelling got to be too much in the house, and later it was my escape from my dad. From where I sat, I could see the whole neighborhood, and I used to pick out a pretty house and pretend I lived in it and had a normal life. Anyway, I slipped and fell and had a bad break from my knee down. The doctor said I had a severe displaced break. I didn't know what the hell he was talking about. All I knew was that it hurt real bad. Then he said something about my growth plates and how my bone would stop growing. He said I'd have a limp. There was nothing he could do to prevent that."

He wrapped his arms around her and covered the side of her face and neck in feathery kisses. "I'm so sorry, Fallon."

She shrugged. "I'm used to it."

"Are you telling me the whole story?" He moved back a bit.

Her head jerked up. "Yeah. Why?"

"In your dreams you're telling someone to get away from you. That you want them to stand back. You scream and it sounds like you're falling."

"I say all that when I'm asleep? It's obvious I'm having a nightmare."

"The same one over and over? You need to trust me, Fallon. I know it comes hard for you because it comes hard for me. I see some of me in you, but we've found each other through all the fuckin' landmines we've had to dodge in our lives. Take a chance and trust me. I know you're scared as fuck, but I'll make sure to keep you safe. By trusting me, you're giving *us* a shot."

Staring ahead, a dazed look covered her face. He let her be, waiting for her to respond. A few moths flapped against the window, their wings frantic against the screen as light poured out from the room. After what seemed like a lifetime, her monotone voice cut through the frenetic beating of the wings. "That day, I'd run up there to hide from my dad because he was in one of his moods and I wanted to get away from him so he wouldn't beat me. He searched the house, getting madder and cussing louder. Then he stuck his head out my window and looked down. I tried to hide against the brick, but he saw my feet and came out to get me. He smelled like sour musk and I thought I was going to throw up. I scrambled to get away from him, but he grabbed me and pulled me back. He was so angry. He told me that if I wanted to get away from him that badly, then he'd help me. He pushed me off the roof.

"At first he wasn't going to take me to the doctor, but it hurt so much and I was running such a high fever that he got scared and took me to the emergency room. The whole way there, he kept threatening that if I told them what really happened, I'd be sent to a foster home where I'd be raped and sexually abused daily by all the men in the house. He kept telling me he loved me, that it was an accident, and that I'd made him so mad he didn't know what he was doing. So when the doctor asked me if my dad had anything to do with what happened, I said no. He'd been concerned because he saw some fading bruises I had from a beating, but I'd told him I was a tomboy and loved climbing trees and roofs."

The room was totally quiet—even the moths had stopped beating their wings. *I'm gonna kill the fuckin' bastard. I'm not gonna tell her, but I'm gonna do it.* He untangled her arms, gently pushed down her knees, and drew her into his embrace. As she cried, he ran his hands up and down her back. *How could the bastard do that to his own kid? Fuckin' sonofabitch!* But then he remembered how his mother used to spend all the money they had buying meth while her four children went to bed hungry night after night. If it hadn't been for the free breakfast and lunch the school had provided for indigent kids, they rarely would've eaten.

"Why the fuck do parents have kids if they don't want to love them?" she whispered.

"Fuck if I know."

"Tonight, when you beat my dad, I was all twisted inside. I actually hated *you* for hurting him. Is that fucked or what?"

"Fuck if I know. My mom loved getting high more than us. It used to piss the shit outta me when I'd come home from school and my youngest sister would be sitting on the floor eating crumbs off it 'cause she was so damn hungry. And our mom would be strung out on the couch, staring off into space. At those times, I hated her more than anything. But when she went through a period of getting clean, and the house was tidy, and dinner was on the table, and she smiled a lot, I fuckin' loved her."

"Do you still love her?"

"Fuck if I know. Some days I do, and some days I wanna slit her throat for fucking up our family the way she did. But I mostly don't think about her anymore. When my brother died from an overdose, my mom died for me as well. I never want to see her."

She tilted her head up and kissed him. "I'm sorry. It must've been awful. I just wanted what all kids want—my parents to love me. My mom left and my dad stayed. I guess I'm still trying to please him. Even though I'm grown up, the child who wanted to win his love and approval is still inside me." Her voice hitched.

He stroked her hair. "I get that."

"But sometimes I really hate him. I used to feel awful thinking that way. I mean, he's the one person in my life who's supposed to be on my side when and if no one else is. Fuck!" She slammed her hand down on the mattress.

"The fact that you can hate him shows that you can see through his bullshit. And you wanting to live on your own is the best decision you can make right now."

"I know but it's so damn scary. I'm afraid," she whispered.

"You've got me. I'll always have your back. If you're scared, lean on me."

She threw her arms around his neck, kissing him passionately. "I'm so happy I have you in my life," she said against his lips.

He kissed her back; she tasted sweet and smoky. "I gotta take a shower, sweetness." Standing up, he went to the bathroom and winked at her before shutting the door.

Clean and refreshed, he smiled when he saw her. He dropped his towel and joined her on the bed. She was lying on her side and he was lying on his, and she had those warm honey-colored eyes and long lashes that captured his heart as he gazed at her. Things he'd never felt before stirred deep inside him. They went past the erection he had, past the lust churning in his gut, and past the hunger he had for her at that moment. He couldn't explain or articulate it; he just knew Fallon moved him in ways no other woman ever had.

"You have such a reflective expression on your face. What're you thinking about?" she asked as she traced his face with her finger.

"How much I care about you." He caught her finger and put it in his mouth, sucking on it.

"Why do you care about me?" She ran her foot up and down his shin.

"Because you do something to me. You fill a hole deep in me I didn't even know I had. You calm the storm in me, bringing me peace. The best way I can say it is that you make me feel complete."

Fallon's eyes glistened and she looked deep into his gaze. "You're my one stability in a world filled with chaos. You never leave my mind. You're always there. And the feeling I have for you stretches throughout my whole body. It's overwhelming, but it makes me feel complete too. I have to admit I'm scared of having my heart broken… of losing you."

Diablo tugged her to him. "I'd never break your heart because if I did, I'd end up breaking mine too. Look, we were betrayed by people who should've always had our backs but didn't. Besides my brothers, I've never trusted anyone. You're the first woman I've trusted in a long time. It seems like you're trusting me too."

She nodded. "You're the only man I've trusted and the only one I know I can depend on. Even though I've only known you for a short time, it's like you've always been there just waiting for me."

"We need each other." He gently pushed her on her back and hovered over her. Bending down, he kissed her deeply while she ran her hands over his strong back. "I want you to know that whether my heart beats another day or another hundred years, it's yours," he said against her lips. She began to say something but he swallowed her words, then slipped his tongue into her mouth. Through her T-shirt, he felt her hardened nipples press against him.

"Let me take off my shirt," she whispered.

"I'll take care of it." He nuzzled her neck as he took hold of her shirt's hem and pulled it up. He straightened up and slowly took her clothes off, piece by piece, kissing and caressing her skin as he revealed it. Seeing her shiver under his touch made his cock grow more. "You're so beautiful," he said as he covered her pert breast with his hand. She moaned and reached out to him, her nails digging into his chest as he flicked his finger over her nipples before taking one in his mouth, cradling her other breast in his callused palm. A throaty moan fell from her lips.

"When I'm with you like this, nothing matters but you and me. Nothing can hurt me and the memories are gone. It's like you're me and I'm you, melting into each other. I feel safe."

"That's all over. From now on it's us and nothing else matters." He pulled her bottom lip into his mouth, sucking hard and knowing it'd be bruised, but he couldn't stop. He wanted all of her and he couldn't get enough of her. He wanted to possess, claim, and devour her; his hunger for her—all of her—was insatiable.

Peppering her shivering body with nips and licks, her moans and squirming underneath him went straight to his dick and fired every nerve in his body. His mouth trailed down to her belly while his hand slid under her and grabbed her ass cheek, squeezing it tightly. Again her moans drove him crazy; their raw desire was intoxicating. As his mouth lowered, she spread her legs, the scent of her arousal fueling his fire. When he licked her inner thighs and the area around her pussy, she bucked forward, pressing her sex against his face.

A chuckle rumbled deep from his chest. "I'll get there." A whimper escaped through her parted lips, and when he looked at her, unadulterated lust shone in her eyes. "Fuck, sweet pea." His desire grew and his pulse quickened as he held her gaze.

More kisses, more licks, more nips to the softest skin he'd ever touched. More moans, more groans, more whimpers as she writhed underneath him. She was the fire in the core of his being. White-hot in intensity. He lifted his head and looked at her pussy pulsing in glistening need. "I love how wet you are," he said as he slid his fingers between the velvety folds of her slippery pussy.

She gasped. "That feels so good."

"I'm gonna make you feel a whole lot better." He explored her aching wetness, then spread open her puffy lips and ran his tongue from her wet slit all the way to the top of her mound. Over and over he licked while he looked up at her, loving her perky nipples and her body moving around uninhibited. The scent of her, the feel of her, the taste of her fueled his fire. He dipped in and flicked his tongue against her clit while his index finger sank deep inside her.

"Oh my God," she gasped, arching into his touch.

Picking up the pace, he shoved his finger in and out while his tongue flicked her hardened spot over and over. He licked her like he was possessed. He craved to hear her cry out, arch her back, come harder than she ever had. Then he felt her body tense under him; her belly was as hard as a board. He kept the steady pace until she cried out and clutched his head between her palms. His tongue kept going as she rode the wave of her climax, pure pleasure surging through him.

As her breathing returned to normal, he sat up and leaned back, his gaze capturing her contented one. He reached over, opened a drawer in his nightstand, and took out a packet. Putting it to his mouth, he ripped it open with his teeth.

Wiping her hair from her face, she breathed, "No. Don't. I'm on the pill." He jerked his head back. "I'm on it for bad periods. I want to feel you inside me."

He growled in pleasure. "I'm good, sweet pea. You're the only one I've been with since I last tested. I can't wait to feel you."

His hand went behind her knee to lift her leg over his shoulder. He was more than ready to bury himself between her thighs. Taking hold of his cock, he placed it at her wet slit and slipped it in. Being inside was like being burned alive with the sweetest heat. He stayed still, loving how her warm walls clutched his throbbing hardness. Then he pulled out and thrust in hard and deep, her moans music to his ears.

"You want it hard?" he panted.

"Hard and fast." She scratched his shoulders with her nails.

"That's my woman." Diablo pulled out and shoved back in, pummeling her tightness over and over. The sound of her wetness mixed with the slapping of his balls with every deep thrust filled the room. "It feels so fuckin' good. I love watching you as I fuck you," he growled. He fucked her fast, hard, and deep. He felt like he was about to burst wide open, and he'd never felt that way before. It was the strangest sensation.

He could tell she was ready to come: tight, swollen, gripping down on his cock. He kept pumping her up and down, wanting her pussy squeezing his hardness as he exploded in her. Then he shot into her still-pulsating wetness, and she cried out as her spasms clamped tightly around his thrusting dick. As they came together, panting, moaning, grunting, and sweating, it felt as if something special inside her made its way through his dick into him. It overwhelmed him, and he didn't know what to make of it. He'd never experienced something like that before.

For several minutes, he lay on top of her, his face buried in her neck, her fingers running over his shoulder like brushstrokes on a canvas. It was the most intense orgasm he'd ever had. He finally rolled over and tucked her against him. She curled her arm around his waist.

Her voice broke through the silence. "I've never been in love before, but it must feel like the way I'm feeling." She pushed her head back and looked up at him.

"I've only felt something for a woman once, but what I feel for you doesn't even fuckin' compare to that. This is what love feels like, sweet pea." He leaned down and kissed her.

"It's awesome and scary at the same time."

"Loving someone is always a risk, but it's worth taking. Nothing's perfect in life, but now that I met you, I'm willing to take all the risks in the whole fuckin' world for a shot at us."

"Me too." She pulled his hand to her lips, kissed it, and tucked it under her chin.

Warmth spread through him. He knew that no matter what, he'd never stop desiring her or loving her. Life had been tough for both of them thus far in their journey, but through their suffering, they'd found each other. They stirred the deepest desires in each other. And at the same time, they'd become each other's comfort from the storm of life.

# Chapter Eighteen

THE FOLLOWING MORNING, Fallon woke up refreshed and happy. Bitterness had stopped running through her veins since she'd finally opened up to Diablo. Telling him about her father pushing her off the roof was like an elephant had been lifted from her. She didn't realize what a heavy burden she'd been carrying with her.

She glanced at Diablo as he slept and elation and desire swept through her, curling her toes. *I love him. He's my anchor, my salvation, my life. My one and only.* Diablo had taken her out of existing and into living. Being in love felt unbelievable. She giggled and reached out to touch his beard. It was soft with just a hint of roughness. She loved it, but then, she loved everything about him.

Smiling, she rolled out of bed, careful not to wake him. Heading to the bathroom, she took a quick shower and washed up, then went over to his chest of drawers, took out another T-shirt, and slipped it over her head. The fabric was soft against her skin as it skimmed down her body. She inhaled deeply as Diablo's fresh, clean scent surrounded her. How she loved his scent. She wished she could bottle it so she could smell it when he wasn't around.

Shaking her head at her silliness, she picked up her phone and curled up in his recliner.

She opened her e-mails and covered her mouth to suppress a shout. There were two job offers: one at the library and one at the bookstore. As she reread the e-mails, she quietly clapped her hands. Since she'd met Diablo, her life had taken so many turns that her head was still spinning.

"I'm hoping our fucking from last night is the reason you have that big smile on your face." Diablo's voice, low and gravelly, stroked her senses like velvet.

"You always have the first smile on my face." She went over to him and slid between the covers. The warmth of his body radiated from him and she cuddled close. His strong arm curled around her and her insides tingled from the scent, feel, and essence of him.

"Did you sleep well?" he asked.

"Best sleep I've had in a long time." She hooked her arm around his chest.

"You up for looking at apartments? Muerto texted and said he had a few."

Excitement skimmed up her spine. "I'd love to. I can't believe I'm doing this."

"You know you can always stay with me," he said gently.

She kissed his skin. "I know, but I want to try to do this on my own. But I want you to feel comfortable to come over whenever you want. I just have to be able to stand on my own two feet."

"That's cool. I get it. I'll be over a lot, so I won't worry so much about you when I'm not there."

"You're too sweet." She sat up and kissed him on the lips, pushing her tongue into his mouth. They kissed and ran their hands over each other's bodies until she pulled away and playfully smacked him on the chest. "Get moving. I want to see what Muerto has to offer."

He laughed and rolled out of bed, shuffling away to the bathroom while she jumped up and got dressed.

They went downstairs to the kitchen, where a woman with heavily highlighted brown hair turned away from the stove and smiled broadly at them. "Diablo. You've been a stranger for a while." The woman's eyes darted to Fallon and then back to Diablo.

"Been keeping busy. This is Fallon." He moved her in front of him. "And this is Lena. She's the one who keeps us fed with all her fuckin' good cooking."

Fallon laughed and extended her hand. "I've tasted some of your dishes and they were delicious. It's so nice to meet you."

Lena nodded, scanning Fallon from head to foot and back up. "You two want some breakfast? I'm making eggs and bacon."

"Sounds good to me. You good with that?" Diablo said. She nodded.

"Go on out and sit down. I'll have one of the club girls bring it out." Lena turned her back to them and opened the refrigerator door.

Diablo grasped her hand and they walked to the main room, securing a table closest to the door. A few minutes later, a pretty blonde with Daisy dukes and a tight tube top came over to the table with two dishes. She winked at Diablo and leaned down real low when she put his plate in front of him, then slid Fallon's plate to her.

"Hey, handsome. You want some coffee and orange juice with your breakfast?" she asked softly.

"Coffee's good." He leaned over and put his arm around Fallon's shoulders. "What do you want, sweet pea?"

She glanced at the woman, who stared coldly at her. "Coffee with cream." She lifted her chin and threw a don't-fuck-with-me stare. The woman snorted and sashayed away. Fallon had to admit she had one of the sexiest walks she'd ever seen, and by the way the other men watched her wiggling ass as she left the room, she knew they'd agree with her. "She's got a killer walk. All the men in here are drooling, and they probably see her every day. She's pretty too."

"Ruby? Yeah, she's popular around here."

"Have you been with her?" She regretted the question the second she uttered it. Did she really want to know which club women he banged?

"A few years ago. Didn't mean anything." He shoved a forkful of eggs in his mouth.

Ruby came back out with two steaming mugs of coffee. She gave Fallon hers without even a glance and made eye contact with Diablo as she put his down. "How've you been? It seems like I don't see you much."

Diablo bit off a piece of bacon and munched on it. "I've been hanging out with my woman." His hand went over Fallon's.

Ruby pursed her lips. "You need to party a little so you can unwind.

We're all missing you."

*This bitch has a lot of fucking nerve. I bet she's waiting for me to say* *something. She's purposely trying to get under my skin.* Not wanting to play into Ruby's hands, she didn't say anything. Instead, she leaned into him and ran her fingers over his head. From the corner of her eye, she caught Ruby's face darkening.

"My woman's taking care of me fine." Diablo's words had a sound of finality to them, and Ruby walked away.

"I don't think she likes me. Actually, I don't think any of the women like me."

"Do you give a shit about it?" Puzzlement crossed his face.

"Not really. I'm used to bitchy women not liking me. I just don't know how I feel about all of them hanging around wishing you'd screw them." She pushed her barely touched plate away.

"It's the way they are. It's the way our world is. If a brother wants one of them, they go. If he doesn't, then they move on to the next. It's pretty simple. Nothing to be worried about."

"Okay. I'm just going to come out and ask. Are you the type of guy who thinks it's okay to screw a woman just for sex but still love and stay with a girlfriend or wife?"

Diablo pushed his empty plate away and cocked his head, his gaze locked on hers. "You're the only woman I've been serious about, and I'm not gonna stick my cock in any other pussy but yours."

Her cheeks warmed as she looked quickly around the room. A few men sniggered, and she wished Diablo didn't have such a loud voice. In a hushed voice, she said, "But do you think it's okay for a man to have fun on the side when he's in a serious relationship?"

"I think I just answered you. I don't roll that way. If a guy does, it's his fuckin' business. I'm not the goddamn moral badge." He took a big gulp of coffee and grabbed his phone when it vibrated on the table. "Muerto's asking when we're gonna go look at his places. You ready now or do you wanna keep talking about whether I'm gonna fuck a club girl?"

"I'm ready, and I was just wondering because I'd think it'd be hard for a man to resist a woman if she keeps throwing her boobs and twat in his face."

He stood up. "For some men it is. For me it's not. And I trust you don't think it's cool to go behind your man's back and fuck another one."

"Of course not. I'm totally not that way." After grabbing her purse off the chair, she followed him out.

"Good. Then we're on the same page." He helped her on his bike and they flew out of the parking lot.

Muerto was waiting for them at a three-story stucco building that had a red-tiled roof, double glass doors, a lobby decorated in Native and southwestern designs, and two sets of elevators. A pretty woman with long black silky hair stood next to him in a pair of skinny jeans that looked like she'd painted them on.

"Hey, dude." Muerto bumped fists with Diablo. "Fallon." Muerto tipped his head.

"Hi." She glanced at the woman who had her face buried in her phone.

The woman looked up and her lips pulled up. "I'm Raven. I'm Muerto's old lady." She laughed. "I've been wanting to meet you."

"I'm Fallon." She shoved her hands in her jean pockets.

Her gray eyes slid up and down. "So, your Diablo's woman. We gotta grab lunch sometime. I'll ask Breanna to join us. Have you met Breanna?" Fallon shook her head. "You're going to love her. She's so sweet and caring. Anyway, we've been wanting to meet you and get to know you. Give me your number and we can set up a day for lunch."

"Okay." She liked Raven. She seemed to be the antithesis of her: extroverted, confident, and strong. Fallon admired those qualities, and was starting to see them in herself somewhat. Since she'd met Diablo, she noticed that she didn't always look at life as a series of obstacles which had been her habit. She'd begun seeing it as a series of opportunities. And now that she'd confided in Diablo about the truth of her "accident," the urge to face her childhood and overcome it took hold of her. She knew she had a long way to go, but for her, being happy and hopeful were new emotions. She embraced them, wanting to foster and grow them until they became her new habit and norm.

"You guys ready to see the unit?" Muerto's voice took her away from her inner musings and she focused back on the situation.

"I'd love to see the unit." She slipped her hand into Diablo's and followed Muerto and Raven into the elevator.

The apartment was perfect. It was only one bedroom and one bath, but it looked huge to her. Considering she spent most of her time in her bedroom at home, having a small kitchen, family room, and dining area seemed gigantic. It was a corner unit, so the kitchen had a window and the living room had sliding doors that led out to a nice-sized balcony. *No more roofs for me.* She giggled to herself as she followed Raven out onto the balcony. Green grass and tall maple and evergreen trees dotted the landscape. Next to her unit was a wonderful weeping willow—her favorite tree. *This place feels so right.* Warmth radiated throughout her body and she tipped her head back, turning her face to the sky.

"It's so beautiful. I can't believe how perfect it is. Just so beautiful," she kept repeating.

Raven laughed. "I guess that means you're going to take the apartment?"

"Oh yeah." She knew she had a silly grin on her face, but she couldn't help it. *My first apartment.* The thought thrilled and liberated her.

"I can help you paint the walls. You need color. White walls are so generic and boring."

"I would like to add some color." Painting the walls would be symbolic for her; it would mirror her life. She was leaving her beige life for one filled with color. She'd taken the first step by going out with Diablo; he certainly wasn't beige.

"We can go to Shineman's. They have the most awesome variety of colors in the county. This will be so much fun."

"Is Muerto cool with me painting the walls?" Fallon glanced inside at Muerto and Diablo, who stood talking by the kitchen counter.

Raven shook her head. "Nope. But don't worry about that. I never did. We can go shopping whenever you want. Call me."

"I will." She opened her phone and plugged in Raven's number as she said it. *She's the third number I have in my directory for women friends.* She had Sylvia's, Annie—the girl she'd met the previous week—and now Raven's. *Awesome.*

"You wanna look at another place? I have a two-bedroom a couple of miles from here. I thought I'd show you this one first because it has security doors, a pool, stackable washer and dryer, and a group of quiet, decent tenants. A bit older, but that can be a good thing." Muerto hooked his arm around Raven's waist.

"I love it. Do you?" Fallon looked at Diablo.

"Yeah. It's cool. You think it's big enough? Maybe you should check out the two-bedroom."

She shook her head. "No. This is the one for me. I'll take it." She went over to Diablo and hugged him.

Muerto headed to the kitchen counter and took out papers from a folder. "I'll have you look the lease over and sign it. Since you're Diablo's woman, I'll forgo the security deposit and first and last months' rent. You can move in today if you want."

She reviewed the lease, noting the clauses about only one pet and no painting the walls without permission. She figured Raven would have her back on that one, so she signed it, a bolt of joy sparking up her spine when he gave her two sets of keys. *This is really mine.* The keys cut into her tightly clenched hand.

When Raven and Muerto left, she whooped loudly and walked around the apartment. "It's all mine!" She fell into Diablo's arms, kissing and hugging him.

He laughed. "It's yours, sweet pea. Do you wanna go to Tula to get some of your stuff? I can get a truck if you want to bring some of your furniture with you."

"I don't really have any furniture. My dad bought everything I have. Anyway, I want to start over. I want to buy my own things and furnish my place the way I want to. I do have a lamp my mother bought me when I was a kid. I'd like to get that along with my clothes and books. I'm not sure if you should come. I mean, my dad may call the cops about what you did to him. I don't want you to get into any trouble."

"No fuckin' way is your dad gonna call the badges. He's in too deep with illegal fighting. The badges would haul his ass in, and the feds would get involved since there's gambling. Anyway, there's no damn way I'm letting you go up there to face all that shit with him alone."

She stroked his cheek. "You're so good to me. I would like you to be there. My dad's still mad, but he's been texting me and asking me to come home. I haven't wanted to deal with it, so I only sent one text asking how he is. He said he's better but he wants me home. I'm pretty sure he won't be home now, so we should go. I really don't want to bump into him."

"We'll take the SUV. Let's go."

"On the way back, we can stop at Furniture Mart. I want to pick out some things." She giggled. It was like she was a kid in the candy store and could have anything she wanted. "Let's go." She pulled his arm impatiently, trying to drag him with her to the front door.

"Hold on. I wanna make sure all the windows are locked along with the sliding glass door."

After determining everything was secure, they walked out of her new apartment. Settled into the SUV, Diablo turned out of the lot and picked up the old highway as they drove to Tula.

When they arrived at her house, Fallon turned to Diablo. "I think it's best if you wait in the car."

"No fuckin' way." He turned off the ignition and started to open the car door.

She grabbed his arm. "Hear me out. If my dad is there, it'll be a big scene if you're with me. I know how to handle him."

"I haven't seen any signs of that. I'm going in."

"Okay, but give me twenty minutes alone. If I'm not out by then, you can come inside. Deal?"

He narrowed his eyes as he pulled at his beard. "Five minutes."

"Come on… I can barely put anything in my duffel bag in five minutes. Fifteen." She smiled sweetly and brushed his cheek with the back of her hand.

"Five fuckin' minutes, and don't give me that sexy smile."

She leaned over and kissed the side of his mouth, licking it with the tip of her tongue while she brushed her hand across his crotch. "Ten minutes," she breathed against his face.

A grunt tumbled from his mouth and he ran his hand over his head quickly. "Fuck, woman. You better get going 'cause you got nine minutes left."

After giving him a quick peck on the cheek, she flew out of the car and opened the garage door with her remote. A breath of relief escaped her as she looked at the empty spot where her dad's car should be. Only Shanna's was there.

She strode over to the door leading into the house and turned the knob slowly; it swung open and she went inside. Cautiously approaching the hallway, she glanced all around but no one was there. *Shanna probably went with Dad.*

As she walked up the circular staircase, she heard muffled sounds coming from the master bedroom. She froze on the stairs and strained her ears. Nothing audible, just garbled sounds. She slipped off her shoes and went up the rest of the stairs, pausing in the hallway. The sounds were louder and more discernible: grunts and moans in varying octaves. She padded over to the master bedroom and noticed the door was ajar.

Sucking in her breath, she went to the door and peeked in. Her eyes widened when she saw Shanna on her knees, her butt high in the air, and a fit man with long black hair and tattoos all over his back, arms, and shins pounding into her. *Oh shit. Shanna's screwing around on Dad.*

Out of the corner of her eye, she caught a glimpse of something black. Moving her gaze from the bed to the vanity chair, she saw a leather jacket with a bright patch of a devil holding what looked like flaming pistons. She noticed the name "Satan's Pistons" over the top of the devil, and on the bottom it read "Arizona." *Fuck! I can't let Diablo come in here.* Backing away quietly, she glanced at her phone: seven minutes to go.

She hurried to her room and closed the door, sending a quick text to Diablo telling him everything's cool and her dad wasn't home. She'd be out real soon. Grabbing the duffel bag from her closet, she went into her bathroom and threw things inside it. Her heart sank when she looked at her bookcase. She'd never be able to take all the books with her without having Diablo help her, and she couldn't do that. Throwing just a few of her favorite books into the bag, she went to her closet and groaned. The majority of her clothes were shapeless, oversized tops and baggy pants, the predominate colors beige, tan, and white. She folded a few T-shirts and jeans and decided to leave the rest. A large part of her craved a new wardrobe with color and some style. *I'll ask Raven to go shopping with me.* She smiled. Going shopping with a friend was totally new to her.

Glancing around the room, she spotted her extra bottle of the lemon body spray she'd bought with Sylvia a few weeks before. She scooped it up and threw it in a plastic bag. Before she left, she looked around, her gaze landing on an antique lamp with hand-painted flowers on the milky-white glass shade. Her mother had bought it at a flea market when Fallon had been six years old. She still remembered the day her mother had brought it home, gushing about how old it was and how she loved it. It was the one thing her father had allowed her to keep from her mother. When she'd run away, he'd been so angry and upset, he'd thrown everything away that had belonged to her. Even photographs weren't safe.

*That's right. The photos I hid under the loose floorboard in my closet.*

Fallon had been desperate to save as many photographs of her mother as possible, so she'd gone up to the attic where boxes of pictures had been stored before she'd even been born. She knew her dad had been planning to throw them away when he got home from work, so she took as many as she could without even looking at them and ran down to her room. She'd worked hard prying up the floorboards in the closet, but she finally loosened them and stashed all the pictures there. The only one she kept was of her sitting on her mom's lap with her mom's arms wrapped around her. Fallon figured she must've been about seven years old in that photo. She'd kept it in a slit she'd made in her mattress. Her dad never found it. She'd look at it often.

With duffel bag, photographs, and Victorian lamp in hand, she left her room and headed for the stairs. A man's voice floated into the hallway. "Bloody Knuckles don't know how to fuck you. Each time we hook up, you're so fuckin' hungry for my cock. Was it the money you wanted?" The sweet scent of weed filtered out of the room.

"You got the cock but he's got the bucks. I got myself covered. Let's go for another round before he gets home. You want me riding that big thick dick of yours?" Shanna's giggles repulsed Fallon.

Standing at the top of the stairs, she waited until they got things rolling again before she gripped the bannister and went down the stairs. As she came out of the garage, she bumped into Diablo. "What are you doing here?" Her muscles tensed.

"Going to get you. Fuck, it's been more than twenty minutes. I was worried."

Handing him her mother's lamp, she walked to the car. "I forgot about some photographs I wanted to bring with me. Let's go. I don't want to bump into my dad."

It wasn't until they had put some distance between her house and them that she relaxed. For the first fifteen minutes, she acted like she'd hadn't noticed that Diablo kept looking at her. She uncrossed her arms and leaned back in the seat, watching the landscape slip by.

"What the fuck happened back there? You're as wound up as a god-damn top."

She pulled at a piece of dry skin on her lips, then took out a cherry-flavored balm and spread it on. "It was just weird being at home."

"Bullshit. Don't shut me out, Fallon."

Turning to face him, she breathed out. "Okay, but I don't want you freaking out or turning back around. Deal?"

"Just fuckin' tell me. I'm not making any damn deal."

Inhaling and exhaling slowly, she rubbed her palms against her jean-clad thighs. "I saw Shanna fucking another guy."

"That's it? I knew she was a slut the first time I met her. You feeling bad for your dad?"

"No. Yes… a little. Anyway, that's not what made me freak. The guy she was with belongs to a motorcycle club. I saw his leather jacket. It said Satan something and the bottom said 'Arizona.'"

"Fuck!" Diablo slammed his hand against the steering wheel, then pulled over. "We're going back so I can beat the fucker's ass. You shoula told me when you got in the car."

"This is exactly why I didn't tell you. We're not turning around. I don't want you and this loser punching it out. I don't want you getting in trouble with the law."

"If I'm not in trouble with the goddamn law then something would be fuckin' wrong in my life."

"I'm not joking. I'm serious. I don't want to lose you. Let's just go back to Alina."

He stared at her for a long while but she held her own, and he finally turned the ignition and pulled the car back onto the highway. They didn't speak for the rest of the ride back, but when she placed her hand on his shoulder, he grasped it and intertwined her fingers with his. She smiled inwardly; she hadn't backed down.

Bringing his hand to her lips, she kissed it, then rested her head against his shoulder. He was her strength, but she now realized she was his as well. A sense of ease shrouded her, and she knew she no longer needed to pretend to be living a different life. Her life had good feelings in it now and she wouldn't trade it for anything.

"We'll get you some furniture. You good?" Diablo said as he turned off the exit for downtown Alina.

Giving him an easy nod, she squeezed his hand. "I'm good. Very good."

# Chapter Nineteen

DIABLO SAT AT the bar, watching Brutus and Army play a game of pool. It'd been one week since Fallon had moved into her own apartment. Each time he caught her standing in her kitchen admiring the appliances, he had to laugh. In many ways she was just starting to grow up. Her dad had kept her sheltered and dependent on him for all of her life. Diablo narrowed his eyes. Her dad probably didn't want her telling people what he'd done to her, so he made her afraid of life and living.

"How's Fallon liking the apartment?" Muerto asked as he sat on the barstool.

"Loves it. You'd think she was living in a fuckin' mansion the way she's been carrying on. It does look better with the new paint."

Muerto jerked his head back. "Paint? What the fuck?"

Diablo shrugged. "Raven brought over several cans a few days ago. I gotta admit the colors look better than all them white walls."

Muerto guffawed. "Raven really pushes my buttons sometimes."

"No control over your woman?" Chains said as he came over to them.

Muerto shook his head. "But I fucking love it."

"That's why I like to fly solo," Chains said.

"Flying solo's the only way I'm going. I don't need a woman around my neck telling me what to do, or tying me down. I like the variety pack when it comes to fuckin'," Goldie added as he came up to the bar.

"I heard you got a Road Glide Special." Diablo curled his fingers around his beer bottle.

Goldie's blue eyes lit up. "It's a fuckin' beauty. Just what a Road

Captain needs. I fuckin' loaded it, spared no expenses. It's metallic silver and looks like a flash of lightning when I'm speeding down the road."

Soon all the brothers who were in the main room formed a circle around Goldie. A new Harley was big news; no other conversation could rival it. They all followed him outside, his bike gleaming under the sun.

"It's fuckin' wicked," Diablo said as he hunched down on his knees to inspect it.

"Awesome, bro." Army ran his hands over the shiny silver body.

For the next hour, the brothers admired the newest addition to their family. The club girls sat on the front porch scowling and shaking their heads, griping about how a metal and chrome bike could get all the attention for the last two hours.

"We gotta celebrate, dude," Army said. The other brothers voiced their agreement.

As they discussed the particulars of the celebration, Steel rode up on his Harley. He walked over to Goldie's new bike. "Fuck, this is gorgeous. You just get it?"

Goldie nodded.

"We were just saying that we need to celebrate," Cue Ball said.

Steel ran his hands over the handlebars. "For fucking sure. Why don't we go over to Cuervos?" Steel was part owner of a non-biker bar in town. His buddy from back in the day, Jorge, was the other owner.

"Sounds like a plan," Goldie said.

"But this is for brothers and club women only," Army said. Many of the brothers agreed with him.

"That's cool. I'm sure our women don't want to hear about Harleys all night. I'll tell Jorge to expect us around eight," Steel replied.

As the brothers continued talking, Diablo went around to the side of the clubhouse and took out his phone.

**Diablo:** *Hey. How's work?*

**Fallon:** *Great! I love this bookstore.*

**Diablo:** *Goldie got a new Harley. It's fuckin' badass. Brothers r* *gonna celebrate tonite.*

**Fallon:** *You celebrate when someone buys a bike?*

**Diablo:** *Fuck yeah! Major event. I'll come by around 11 tonite.*

**Fallon:** *Ok. You can stay longer if you want.*

**Diablo:** *I know. U b careful. I'll have a prospect make sure u get home ok.*

Ever since she'd told him about inheriting the money and that someone had tried to impersonate her, he made sure to watch her. He had to keep her safe. Her birthday was approaching, and then she'd fall into a shitload of money. It made him feel more than uneasy.

**Fallon:** *You don't have to do that. I'll be fine. Promise.*

**Diablo:** *It'll be either Patches or Ruger. U know them both. See u later.*

In his mind's eye, he could see her frowning, her lips pursed together the way she did when she didn't agree with him.

**Fallon:** *You're going to do it regardless of what I say, right?*

**Diablo:** *Ya. Gotta go. Text me when u get home.*

**Fallon:** *Ok. Have fun.* ♥

She'd started using hearts to end their text conversations, and for some reason, he found it cute as hell. There were many things he found cute: her freckles, the way her forehead creased when she was pissed, her giggles, the way she ate all the crust off her toast first, her spontaneous hugs. *My sweet pea's got a good hold of me.* He chuckled and slipped his phone back in the inner pocket of his cut.

Walking back to the group of brothers who still congregated around Goldie's baby, heat radiated through his chest. He couldn't remember being that happy with any woman, even Hannah.

Fallon was quickly becoming his everything.

And he was just fine with that.

★   ★   ★

AMBER-SPECKLED BAR LIGHTS illuminated twisted curls of smoke as loud conversations in loud voices competed with the rock music from the jukebox. Shot glasses, beer bottles, and mounds of buffalo wings and nachos littered the counter and tables. Most of the room wore denim and leather; the ones not wearing it gazed at the rough-looking men with fear and admiration. A few citizen women ventured over and struck up a conversation with some of the men, but they soon retreated to their tables in the back when the club girls rushed over.

Goldie laughed and tugged Angel close to him. "You girls don't want any competition tonight."

Shaking her dark brown hair, she grabbed hold of the back of his neck, pushing his face toward hers. Their lips met and Goldie's hands slid down to Angel's ass. Diablo threw back his shot, wishing Fallon were there. He had a real bad urge to kiss her deep and wet, but it'd have to wait until later.

"You look like you wish you had a woman," Maria said as she ran her finger up his arm.

"Only one." Diablo tossed the whiskey down his throat.

"Fallon. That's her name, right?" He nodded. "I'm not gonna lie to you and tell you I'm happy about it, but I'm used to it now. That's something, right?"

Smiling, he picked up another shot glass. "How's your brother?"

"Not good. Thanks for asking. No one else has." She picked up her beer bottle and took a long pull.

"Did you wanna eat something? It looks like you've lost some weight." He pushed the plate of nachos he'd been munching on close to her.

She smiled and squeezed his arm. "You're really a gentle person. I hope your girl's treating you special."

"She is."

Wiping her eyes, she laughed. "She better be or I'm gonna beat her ass." A pause ensued. "You must be loving Goldie's new bike. It's so fuckin' cool."

As the two of them spoke, Diablo saw two men walk in and his senses went into high alert. There was something about the men that raised red flags: sweat poured down from the skinnier one's face, and both men darted their eyes around constantly.

*They seem outta place. Like they're not comfortable. Why the fuck are they hanging by the door?*

Diablo went over to Steel, who was talking to Paco, Crow, Muerto, and Shotgun about some of the best road trips he'd been on. Diablo stood close and Steel stopped in mid-sentence, turning to look at him. "What's up?"

Diablo jerked his head slightly toward the two men standing near the entrance. "You know those two?"

Steel shook his head. "They seem nervous." He motioned for Jorge to come over. When Jorge didn't recognize them, the cluster of brothers stiffened.

The tension between them wound around the other Night Rebels, and Army joined them. "What the fuck?"

"Something's up with the two dudes by the door," Paco said as he slipped his hand inside his cut.

"We better watch them. I don't have a good feeling about them," Diablo said, reaching inside his cut as well.

Before he could take out his Glock 9mm, there were two pops, one right after the other. Shrill screams, scraping tables, knocked-over chairs, and more shots drowned out the music. Citizens were ducking under tables while the brothers were shooting at the two men by the door who'd caused the panic.

"Get down!" Steel yelled out to the club girls, who stood hugging each other.

Another shot. Diablo saw Maria as she hit the floor. "Fuck!" As he ran over to her, he saw the two men dash out the door. "Maria's been hit. I'm going after the fuckers." He ran to the front door and saw Chains lying on the floor, blood pooling under him.

"I got this, bro. Just go," Crow said.

Diablo barreled out of the bar and saw the two men leaving the parking lot on a couple of Harleys. Jumping on his, he tore after them. As they sped toward the highway, Diablo could see the back of one of the men was covered in red. He pushed his bike harder. Cams and engines screamed behind him, and he looked in his mirror to see Muerto, Army, and Goldie coming from the rear.

Harder and faster they pushed. As he gained on the two assholes who'd opened fire on them, one of them fired his gun, the rush of bullets whizzing by Diablo. He took out a tire iron from one of his saddlebags and threw it at the wheel of the rider soaked in blood. The bike careened out of control and crashed, throwing him off. The smell of burning rubber filled Diablo's nostrils as he watched the rider slide down the pavement, leaving his skin on the asphalt. Diablo passed by him, figuring he was most probably dead, with Army, Muerto, and Goldie in hot pursuit.

The other rider slowed down to avoid a dip in the road, those few seconds allowed Diablo to overtake him. He pulled in front of him, Muerto and Goldie on each side, and Army in the back. The rider slowed down and they forced him off the road. Diablo leapt off his bike and dragged the guy off his.

"You motherfucker!" He punched and threw him on the ground, kicking him over and over. Goldie, Army, and Muerto joined in, taking out all their anger on him.

"Who the fuck are you? Did someone send you?" Army yelled in the man's battered face. He remained silent.

Diablo spat on the sand. "Muerto, call and tell Steel to send a truck. We're gonna take this fucker to the cell and get some answers." Through the swollen slits of the rider's eyelids, Diablo saw fear building. He kicked him hard. "You better be scared, you sonofabitch." He turned around and went to his Harley, pulling yards of brown rope out of his saddlebag. Goldie took it from him, went over to the downed rider, and began hog-tying him.

A white pickup truck kicked up dust as it skidded to a stop near the four bikers and their prisoner. Jigger jumped out and rushed over to the quartet.

"What the fuck's going on back there?" Goldie asked as he helped drag the restrained man to the truck.

"A fucking mess. Badges everywhere. Citizens freaking out."

"Besides Chains, did any other brothers get hurt?" Army rolled the grunting man into the back seat of the truck.

"No. Chains was shot in the shoulder. He should be good. Paco got him back to the club house and called Doc."

"How's Maria?" Diablo asked in a low voice.

"She didn't make it. Took a bullet in her chest."

"Fuck." Heaviness pressed on his chest as Maria's face flashed through his mind. In his world, death was a common occurrence and could happen in the blink of an eye; each day they lived was a cause for celebration. But Maria was a club girl. Even though she was part of their world, her role was to please the brothers. In many outlaw clubs, the girls were inconsequential. *She didn't deserve to die. She never did shit to anyone.*

After they loaded the guy's bike in the bed of the truck, they went to where his buddy had gone down with his Harley. The dead rider lay face down in the sand. Diablo picked up his tire iron while the others loaded the man's crumpled motorcycle in the truck's bed. They picked up the dead man, threw him in the back with his buddy, and headed back to Alina.

PACO JOINED THEM in the cell as Diablo picked up a pair of pliers. "This fucker talk?" he asked.

Diablo shook his head. "I got all the time in the world." Goldie, Army, Muerto, and Jigger laughed.

"Fucking badges are all over the damn place. This asshole's caused a shitload of trouble. Coming into a bar with a bunch of citizens. What the fuck were you thinking, asshole?" Paco punched the guy in the face. His head hung down as drops of blood stained the cement floor.

"How're the girls doing?" Diablo paused and looked at Paco.

"They're in shock. They're not talking. The only ones talking are the citizens, and they didn't see shit. What a fucking mess."

Diablo pulled the man's head back by his hair. "What do you want to come out first, your top or bottom teeth?" The man didn't answer. "Let's start with the bottom."

The man's screams filled the small room as his bloody tooth clinked against the glass Diablo put it in. "That one's for Maria, you sonofabitch."

By the time he'd pulled out four teeth, the man told them everything they already suspected: Satan's Pistons were behind the hit. The sobbing jerk opened fire in a crowded bar and killed Maria for a new Harley and a thousand bucks. When Diablo pulled the trigger that took the man out of his misery, he didn't feel any satisfaction. They'd lost one of their club girls. The women wore the "Property of Night Rebels" proudly, and the brothers were supposed to protect them.

By the time all the evidence was destroyed and the bodies scattered, it was three in the morning. He slipped into Fallon's bed and pulled her close to him.

"Goldie must have a really cool bike," she teased. He just held her tighter. "Did you have a good time?"

"Nah." He kissed her head and squeezed her.

"Are you okay?"

"Yeah." *I shoulda taken care of the guys when they first came in. My gut fuckin' told me something was up. Maria would still be here. Fuck.*

She grasped his hand and tucked it under her chin, and he smiled. For a long time, he lay looking at the curtain as it billowed in the wind.

Sleep would elude him.

And Maria would haunt him.

# Chapter Twenty

A S THE CLUB girls sobbed, the brothers spoke in somber voices. Fallon helped set the reception table along with Breanna and Raven. The other two old ladies, Sam and Shannon, refused to attend the funeral and reception of a club girl. Fallon figured it was because their husbands indulged on occasion with them, but a life was still lost.

"Let's put the barbecue brisket at the end of the buffet," Breanna said to Fallon. Lena had been cooking up a storm for the past couple days and appreciated the help Breanna and Raven offered. Fallon loved being included in the circle of club life even though she wasn't a true old lady. Diablo hadn't asked her to wear his patch, but they were still in the early part of their relationship. She needed to get to know him and his world better.

"Maria was one of Diablo's favorite club girls," she said softly.

"Does that bother you?" Breanna asked as she covered the baked beans with foil.

"I keep thinking it should, but it doesn't. I mean, all these guys probably went with her, but that was before any of us knew them."

Raven smiled. "You got a healthy dose of confidence, girl. I'm with you. When I started going out with Muerto, Ruby showed me her attitude, but I knew my man and that me being in his life had stopped all that."

Fallon giggled. "I never had anyone tell me I had confidence."

"You do. Living on your own has been good for you." Raven smiled.

"I guess. I mean, I'm living the life I always wanted. Sometimes I think it's just a dream and I'll wake up back in my old bed." She shuddered.

"Just keep going forward. Life doesn't wait for us. Bad things and wonderful things happen. We just have to keep going," Breanna said.

Fallon nodded and looked behind her. Diablo leaned against the bar, a faraway look in his eyes. "I'm going to see if Diablo's okay. Do you need me to do anything more?"

Breanna touched her forearm lightly. "We're good. Go over to your man."

Fallon walked over to him. He smiled when she gave him a quick hug. "Are you doing okay?"

"Yeah. I just can't believe I let this shit go down. I knew something was up with those two fuckers."

"Don't do this. In every situation, we can look back and say we wished we would've done something differently. And maybe we would if given the chance to go back. Believe me, I'm the queen of wishing I'd done things differently in my past. But ever since I got away from the situation at home, I realize that I spent most of my life living in the past so I missed out on the present. You weren't the only brother in there. All of your brothers were there. Don't put all of this on your back."

"She was only twenty-three. Fuck."

"I know. It's such a sad waste of a life."

Diablo stared at her, his gaze soft and tender. "You're fuckin' incredible. Most women would be so bitchy about me being sad over Maria. They'd be jealous." He stroked her cheek with his fingers.

"I know you guys were friends. It's terrible to lose a friend."

He bent over and kissed her, then trailed his mouth to her ear. "You're very special to me, Fallon."

Excitement tingled through her, and she ran her hands over his shoulders. "You're special to me too. More than you'll ever know."

And he was. Since he'd come into her life, her world had exploded. After all those years, the woman who'd wanted to emerge was finally able to do so, and it felt so fucking liberating. Where life had been gray and beige, it was now full of color. Where there had been sadness and lethargy, there was now joy and boundless energy. Life had never been so wonderful. And she was in love. *In love.* The emotion vibrated through her. The only thing that could make her life more over the top was to hear him tell her that he loved her.

"You gonna get some chow?" Paco said as he passed Diablo and Fallon.

"Yeah. You ready?" Diablo said, looking at Fallon. She nodded.

The rest of the afternoon was spent eating, toasting, drinking, and sharing stories, but a tense undercurrent of white-hot anger rumbled in the brothers' voices. Maria's death would not go unavenged.

As Fallon covered the last bowl of potato salad with plastic, Breanna came into the kitchen. "I would've helped you put things away," she said, sitting on one of the stools. She took her high heels off and rubbed her foot.

"No problem. It was a nice tribute to Maria. I'm glad. None of her family came to her funeral. At first I thought it was heartbreaking, but then I realized that her family really was the Night Rebels."

"That's right." Breanna took off her shoes and sighed in relief. "My feet are killing me. Are you and Diablo going to take off? I know Steel is ready to go."

"I'm not sure what he wants to do. Raven left a while ago with Muerto. She told me to tell you goodbye. You know, she's been helping me decorate my apartment. She's got a real flair for it."

"She's the best. We'll have to do a girls' night out. We can go to Alfonso's for margaritas and tacos. Have you been there?"

"No. Diablo and I usually go for barbecue. If we eat Mexican, we go to La Cantina."

"We've got to go to Alfonso's. They have the best margaritas in town. I'll talk to Raven and we'll set a date."

"That sounds like a lot of fun. Let me know."

Steel walked in, placed his hands on Breanna's shoulders, and kissed the side of her neck. "Ready to head out?"

She tilted her head back and caught his lips.

Fallon turned away and opened the refrigerator, putting the leftover food inside.

"I'll give you a call," Breanna said.

Fallon turned around. "Great. Bye." She watched them walk out, then smiled when Diablo stood in the doorway. "Did you want to go?" she asked. He nodded. She washed her hands, then went over to him.

"I feel like a ride to Chaco Canyon. You good with that?"

Grasping his hand, she smiled. "I'd love to go there. We've talked about it for a while but it seems like something always came up to keep us from going there."

They said their goodbyes as they walked out of the clubhouse. Fallon couldn't wait to wrap her arms around her man and feel the vibration of his Harley under her.

THE DESERT LANDSCAPE spread out before them, and shadows danced across the road in the late afternoon sun. The wind whipped around them, pressing Fallon closer against Diablo. The bike veered to the left and they left the main highway, climbing and twisting around roads carved out of the mountains. The heat from the desert dissipated the higher they climbed, and the brown scenery melted into green.

When they'd finally reached their destination, Diablo killed the motor and helped her off the bike. He seemed small in comparison to the noble walls carved by nature. All around there was raw beauty. The only sound she could hear other than their breathing was the distant rush of water echoing against the sandstone flanks.

"It's beautiful here," she said as she walked to the edge of the canyon. Looking down, the gorge spread beneath her, a river flowing in a dusty bed fringed by evergreens and pines. The water shimmered blue under the clear sky, the rocks sparkling like jewels.

Diablo came over and put his arm around her. "I've been wanting to share this with you for a long time."

She rested her head on his shoulder. "I'm glad we waited. We know each other better, and I feel closer to you than I have to any other person."

"It's good to hear you say that. You mean more to me than anyone."

She glanced at him. "What about your sisters? You never really told me about them. I'd like to hear about them if you're up to it."

Sighing, he walked over to his bike and took out a Native American woven blanket. He spread it on the ground and held out his hand to her. She came over and he helped her to sit down. Smoothing her fingers over the soft cotton, she said, "This is gorgeous. Where did you get it?"

"Steel gave it to me. He's got an aunt who makes these blankets." He stared out at the red cliffs for a while, then turned to her. "I don't have any contact with Clarissa. She's a couple years older than me. After we were farmed out to different foster homes, we lost touch. When I turned eighteen, I looked her up, but she didn't want anything to do with me, Beau, or Taya. She's been divorced twice and had her three kids taken away from her. She's going the route of our mom—a meth junkie. As far as I know, she's still in Salt Lake. I haven't spoken to her in years."

"You don't have to talk if it upsets you."

"It doesn't. It's just the way it is. My brother ODed in a back alley surrounded by trash. I couldn't help him. The drug was too powerful. I did a stint in prison 'cause I beat the shit outta the perv who was messin' with Taya."

"I didn't know you were in prison," she said softly.

"Yeah. I lost my head when I saw what Taya's foster fuck was doing to her. If I had to do it all over again, I still would've beaten his ass. No regrets there."

"Do you ever see Taya?"

He blew out a long breath, leaned back on his hands, and stretched his legs out in front of him. "When I got out, I tried to find her. Word was that she was using and selling herself to support her habit. One day, I bumped into her and took her to the motel where I was staying. She told me she wanted us to get a place together and start over as a family. I was good with that. After she took a long shower, we went out to dinner. She ate like she hadn't had a decent meal in weeks. Taya was so talkative and friendly, but I cut through it all and told her that I knew the score. Of course, she denied turning tricks for dope. I told her I didn't care what she did before, but we had a chance to have the life we should've always had. She agreed and I had a good feeling about it. I told her to crash with me until I made enough to get us an apartment. She told me she wanted to go into rehab and really turn her life around." He pressed his lips together.

"Did it work out?"

He laughed dryly. "Something woke me up at about three in the morning. I saw Taya by the dresser. I asked what the fuck she was doing. She said she needed some aspirin. I told her I had some by the nightstand and went to sit up. She rushed over and before I could switch on the fuckin' lamp, she clobbered me in the head with something hard. I blacked out. When I came to, she was gone and so was my wallet, money, watch, knives, and cell phone."

"That's awful," she said, her hand over her mouth.

"It's my fuckin' family. I didn't even bother to look for her. I took off for Colorado that day."

"So you never heard from her?"

"It'd been a few years, but then she started calling me whenever she needed money. I know she's still using."

"I bet you give her money." Her tone was matter-of-fact, not judging. She already knew the answer because she'd discovered that, deep down, he had a heart of gold.

"Yeah. I shouldn't but I do. Fuck if I know why."

She moved closer and straddled him, her hair brushing against him as she bent over. "Because you're a wonderful person. I wouldn't expect anything less of you." She kissed him passionately, hard and wet, while he grabbed a fistful of her hair, pulling her down even farther.

"You do something to me, woman. You're the first woman who has my heart—all of it." He sank his mouth into the curve of her neck and shoulder and an electric charge zinged through her.

"Oh, Diablo," she murmured through parted lips.

"I fuckin' love hearing you say my name, sweet pea." He sat up and rolled her onto her back, his face hovering over hers. His mouth crushed hers with such intensity it took her breath away. It was like he wanted to devour her whole, claim her mouth as his alone.

She snaked her arms tightly around his neck as they kissed wildly under the blue sky, the river below them rushing over rocks, in sync with their fevered desire. Diablo glided her shirt over her head and then unclasped her bra, her breasts falling out. Like a starving man, he gorged himself on her creamy flesh, sucking her nipples to hard, reddened points.

Lust mingled with love crashed inside her like a tidal wave as her sexual hunger grew. His touches, his scent, his taste fueled her arousal, creating delightful shivers from the tips of her buds straight to her throbbing pussy. As he played with her tits, he pushed her pants down over her hips, his callused fingertips catching on her panties.

"I can't fuckin' get enough of you," he rasped as he placed little kisses all over her body, making her wiggle from want. Then his fingers slipped between the slick puffy folds of her sex.

Frantically, she searched for his zipper. "I want you inside me." He guided her hand to his crotch and she unzipped his jeans, releasing his granite-hard dick. The beads of precome left a small wet trail on her belly as he shrugged off his pants.

And then he was at her entrance, shoving into her while he kissed her deeply. She wrapped her legs around his waist, urging him to go faster until they were one rhythm. They clung to each other, fused together by their raw passion and lust, never wanting to let go.

Their cries of euphoria and surrender echoed in the canyon. As Diablo gripped her, his breaths short and shallow, her body and mind yielded to him completely.

She'd never felt such intense senses and emotions, and she realized she'd just experienced a life-changing moment. From that moment on, they were one, fused together by love, trust, desire, and friendship.

After he rolled off her, she cuddled in his arms, knowing she'd never be the same again.

He was her anchor and she was his, and together they could face anything.

As she gazed up at the sky, she wiped a tear that had trickled from the corner of her eye.

*And then there is life.*

Her smile matched the radiance of the sun.

# Chapter Twenty-One

I N A WOODED area near Bison Peak, Sheriff Wexler stood with several of his deputies, looking at the bones in the shallow grave. He glanced to his side and saw the two hikers who had made the frantic call. His jaw worked overtime, chewing the two sticks of gum he had in his mouth; he always chewed gum because it calmed him and made him think clearer.

The bones on the ground were discolored, and the skull had long strands of light brown hair. A red tattered blouse and a patterned scarf were partially covered by seasonal debris. He opened a large plastic bag and placed the worn items inside.

"Cordon off two hundred yards and see if you can locate any more bones," Wexler said as he went down on his haunches. With a steel rod, he lifted the skull and examined it; there was a large hole in it and a few teeth still intact. He knew that, to make a dental identification, his deputies would have to find more of the person's teeth. Based on the remoteness of the location, the shallow grave, and the hole in the skull, the sheriff turned to one of the deputies and stated, "Looks like we got a homicide here."

Doug Wexler had been the sheriff for Alina for the past twelve years. In his twenty-two years in law enforcement, he'd learned to ask for help in cases that mirrored big city ones since his deputies didn't have the experience to investigate them properly. Alina had maybe one murder a year or every other year. Of course, the sheriff wasn't counting the "taking care of business" the Night Rebels engaged in. He had a tacit agreement with them to keep hard drugs out of the county, and in turn he'd look the other way for some of their illicit activities. It was a tenuous relationship, but it seemed to work.

Staring at the skull and bones, he knew his department was in over its head. He needed the expertise of a team that investigated murders every day. Taking out his phone, he plugged in the number for the sheriff's department in Durango—a larger city an hour north of Alina.

"This is Sheriff Wexler of Alina County. I need to speak to your captain in homicide."

Fifteen minutes later, he cracked his gum, then cleared his throat. "Durango is sending over CSI and a homicide detective. They should be here in a while. In the meantime, let's sift through the soil to see if we can find any teeth or bone shards." He went over to interview the hikers.

Less than two hours later, a navy blue sedan pulled into the area and four men stepped out; two looked to be in their early forties, the other two in their late thirties.

The man with the tan pants, brown sports coat, and yellow-striped tie held out his hand.

"I'm Detective Feliz Contreras with the Durango Sheriff's Department." He introduced Vince Onofrio as his partner, then Brandon Manning and Roberto Anchondo as the CSI team. After a short briefing, the men went to work, scouring the area.

A half hour later, one of Wexler's deputies cried out, "I found another skull and some bones."

The sheriff and the Durango law enforcement team went over and stared at another skull. This one had two holes in it: one in the back and one in the right temple. A pair of worn black jeans, a badly soiled blue windbreaker, and a black baseball cap were near the skeletal remains. The men silently went to work collecting and bagging evidence. They didn't have to say anything: they had another victim.

Wexler wiped his forehead with a handkerchief. *Shit. A double homicide.* From the clothing, it seemed that the skull and bones might have been a man in life.

As the CSIs worked the scene, bagging and labeling evidence, Contreras came over to the sheriff. "The holes in the skull look like bullet holes. We found a bunch of bones and some teeth about two hundred yards from the original site. From the way it looks, I'd say the victims were killed at the site. Your men are sifting through more of the soil, so hopefully we can find most of the teeth. Since the bones were scattered, we have to assume there was some animal scavenging. CSIs will collect and screen the soil and seasonal debris."

"Once you have a report, I can try and see if our Jane and John Doe are in the missing person's database."

"We'll call in a forensic anthropologist to analyze the bones so we'll know the age, sex, condition and any other particulars of the victims. Hopefully we can put a name to them."

"I'll look for that report," the sheriff said as he watched bags of evidence being removed from the scene. Grim-faced, he walked to the patrol car, his footsteps muted by the fallen pine needles.

# Chapter Twenty-Two

THE AIR WAS tense and punctuated with rage as the brothers talked loudly amongst themselves before Steel called the meeting to order. The only thing on everyone's mind was when they were going to exact vengeance on the Satan's Pistons. Diablo's clenched jaw twitched as the memory of Maria's fallen body on the barroom floor played in his mind.

The gavel went down and the brothers focused their attention on the president and vice president. Both Steel's and Paco's faces were etched in fierceness.

"You all know why I called church."

"The fucking Satan's Pistons," Crow grumbled.

Steel and Paco nodded. "What the fuckers did was a declaration of war." Steel waited until the noise died down.

Paco pushed off from the wall with his foot. "Army secured the arms deal. Hawk and Banger were right—Liam's trustworthy. We're gonna blow their fuckin' clubhouse up."

"They've been itching for a fight ever since they set up shop in Alina with that fucking strip bar. Then they put money into the warehouse fights. They're trying to get a goddamn hold in southwest Colorado. Count me in on going to Arizona to beat their asses," Crow said. Many brothers voiced their support.

"That's never gonna fuckin' happen. The Insurgents aren't happy at all with these fuckers. They own Colorado. Banger told me that they're taking what the Piston assholes are doing as an act of aggression. I told him we'll handle it, but he's ready to come down with a few of his brothers and join us in beating their asses." Steel crossed his arms and scowled.

"How deep is Bloody Knuckles in with these fuckers?" Paco asked Diablo.

"Seems like he hooked up with them for the money to get the warehouse going, but when he tried to pay them back, they didn't want it."

"You mean this dumbass thought he could just pay up and they'd be gone? What a fuckin' loser," Goldie said.

"Is he with them or just tied to them?" Paco picked up his bottled water.

"Stuck with them. From what Sam told me, Charlie wants out real bad, but the fuckers aren't letting him." Diablo crossed his arms.

"What a bunch of yellow-bellied pussies. First they hide behind some punk gang to open their strip bar, and now they're hiding behind this dumb fuck for their interest in the warehouse," Skull said.

"Yeah. It's time we show them what happens when they try shit in Night Rebels territory," Diablo added.

Steel fixed his gaze on Diablo. "Is Fallon involved with any of this?"

Diablo kicked over a chair and pounded on the table. "Why the fuck would you ask me that? You think I'd be with her if she was? Fuck no. She's clean."

"You know I had to ask. Sometimes a woman can make a man blind to some things," Steel said, all eyes on Diablo.

He shook his head. "She's not. But her step-bitch is fuckin' a Piston. Fallon saw them together in the bedroom when we went to get some of her things. She told me later. Otherwise, I would've gone in and beat the shit outta him."

"Did they see her?" Paco said. Diablo shook his head. "I bet he was probably fucking the bitch and some of his brothers came down with him to see the fights the first time you ran into them."

"I'm fucking sure they weren't expecting us. Ran away like a bunch of pussies," Sangre said, and the room exploded in laughter.

Steel held up his hands and they quieted down. "I'm sending ten of you down there to torch their fucking clubhouse. The first couple of nights you scout to get the layout, see what security is like and when it's best to attack."

"We got to make sure we don't kill citizens," Paco said.

"Right. I want you to move in and out fast. You'll take the cages so you don't announce to the whole fucking town you're there. This town is small, like two thousand people, but that's good for us since law enforcement is practically nonexistent. I'm sending Diablo, Army, Chains, Paco, Sangre, Goldie, Brutus, Skull, Muerto, and Eagle."

Crow jumped up. "What the fuck? I need to go. I've been waiting for this day ever since they cut me." He lifted his T-shirt, showing off the red, angry scar from his ribcage past his belly button that decorated his skin.

"I need you to watch Balls and Holes. Muerto will be with the group going to Arizona."

"Let Muerto stay and watch it and fucking send me."

"You're too involved with this. To make sure no mistakes are made, you have to be detached and cold."

"I can be. Anyway, that was my home turf for a couple years. I know it real well."

"He's got a point. It'd be to our advantage to have him," Diablo said.

Steel slowly nodded. "Okay, but don't fuck this up. You'll leave early morning."

The slamming gavel adjourned church.

When the brothers went into the main room, Diablo declined the beer the prospect handed him. He turned to his team. "We'll meet here at one thirty in the morning. Army, make sure we got the stuff we'll need to make the bombs. Crow, is there somewhere we can camp out where we won't be detected?"

"I know just the place."

"Good. I'll see you all at one thirty."

Diablo hurried out of the club. He wanted to spend as much of the night as he could with Fallon. In his world, one never knew when death would come calling.

He revved his engine and then sped into town.

THE RESTAURANT WAS small and quaint, and the owner, Adelita, greeted Diablo with a warm smile and embrace. Her dark eyes darted to Fallon and she put her hand out.

"I'm Adelita. Welcome to my restaurant." She shook Fallon's hand heartily, then said in a low voice to Diablo, "About time you bring a woman around."

Diablo narrowed his eyes, but there was a twinkle in them as he feigned being cross. Adelita had become like a mother to him, and he often attended her family's fiestas, christenings, and weddings. She was also a good listener and knew him better than he cared to admit. She was always on his case about settling down and starting a family, parading woman after woman in front of him, but he wasn't interested.

No woman had captured him physically, emotionally, or sexually until he met Fallon. And as he got to know and spend time with her, he became more and more hooked. Her fragrance, her touch, her softness, the sweet electricity that ran through his body when her loving hand caressed his head, rested on his chest, or gently stroked his forearm opened entire circuits of emotional feelings for him. Ones he'd never experienced before with any other woman. That's how he knew she was the one for him. But he wasn't going to share that yet with Adelita. *I'd never hear the end of it.*

The robust woman showed them to a table by the window. The window looked out to a garden replete with flowering trees and vegetation. It was a slice of lushness in a barren landscape.

After giving Diablo a bottle of Corona and Fallon a sangrita, Adelita hurried off to the kitchen. "It smells awesome in here," Fallon said as the aroma of grilled meat and green chilies wafted from the kitchen.

"The food is killer. They have the best fuckin' chile relleno burrito."

"Sounds like it'd be a lot of food. I think I'll just have an order of carnitas tacos," Fallon said as she stirred her drink.

"You don't eat much." He grasped her hands in his and brought them to his mouth, kissing them tenderly. "I gotta go away for a bit on club business."

Her eyes widened. "When? And what's the business?"

"Very early in the morning, and club business is just between the brothers."

"What does that mean? Why can't you tell me what you're doing? Is it something bad?"

He squeezed her hands. "There are certain things that go on in the club that only the brothers can know about. Club business is for brothers only. That's just the way it is, so don't ask me about it."

She shook her head. "I don't really get it."

"You don't have to. All you gotta do is trust me."

"When will you be back?"

"Dunno. I'll try to contact you if I can. If you don't hear from me, don't think you're not on my mind, or that something's wrong."

"I'm afraid you'll get hurt. I can't lose you," she said softly.

"I'll be good. Don't think about it. Let's enjoy our dinner. Then I'm going to show you how much you mean to me when we get back to your place." He winked at her, but her wrinkling brow hit him in the gut. *She's gonna have to get used to this.*

The food was delicious, and even though they laughed, talked, and ate too much, Diablo knew anything could happen in Arizona. And from the way she'd been pinching the skin at her throat, she suspected he may be hurt or killed. He wished he could promise his safe return, but in a world of violent confrontations, nothing was guaranteed. *Hell, nothing's a sure bet even in the citizen world.* He knew that all too well.

When they arrived at her apartment, Diablo took her in his arms and kissed her deeply, loving the way their breaths mingled. They took turns undressing one another, and when they slid between the cool sheets, he pressed her warm body to him, running his hands over every inch of her. She sat in his lap as he leaned against the padded headboard. Then he was inside her and they sat like that for a while, mouths together, chest to chest, not moving. She started to move, grinding against him, and he pushed up hard and deep inside her. Her small moans drove him wild, and he took her into his arms and pushed her back on the bed. Brushing away the hair from her eyes, he thrust hard and their sounds filled the room.

After it was over, he held her close to him, content that she'd fallen asleep. When his alarm went off, he gently slipped away from her and put on his clothes. He secured his Glock in his cut's pocket and shoved the hunting knives down his boots.

"Are you leaving?" Her voice trembled.

"Yeah." He came over and kissed her. "Be a good girl and don't cry. Before you know it, I'll be home."

"Promise me?" she said in a low voice.

"I'll see you. If you need anything, call Breanna or Raven." He kissed her again and left the room. When he took off, he glanced up at the window and saw her standing there. He wanted nothing more than to go back up and be with her, but he turned away and drove to the clubhouse.

Everyone was ready when he arrived. Rushing up to his room, he retrieved his industrial flashlight and another 9mm, then joined the others as they piled into two SUVs. It'd take them less than two hours to arrive in Arizona, where Crow would guide them to the Satan's Pistons clubhouse. They'd have it under surveillance for a couple of nights, then make their move.

The second night, Diablo texted Fallon, telling her he missed her.

**Diablo:** *I miss u, woman.*

The ping came in less than a second, and he smiled.

**Fallon:** *I miss you too. I can't wait for you to come home.*

**Diablo:** *U doing good?*

**Fallon:** *Other than missing you, yeah, I'm fine. You?*

**Diablo:** *Not bad. I gotta go. Nite.*

**Fallon:** *Goodnight. I'll dream of you.* ♥♥

Diablo looked at the screen until it went dark, and then slipped his phone inside his pocket and pulled off his boots. In late September, nighttime in the desert could be cold. He pulled the sleeping bag over his shoulders and hunkered down for another long night without his woman.

By the time they'd figured out how lax the Pistons' security was, they'd made a ton of Molotov cocktails from liquid laundry detergent and two parts diesel fuel. At two forty-five in the morning of the third day, the dark sky lit up with blasts of fireballs. Screams and yells from inside were music to the Night Rebels' ears. A few flashes of gunfire came from the club, but the Satan's Pistons were no match for the Night Rebels.

Not wanting the badges to get involved, they left the burning clubhouse behind and headed back to Alina. They were pretty sure several Pistons had been killed or seriously injured, but they were certain that the fuckers would think twice before they came back into Colorado. Diablo knew the next hit would be the warehouse; that was the last stronghold the Pistons had in their territory.

The group of outlaws drove back in the dead of night, congratulating each other on a job well done.

# Chapter Twenty-Three

SINCE DIABLO HAD been gone, all sorts of awful scenarios played out in Fallon's head. She didn't know what she'd do if something happened to him. He was her life, her love, her everything, and she couldn't dare entertain the thought that he may be killed. *Stop acting like a weak ninny. He's been in the club for a long time. He knows what he's doing.* But she also knew that life could change in an instant without any warning.

"I'd like to get this," a thin man said as he laid his book on the counter.

The customer's voice brought her out of her reverie. She rang up the book and bagged it, grateful for the line forming at the cash register; if she kept busy, she wouldn't think of Diablo and that he may be hurt.

As she rang up the last customer in line, her phone pinged. Her heart jumped, hoping it was Diablo. She quickly opened the text, but disappointment settled in. It was from Annie, the woman she'd met in Tula several weeks before. They'd gone out for coffee the previous week.

**Annie:** *Hey. R u up for dinner and music. Bored out of my mind.* ☺

Fallon sighed. She wasn't really in the mood to listen to music, but she figured it'd be better than sitting alone and thinking about Diablo.

**Fallon:** *Sure. Where and what time?*

**Annie:** *The Burger Hamlet @ about 7?*

**Fallon:** *That should work. See you then.*

Happy that she had plans for the evening, she went over to the boxes stacked against the wall and opened them. After picking up several books, she began arranging them on a nearby table. As she worked, a strong sense of foreboding hit her. Her eyes watered and she quickly said a prayer for Diablo's safe return.

For the next half hour, the feeling of doom grasped her no matter how hard she tried to shake it. The hairs on the nape of her neck stood up and an icy chill seized her. *What's the matter with me?* She turned around and her breath caught in her throat when her gaze fell upon a man of medium height with dreadlocks. His face had numerous piercings and the coldest eyes she'd ever seen. He speared her with his stare, and shivers shimmied up her spine. She turned away, but she still felt his eyes on her.

"Did you open the boxes that came in this morning?" her colleague, Jerry, asked.

His voice startled her and she jumped.

"Are you okay?" Jerry said.

She giggled nervously. "You just startled me. I opened the boxes and am arranging some of the books on the display table." She shifted her glance to the front and searched for the man who'd creeped her out. He wasn't there. Looking around the small bookstore, she didn't see him anywhere.

"Did you see a guy with dreadlocks standing by the door?" she asked Jerry.

Shaking his head, he said, "No. Why?"

"Oh nothing. He just looked kind of scary." *I wonder if I imagined him. This thing with Diablo has got me all jumpy.* Grabbing more books, she continued displaying and stacking them until it was time to close the bookstore.

When she was home freshening up, her phone pinged. *I hope it's Diablo.* She went over to it and opened the text, grimacing when she saw it was from Shanna. *What the hell does she want?*

**Shanna:** *Ur dad is sad that u haven't returned any of his calls.*

**Fallon:** *I've been busy.*

**Shanna:** *It'd be nice if you talked to him.*

Fallon scrunched her face. "What are you up to, Shanna?" she said under her breath. She'd had enough of her fake concern.

**Fallon:** *Gotta go.*

She didn't answer Shanna's subsequent texts. Not trusting her at all, a sense of foreboding overcame her again. It wasn't as strong as it'd been in the bookstore but it was there, seeping through her pores and wrapping around her nerves, and she couldn't shake it.

Forcing herself to get ready for her night out, she jumped into the shower, applied a small amount of makeup, and slipped into her short black skirt and knit top. The skirt was much tighter than what she was used to wearing, but Raven had insisted she buy it, and she had to admit she loved the way it looked on her. Grabbing her purse and glancing one last time in the mirror, she made her way to The Burger Hamlet.

Annie sat at a two-seat booth along the wall. Fallon liked her. Annie was very different from her: vivacious, adventuresome, and calm. She was also pretty with her dark hair and chestnut brown eyes.

"This hamburger is amazing. I heard it was a good restaurant. Have you been here before?" Annie said before taking another bite.

"No. I'm new to Alina. Did you move here?" Fallon replied.

Annie nodded, her curls bobbing around her face. "My boyfriend got a good job offer at one of the farms around here. I like it better than Tula. It's bigger and there's more to do. How do you like it?"

"This is the first time I've been out on my own, and I love it. I work part-time for Just One More Chapter. It's the bookstore on Main Street. I really like it. How long have you been with your boyfriend?"

"A few years." Annie picked up a fry and popped it in her mouth.

Before Fallon realized it, three hours had gone by. It felt good chatting with Annie about everything and nothing. Fallon had never really had a close friend, and she thought Annie may end up being her best friend. They had so much in common.

"I thought we could listen to some music at the D Note. You game?" Annie pressed her remote and her car lights flashed on.

"That'd be good. I heard they have live bands."

"See you there."

THE TWO WOMEN sat near the front of the stage as a cover band crooned out hits from the 80s and 90s. Fallon ordered a margarita while Annie had a beer. People danced, and Fallon found herself wishing Diablo were there so she could sway to the music in his strong arms. She couldn't wait for him to come home. She missed him so much. He was such a big presence in her life that it seemed strange to remember her life without him in it.

*I wonder if he's in love with me.* From the way he acted and the things he said, she thought he was, but he hadn't told her he loved her. She wanted to hear those words from him. She loved him with everything she had, but she was afraid to tell him in case it scared him away.

Annie excused herself to go to the ladies' room, and Fallon ordered another margarita. As she sipped her drink, she felt someone staring at her. Shifting in her chair, a slight chill ran through her. Rubbing the back of her neck, she looked behind her and straight into the flat eyes of the man she'd seen at the bookstore earlier that day. Hair lifted on the back of her arms and her heartbeat raced, nearly exploding.

The man with the dreadlocks didn't move a muscle, just leaned against the wall, his dark eyes fixed on her. She stared straight ahead. Fear bubbled in her chest, but she didn't want to show it. Turning sideways, she looked at the threatening figure from sidelong glances. He hadn't moved from his spot. Although every nerve in her body tingled, she plastered on a placid face, showing him that she wasn't easily intimidated.

Annie pulled out the chair and sank down on it. "What's going on? You look as white as a ghost. Are you sick?"

Fallon shook her head. "Look behind you. Do you see that man with the dreadlocks? He keeps staring at me."

Anne turned around. "What guy? I don't see anyone with dreadlocks."

Fallon twisted around in her chair and looked at the empty spot. *Where did he go?* She scanned the bar but couldn't find him. *He must be here somewhere. I know I didn't imagine him this time. Or did I? Am I going fucking crazy?*

"Are you sure you're all right? You don't look so good right now. Do you want to go home?"

Her breath came out choppy. "I am feeling out of sorts. I should go home. Sorry if I spoiled your evening."

"You didn't. I've got to work in the morning. Let's go."

The two women paid their tab and left the establishment. Outside, Fallon kept looking around to see if she could spot the man with the dreadlocks. No one was there.

"I had a good time. We'll have to do it again soon," Annie said.

"For sure." Fallon climbed into her car and started the motor.

On the way home, she had a sense that someone was following her. Every few seconds she glanced in her rearview mirror, but nothing seemed out of the ordinary. *You're just being foolish. Why would anyone want to follow you? That guy's just got you all spooked.*

She pulled into her parking space and got out. As she walked down the path leading to the front glass doors, she heard a shuffle behind her, like a shoe against the pavement. She stopped. Nothing but the soft rustling of the leaves by the night breeze.

*I know someone's here. I can* feel *them.* Iciness traveled through her veins as she took another couple of steps, the light scraping behind her picking up once again. *I just need to make it to the front door. I can do this.* With her heart slamming against her chest, she pushed onward, ignoring the footsteps. Then a stench like stale cigarettes and beer invaded her nostrils and she looked back. The dreadlocked man's burning stare—lethal and penetrating—slayed her. His warm breath touched her skin.

"No!" she screamed as she struggled to make it to the front door.

He didn't say anything before he reached out and grabbed her arm, his jagged nails tearing at her skin. Then the front door opened and a couple came out. The man let go of her and dashed away, and her head spun. Stumbling to the front door, she murmured her thanks to the couple who held it open for her, and she went to her apartment.

Clammy sweat drenched her skin as she leaned against her closed door, gasping for breath. *He must have followed me home. He knows where I live.* Panic seized her. She felt the urge to run, escape, hide. It was no different than when she was a child fearing the belt, the hairbrush, or whatever her dad came to beat her with. She wanted to jump out of her skin, make her heart stop racing, and catch her breath. It felt as if someone was choking her. Her heart was racing, and all she wanted to do was curl up into a ball and wait for Diablo to come back to her. She sank to the floor, gasping like a fish out of water, the room spinning out of control.

A long time later, she pushed up from the floor and brushed her hair from her damp forehead. Securing a straight-backed chair, she dragged it over to her front door and placed its back under her doorknob. Then she arranged the sticks she had the man at the hardware store cut down for her in her window and sliding door tracks. She splashed cold water over her face and shrugged off her damp clothes. Lying down on the bed, she took out her phone and sent a text to Diablo.

**Fallon:** *I'm missing you like crazy. Hurry home.* ♥♥

Wrapping the comforter around her, she fell asleep waiting for his reply.

# Chapter Twenty-Four

"T HE BITCH FOUND out about her grandma. Damnit. Can't you do anything right?" he said.

"Why're you always blaming me? She probably got a letter from the law firm on a day that I was away. She thinks she's so clever. I knew something was up when the lawyer canceled my appointment."

"We'll have to go with plan B." He went over to the window and looked out.

"Damn right. There's no fucking way I'm letting her get all that money. I've had to stay in this godforsaken town and now it's payday."

"She must know something's up. Do you think she's suspicious of us? I'm sure the lawyer told her someone made an appointment pretending to be her."

"I was so careful with the damn mail. I can't believe she found out. It would've been much simpler if she hadn't. She thinks she's something with her new apartment, job, and biker boyfriend. I'm sure she got some money from the law firm. Fuck."

"Let her think she's got us fooled. It's when they're cocky that they put down their defenses. And I need a new car," he said as he looked at his parked in the driveway.

"That fucking cunt has been more trouble than she's worth. I've had to put up with so much shit."

He sighed. "I know. Pretty soon it'll be over. Did you already open an account in her name at Bank of the Rockies?"

"Yeah, I'm on top of things. Don't worry about me. The only problem we have is Diablo. I'm not sure she told him about the money. I still don't know what he sees in her."

"Why're you so obsessed with that? Are you mad that he gave attention to Fallon and not to you?"

"Fuck off."

"Anyway, we got a couple weeks before she turns twenty-two, and I want to make sure we're all set." He turned away from the window and sat in one of the chairs in the master bedroom.

"We will be."

"It's about time the bitch paid off." He laughed.

# Chapter Twenty-Five

D ETECTIVE CONTRERAS POURED coffee in the mug his seven-year-old had painted for him the previous Christmas, then grabbed a glazed donut and sat down at his desk. The report from the forensic anthropologist on the Jane and John Doe found in Mesa County laid on top. After taking a swig of coffee and a bite of his donut, he opened the report.

> **First Skull:** Female, Caucasian, slight stature, age from twenty-five to thirty-three years old. No soft tissue present on bones. Bones found indicate animal scavengers chewed on some of them. Other bones discovered were rib bones. Fractures to bones of the face and ribs show they were in various stages of healing, which may suggest a history of violence in the domestic setting. The immature molars and premolars were intact. Incisors and canines were absent but located in the soil underneath the remains. From the shape of the teeth, absence of fillings, and possibility of braces, it is presumed that Jane Doe might have worn braces, thus suggesting she came from a family of some means.
>
> Skull showed bone breakage patterns without any sign of healing, which indicates that the injury occurred at or near the time of death. Since the bone was still fresh when the trauma occurred, the fracture edges were sharp and clean. The blunt force skull injury to fresh bone left identifying marks of the weapon used to inflict the trauma—a blunt, oval-shaped club.
>
> Taking into account the surrounding environment, the climate, and the existence of insects and feeding animals, the

determination is that the victim has been there for twelve years.

**Due to the injury, the determination is that foul play caused the death.**

**Second Skull:** Male, Caucasian, medium build, age around thirty to forty years old. Hand and feet bones indicate animal scavengers chewed on them. Premolars were intact; however, the rest of the teeth are missing and have not been located.

Skull shows two holes, one in the back of the head and one in the left temple, without any sign of healing, which indicates that the injury occurred at or near the time of death. Since the bone was still fresh when the trauma occurred, the fracture edges are sharp and clean. The holes indicate that a firearm caused the injury.

Taking into account the surrounding environment, the climate, and the existence of insects and feeding animals, the determination is that the person has been there for twelve years.

**Due to the injury, the determination is that foul play caused the death.**

Contreras read the report a couple more times and then placed the information he gleaned from it in the National Missing and Unidentified Persons Systems to see if any hits came up. Several images appeared and he shook his head, surprised that so many people were listed as missing.

"What you got there?" Detective Onofrio asked.

"Just reading the report that came in on the Jane and John Doe in Mesa County. I'll send a copy to Wexler. Haven't found anything in the database so far. I think we should put it in the papers and television in the area. There was that locket that was found buried in the dirt. Probably fell off the female after decomposition set in. Maybe someone will recognize it."

"Sounds like a good idea. If they're not in the national database maybe they weren't reported as missing."

"That's what I'm thinking. Anyway, I'll get a picture of the locket from forensics. You never know."

"How long did forensics say the two victims have been in their shallow graves?"

Contreras laced his fingers behind his head. "About twelve years, give or take a year."

Onofrio whistled under his breath. "Damn. There's definitely people missing them."

"Yeah. Jane Doe was someone's daughter or sister or mother, and John Doe was someone's son, brother, or father. Their families deserve to know what happened to their loved ones. They've been wondering after all these years. I hope we can identify them." Contreras knew that in some cases an identity was never made. He hoped that wasn't going to be the case with the recently discovered victims.

"You going to Mirabella's dance recital?" Onofrio said.

"Yep. I have to cut out of here in a couple hours. I'm going to send this off to Wexler, then check the database another time. Then I have to interview the old lady who says she saw something suspicious in the parking lot when Rachel Dunleavy was murdered. I'm still betting it's her ex-husband who did her in. Some people just can't let go." Contreras sighed and went over to the copy machine, placing the forensic anthropologist's report in the feeder. As he watched the papers move, he wished they could solve this case and finally let these two victims have the peace and closure they deserved.

# Chapter Twenty-Six

T HE NIGHT REBELS flocked into the clubhouse, weary-worn from their mission in Arizona. When the brothers entered the main room, they received a warm welcome from those who stayed behind and the club girls. Brown bottles and short glasses filled with clear and amber liquids glistened in the morning's light.

Diablo went up to the bar and downed two Jacks, the whiskey going down smooth like liquid fire. After a few days without any alcohol—when on a mission, no drinking was allowed—the smoky whiskey tasted damn good.

"Mission accomplished?" Rooster Mike said as he came over to Diablo.

"Yeah. The fuckers got what they had coming." Diablo's jaw twitched.

"Lena's been cooking up a storm ever since Steel told her you'd all be back today."

"Smells fuckin' awesome," Skull interjected.

"I gotta go see my woman." Diablo downed another whiskey, then spun around and headed to the kitchen. After talking briefly to Lena, he headed to his room to freshen up and get rid of his dusty clothes. He couldn't wait to see Fallon. The whole time he was gone she was always on his mind. He'd never felt such a strong pull toward another human being in his life. It was amazing that out of the sea of seven billion people on the planet, she'd entered his orbit softly and unassumingly. But her impact on him was like a galactic storm. He'd made up his mind while he was away that he'd never let her slip out of his life.

Freshly showered and changed, he locked his door, pumped his fist in the air as he walked through the main room, and straddled his Harley before he switched it on and rode to the bookstore.

The store smelled like ink and paper. It was the only one in town that had such a varied collection of both used and new books. The owner, Hattie, had opened the town's favorite gathering hole for bibliophiles thirty-five years before, and her friendly staff and willingness to find out-of-print books gave the shop its stellar reputation.

When Diablo entered the store, the chiming bell announced his arrival. He scanned the area but didn't see Fallon. Jerry came up to him, smiling. "You're here to see Fallon, right?" Diablo jerked his head. Jerry licked his lips quickly. "She's in the back room opening some boxes we received earlier. Just go on back."

Diablo went to the back of the store and opened the door that had an "Employees Only" bronze sign on it. He went down a short hallway and stopped when he heard the rustling of paper and the ripping sound of a box cutter. Walking inside the room, he saw Fallon with her back to him, breaking open boxes and taking books out. The way her hips swayed when she'd pull open the top of a cardboard box made his dick punch against his zipper. The truth was he'd been sporting a hard-on ever since he'd come back. It was all he could do to freshen up and come over to the store without losing it.

His woman had changed her wardrobe nicely. Instead of the baggy, shapeless tops and pants she used to wear, she now sported leggings and fitted tops, and she looked mighty damn fine. Her change in wardrobe reflected her growing confidence in herself, something he loved seeing as the weeks went on. Forging out on her own seemed to have really helped her come out of her shell. As much as he wanted her to live with him, he had to admit that she'd been right to have some time to herself to get to know who she really was.

As if sensing him, she stopped and whirled around, a huge smile lighting up her face. Without a word he went to her, pulling her into his embrace and kissing her. "I'm so happy you've come back safely," she murmured against his mouth.

"I've missed you so much, woman," he rasped as his hands skimmed over her hips and cupped her buttocks. He walked her backward to the wall and pushed her against it, his mouth never leaving hers.

"I had no idea when you were coming home. I didn't hear from you," she said in small pants as he ran his tongue down the side of her neck, nipping and sucking between the licks.

"You were on my mind the whole time, sweet pea. I'm ready to burst here. I want you so fuckin' bad."

"Me too." She glided her hands underneath his shirt and raked her nails down his muscular back.

In one fluid movement, he'd turned her around, taken off her leggings and panties, and shoved her against the wall so her palms were flat on it. He spread her legs wide and pushed down on her lower back so her ass was up higher. She moaned and looked behind her shoulder, her desire-filled eyes catching his and making his cock hard as steel.

"What if Jerry comes looking for me?" she whispered.

"Then he'll find us fuckin' good and hard." He unbuttoned and unzipped his jeans, shrugging them down. His hardness poked against her quivering flesh, and he placed his hands on her ass cheeks, squeezing them hard, loving the way she moaned and squirmed when he dug into her skin. Leaning over, he kissed her lower back, then trailed his lips up her spine, landing on the nape of her neck. "So fuckin' beautiful."

Shoving her top up, he grasped one of her tits in his hand and massaged it, then ran his hand down her belly to her pussy.

"That feels so good," she muttered.

"I bet it does. And I love how wet you are," he said against her skin as he ran his finger up and down her wet mound. "Do you want me to fuck you, sweet pea?" he asked as he slid his finger next to her hardening sweet spot.

"Yes. I really want it," she breathed.

"Want what?" he asked as he flicked her nub.

"I want you to be inside me. Please?" She turned to look at him and the lust he saw in her gaze sent him over the edge.

He grabbed and squeezed her ass cheeks roughly, then jackhammered into her hard. She cried out in a mixture of pleasure and pain. For each thrust, he pulled all the way out and then buried his dick to the hilt, his balls slapping her pussy lips and clit. Each time he plunged his cock into her, Fallon's body was pushed forward, causing her tits to sway. Grabbing one of her breasts, he said thickly, "I'm gonna make you come until you can't breathe."

With each thrust, her wet and warm walls clamped onto his cock, drawing it in and coaxing it deeper. Sweat misted over their bodies as their frenzied desire mounted. Then he pulled out quickly, yanked her up, turned her around, and flattened her back against the window. Diablo lifted her and she wrapped her legs around his waist before he shoved into her again. He dipped his head and kissed her while he pounded her pussy, an enticing combination of wickedness and seduction.

Diablo's balls tightened and the pressure was strong, overpowering. He stiffened and then grunted, his release ripping through his hardness, his balls emptying thick, hot streams of ecstasy into her. Fallon's nails dug into his skin as she followed his release with her own pleasure-filled one. Her high-pitched cry rang through his ears as he placed his damp forehead between her heaving breasts.

"Fuck, sweet pea," he grunted as his breathing slowly returned to normal. She had her arms around his neck, her head buried in the crook of it. It was the best fucking he'd had since the last time they'd come together.

Gently he eased her down and she fell against him. "My legs feel like jelly." She chuckled. He helped her onto a chair. "I'm so glad you're back," she whispered.

Kissing her gently, he stroked her cheek. "Me too," he murmured against her lips.

"Can you please close the door now? I feel like we're tempting fate. I really don't want Jerry to see me half-naked."

"Neither do I." He zipped his pants, winked at her, then strode over and shut the door. "What time do you get off work?"

"At five. Did you want to go out to eat? It'll be my treat."

"We can get some barbecue. And I'll pay. No arguments about it. You know I'm old-fashioned that way. No way am I gonna have a woman pay for me." He held his hand up and came over to her, his finger tracing her jawline. "Having you in my life is a treat. I'll pick you up at six thirty. I got some shit to do right now."

Shaking her head, she leaned forward and hugged him. "You're too sweet. Six thirty is good. I better get back to work. I have all these boxes to unpack and inventory." She swept her hand over a stack of boxes to the left.

"I'll see you later, sweet pea." He brushed his lips across hers and left the room.

As he walked down Main Street, he bumped into Goldie. "Hey, dude. What're you up to?" Goldie said.

"I just stopped by to see Fallon. I'm going to get her something for her birthday. It's coming up soon and I have some time to kill, so I thought I'd get it today."

"I don't have shit to do. I'll hang with you and afterward we can grab a beer. I just got back from visiting my grandma."

Diablo's face softened. "How's she doing?"

Goldie raked his fingers through his thick blond hair. "About the same. She still recognizes me, so that's a plus. Alzheimer's a fucking awful disease. I can't believe she got it. I mean, she's always been the nicest, sweetest person I've ever known. If it weren't for her, I don't know where I'd be. She took me in when my mom bailed."

Diablo clasped Goldie's shoulder. "It fuckin' sucks when bad shit happens to the good ones and great shit happens to the fuckin' assholes. Life can be a twisted puppet master. Fuck."

Goldie nodded. "What're you planning to buy for Fallon? Before you answer that, I gotta admit I never thought I'd live to see the day where you'd be shopping for gifts for a woman. Dude, you're so hooked." He chuckled.

"I'm shopping for Fallon, not just any woman. And… yeah. I'm fuckin' hooked in a big way."

They went into a shop at the end of Main Street. Lace 'N' Things catered to women and had a little bit of everything, from beautiful stationery to naughty lingerie. The saleslady's eyes widened when the two bikers entered. "May I help you?" she said, the lines around her eyes deepening when she frowned.

"Need to get something sexy for my woman," Diablo said as he glanced around the store.

"Like lingerie? We have some very pretty pieces and they go from sweet to… well… to not so sweet. The ones we have are against the back wall."

Diablo turned to where she pointed. "I'll check 'em out."

"Do you have stuff that has cutouts, like where the tits and pussy are?" Goldie said.

The woman's face blanched and Diablo chuckled. Goldie didn't have filters. "Uh… no. We don't carry *that* kind of lingerie. Maybe you'd have some luck online." She turned away quickly and started rearranging a stack of lace scarves on one of the display counters.

"What the fuck's her problem?" Goldie asked.

"You're fuckin' clueless, dude. Let me check out what they got."

The two men looked at the different teddies, babydolls, and two-pieces. "I like them with the cutouts. I think it's sexy as fuck." Goldie had a black teddy in his hand.

"I like where you can untie shit. Covering up can be sexier than showing everything right off." Diablo pulled out a sheer lilac teddy with pretty satin ribbons over the breasts and crotch. He knew Fallon would love that the ribbons had tiny flowers on the end, and he loved that the back was a thong. They could have some real fun with that one. "I'm gonna get this one. Let's go."

As they exited the shop, Goldie laughed. "I bet we're gonna be the topic of discussion at that uptight lady's next potluck. Now let's grab a beer."

"I need another gift that's all for Fallon. If you were a woman, what would you want?"

"I know what I wouldn't want—you. I'd prefer a blond, blue-eyed stud like me."

"Fuck you," Diablo said as they headed to Eldorado Street.

They walked down the street and a small shop with different shaped perfume bottles caught his eye. Twenty minutes later he came out of the shop with a perfume bottle of a bejeweled woman dressed for a masquerade and a bottle of Chanel perfume Chance Eau Fraîche. When the lady had spritzed it on a piece of paper and he smelled it, he knew it'd be perfect for Fallon. Its scent reminded him of her, and he knew she'd love the light, airy perfume that had a woody lemon-infused fragrance.

"Are you done spoiling your woman? I need a beer." Goldie said.

"Done. Let's go to Bulldog Pub."

The pub was a mass of people and noise as the two bikers took the booth next to the front window. They placed their order for two drafts, two orders of buffalo wings, and a basket of fries. They talked about Goldie's new Harley and the customizing Diablo wanted to add to his bike as they scarfed down the wings and fries, ordering another round of draft beer.

"Whoa," Goldie said as he set his glass down. He motioned the waitress to come over. "Send that cutie a drink."

"Do you want me to tell her it's from you?"

"Why not? I may get lucky." He laughed and the waitress walked away to fill the order. "She's a looker."

Diablo looked over, but from where he was seated, he could only see the back of her. He turned back to Goldie. "She's a citizen. You know how you regret taking up with one of 'em."

"Yeah, but it's fucking fun while I'm with them. Oh yeah, she's smiling at me. Wait, she's coming over here. Now don't scare her away."

Diablo jerked his head back. "What the hell does that mean?"

"Don't give her the evil eye. You do that a lot, you know. It intimidates the hell outta citizens."

"This is the way I fuckin' look."

"Here she comes."

The woman came over and smiled at Goldie; then she turned to Diablo and her face fell. He took in her tight jeans, low-cut top, and heavily made-up face and shock tore through him. "Taya? What the hell are you doing in Alina?"

"Diablo," she said as she brought her hand to her mouth.

"You know this delicious-looking woman?" Goldie smiled at her.

"Lay the fuck off. She's my younger sister," Diablo growled.

Goldie pushed back. "What? Seriously?"

Diablo nodded. Looking at Taya, he said, "Let's go back to your table. I wanna talk to you." He followed her back and slipped into the seat across from her. "Level with me. Why're you in Alina?"

"How are you?" she asked as she picked up her paper napkin and began ripping it.

"Cut the small talk. What the fuck are you doing here?"

Avoiding his gaze, she looked at the napkin in her hand. "My boyfriend got a job here so we came out. Nothing was happening in Salt Lake City, so we decided to see if this job panned out. So far so good." She giggled.

"Why didn't you call me? How long have you been here?"

"We've only been here a few days. I thought you lived in Pueblo. I totally forgot it was Alina. If I'd remembered, I would've called for sure. Now that I know you live here, I want you to meet my boyfriend. You'll like Tae. He treats me real well. We're really serious."

"Is this the one who's your pimp?" His eyes narrowed.

She shook her head vigorously. "No. No way. Tae is great. You'll like him. I want you to meet him. I'll call you and we can get together for dinner or something. This is gonna be so much fun living in the same town. We can catch up on the years we've spent apart."

"Where you living?"

"We have a place at Empire Apartments. It's not fancy, but it's perfect." She glanced at her phone. "I'm sorry but I have to go. I didn't realize it was so late. I got a job as a dog walker, so I have to go get the dogs. I like it, and the pay is way more than I thought it would be." She stood up and took out her wallet.

"I got it," Diablo said.

She smiled. "Thanks. I'll give you a call." She rushed out of the eatery.

When Diablo came back to the table, Goldie shook his head. "Man, what a fucking small world. Imagine you seeing your sister in Alina of all places."

Diablo scowled. "Yeah... imagine that." He didn't believe a thing Taya had said. She was up to something, but he couldn't figure out what it was. He was pretty sure whatever it was involved money. *Maybe she moved here so she could be closer to me to get money out of me more often.*

"Maybe she's been missing you and wanted to get closer to you." Goldie motioned the waitress for the bill.

"Maybe." He didn't think that was it, but she seemed happy and clean; he hadn't seen the scabs and sores indicative of crank. *Maybe she's telling the truth. Maybe she left Salt Lake to get away from her pimp.* It seemed plausible, but he didn't trust anything she told him. He'd never forget how she'd betrayed him when he'd only been trying to help her out.

*I'll see if she calls me. I wanna check out this boyfriend of hers.*

WHEN HE AND Fallon arrived home from the restaurant, they walked up the sidewalk to the front doors of her building. From his peripheral vision, he saw something in the distance. A form. A shape. Something that triggered his internal warning system.

"Go inside. Lock your door. I'll join you in a minute."

"What're you talking about? Where're you going?" Fallon gripped his hand.

Gently he shrugged it away. "I thought I saw someone. Go on, do as I told you."

He waited until she went into the elevator, hating that precious time had slipped away. When the doors closed, he sprinted across the grass to the semiwooded area across from the complex. He didn't see anyone so he walked around, his ears alert to any sounds: footsteps, car door closing, car engine, snapping of a twig. Nothing. He walked back around and stood behind the lilac bush, a sliver of his body partially exposed. From that position, he could see the front of Fallon's apartment building perfectly.

The faint scent of smoke curled around his nostrils. He looked down and saw several cigarette butts on the ground. Bending over, he picked one up; it was still warm. He smelled it, noting it'd been recently extinguished. Someone had been watching them. He waited in hopes the person would come back, but after a long while, he crossed the street and went back to the front of Fallon's building. He buzzed her apartment and she let him up.

When he got off the elevator, she was waiting for him in the hallway.

"Did you see anyone?" she asked.

"No, but I know someone was out there."

"You're right." She followed him inside her place.

Stopping in the middle of the room, he spun around and looked at her. "What do you mean?"

She told him about the man with the dreadlocks who'd been spooking her for the last couple of weeks.

"Why didn't you tell me this?"

"At first I thought he was just a random nut and it wasn't a big deal, but when he followed and came after me a couple days ago, I knew that wasn't normal. I didn't want to spoil your homecoming, but I was planning to tell you about it tomorrow morning."

Fire coursed through his veins. "He tried to attack you? Fuck! I'm gonna find this sonofabitch and teach him some respect. It won't be too hard to get this fucker. There aren't many guys with dreadlocks in Alina. Sounds like he's stalking you."

"I don't know why. I first noticed him at the bookstore a couple of weeks ago, and like I said, it didn't seem like a big deal. I mean, I thought he was creepy and all that, but it seemed like it was an isolated thing. But then I started getting a feeling like he was following me and watching me even though I didn't see him a lot of the time. It was like I knew he was there. Then I would see him at places I went, and it ended with him coming after me. That time it was different because it felt like he not only wanted to hurt me, but that he wanted to do something nasty to me too." She shivered and he drew her in his arms.

The thought of another man even touching her made his blood boil, and the fact that the asshole scared his woman put him over the top. He'd make sure to find him and make him pay for what he'd done. He rubbed her back. "I'll find him. In the meantime, I'm installing GPS on your phone and picking you up from work. I'm also moving in."

She smiled. "Yes, sir."

Nodding, he led her to the couch and turned on the television, but his mind was on the man with the dreadlocks. Chances were high he was the one watching them earlier. He wished he would've caught him. He'd do anything to take the worry out of his woman's eyes.

*I'm gonna find this bastard and tear him from limb to limb.*

He had to keep Fallon safe.

She was his world. His life. His love.

And there was no way he was going to lose her.

# Chapter Twenty-Seven

THE FOLLOWING MORNING, after Diablo made Fallon promise to call him before she left the apartment, she sat at the kitchen counter and unwrapped the *Alina Post*. One of her favorite things to do in the mornings was read the local paper while she sipped on a big mug of coffee laced with hazelnut creamer. As she sipped, her eyes scanned the headline "Skeletal Remains found in Mesa County." She skimmed the article, then stared at the computerized images under the caption "Do you know this man and woman?" Her breath caught in her throat as she stared at the woman's image.

All of a sudden, the room became hotter and stuffier, and it was like she was going to choke. She went over to the sliding door and opened it, a welcomed rush of air calmed her down. The scent of crisp apples, firewood, and earth wafted around her as she watched the red, yellow, and gold leaves shiver in the wind. After taking in the cool air for several minutes, she went back to the counter and looked at the images in the paper. The computerized rendition of the man and woman haunted her, especially the woman's. There was something familiar about her, something tugging at the back corners of her mind.

She looked at the next set of pictures, which were the clothing and some items found near the bones. When her eyes landed on a gold locket with a Victorian floral pattern on it, she covered her mouth, gasping. Her skin tingled as a clear image of her mother wearing the locket popped into her mind. "Oh my God," she cried aloud.

Her mother had bought a locket very similar to the one in the paper at an antique shop in Durango. Fallon remembered it clearly because her dad had been out of town and her mother had decided that they'd have an adventure. For some reason—she really didn't know why—her mother had sworn her to secrecy. She hadn't wanted Charlie to know they left Tula. Fallon recalled that it had been a wonderful day and that her mom had fallen in love with the locket. She'd bought it and when they'd returned home, she promptly placed Fallon's picture in it.

Fallon's heart lurched as she remembered that day, and she stared at the picture in the paper. She couldn't be a hundred percent sure, but the minute she'd seen it, it'd jogged a lost memory. Clutching her arms to her chest, she rocked back and forth, the monotony of the movement calming her. Then she remembered the pictures she'd taken from her home. The pictures she'd kept hidden for years, too afraid to look at them for fear her father would find out she had them and take them away from her.

She went into her walk-in closet and pulled out a shoebox. Sitting on the floor, she opened the box and stared at the images piled on top of one another before dumping them out on the floor and sifting through them. They were all mixed up: pictures of her mother when she was a teenager, when she was a little girl, when she first had Fallon, older pictures of them as a family. Fallon didn't know a lot of the people in the pictures, though she guessed some of them must've been her grandmother and grandfather. They were in a lot of the pictures of her mother when she was a teenager.

Then she found the pictures of her mother wearing the locket. In many of the photos, she had it on.

She grabbed those photos and went to the kitchen, comparing the locket and her mother to the pictures in the paper. Her pulse pounded as the blood rushed to her head, the room spinning. *This woman is Mom. Oh God. Someone killed Mom.* The thought was surreal, and in an instant, Fallon's world had been turned topsy-turvy. She glanced at the man. *Is this Rich?* She couldn't really remember what he looked like.

Picking up her phone, she plugged in the phone number listed in the article.

"Detective Contreras."

"Uh… I'm calling about the article in the *Alina Post*. The one about the bodies you found."

"Do you have any information about them?"

She took a deep, shuddering breath. "I think it's my mother." Her voice cracked.

"What's your mother's name?"

"Joanna Richardson."

"How long has your mother been missing?" he asked.

"We thought she ran away with Rich. That was about twelve years ago. I recognized the locket. The article didn't say if there was a picture in it. My mom had a photo of me in it. Does the locket you found have a picture of a little girl?"

"It does. We didn't release that information because we wanted to be sure that anyone who called wasn't just an attention-seeker."

"So someone killed my mother?"

"I'm afraid so. I'm so sorry. I need to talk with you. When can we meet?"

"Anytime. All this time I thought she left me behind. I should've known better. I knew she loved me even though my dad kept telling me she didn't. How did she die?"

"The results indicate a blow to the head."

A small whimper escaped through her parted lips. "Why would someone kill my mom? Everyone loved her. She was such a loving, nice person. I don't understand this."

"We'll have to do a positive identification. Do you remember the name of your mother's dentist?"

"Dr. McClure. He retired a few years ago. I think he's still in Tula. I can't believe any of this."

At the end of the conversation, Fallon had made arrangements to meet with Detective Contreras, give a sample of her DNA, and give a statement. He'd asked a lot of questions about her father.

When she put the phone down, numbness prevented her from doing anything, even thinking. She sat staring out the sliding glass door to the maple trees, the cloudless blue sky, and the mountain's craggy peaks that already had a white dusting on them. Snapshots of her life with her mother whipped through her mind like a fast-paced slideshow.

In one morning, her reality had changed. What she'd believed for more than a decade had been proven false. The enormity of it was too much to comprehend. When she'd thought her mother had run off, hope had always been there, nudging her that one day her mother would make contact with her. Hope was now dashed forever. Her mother would never contact her. Her mother was dead. It was so final.

She wished she never would've opened the paper. Hope was better than knowing the truth.

Her phone rang and she picked it up. "Hello?" Her voice sounded faraway.

"Fallon? What's happened?" Diablo said.

"I found out my mother is dead," she said. It felt like she was out of her body, watching herself sitting at the kitchen counter talking with Diablo. *None of this feels real.*

"Fuck! I'm so sorry, sweet pea. I'm coming over now. This must be hard for you."

"She was murdered. She never left me. She was taken from me. Why would someone want to do that?"

"You're not making sense, sweet pea. No matter. I'm on my way."

She put the phone down and continued staring until Diablo came in. He rushed over to her and hugged her. After a while, she was able to tell him what had happened. She showed him the article in the paper and the photograph she found of her mother with the locket.

Then she broke down and cried. The thought of her mother dying on the cold ground in the middle of nowhere haunted her, and she knew that thought would forever be part of the fabric of her mind. Diablo stroked her hair as she had her meltdown. He didn't offer platitudes or cheerful sayings—he was just there. And that's exactly what she needed.

As the blue sky began to turn amethyst and cranberry, Fallon drew away from Diablo and smiled weakly. "Thanks for just being here for me."

"Of course. You're my heart, sweet pea. When you're in pain, I am too."

"You're the best. I have this urge to call my dad. I guess I just need to talk to someone who knew her and loved her too."

He nodded. "I can see that. You should call him. It'll be good for you."

She went into her bedroom for privacy and plugged in her dad's number. When he answered, she almost hung up. "Hi, Dad," she said meekly.

"It's about time I heard from you. Why the fuck have you been ignoring me? And why the hell did you move out?"

"Dad, I didn't call for that."

"And you moved in with that biker scum. Fuck, Fallon. Didn't I raise you better? Do you think your mom would've wanted you to end up with a low-life biker? I can tell you no fucking way she would've wanted that."

"I didn't call to argue. I called because I have some real disturbing news to share with you about Mom."

"What is it?" he asked in a low voice.

"The cops found her body... or at least what's left of it. She was murdered, Dad. The detective said she died from a blow to the head."

Total silence. Thinking she'd lost the connection, she glanced at her screen. Her dad was still connected.

"Dad? I know it's a shock. I'm still reeling from it."

"Are they sure it's her?"

"Pretty much, especially since they found the locket with my picture in it near her. I can't believe someone killed Mom." Her voice hitched.

"Where was she found?"

"Bison Peak. Remember how Mom used to love to go hiking there?"

"Vaguely."

"I still can't believe it."

"When will the cops be talking to you?" he asked.

"Tomorrow."

"No reason to tell them about our fights. You know how innocent people get railroaded when they want to solve a case."

"I was young. I don't remember a lot."

"You know I loved your mother very much, don't you?"

"Yes, Dad. I know you took it real hard when she left."

"I never wanted the three of us to break up, but she did. You didn't know a lot about your mother. I shielded it from you because I didn't want to taint your love for her, but she really was a slut." His voice was cold and detached.

A shiver ran down her spine. "I don't think that matters now."

"Yes, it does. People always paint a dead person as a saint even if he was a bastard in life. It's human nature to do that, I suppose. I'm not that way. Your mother didn't care about you. She was planning to leave us… you behind." He chuckled when she gasped. "You didn't think I knew she had a lover? I did. Everyone did. It was the talk of the town, and I was made out to be the cuckold husband. You were too young to understand any of it. It's too bad your mother was killed, but I can't help but feel that she got exactly what she deserved."

"I know you're angry, Dad, but how can you say that?" she whispered.

"In all the years we were together, I never once cheated on your mother. Not because I didn't have the chance—I had a lot of women hit on me when I was out on the road—but I never strayed. I loved her. And what did she do? She let another man touch and fuck her. What she did was disgusting and wrong. And eventually, the bad always end up punished."

Fallon had called her father to commiserate and talk about the times they shared with her mom. She hadn't expected his cold fury, his spite, and his detachment.

"And you need to get your ass home and stop fucking the scum. You're turning out to be just like your mother."

"I have to go. I just wanted to tell you about Mom," she mumbled, then disconnected the call. A few seconds later her father called back, but she let it go to her voice mail. She went back into the living room and curled up next to Diablo on the couch.

"How'd it go with your dad?" he said as he caressed the top of her head.

"Strange."

"Do you think he's involved?"

"I didn't before I called, but.... It was just a strange conversation, that's all. He said he knew my mom was having an affair. I know she didn't think he knew." She rubbed her temples. "It's just too much to think about right now. I can't believe my dad would do anything like that. He's just still angry about my mom having an affair. I guess I can get that. Time sometimes doesn't heal all wounds."

"Yeah. Betrayal's a hard one to forget. I don't think people ever do. They may say they do, but when trust is broken, it's almost fuckin' impossible to mend it back again."

"It is. I'm sure that's what's going on with my dad. Me telling him about my mom opened the old wounds. The anger is still there. I know he wouldn't have hurt her. He loved her too much."

She burrowed into him deeper, loving the way his closeness, his scent, and his touch made her feel like she'd finally found her place in the world. She looped her arm around his waist, and as her eyelids drooped with the drone of the television, she welcomed the refuge of sleep.

# Chapter Twenty-Eight

*Three weeks later*

GIRLS' NIGHT OUT had become a weekly date for Raven, Breanna, and Fallon, and even though they occasionally tried a different restaurant, they always returned to Alfonso's and their killer margaritas. Having girlfriends was enriching to Fallon, and she cherished each of them. Even though she enjoyed her friendship with Annie, she couldn't talk about Diablo or the Night Rebels because she just didn't think a citizen would understand. With Raven and Breanna, she was free to talk about the fears, joy, and confusion of loving an outlaw biker.

As the three women sipped their margaritas and dipped their chips in the killer tomatillo salsa Alfonso's was known for, Fallon sensed him. She felt his piercing icy eyes on her, and goose bumps shivered on her skin. Not wanting to but unable to resist, she slowly looked over her shoulder. The man with the dreadlocks was across the street, watching her. His hair was pulled back, but there was no mistaking his flinty eyes. She was sure that she'd never forget them as long as she lived.

Instead of turning away quickly, she swiveled in her chair so she had a better view of him. She stared back. At first it seemed to startle him, but then his lip curved up in a half smile as he leaned against the oak tree.

"What're you looking at?" Breanna said.

"That man across the street. He's been stalking me for the past month."

When Breanna and Raven craned their necks, her stalker blew a kiss to her, then disappeared into the darkness of the night.

"Where?" Breanna squinted.

"I don't see anyone either." Raven stood up from her chair and leaned over the table.

Fallon turned back around. "He's gone. He does that. It's like he wants people to think I'm crazy or something."

"Or he's trying to drive you crazy. I once saw a movie where the husband was trying to drive his wife crazy so he'd inherit all her money," Breanna said.

"Don't you have to be a bit crazy or unstable for that to work?" Raven sat back down.

"In life, probably, but in a movie pretty much anything can go." Breanna laughed.

"Did you tell Diablo about this?" Raven said.

"Yes. He's checking around. You know, I'm inheriting some money on my twenty-second birthday. It's from my maternal grandmother. I never knew her."

"Do you think the creeper knows about it?" Raven dipped her chip in the salsa.

"I have no idea. I don't know how he would. The only ones who know for sure are Shanna and my dad." Her stomach tightened when she thought about her dad.

"He's probably a weirdo who's got a bug on you. Weirdos can be totally dangerous. I know," Raven said.

"I'll call Diablo when we're ready to leave. He'll come over and follow me home. He's been doing that since I told him about the guy. It seems to work."

For the next couple of hours, the women enjoyed themselves, and Fallon hated to see the evening end. She texted Diablo when they were finishing up, and he pulled up a little while later and waited on his bike in front of the restaurant.

"I never thought Diablo would have a girlfriend, but I'm so glad he found you. You're made for each other," Breanna said.

"Thanks. I didn't believe I'd ever have a boyfriend. I was so not into guys, but then Diablo came into my life and made it colorful." She giggled.

"He doesn't talk much, does he? Muerto said he's a quiet man but a good, loyal brother." Raven placed her credit card on the bill tray.

"I'm a quiet person too. Sometimes we'll sit in silence, but it isn't awkward or anything. It's great, actually. We enjoy each other's company even when we're not doing anything. It's hard to explain." Fallon smiled and looked at Diablo, who winked at her. *Whenever I look at him, I turn to mush. I love him so much.*

"Steel would be frowning about now," Breanna said as she stood up.

"Muerto too." Raven pushed away from the table.

"Diablo is the most patient man I've ever known," Fallon said as she followed the two women out of the restaurant.

They went over to Diablo, and Fallon gave him a big hug. Breanna and Raven spoke briefly to him, then headed to their cars, waving their goodbyes to Fallon. Diablo followed her back to the apartment. "It fuckin' kills me that I keep missing this fucker," he said as he threw his keys on the counter. "I told the brothers about the asshole and they all have their radar up for a guy in dreadlocks, but nothing's coming up. You'd think one of us would spot him. Even the prospects haven't seen him when they've been tailing you. Fuck."

"He's unpredictable. He's not always around. It's been days since I've seen him, and the last couple of times, I only sensed him. He's such a nut."

"Did he do the same shit as the last time, just staring?"

She nodded and placed the tamale platter she'd ordered for Diablo from Alfonso's in the microwave. "The same. This time I stared back. He seemed surprised I did that."

He laughed. "That's my woman." He kicked off his boots, placed his cut on the back of the chair, and sat on the couch. "Food smells good. I didn't even ask you to bring me anything. You know me, sweet pea."

His words made her all warm and fuzzy inside. *We're a real couple.* Even though she'd fought hard to be on her own when she first moved to Alina, she had to admit she loved living with Diablo. Her stalker had sped up their courtship, and she'd thought it was too soon to live together, but it was perfect. They had grown even closer, and she loved his presence.

She brought his dinner to the coffee table along with a beer and sat down next to him. He'd turned on a zombie movie, and she laughed. Her honey was obsessed with zombie movies, and since they'd started going out, she'd gotten into them as well. The movies were a good distraction, and now more than ever, she needed the distraction. She still hadn't heard from Detective Contreras about the DNA results. Unfortunately, the dentist had destroyed all dental records older than seven years upon his retirement, so there was nothing on the teeth that had been found. Thus, the DNA results were essential, even though everyone knew the remains were of her mother and Richard. She'd seen the locket with her picture tucked inside it, and it'd broken her heart. At that moment, reality had come to stay.

She'd told Diablo that once the investigators released the remains, she wanted to give her mom a proper burial. He'd agreed and told her he'd stand by her in whatever decision she made.

Fallon wiped away the tear that had leaked out of her eye. *Concentrate on the movie. I know you're looking down on me, Mom. I hope they find the bastard who killed you. Oh Mommy.* She gasped and Diablo paused the movie.

"Talk to me."

"I was just thinking about my mom."

"I know this is hard and it fuckin' sucks." He cupped her chin and tilted her head back, then kissed her.

"I spent the last twelve years angry at her for leaving me behind. I kept hoping she'd come back into my life. I never knew she was dead. It's like she just died. Like I just lost her."

He eased her head onto his chest. "You did just lose her, and you need to grieve for her. Cry, yell, smash shit—whatever you need to get you through the grief. I'm here for you, but it's something you gotta go through. Don't play it brave. Grab it with both hands and deal with it.

It'll be painful, but you'll get through it. You're tough. I saw it in you the first time our eyes met."

"I'm so lucky to have you in my life. If my mom were here, she would love you. I know it."

"She's looking down on you, sweet pea. She's happy you found your way."

As she cried, he held her until she didn't have any more tears left. Even though she knew she'd always feel like a piece of her died inside, she'd get through it because her mother would want her to, and Diablo was her pillar to hold her up when she faltered.

FALLON CHECKED HER messages, hoping the detective had left her one, but he hadn't. Sighing, she pulled herself off the bed and tried to smooth down her bed hair. Diablo had left early that morning, citing club business as his reason.

She went into the bathroom and looked at the reflection in the mirror: dark circles, pale skin, and a couple of zits. "Happy birthday," she said under her breath. She'd figured Diablo had forgotten it was her birthday since he hadn't said anything to her after he kissed her goodbye. It didn't really matter. Once her mother had left—died—her dad had stopped any celebration of it.

She splashed cold water on her face. She hadn't heard from her dad since that strange conversation they'd had three weeks before, and that suited her just fine.

Fallon slipped on a light robe and went into the living room. As she sank down on the couch, her phone pinged.

**Diablo:** *B ready @ 7. Dinner @ Antlers.*

She reread the text. Antlers Steakhouse was one of the most expensive restaurants in a sixty-mile radius. She'd heard the food was excellent, and she'd been wanting to take Diablo there as a way of telling him she appreciated everything he did for her, but they'd never made it.

**Fallon:** *I've been wanting to take you there for a while.* ☺

**Diablo:** *I'm taking u.*

She could almost hear him growl.

**Fallon:** *K. You just feel like a steak?*

**Diablo:** *Ya & it's ur bday.*

Fallon grinned. *He remembered.* Her skin tingled.

**Fallon:** *Didn't think you remembered.*

**Diablo:** *Of course.*

**Fallon:** *Just haven't had anyone remember it in a long time.*

**Diablo:** *I'm in ur life now. Things r different.*

**Fallon:** *So true and I love it.*

**Diablo:** *Dress sexy. I like the way u look. See u @ 7.*

**Fallon:** ♥♥

The gloom that had fallen over her lifted, and she went to her closet to pick out her outfit. She chose a pale orange satin camisole that fitted her snugly and a pair of tight-fitting black pants, preferring pants to dresses since they didn't draw as much attention to her built-up shoe. She used to be so self-conscious about her shoes, thinking everyone was staring at her, but since she'd changed up her wardrobe, bought some killer made-to-order shoes, and stopped being so paranoid, she was surprised by how many people didn't even look at her shoes. Taking out her black pumps, she smiled when she thought of how she used to be only a sneaker and Croc type of woman.

In the bathroom, she took out a small jar. She'd bought the charcoal mask the other day when Sylvia had come to Alina to go shopping with her. She'd been thrilled since she hadn't seen Sylvia since the night Diablo beat up her dad. Sylvia talked her into buying the mask, telling her that charcoal facials were all the rage in Hollywood.

While slathering the cool black cream on her face, excitement tingled inside her. Celebrating her birthday with Diablo was beyond special. After rinsing her hands, she laid down on the bed while the mask tightened her face as it dried. Sylvia had also talked her into buying a skin exfoliator and several body creams, so her idea was to pamper herself to the max and make her skin as smooth and satiny as possible. Fallon had never spent a whole day getting ready and it felt decadent to her.

As the mask continued to tighten on her face, she closed her eyes and let her mind drift.

WHEN DIABLO CAME at seven o'clock, the desire in his eyes as he checked her out from head to toe made her day of pampering worth it. Without saying anything, he yanked her into his arms and peppered the side of her neck with kisses. "You smell and feel real good, woman," he said against her skin.

Pushing back, she tugged his beard and kissed him on his soft lips. She stepped back and looked at his amazing physique covered in tight black jeans and a black shirt with blue pinstripes that hugged his defined biceps and pecs. The way his muscles rippled when he moved made her nipples tingle and her panties dampen. "You look so sexy and hand-some," she said in a soft voice.

Diablo tugged her back to him and cupped her ass cheeks, digging his fingers into her pliable flesh. "You look fuckin' hot," he said thickly as he bent down and kissed her.

Moaning into his mouth, she looped her arms tightly around his neck and brought him closer to her. She would never get tired of kissing him; he had a way of turning even a simple kiss into the most intense experience.

"We better get going or we'll end up staying in tonight," she said while pulling back.

"That works for me." He winked at her, then swatted her butt.

"I figured it would, but you promised to feed me." She smiled as she took out her compact. From the corner of her eye, she saw Diablo watching her intently as she reapplied her lipstick and gloss. She snapped her compact shut. "Ready?" He nodded, putting his hand on the small of her back as they left the apartment.

Antlers Steakhouse had been the premier restaurant for the past forty years. Its quality service, food, and atmosphere came at a steep price, but for the diners who came from as far away as Durango, it was worth it. Dark mahogany walls and rich burgundy leather chairs gave the restaurant its old-world charm.

Fallon sipped on a glass of Chianti while Diablo drank a Corona. Light jazz slowly played on the overhead speakers, and the soft lighting made his eyes glow. He gazed at her with such tenderness in his eyes that she thought she was going to lose it. All through dinner, he'd leaned over and given her small kisses and soft strokes against her cheek. Each time he touched her, a spark ignited inside her, sending her arousal to new heights. By the time they were finished eating, it was all she could do to keep herself from jumping in his lap and grinding her aching sex against his bulge.

"Do you want anything else?" the waiter asked as he cleared the crumbs from the tablecloth.

"Bring us a piece of your chocolate cake, with two forks," Diablo said.

Fallon laughed when the waiter placed a large piece of cake in the middle of the table, gave each of them a fork, then left. "This looks so good. And the frosting is dark chocolate."

Diablo scooped some with his finger. "Taste it."

She opened her mouth and her lips clamped around his finger, licking and sucking the velvety frosting off it. "Delicious."

A low growl came from his throat as he broke off a piece of cake and fed it to her. Then he put his fingers in his mouth and licked them. She captured his smoldering gaze with hers, and when his hand slid under the table and onto her thigh, she gasped at his touch. "You're the most beautiful woman here tonight," he murmured. His fingers inched closer to her throbbing sex, making her shift in her seat. "If I put my hand on your pussy, are you gonna be wet?"

His words sent electric sparks from the top of her head to the opening between her legs. She could feel the wetness coating her panties, and his hand was so painfully close. Her need for him was great, and at that moment, she wanted nothing more than to feel his long fingers slip between her aching folds.

Then, somehow, he undid her zipper. The desire coursing through her had been so great that she hadn't even felt it. *Oh God! It feels so good.* His fingers had slipped under her crotch and were sliding between her puffy folds. She was sopping wet; she could feel it, hear it as his fingers moved back and forth slowly, and smell it. *I can't believe I'm letting him get me off in public.* But it didn't matter. The only thing she was aware of was how exquisitely Diablo was doing just that. The pleasure was off the charts, and she slid down slightly and spread her legs wider to give him better access. Diablo flicked her aching spot with his fingertip as his middle finger broke through her wet slit and plunged deep inside her. Pleasure and release racked her body with a series of shudders. She soared with delirious pleasure as his mouth covered hers, swallowing her moans.

Grateful that they were nestled in a corner, looking out at the town's lights sprinkled below them, Fallon straightened up and zipped her pants after Diablo removed his hand. He slowly licked his fingers, his gaze locked on hers. With reddened cheeks, she gripped her water glass and took a big gulp.

"Don't be embarrassed," he said.

"I just had an orgasm in a restaurant." She took another gulp of water.

"I know. I gave it to you." He winked.

Smiling, she shook her head. "You're older than me. You're supposed to mentor me, not corrupt me."

"Corruption is a helluva lot more fun." He kissed her cheek.

"It is." She took his hand and kissed it.

After Diablo paid the bill, they went to the Twilight Lounge where they danced to tunes from the 50s through the present. By the time the evening was over, Fallon was exhausted, tipsy, and happier than she ever thought was possible.

On the ride home, she let the cool October wind dry her sweaty body. She'd never danced so much in her life, and the big surprise was how agile Diablo was on the dance floor. *Tonight was perfect.* She gazed up at the stars strewn over the dark sky and hoped her mom was looking down and smiling at her. *I'm okay, Mom.* Even though the DNA results hadn't come through, she knew it was her mother; the locket proved it. And it made her feel better to think of her mother watching over her.

When they arrived home, Diablo surprised her with two beautifully wrapped gifts. Holding up the sexy teddy, she winked at him. "It's beautiful, but I think this is your gift too."

"Fuck yeah, sweet pea. I want to see it on you in a few minutes."

She laughed as she opened the gold foil wrapping. The perfume box made tears spring to her eyes. She quickly wiped them away. Opening it, she inhaled deeply, then dabbed the perfume on her pulse points. "I love it. The scent is me. It's so light and aromatic. Thank you, honey. You're the best." She threw herself into his waiting arms and held him for a long time.

She stood up, her perfume bottle in one hand and the teddy in the other. "Let's go into the bedroom so I can show you how grateful and happy you've made me."

He leapt from the couch and followed her.

A couple hours later, Fallon sniffed her wrist for the umpteenth time, then ran her hand across his smooth chest. Diablo was already sleeping and her eyelids were drooping. She watched the slivers of moonlight as they slid through the curtains and cast patterns on the carpet. Memories of the evening filled her mind as her eyes began to close.

*Best birthday ever.*

And then all at once, sleep overcame her.

# Chapter Twenty-Nine

A FEW DAYS after Fallon's birthday, she received a phone call from Detective Contreras. She was at work, and when she saw his number, she quickly ducked out of the store. Except for Diablo and her dad, she hadn't told anyone about her mother.

"Hello, Detective. I hope you have the results," she said as she walked around the corner.

"I do. From the DNA tests and the positive identification of the locket, your picture, and the clothing that has been identified, I regret to inform you that the remains found at Bison Peak are that of your mother and a man named Richard Blather."

Even though she'd been absolutely sure, hearing it aloud tore at her heart. "I knew it. I guess I was just holding out a sliver of hope that it wasn't," she whispered.

"I understand. I'm sorry for your loss. You had some of your mother's DNA in your test. We also tested your father's DNA."

"Why? He wouldn't have my mother's in his."

"Just a comparison since you'd have some of his. A person doesn't inherit all her parents' DNA, but she will have some of each. Is your father your biological dad?"

"Yes. Why're you asking me that?" Ice filled her veins.

"It's just that your DNA didn't have any of his. Have you ever seen a copy of your birth certificate?"

"No, but my parents used it to get me into school and I have my dad's last name—Richardson."

"Maybe he adopted you."

"He didn't. It's my dad. I think my mom would've told me if he wasn't. Why would she lie to me?"

Contreras's sigh was audible. "I didn't mean to upset you. It's just that you don't have your dad's DNA, which indicates that you and he are not biologically related."

"Your test is wrong." The pounding in her ears made her head ache.

"It's not. The lab tested and retested it many times."

*Dad's not my real dad? What the fuck?* Her mind spun as she tried to concentrate on what the officer was saying. *How could that be? Why would he raise me if I wasn't his kid? This doesn't make sense. Something's obviously wrong with the test results.*

"I'll need you to come to Sheriff Wexler's office tomorrow. I want to go over a few things you've told us about your father."

His words jarred her back to the conversation. "Is my dad a suspect?"

He cleared his throat. "We always look closely at the ones closest to the murder victim. It's just routine."

*Bullshit! They suspect Dad. I wondered why they took his DNA. That phony reason the detective gave me doesn't make sense. They think Dad killed Mom and Rich.*

Her father's cold, mean words when she'd called him after she learned of her mother's death rang through her ears.

"Does tomorrow at noon work?"

"Uh… sure. It works." *This is too much. I don't know what the fuck's going on.*

"Good. I'll see you tomorrow. Again, Fallon, I'm sorry for your loss."

Fallon stared at the screen as she slumped against the brick wall. *I'm going to be sick.* She bent over and dry heaved. *He can't be right. Dad wouldn't hurt Mom, and Dad's my real dad.* But he'd been so mean to her over the years. *A lot of biological parents are mean to their kids. I can't stand this.*

Walking back to the store, images of her dad filled her mind. *Everyone always said we didn't look anything like each other, but I've seen kids who don't look like both parents.*

"You look sick," Jerry said as she reentered the store.

"I am. I have to take off. Stomach flu, I think." She pushed her hair off her damp face.

"Go on. Take care of yourself."

Head bowed, she said, "Thanks, Jerry. I owe you."

In less than fifteen minutes she was sitting in her apartment. She'd been so upset that she'd forgotten to call Diablo to tell him she was leaving so he or a prospect could follow her home. At that time, it didn't matter; all that mattered was finding out what the hell was going on. She grabbed a bottled water from the fridge and sat at the kitchen counter. With shaky hands, she plugged in her father's number.

"I didn't think I'd hear from you. You've been ignoring my calls," Charlie said.

"I didn't like what you said about Mom. You acted like you didn't care about her."

"I was angry. Your mother hurt me a lot by what she did. I shouldn't have said those things about her to you."

Her cold hands tingled. "The detective called me. He said it's Mom for sure. He took my DNA and compared it to hers. He said he asked you for DNA too."

A long pause. "I heard they made a positive identification. They take everyone's DNA in these cases. It doesn't mean anything. How've you been? You had a birthday this past Friday. Happy Birthday."

She froze. In that instant, she knew he wasn't her dad. She knew he'd murdered her mother and her lover. "You're not my dad, are you?"

A much longer pause.

"What the fuck made you say that?"

"I don't have your DNA. I put up with all your abuse, your hate, your punishment and you aren't my real dad?"

"I fucking took care of you. I fed you, bought you clothes, gave you a place to live. That's what a father does, Fallon."

"But you never loved me! Why did you keep me after Mom was gone? All you did was hurt me."

"You ungrateful bitch! I gave you my name and a home. It was a helluva lot more than your *real* dad ever did. He never wanted you. He wanted your mom to have an abortion. You want to know about your dad? He was married with a family of his own. He couldn't have you tainting his good name and standing in his community."

*Married? No. He's lying. He's still trying to hurt me.* But then she remembered the lawyer telling her why her mother and grandmother had a falling out. It'd been about her going out with a married man.

"Your mother spread her legs for him and got herself knocked up. Your high and mighty grandmother threw her out, so she came to me. We'd been friends, but I always loved her. I watched her fuck half of our high school, but when she needed help, she came to *me*. She said she'd try and make me a good wife. I gave her fucking respectability and you a name. And what did Joanna do? She turned you against me and took on a lover. She deserved what she got." He laughed dryly.

"She didn't turn me against you—you did. Why did you keep me?"

"Would you rather have gone to foster care? No one would've kept such an ugly, stupid girl around. You should be thanking me instead of accusing me, you cunt."

"You're sick. Hate and vengeance have made you crazy. You crippled me, you fucking asshole!"

"You think you're something now that you're living with biker trash? You're nothing but a whore, just like your mother. The only difference is that she was beautiful and you're fucking ugly. Shanna was right. I should've thrown you out years ago."

"I wish you would have. I hate you. And I know you killed Mom and Rich. You're the worst thing that's ever happened to me."

"You better watch what you tell the cops. I know where the fuck you live. I know where you work. I know everything you do." His words curled around her nerves and squeezed hard.

*He put the dreadlock guy up to spying on me.* "Don't threaten me. You're going to get exactly what you deserve. And Mom did love you. You just destroyed it like you do everything."

"Don't say a word—"

She hung up, her teeth chattering and her body shaking. Everything in her life was different from what she thought. A few days before, she was on top of the world, and now she was reaching the dark abyss of despair.

*How could he be so cruel? He killed Mom. He tortured me. I have to tell Detective Contreras.*

Ignoring the incoming calls from Charlie, she called Contreras and told him everything that had happened. She even told him about the monster throwing her off the roof years before. He told her to be careful and he'd see her the following morning. Somehow, she'd felt better telling him about everything. Charlie had destroyed her life and her mother's.

She went to the closet and took down the shoebox of photographs, scrutinizing the face of a man who was with her mother in many of the pictures. Her mother's eyes shone with love in a lot of them as she looked endearingly at him. Looking at them objectively, Fallon saw that she shared similar facial features with him, especially his mouth and freckles.

*He's my father, but he didn't want me.*

Her cheeks glistened as she stared at him for a long time. Then she wiped the dampness from her cheeks and ripped the picture to shreds.

# Chapter Thirty

CHARLIE HAD BEEN sitting on one of the straight-backed chairs staring out at the street. He knew it was only a matter of time before they'd arrest him. That fucking Contreras and his sidekick executed a search warrant. He cursed himself for keeping the photographs he'd taken of Joanna and Rich when he was surveilling them. Many of the sales trips he'd told her he had didn't exist. He'd stayed in town at the hotel, following them as they frolicked and flaunted their depraved love in his house. And the way Fallon had laughed and hung on to Rich whenever he'd come over made him hate her even more.

*I know Fallon's been yapping her mouth off. Ratting me out. What a bitch. Just like her mother. I should've killed her when I had the chance.* He'd thought about it the night he'd come home from murdering Joanna and her lover. He'd been trailing them that morning, and when they'd gone to Bison Peak for one of their hikes, it'd been easy. He'd put two bullets in Rich's head, enjoying how devastated Joanna had been, and then he'd raped and beaten her to death. When he'd gone home, Fallon had been surprised to see him. He'd told her that her mother had called and said she was leaving them. Fallon had been inconsolable.

*I should've killed her that night.*

But he hadn't. The little bitch had always had the love of Joanna— the love he should've had. Fallon had reminded him so much of Joanna that, in a perverse way, it'd been like she was still there. When his darkness overtook him and rage set in, the beatings he gave her, he was giving to Joanna.

And now the little cunt ratted him out. Probably told the cops he pushed her off the roof. That he made her a cripple. He shook his head.

He never thought any man would want her. *I should've thrown out the biker scum the minute he looked at her. And I am her father. I've supported and cared for her better than most biological fathers do. I did Joanna a huge favor.*

"This is all your fault, Joanna," he said.

A door slamming drew his attention to a car across the street. *Where's Shanna?* The minute she came home, he was taking her and getting the fuck out of Tula. He knew she didn't like the small town, so she'd be happy to leave. *There's no fucking way I'm going to prison.* After all these years, he'd figured Joanna and Rich would never be found. It was fucking bad luck they were. It messed up his life in a big way, but once they were out of the country, they could have a new life.

He brought the glass of scotch to his lips and took a sip, savoring the flavor as it exploded across his taste buds.

The bedroom door slowly opened.

"What did you tell the cops?" He took another gulp of scotch. "You don't want to tell me? Did you betray me?" He watched as she slipped something out of her purse. The fading light cast the gun in an eerie glow. "What the fuck?"

He tried to rise from the chair, but the room was spinning and he couldn't feel his limbs. *What the fuck is going on?* Charlie saw her glance at the bottle of scotch and smile wryly. *She put something in the bottle.*

He tried to talk but couldn't; all that came out of his mouth was spittle. He was paralyzed, watching a horror film in which he had the starring role. She came over to him and picked up his hand, placing the gun in it. She wore green latex gloves. *She's going to make it look like suicide. How clever. Ungrateful bitch! I can't even move a muscle. I can't believe she'll go through with this. After all I've done for—*

The deafening roar from the gun echoed in his ears a second before life seeped out of him.

# Chapter Thirty-One

S TANDING TALL, LEGS spread wide, Diablo watched as his brothers bowed their head during the final prayers before laying Joanna Richardson to rest. They had come out to support his woman even though she wasn't his old lady. The camaraderie and love his brothers had shown Fallon since he'd brought her into his life touched him deeply. And the way they rallied around her after the news broke that the remains belonged to Fallon's mother was the reason he was in the Night Rebels.

A small sob escaped from Fallon and he pulled her closer to him. His heart broke for his woman, and by the forlorn looks of his brothers, they were feeling her pain too. He and Army locked gazes, and Diablo jutted out his jaw and lifted his chin. Army nodded and turned away. Down the line, his brothers gave him their support. They had his and Fallon's back in whatever way they needed. He wanted to tell them thanks, give them a hug, but that wasn't his way. They knew he appreciated them, and that he'd do the same for each and every one of them.

The crunch of leaves mingled with hushed voices as they left the cemetery. Fallon had wanted her mother buried so she could have a place to visit. He could understand that. Rich's sister had claimed his remains; he was buried in Pueblo where his family was.

Goldie came over and bumped fists with Diablo. "You guys coming to the clubhouse? The women prepared some food."

Diablo looked at Fallon and she nodded. "Yeah. I guess we'll be there."

Several brothers came over and chatted with Diablo while throwing furtive glances at Fallon. It was the way of the brotherhood. Women were not part of the whole group but earned the support, loyalty, and respect through their man. Each brother would defend and kill for an old lady, but they wouldn't disrespect her man by initiating a conversation with her, or spending time with her. It was the way their world was, and it worked for them.

As they walked toward their bikes and cars, Raven and Breanna came over and hugged Fallon, whispering words of comfort to her. Diablo appreciated how they'd helped her through the ordeal of losing her mother and then finding out Charlie wasn't her biological dad. He was surprised when he heard that because Charlie was always so protective of her. The only regret Diablo had was that he hadn't killed the scumbag when he had the chance. The way Charlie had hurt his woman was something he would never understand.

Sylvia and Annie had also offered their support to Fallon, and even though they hadn't been able to attend the funeral services, they had been there for her when she needed them. Diablo was happy his woman had a network of friends she could count on.

When they arrived at the clubhouse, a table of food awaited them. The prospects had beer, tequila, and whiskey poured and ready for consumption. Diablo brought a shot of brandy to Fallon. "This will make you feel better," he said.

"Thanks." She brought the honey-colored liquid to her lips.

During the next hour, the brothers made toasts to Fallon and her mother. From the way his woman's eyes shone, he knew she was touched by the gesture. His body hummed with pride at being part of the brotherhood.

After eating hardly anything, Fallon told him she wanted to lie down. Her red-rimmed eyes and nose accentuated her pallor. He held her hand and led her to his room, gently easing her on the bed. He slipped off her shoes and black pants, then sat her up and pulled her black knit top over her head. She didn't say a word, just watched him with those mesmerizing eyes that had first drawn him in many months before.

He went over to his dresser and pulled out a T-shirt, then came back to her. Taking off her bra, he slipped the T-shirt over her head and guided her under the sheet. He tucked it and blanket under her chin and ran his fingers through her hair until she fell asleep. Switching the table lamp to low, he quietly left the room.

When he entered the main room, Crow came up to him. "She doing okay?"

Diablo nodded. "She's been through a lot, but she's a fighter."

"I can't believe Bloody Knuckles offed her mom. What a pussy," Jigger said.

"I never liked the bastard. My gut told me there was something up with him." Diablo threw his Jack back.

"Figures the pussy would take the chickenshit way out. Fuck. He shoulda manned up to what he did." Goldie took a bite of his burrito.

"I didn't think he had the guts to kill himself. Fallon was shocked too. You never know." Diablo smiled when Lucy set a plate of enchiladas, tacos, rice, beans in front of him. "Damn, that's a lot of food."

"You hardly ate anything."

"You still watching out for me?" He laughed, then put a forkful of rice in his mouth.

"Always. We're still friends." She walked over to the other club girls who were busy clearing away the dirty dishes.

Raven walked up to Diablo. "Here you go," she said as she gave him the bag in her hand.

He smiled and opened it. Inside was a black leather vest with the most beautiful embroidery he'd ever seen. "You did a good job," he said, tracing his fingers over the soft lettering.

"What the hell is that?" Muerto asked as he put his arm around Raven's waist.

"None of your fuckin' business," Diablo replied, and several brothers guffawed.

"Raven?" Muerto looked at her.

Raven glanced at Diablo and he nodded slightly. "I did the embroidery on the cut he's giving Fallon. The guy you all use does a shitty job."

Breanna clapped. "I love that you're asking Fallon to be your old lady. You guys make the perfect couple."

"What about us, babe?" Steel asked as he came up behind her, circling his arms around her waist.

"That's a given." She craned her neck and kissed his chin.

Diablo sniggered. *She knows how to handle him.* "Raven saw what Jeb did and she was horrified. She snatched it from me, telling me there was no way Fallon can wear her cut like that."

Muerto jerked his head back. "Jeb did your cut and Breanna's."

"And that's why I redid them. I'm not going to wear a beautiful vest with some shitty work on it." She tossed her head.

Muerto laughed. "You're really something, woman."

Steel shook his head and pressed Breanna closer to him.

"Forget about the fuckin' embroidery. I can't believe Diablo's taking an old lady." Paco gestured to the prospects for another round.

"I'll drink to you taking an old lady, but you, Muerto, and Steel need to stay away from me. There's no way I wanna catch what you guys got. Life's too short." Goldie winked at the club girls, who giggled.

"Enough lovey-dovey shit. Who's up for a game of poker? I have a wad of cash and I want to make it grow fatter." Army picked up his tequila from the bar.

"I'm in," said Paco.

"Me too." Skull walked over to the poker table.

"I need some cash, and Army's is as good as anyone's," Brutus said as he picked up his drinks, with Sangre, Eagle, Shotgun, and Cue Ball following him.

Anxious to be with Fallon, Diablo picked up the bag and went up to his room. When he came in, Fallon was sitting up, leaning against the headboard.

"Did you have a good rest? Your color's come back." He sat next to her on the edge of the bed.

"Yeah. I was doing okay, but then all of a sudden this wave of exhaustion hit me."

"You've had a rough few weeks."

She nodded. "I'm trying real hard not to dwell on it. I know I have to deal with it and let the grief and anger work its way through. Breanna's helping me with it. She's been great."

"She's good with stuff like that."

"I don't ever want to think about Charlie again, but I know I have to."

"It'll take time. Do you want anything? I can get one of the girls to bring you up some food."

She shook her head. "I'm not hungry. What do you have in the bag?"

He pulled off his boots, then stood and took off his jeans. He hung his cut up in the closet and crawled next to her. Grasping her hands, he caught her gaze. "My heart goes out to you 'cause you've had a lotta shit you've had to handle in your life. Your strength has amazed me. You need to know that no matter what happens in life, we have each other. I love you, woman. I've never loved a woman the way I love you. I need you to fill in the dark spaces of my heart, and you need me to hold you through the dark shadows of your memories. We need each other, and I want you more than I've ever wanted any woman. I thought I was content just living life with the brotherhood until you woke something up inside me. I want us to be together forever. I want you to wear my patch." He handed the bag to her.

With trembling hands, she opened it and pulled out a black leather vest. Her gaze darted to him, then back to the vest. She held it up and turned it around. In scrolling lettering, it read "Property of Diablo."

"Do you know what that means?" he said in a low voice.

"Yeah. Raven told me. It's beautiful. The lettering is so intricate and artistic. Simply lovely."

Diablo chuckled.

She leaned forward and slipped it on, then stood up and went into the bathroom. He watched her as she modeled it in the mirror, turning this way and that to see how it looked on her.

"You look beautiful with it on," he said, pride swelling inside him.

"I love it." She walked over to him and sat next to him. "For so long I'd been afraid, lonely, and miserable. Charlie kept telling me that no man could ever love me, but a spark of hope lived inside me. But as the years went by, the spark faded more and more until it was practically nonexistent. Then I met you and you made me believe in myself again. You made the spark reignite, and now it's a bonfire inside me, burning with love and admiration for you. I love and want you more than anything else in my life. I can't imagine a life without you. I love your patch, and I'll wear it with love and pride. I'll work hard to be a good old lady."

"I'll make sure you never regret opening your heart and life to me. I love you, sweet pea." He took her mouth in a deep, wet, claiming kiss. She arched her back, pressing her tits against him, her hardening nipples against his taut skin sending electric jolts straight to his hard dick. Grunting, he slipped his hand over her breasts and rolled her nipple between his fingers.

He gently pushed her down on the bed. When he saw a tear trickle down the side of her face, he wiped it away with the corner of his thumb. "What's wrong, sweet pea?" He feathered her throat with kisses.

"I'm so happy and sad at the same time. I have a whirlwind of opposite emotions inside me. Today is the happiest day of my life and the saddest."

He hovered over her, his face a scant couple inches from her face. He lightly kissed her forehead, eyelids, cheeks, nose, chin, and lips, then sat up and pulled her with him. He took her cut off, touching her protesting lips with his tongue, then hung her cut next to his before coming back to the bed.

Lifting the sheet, he motioned her over. She slipped in and he followed her. Gripping her in a smothering hug, he whispered, "Just let go. Breathe and let go."

Her body melted into his and he rocked her until she surrendered to sleep. He leaned over and switched off the lamp, they lay down on the pillow with Fallon tucked snuggly in the crook of his arm.

He watched the clouds swirl like spilled ink in water against the midnight blue sky. An occasional glint of bright light peeked through the ever-spreading clouds. The scent of damp earth and decaying leaves lingered in the air. Fallon moaned in her sleep and he held her tighter to him.

The whirling clouds entranced him, and as he held his old lady, watching their movements, sleep overtook him.

# Chapter Thirty-Two

"THE MONEY FROM your trust fund has been wired to your account," Scott Garber said.

"It's a lot of money. It's scary. I'm glad you kept pestering me about the will. I feel better now that I have one." Fallon tapped her fingers on the counter.

"I suggest you invest it. If you want to set up another trust, you can call me. I can easily do that for you. Of course, I don't want to tell you what to do with your money, but I wouldn't advise just leaving it in your bank account. You'll want it to grow."

"Diablo and I are planning another trip to Denver. He and some of his buddies are going to see a motorcycle show at the convention center. I'll definitely make an appointment and have you help me set things up."

"Sounds good. I wanted to tell you how sorry I am about your mother. I heard about it on the news. How're you doing?"

"Thanks for mentioning it. I'm taking it one day at a time. I'll call you in the next week or two. Thanks for everything."

Fallon set her phone down and glanced at the time. She had to meet Annie in less than half an hour and she wasn't even dressed. She slid off the chair and went into the bedroom. In her closet, she pulled out her cut and ran her fingers over the embroidered letters. A thrill ran through her each time she looked at it. A few nights before, they were out with some of the brothers at a biker bar and she had on her cut. When a biker hit on her, she'd just pointed over her shoulder at her back. The moment he'd seen her "Property of Diablo" patch, he'd mumbled something and walked away. She loved wearing her man's patch. For her, wearing it meant she was his and he was hers.

She pulled out a pair of jeans, a long-sleeved green T-shirt, and a cardigan to ward off the bite the late October wind carried. As she combed her hair, her phone rang and she rushed into the kitchen to pick it up, grimacing when she saw it was Shanna. Hesitating for a couple seconds, she answered.

"I'm just calling to see if you want anything before I clear out the house."

"You're moving?"

"Yeah. There's no way I want to stay in this house with all the memories. Did you want to take anything? Like some mementos?"

She snorted. "Of what? I'm good. Whatever you don't want just throw away."

"How're you doing?"

Shanna still didn't fool her. She'd known from the day Charlie brought her home that Shanna hated her. Why she did, Fallon didn't know, but now it didn't matter. "I'm fine."

"I missed you at the service. I know you had some issues with Charlie, but he did care about you. He was so distraught with the investigation and the way the cops were trying to pin your mother's death on him that it got to be too much. He was suffering—"

"I have to go. I have an appointment. Like I said, throw out whatever you don't want. Have a nice life." *I hope I never hear from her again. I'm sure her plans to take my money were thwarted by the law firm and Charlie's death. They sure in hell deserved each other.*

She went back to her room and dabbed on her perfume, the scent enveloping her and making her think of Diablo. She slipped her shoes on, slung her bag over her shoulder, grabbed a jacket, and left her apartment.

When she arrived at Burger Hamlet, Annie was already seated at a table near the fireplace. Fallon waved and made her way over, smiling at Annie's obsession with hamburgers; it was all she ever wanted to eat. During lunch, they talked about books and the upcoming holiday.

Annie said she wanted to have Thanksgiving at her place. Fallon was pretty sure the club would be celebrating the holiday with the brothers. Diablo told her that they did the main holidays together.

Fallon hadn't shared any information about Diablo with Annie. She wasn't sure her friend would understand the outlaw biker world. She also didn't share too much about herself with others. It was a throwback to her growing years, and she still had trust issues.

On the other hand, Annie talked nonstop about her boyfriend. She adored him, and he was almost like a god to her. Fallon thought it was funny that Annie's boyfriend could do no wrong.

"Is there anything else I can get you?" their waiter asked. Both women shook their heads and he placed the bill tray on the table. "Whenever you're ready I'll take it." He sauntered away.

"I'm having such a problem trying to decide which paint color to use on my walls. I also want to replace the window coverings. I wish I had an artistic eye," Annie said as she took out her wallet.

"I'm not that good either, but I have a friend who's an artist. She's amazing. She did a fantastic job with my place."

"I'd love to have her help me. I'd pay her. I really need some guidance. Do you think you could come over and take a few pictures to show her? If she's interested, I can set up an appointment with her. I live only a couple of minutes from here."

Fallon looked at her phone; Diablo was coming by to pick her up in a couple hours. "I can go, but I can't stay too long."

"I understand. It shouldn't take too long to take the pictures. My place isn't that big." Annie laughed and stood up. The two women left the restaurant. "Follow me."

Fallon went to her car and followed Annie to a small apartment complex. "What floor are you on?" she said.

"The second."

Fallon climbed the stairs slowly, then entered her apartment. Annie's place was practically bare. There were a few boxes against the wall, three chairs, a small table with a television on it, and a small love seat. It didn't look lived-in, and there wasn't a warm feel to it. The ambience was cold and sterile, and Fallon shuddered involuntarily as she sat on the love seat.

"It needs work, huh?" Annie said.

"A little. Raven will make your place look awesome. I better take some pictures."

"Let's have a drink first. Do you want a glass of wine?"

"No. A Coke would be fine. Remember, I don't have a lot of time."

"I know."

"How many bedrooms do you have?"

"Two. What about you?"

"Only one. My place is tiny but I love it. It's my first apartment." Fallon took a sip of Coke.

They chatted about the neighborhood. Annie had some wild stories about some of her neighbors. As Annie told her another story, Fallon began to feel sick. Nausea hit her and she started sweating. Annie kept talking, but her voice seemed distant and unintelligible as Fallon's pulse pounded in her ears. Everything looked blurry and it felt like she was in a dream state. She tried to get up but just fell back against the cushions.

"I don't feel so well," she said, her head pounding. *What the hell is wrong with me? I feel like I'm drugged, but that doesn't make sense. It must've been something I ate.* She forced herself to focus on Annie's smiling face. "I'm sick, Annie. Real sick."

"Is the room spinning? Do you feel out of it, like wading in a pool of mud?" Fallon nodded as best she could. "Bedtime scoop will do that."

*What the hell is she saying? And why the fuck is she just sitting there smiling at me?*

"I bet you can't talk so good now. Bedtime scoop is the street name for GHB. That's a synthetic sedative. It's made in underground labs."

"Why did you give it to me?" Fallon slurred.

"I have seven hundred thousand reasons why." She laughed. "You're worth a lot of money. I mean, my share will only be two hundred thirty thousand, but fuck, that's a fortune for someone like me."

"You want my money? Who are you?" It felt like there was cotton in her ears.

"We gotta get going, Fallon. We can chat later."

One of the doors opened and a man of medium height came out. Fallon tried to take him in through her blurry vision, and she gasped when his penetrating eyes speared her.

*That's the guy who's been following me. But he doesn't have dreadlocks. I know it's him. I'd never forget his eyes. No! Oh God, who are these people? I can't keep my eyes open anymore. Fuck, I'm slipping away....*

FALLON BLINKED SEVERAL times as she tried to adjust her eyes to the dimness of the room. *Where am I? What the fuck happened?* She couldn't remember much of anything except that she'd gone over to Annie's apartment to take some pictures. She tried to move but her body felt like it weighed a thousand pounds. Then she heard voices and knew she had to pretend to be sleeping.

"We have to get this shit wrapped up tomorrow," a woman said.

*I know that voice. It's familiar. Fuck, it's Shanna. The bitch outdid herself.*

"How do you know she's going to go along with us? I mean, seven hundred thousand is a lot of money to just sign over," Annie said.

"She'll sign it over or I'll make her sorry she didn't. Although fucking her would be fun. She's pretty hot," a male voice said.

*I don't know who that is. They can have the damn money. I just want to be back with Diablo.*

"You asshole. You're not fucking anyone. If she doesn't go along with it, I'll pretend to be her. I already got her handwriting down, and you got all the IDs fixed. It'll be a snap," Annie replied.

"It's better to have her sign it over. It's cleaner that way. I don't believe in complicating things. It was luck that the cops found her mother's bones. It gave Charlie the perfect motive to kill himself." Shanna laughed.

"We lucked out on that one," Anne replied.

"You bet we did. I was trying to find a reason why Charlie would kill himself. He wasn't the suicide type. But then this murder investigation fell into my lap. I knew I could make it look like suicide, and given the circumstances, it made sense that he'd do that. I couldn't have planned it better. Now that he's out of the way, Fallon is the last loose thread. Once we get the money, she's history too." Shanna chuckled.

"I'll take care of her. Don't sweat it," the man said.

*Shanna killed Charlie, and the bitch is going to kill me. Wait. That man. The one following me. I saw him.* Images pierced through her drug-addled brain. *He was at Annie's. That's right. How are they connected with Shanna? How the fuck am I going to get out of this?*

"She'll be coming out of it in a couple of hours. I'll tell her the choices and she can decide. I can't wait to get the fuck out of this hick town. I was made for a city like Los Angeles."

"Two hundred thirty thousand won't go very far in LA," the man said.

"You should go somewhere in the south where things are cheaper," Annie added.

"My hair would be a mess in all that humidity. Anyway, I didn't say I was actually going to move to LA."

Fallon peeked out from under her eyelids; she didn't dare open her eyes all the way. All she could see was their feet: Shanna's stilettos, Annie's sneakers, and black boots worn by the man with the cold eyes. Despair began to wrap around her nerves, strangling them. She had no idea where she was; her only hope was that Diablo would be able to track her location from the GPS device he'd installed on her phone. The three of them acted like amateurs, and she prayed it didn't occur to them that she'd have a GPS tracking device. In her heart she knew Diablo would come for her.

Until then, she'd have to play the waiting game.

# Chapter Thirty-Three

DIABLO LET HIMSELF into Fallon's apartment. "Sweet pea?" His voice echoed eerily. He went into her bedroom and checked around. Nothing seemed out of the ordinary, but concern punched his gut. He called the bookstore. She wasn't there. Scrolling through his phone, he checked to see if she'd sent him a text message he'd missed. Nothing.

He called Muerto and asked him if Raven was out with Fallon.

"No. Raven's right here."

"When's the last time she saw her?"

"Hang on, I'll put her on." A few seconds passed, and then Raven's phone filtered into his ears.

"When was the last time you saw Fallon?"

"When Breanna and I went out with her for our girls' night at Alfonso's. It was last Thursday. Has something happened to her?"

"That's what I'm trying to figure out. Do you have any idea where she could be?"

"Wait a minute. She went out to lunch with her friend Annie. I received a text from her saying she was at Annie's apartment taking pictures. She was doing it because Annie wanted me to help her decorate the place. I told Fallon to send me the pictures when she was done, but I never got them. I texted and called her a few times but I haven't heard from her. I was getting worried. It's not like her to not return my calls or texts."

As Raven spoke, his gaze flitted around the room and his mouth went dry. He'd been living in his world too long not to heed the warning signs. His gut was telling him that Fallon was in trouble.

Muerto asked if he needed any help, and Diablo told him yes, but he'd call him back. He opened her laptop and went into her photo folder. A series of images of him, club parties, her girls' night out with Breanna and Raven, and photos of him and Fallon popped in front of him.

Then his blood ran cold: his sister Taya was in one of the photos. From the look of the pictures, it seemed that she didn't realize Fallon was taking a picture of her. *Why the fuck does Fallon have a photo of Taya?* He kept staring at the photo and saw a menu on the table along with Fallon's purse. Hitting the Zoom button, the menu pixelated in front of him. The name of the restaurant was Burger Hamlet.

*Fuck.* Fallon had told him her friend Annie was in love with that place. *So Taya is Annie. I fuckin' knew she was up to no good. Why the fuck is she with Fallon?* Diablo stared at the screen as his mind whirled. The only thing Taya wanted was money to support her habit. The only time he heard from her was when she needed money. But what was her connection to Fallon? She didn't have money. Diablo's blood ran cold. *Fallon's inheritance. I don't know how the fuck she even knows about it, but she's involved. And she's in thick. I gotta get to Fallon.*

He checked the GPS app and pinpointed her location: the warehouse. *Fuckin' Shanna's in on it too.*

Diablo plugged in Steel's number.

"My woman's in trouble. I traced her to the warehouse and I know that bitch Shanna's there. I'm betting the Satan's Pistons are in on this."

"Let me get some brothers together. We'll go with you. After we get your woman out of there, we'll demolish the warehouse. That was the only piece we'd left dangling. We'll take the cages since we don't want to announce our arrival."

"We gotta go now. I don't know what the fuck they're doing to her." His voice was tight.

"Be cool, brother. You need a level head. We'll get to her. Just stay cool."

Diablo ran out of the apartment and jumped on his Harley, taking the back roads as he sped all the way to the clubhouse.

*If anything happens to Fallon, I'm gonna spend the rest of my life exacting revenge on every last one of those fuckers.*

# Chapter Thirty-Four

ICE WATER IN her face startled Fallon out of a deep slumber. Stretching her limbs, she wiped her face with her hands.

"Get up, bitch. You got some stuff you need to do for me. And if you give me any lip, I'll beat your ass. This has taken way the fuck longer that it should've."

Fallon glanced behind Shanna and saw Annie, who stared at her. Cruelty etched her face. *How could she pretend to be my friend all this time?*

"Get the skank to the fucking bank so I can blow outta this damn state." Annie lit a joint.

The man who had been following Fallon came in. "Are you up, princess?" He stroked her cheek and she flinched. "Don't you like my touch?"

"Will you stop it, Tae? It's not funny," Annie fumed, shooting dagger eyes at Fallon.

"Shut the fuck up, slut." Tae looked back at Fallon. "You're not a slut, princess. You're a good girl. I don't see many of them." He chuckled and ran his finger over her jawline.

"You're the one who was following me. Did you cut your hair?" she said softly. She caught on that Tae was in charge and he was taken with her. She had to play into it if she had any chance of surviving.

He laughed. "It was a wig. I wanted to make sure you stuck around. Then I got to liking you and wanted to have a little fun with you." He kissed her cheek, and Fallon gritted her teeth to keep from dry heaving.

Annie rushed over and threw her arms around Tae, kissing him. He shoved her away and she jumped back up. "Don't you throw me away.

What do you want with a crippled woman? Have your tastes gone over to the freak side? If you think I'm gonna stand around and watch you flirt with this skank, you're fucking wrong. You need me for this to go down, so don't fucking piss me off!"

Without warning, he punched Annie in the face. The girl howled and fell back. "Don't you ever fucking threaten me again. You're nothing but a trashy whore, spreading your nasty legs for some juice. You pathetic, slut." He hit her again and Shanna rushed in.

"What the hell are you doing, you dumbass? How the hell can she go to the bank now with her face all bruised up? You never were the smart one of the family. Daddy was always beating your ass for stupid shit you did. I should do that now."

*I didn't know Shanna had a brother. He must've been the one she was talking to when I overheard her that day. I'd thought it was Charlie. The dumb sonofabitch got played big-time by Shanna. He never knew about my grandmother or the inheritance.*

Shanna glared at Fallon. "I'm in charge here, and you're going to do exactly what I tell you. You're going to go to the bank and withdraw your money. I'll be with you holding a gun to you in case you try to get cute."

Fallon laughed. "Are you serious? Do you think the bank is going to just give me seven hundred thousand dollars in cash without me calling first? Most banks don't have that much cash. I'd have to call ahead to request it."

"Is that true?" Shanna turned to Tae.

"I don't know. It sounds good."

"Sounds good? I should've done this by myself. I knew involving you and your druggie girlfriend would fuck this up. You should've investigated all this."

"Why the hell didn't you?" Tae snapped.

Shanna sighed in exasperation and turned back to Fallon. "I think you're making this shit up. You're going to go to the bank and ask for the withdrawal."

"I'm not doing shit. And you're not going to do a damn thing about it because you need me. Annie can't go to the bank looking like she just had a round in the ring. You're nothing but a money-hungry bitch."

Shanna raised her hand to slap Fallon but Tae intervened. "You can't bruise the merchandise, sister. Take Annie and leave me alone with the princess. I'll get her to play ball."

Shanna went over to Annie and she flipped out, screaming and crying, her arms swinging everywhere. "I can't control her. You take care of your bitch," Shanna said as she stormed out.

Tae leaned over and whispered in Fallon's ear, "I'll be back, and I promise to show you a good time." He licked her earlobe and went over to Taya. Pulling her up by her hair, he dragged her from the room, the young woman screaming the whole time.

When they'd left, Fallon frantically looked around for a way to escape. At that point she realized she was in the back part of the warehouse. Since Charlie had died, the fighting gigs had stopped and the ring girls had moved out. She knew there was a back entrance behind the partition. As she struggled to stand up, four loud shots exploded. *Bang! Bang! Bang! Bang!* The noise reverberated around the room.

Silence.

*What the hell happened?* Her skin crawled as though she had millions of ants on it. *Maybe Diablo's here.* Hope shot through her but quickly turned to despair when Tae walked back into the room.

"What happened? Who fired those shots?" she said, her voice laced in panic.

Tae sat down next to her and jerked her to him. "Shh, princess. No need to be worried. I took care of some business."

"Where're Annie and Shanna?"

"First off, Annie's name is Taya. She's the sister of your bodyguard. Isn't that a fucking small world? She didn't make the connection until she bumped into him in a restaurant."

"Taya? She knew I was Diablo's girlfriend and she still did this?"

Tae laughed. "What you didn't know about Taya is that she's nothing but a cold-hearted bitch. She'd sell anyone out for a fix. I bet you wouldn't do that. You're a nice girl."

"You didn't tell me where they are."

He smiled. "I'd say they're both in hell, but not sure the Devil wants them." He threw his head back and laughed.

"What does that mean? You didn't *kill* them, did you?"

"I never was good at sharing. Shanna knew that. I never intended to share the money with them. I'm pretty sure she was planning the same fate for me, and Taya would've loved to have offed Shanna. Anyway, there's no way Taya could pull this off. You can't trust a druggie. And besides, she doesn't even look like you." He reached out and stroked her cheek. "You have an innocence about you that she never fuckin' had."

*I have to buy time.* "I can help you get the money. I never liked Shanna, but you're different." *Hurry, Diablo.*

Tae smiled and ran his hand down over her hip. "Now you're talking. Before we go to the bank, I want a taste of you. I've been wanting to fuck you for a while. I like innocent girls, not slutty ones like Taya, although I have to say I got some decent money for her ass."

Fallon's eyes widened. "You were her pimp."

"Yeah. And if you're real good, I'll let you live and be my special girl." He kissed her and she jerked back. He narrowed his eyes. "Don't fuckin' do that." His voice was cold and had an edge to it.

"I didn't mean to. You just took me by surprise. Let's see how much money I can take from the bank. Then we can come back and have the time we need."

"I'm good with going at it now and later." He fisted her hair and yanked her head back, causing her scalp to burn and her eyes to water. "You like it rough, babe? I bet you do since you're fucking an outlaw. I can give it to you real hard." He slammed his mouth against hers and shoved his tongue inside. She tried to push him away but she was no match for his strength.

Right when he slid his hand under her knit top, the door burst open. Before either of them could react, Diablo had Tae by the neck, shaking him like a leaf in the wind. He threw him to the floor and the two men punched and kicked until Diablo was the only one punching and kicking. Tae lay unconscious on the floor.

Steel walked over to Diablo. "He's gone, brother. Go take care of your woman."

Army, Paco, Goldie, Chains, Crow, Shotgun, Eagle, Muerto, and Skull rushed in, AK 47s in hand. "Anyone else in here?" Paco said.

Steel shook his head. "Seems like the two women we found in the next room and this fucking dirtbag were the only ones in on this. Is that right, Fallon?"

"Yeah." She pushed herself up, Shotgun grabbing her elbow when she stumbled. The drug still had an effect on her. She bent down and wrapped her arms around Diablo, his back against her. She peppered the side of his neck and face with light kisses, murmuring, "I love you," over and over.

Diablo stood up and pressed her close to him. Without a word Chains, Goldie, Shotgun, Eagle, and Muerto scooped up Tae's lifeless body and headed out. Fallon buried her head in Diablo's blood-spattered T-shirt and sobbed. He rubbed her back as she heard Steel say in a low voice, "We'll take care of everything here. Take your woman home."

Diablo wrapped his arm around her and led her outside. She saw Taya on the floor and a dark pool of red filled in the cracks in the floor. She glanced at Diablo and her heart splintered when she saw the sadness in his eyes as he stared down at Taya's lifeless body. After a couple of minutes, he shook his head and tugged Fallon closer to him and they headed out into the bright autumn sunshine.

# Chapter Thirty-Five

THE FOLLOWING MORNING the warehouse fire made it on page three of the *Alina Post*. Photographs of flames licking the brickwork and smoke billowing into the sky were in full color and plastered on the bottom of the page.

"The warehouse burned to the ground," Fallon said as she stirred hazelnut creamer into her coffee.

"That must've been the reason for all that haze last night." Diablo took a bite out of his buttered toast.

Fallon glanced up and met Diablo's dark stare, then nodded and continued reading the paper. Of course, they would never speak about what happened at the warehouse to anyone outside of the brotherhood. Fallon knew she couldn't share what had happened to her with Raven or Breanna, even though they suspected something. The women knew their men's secrets were theirs as well.

"You doing okay? You went through a lot yesterday." Diablo reached out for her hand.

"I'm not sure yet. I don't think it's all sunk in."

"Breanna told me that you should see a grief counselor because you've had so much shit dumped on you in such a short time. She gave me a couple of names, said they're very good."

"I think I'll give it a try. I have a lot I need to sort out with my past. I know if I act like it's no big deal, it'll clobber me over the head. Are you doing okay?" She placed her hand over his.

"Yeah, fine. I'm just worried about you. I'm glad you're gonna talk to someone. Of course, some things have to be left unspoken."

"For sure. I know the score. I was just wondering how you're doing with Taya's death."

He shrugged. "The sister I knew when we were young died when our mom quit being a mom. That was a long time ago, and I've already mourned."

"But she was still your sister. I was blown away when I found out."

"I knew she was up to no good when I bumped into her, but I never figured it involved you. I didn't fuckin' see that. The time she split my head open and robbed me was when my trust died, and it never came back. I tried to help her as best I could, but she was lost before our family even broke up. It's the way it goes sometimes. At least she's free from her demons. I hope she finally has some peace. She never did in her short life."

"I wish I could've known her under different circumstances. I'd like to think we would've really been friends."

"Not likely. Her only friend was crack. You never mentioned me to her?"

"Not by name. I didn't tell her I had a biker boyfriend, but that creepy Tae knew because he tailed me. He told me your sister bumped into you in town and made the connection that I was your girlfriend. When she drugged me she knew you were my boyfriend. I can't believe she did that to me... to *you*."

"I can. She stopped being my sister a long time ago. Her heart was ice. When I think of how it was when we were all kids, I never would've thought she'd have grown into a woman without a soul. I guess I have my mom to thank for that."

"Don't you think she deserves a proper burial?" she whispered.

He nodded, his jaw jutted out. "The brothers took her over to Sagebrush. We know a guy who owns a mortuary there. He's got her body. I'm gonna ask him to cremate her then I'll spread her ashes in Chaco Canyon."

"I'll be at your side." Fallon grasped his hand while she shook her head. "What a crazy thing this all was, and just for money."

"People do a lot of shit for money. And as far as the money goes, sweet pea, it's all yours. I'm your man and I'll take care of you, so if you need a car, clothes, whatever, I'll take care of it. You should think about taking the lawyer's advice and investing it, but I'm not gonna tell you what to do with it."

Warmth spread through her as she leaned over and kissed him. "I love you. You're the sweetest man."

He tweaked her nose and smiled. "Now I know you love this apartment. It's cute, and you and Raven did a good job painting the walls and decorating. It pissed Muerto way the fuck off what you did to his walls, and watching all that was funny as hell. But it's too small for us. We need to find a bigger place. There're some new developments I've been reading about and I think we should take a look this weekend."

"Isn't the bike rally this weekend?"

"Yeah, but we don't have to go both days."

"I'd love to find a beautiful home with a gourmet kitchen. I love to bake and having a double oven would be like a dream come true."

"Then I'll buy you whatever you want. Hell, I'll buy you a bakery if you want."

Fallon giggled. "I'll be happy with the double oven."

Diablo held her hands, staring intently into her eyes. "All kinds of crazy thoughts went through my mind when I realized you were gone. Just the possibility of losing you twisted me up from the inside out. All I could see was your face, hear your voice, and feel your touch. I never want you out of my life."

"I was freaking out too. The thought of never seeing you again made my insides freeze. I knew you'd come for me, but I wasn't sure if it would be in time. I feel so connected to you."

Diablo came over to her and tugged her up, then swung her into his arms, his lips gently covering hers. A shiver rippled through her as she drew his tongue into her mouth.

"I love you, sweet pea," he said against her lips, his hands roaming over her body.

"I loved you before I even met you."

He led her to the couch, his lips fused on hers, and pulled her onto his lap. "I'm crazy about you. Some of the brothers think I'm acting like a love-sick pussy, but I don't give a shit."

Fallon laughed and kissed his chin.

"I want you in my life forever, woman. I want you to stand beside me through the good and bad. I want you to ride with me until our last sunset."

"What're you saying?" she said in a low voice.

"I want you to be my wife." He brushed his lips against hers. "I need you."

Joy glistened in her eyes. "I need you too."

"Then it's a yes?"

"A huge yes." She peppered his face with kisses as tears trickled down her cheeks, happiness flooding her to the core.

"You just made me fuckin' happy." His face split into a wide grin.

Sniffling, she wiped her wet cheeks. "I'm ecstatic. I want to always have you by my side."

He nodded, watching her fixedly. "I want a biker wedding, but we can do some of the stuff you want too."

"A biker wedding is fine, even though I don't really know what that means. I can guess Harleys play a role in it."

He laughed. "Fuck yeah, sweet pea. You're catching on."

Placing her hands on each side of his face, she said, "Your world is what saved me, so it's only fitting that we share our love with your brothers."

"You're a kickass old lady."

"I do have one request. I've never been to the ocean. I fell in love with Santa Monica Pier when I first saw the movie *The Lost Boys*. I want to go there for our honeymoon."

"That's a fuckin' awesome movie. We'll go to Santa Monica and make love on the beach. Whatever you want, you got."

She licked his lips, then moved her tongue away when he tried to grab it with his teeth. Running her tongue up his throat to his chin, she kissed him deep and messy. He grasped her hand and placed it on the bulge in his jeans. She sucked in her breath. Dragging his tongue to her ear, he pulled her earlobe between his teeth and whispered, "This is all yours. Always." His hand glided under her T-shirt.

Taking his hand she moved it over her breast. "And I'm all yours."

As his heated eyes caught and held hers, she smiled wickedly and slowly unzipped his jeans.

# Epilogue

*Two months later*

"I LIKE IT better by the other window," Fallon said, pointing behind Paco's shoulder.

"Woman, make up your mind," Diablo gritted as he and Paco moved the seven foot Christmas tree yet again.

"I just want it to be perfect. It's been so long since I had a Christmas tree."

"I get that, sweetie, I really do. But you've also bought a shitload of lights we still have to wrap around this sucker. We've been moving the tree around for the past half hour."

Fallon giggled. *Diablo's so cute when he's trying not to be pissed. Do I dare tell him I like the tree best where it was when we first started?* "Don't be mad, but I like it best right in front of the middle window."

"Where we first had it?" Paco said.

She nodded. "Sorry. I'm baking chocolate chip cookies and butterscotch bars. And I'm making hot chocolate."

"It better have a couple shots of Jack. We're gonna fuckin' need it." Diablo walked backward toward the middle of the family room.

Smiling, she went to the kitchen to check on the cookies. She loved her double ovens and shiny new appliances. Actually, she loved their new home. They'd only been in it for the past few weeks, but she had it practically finished. She couldn't believe that they'd found the perfect house so soon after they'd started looking.

Paco and Diablo came into the kitchen and sat at the counter. She slid the bottle of whiskey to them and place two steaming mugs of hot chocolate. Turning around, she grabbed the oven mitts and took out the cookies and bars from the ovens.

"We gotta get some of the brothers over here to help with the fuckin' lights," Diablo said as he poured the whiskey into Paco's mug.

"And the ornaments," Fallon added.

Paco took a cookie and shook his head. "My Christmas tree duty stops with the lights."

"Call Raven and Breanna. They'll like helping you with the other stuff." Diablo took a bite out of the warm chocolate chip cookie.

"That's a good idea. We can order pizza and salad for everyone and make a party of it." Fallon took out her phone and called Raven.

"Tell her to bring Muerto over here." Diablo poured more Jack into his mug.

Soon the house was filled with Night Rebels stringing lights around the tall tree. Raven, Breanna, and Fallon stood by the fireplace giggling as they saw the men fumbling with the lights, arguing as to how to make them look good, and untangling them numerous times.

"I never thought I'd see the guys so interested in a Christmas tree," Breanna said.

"I should take a picture," Raven added.

"You do that and I'm just gonna delete it," Muerto said over his shoulder.

"If you can get to it before it goes viral." Raven laughed.

Fallon bent down and put another log in the fire and it cracked and spit as the orange flames curled around it. "It's cold tonight."

"It was snowing when we got here," Raven said as she sat on the couch.

"Have you picked a date for your wedding yet?" Breanna asked as she joined Raven on the couch.

Fallon shook her head. "Not yet. I want to be engaged for a while before we get married." She glanced at the white diamond solitaire on her finger. "I'm thinking next October. We're going to California for our honeymoon, and I figure there won't be so many tourists there in October. Not like the summer."

"That sounds like so much fun. I think it's a good idea to have some time before you get married." Breanna smiled and picked up a box of ornaments on the table. "These are lovely. They look old."

"They were my grandmother's. My lawyer gave them to me when we went to Denver last month. My grandmother had a large storage unit and she didn't have anything in the will about it. I ended up inheriting all the stuff in it. It was so much fun to go through all the old photos, heirlooms, and memorabilia my grandma saved."

"I bet there were a lot of cool things in there. If you don't want any of the old jewelry, let me know. I'll buy it from you," Raven said.

"Actually, I was thinking of you when I saw all these old broches and earrings. Some of them look like they could be from the 1940s. I pulled a couple of pieces I wanted, but you're welcome to the rest."

"Awesome. I can't wait to see what you have. Let's plan to get together next week."

As the men finished stringing the lights, the doorbell rang and Diablo went over to answer it.

"Pizza's here," he said as he took out his wallet.

Fallon went over to help carry the bags of salad the delivery boy handed to her. Breanna and Raven jumped up and followed her to the kitchen. In a short time, a huge bowl of salad and numerous boxes of pizza lined the kitchen counter. The men filed in, grabbing a plate and filling it up. A large aluminum bucket contained bottles of Coors.

Several hours later, Goldie, Paco, and Chains stubbed out their joints and heaved themselves up from the couch.

"It's a fuckin' big tree," Goldie said as he walked to the front door.

"Biggest one I've seen in a house," Chains added as he followed Goldie.

"And a fuckin' heavy one too." Paco laughed.

"Thanks for helping out." Diablo bumped fists with the three men.

The brothers walked out into the frosty air, their breaths rising in visible puffs to join the clouded night sky. Diablo closed the door and wrapped his arm around Fallon. "Why don't you fix us a couple of spiked hot chocolates?"

She smiled and went toward the kitchen. When she came back into the family room with two mugs, the flickering tree with its glistening ornaments made her eyes shimmer. "This is the most beautiful tree I've ever seen," she murmured as she placed the cups on the coffee table. She sat down and snuggled next to Diablo. "Don't you think it's magical?"

He reached over and picked up his mug, blowing on the hot liquid before he took a sip. "You make the best hot chocolate. And the tree fuckin' rocks."

"Thanks for making our first Christmas in our new home amazing." She kissed his neck.

"Anything you want, sweet pea, you got."

She giggled. "I can't believe you talked the guys into coming over here to help trim the tree. I mean it was so funny to see all these big, buffed guys hanging lights. You got an awesome group of friends."

"My brothers are the best. We're there for each other even if it's going to Rooster Mike's son's baseball game, helping Goldie with his grandma, or stringing lights around this damn tree. You must've bought a thousand long ass strands, woman."

She laughed. "I guess I did get carried away, but look how beautiful the tiers of lights are. And the ornaments are so vibrant. I love that I have my grandma's baubles on the tree. I know they're the same ones my mom helped put on when she was a young girl. Just thinking about that makes me shiver."

Diablo put his empty mug on the table, then bent down and kissed her. "I'm hoping that soon you'll be passing the ornaments to our kids."

Pushing away a bit, she choked slightly. "We've got plenty of time for that. We're not even married."

He frowned. "Don't you want kids?"

She nodded. "Yeah. I do. I just don't want them for a few years. I want some time for us first."

"I just don't wanna be an old man when our kids are born."

She kissed him gently. "I don't want to wait *that* long. You'll make a great dad. You have a good heart."

"I know I'll always be there for them no matter what. You'll be a kick ass mom."

"One thing's for sure, our kids will always know we love them."

"And they're gonna know how crazy in love I am with their mom." He pressed her to him and kissed her hard.

"Oh yeah?" she whispered.

"Yeah," he said thickly as he eased her onto her back.

The Christmas lights shone in his eyes as he hovered over her. She glanced at the window and saw snowflakes swirling and dancing in the icy wind. "It's snowing again."

Diablo looked over at the window. "That wind's really blowing." He turned back to her and swept his lips across hers.

The warmth from the fireplace covered them but it was nothing compared to the bonfire that his kisses lit up inside her. Shivers tingled her spine and she raised her head off the cushion to meet his scorching lips. The moment was perfect: the glittering tree, the falling snow, the crackling fire, and the love of her life. Every touch, kiss, and whispered word ignited sparks in her.

After years of isolation and sadness, she'd found her place. Never could she have imagined that a tough outlaw biker would ride into her life changing everything. And she wouldn't trade him for the world. He was hers and she was his and they'd have children and live out their years together.

"I love you so much," she breathed against his ear as he nipped her skin.

"I love you too," he rasped, his gaze boring into hers.

In that moment they loved with their eyes, their bodies touching as their souls mingled in the quiet moments between action and stillness.

Then it was all passion—intense and intoxicating. His touch scorched her, his voice melted her, and his kisses blazed a trail to the throbbing between her legs.

*He's the only flame I'll ever need. I'll always love him.*

She captured his smoldering gaze and opened her legs wide.

Make sure you sign up for my newsletter so you can keep up with my new releases, special sales, free short stories, and other treats only available to newsletter readers. When you sign up, you will receive a FREE hot and steamy novella. Sign up at:

http://eepurl.com/bACCL1

Visit me on Facebook
facebook.com/Chiah-Wilder-1625397261063989

Check out my other books at my Author Page
amazon.com/author/chiahwilder

# Notes from Chiah

As always, I have a team behind me making sure I shine and continue on my writing journey. It is their support, encouragement, and dedication that pushes me further in my writing journey. And then, it is my wonderful readers who have supported me, laughed, cried, and understood how these outlaw men live and love in their dark and gritty world. Without you—the readers—an author's words are just letters on a page. The emotions you take away from the words breathe life into the story.

**Thank you** to my amazing Personal Assistant Amanda Faulkner. I don't know what I'd do without you. I value your suggestions and opinions, and my world is so much saner with you in it. You keep the non-writing part of my indie publishing world running smoothly. I so appreciate it. You are always ready to jump in and fix everything when I'm pulling my hair out. You are so cheerful, and when I hear your bubbling voice, it instantly uplifts me. So happy YOU are on my team!

**Thank you** to my editor, Kristin, for all your insightful edits, excitement with my new series, Night Rebels MC, and encouragement during the writing and editing process. I truly value your editorial eyes and suggestions as well as the time you spend. You're the best!

**Thank you** to my wonderful beta readers, Kolleen, Paula, and Barbara. Your enthusiasm and suggestions for DIABLO: Night Rebels MC were spot on and helped me to put out a stronger, cleaner novel. Your insights and attention to detail were awesome, and I take all of your suggestions seriously. I appreciate the attention you always give my books.

**Thank you** to the bloggers for your support in reading my book, sharing it, reviewing it, and getting my name out there. I so appreciate all your efforts. You all are so invaluable. I hope you know that. Without you, the indie author would be lost.

**Thank you** ARC readers you have helped make all my books so much stronger. I appreciate the effort and time you put in to reading, reviewing, and getting the word out about the books. I don't know what I'd do without you. I feel so lucky to have you behind me.

**Thank you** to my Street Team. Thanks for your input, your support, and your hard work. I appreciate you more than you know. A HUGE hug to all of you!

**Thank you** to Carrie from Cheeky Covers. You are amazing! I can always count on you. You are the calm to my storm. You totally rock, and I love your artistic vision.

**Thank you** to my proofreader, Daryl, whose last set of eyes before the last once over I do, is invaluable. I appreciate the time and attention to detail you always give to my books. You ALWAYS deliver, and I love that I can count on you.

**Thank you** to Ena and Amanda with Enticing Journeys Promotions who have helped garner attention for and visibility to the Night Rebels MC series. Couldn't do it without you! Also a big thank you to Book Club Gone Wrong Blog who is hosting and promoting DIABLO. Totally indebted to you.

**Thank you** to the readers who continue to support me and read my books. Without you, none of this would be possible. I appreciate your comments and reviews on my books, and I'm dedicated to giving you the best story that I can. I'm always thrilled when you enjoy a book as much as I have in writing it. You definitely make the hours of typing on the computer and the frustrations that come with the territory of writing books so worth it. You make it possible for writers to write because without you reading the books, we wouldn't exist. Thank you, thank you! ♥

## DIABLO: Night Rebels Motorcycle Club (Book 3)

Dear Readers,

Thank you for reading my book. I hope you enjoyed the second book in my new Night Rebels MC series as much as I enjoyed writing Diablo and Fallon's story. This gritty and rough motorcycle club has a lot more to say, so I hope you will look for the upcoming books in the series. Romance makes life so much more colorful, and a rough, sexy bad boy makes life a whole lot more interesting.

If you enjoyed the book, please consider leaving a review on Amazon. I read all of them and appreciate the time taken out of busy schedules to do that.

I love hearing from my fans, so if you have any comments or questions, please email me at chiahwilder@gmail.com or visit my facebook page.

To receive a **free copy of my novella**, *Summer Heat*, and to hear of **new releases**, **special sales**, **free short stories**, and **ARC opportunities**, please sign up for my **Newsletter** at http://eepurl.com/bACCL1.

Happy Reading,

*Chiah*

# GOLDIE
## Book 4 in the Night Rebels MC Series
## Coming in August, 2017

**Goldie, Road Captain of the Night Rebels MC, loves women and women love him.** He's a simple man who only needs his Harley, whiskey, and women—in that order—in his life to make it hum. Being an officer of an outlaw motorcycle club, the women are more than willing to accommodate the blond, ripped, and tatted biker. His rule is simple: pleasure without commitment. It's served him well until one night when she walked into the club's tattoo shop wanting an ink job on her sexy bottom.

For reasons he doesn't understand, he's drawn to her.

He's never felt such a pull before.

He wants to get to know her.

Then he finds out her name is Hailey Shilley. He hasn't seen her since she moved away from Alina eleven years ago.

She's off limits.

He has to forget about her.

She's his best friend's little sister.

Problem is he can't get her or her sweet tattoo out of his mind.

Hailey Shilley left Alina when she'd first started high school. She's back to help her aunt run her floral shop. When she stumbled into the tattoo parlor with her two friends, she didn't expect to find the most gorgeous guy she's ever laid eyes on. His ripped body, strong jaw, and to-die for tats made her tingle all over. She can't get him out of her mind.

When she finds out he's her brother's best friend, she can't believe what a hunk he grew up to be. But her brother warned her about him. Told her he's an outlaw biker and a player. She always had a crush on him, but now that they're both grown up, she isn't sure she wants to risk her heart to him.

While Hailey tries to put aside her fears and Goldie his loyalty to his buddy, female bodies are turning up all around the county. A madman is loose and he's closing in on the women Goldie holds dear to him. Can he be stopped in time?

**This is the fourth book in the Night Rebels MC Romance series. This is Goldie's story. It is a standalone. This book contains violence, sexual assault (not graphic), strong language, and steamy/graphic sexual scenes. It describes the life and actions of an outlaw motorcycle club. If any of these issues offend you, please do not read the book. HEA. No cliffhangers! The book is intended for readers over the age of 18.**

## Excerpt: GOLDIE

Note: This short excerpt is a ROUGH DRAFT. I am still writing the story about this bad boy. It has only been self-edited in a rudimentary way. I share it with you to give you a bit of an insight into Goldie.

# Chapter One

THE TATTOO SHOP bustled as young men and women filed in to make a statement on their skin. The weekends at Get Inked were crazy since it was the only tattoo and piercing shop that looked decent. Bent Needles, the shop's competitor, had been cited for health violations numerous times by the county. The Night Rebels own Get Inked and customers felt comfortable in the clean, professional-looking establishment. The ochre yellow walls and dark brown laminate floors had a calming effect on people who paid to have needles pierce their designs into their skin.

"Did Flora ever call?" Tattoo Mike asked Goldie as he slipped a wad of cash into the cash register.

"Nope. I tried calling and texting her a bunch of times. It'd be a big help if we had a receptionist tonight. It fucking sucks to have to run the counter and do the ink. We should fire her ass. This is the second Saturday she's pulled this shit." Goldie ran his hand through his short hair.

"I already have an ad online and in the paper. She's history." Tattoo Mike glanced over the appointment book. "We gotta start limiting walk-ins on the weekends. You got any appointments for tonight?"

"I just finished with my last one. You?"

"I got two, and both of them are pretty intense in design. Looks like you, Skull, and Freddy are gonna have to handle the walk-ins."

"No problem. I'm going to get a club girl over here to handle the front desk." Goldie picked up his phone. "Dude. We need one of the girls to help out tonight. That bitch Flora was a no show again. We're slammed and it's just going to get worse. Seems like everyone wants a tat or a piercing after downing a few shots." Goldie chuckled.

"I'll bring one of the girls over. The bitch just lost her job," Paco said.

"Tattoo Mike's already got an ad out. Thanks, dude. See you in a few." Goldie placed his phone down and looked up as Skull approached.

"Freddy's sick as shit. There's no way he can work on anyone." Skull pulled out a bottle of root beer from the mini fridge behind the counter.

"Fuck! Tattoo Mike's got two customs." Goldie clasped the back of his neck and rubbed it hard.

Freddy was the only citizen tattoo artist who worked at Get Inked. He'd been working there for over five years and his work was impeccable. The club had talked about taking on another citizen artist part-time, but they hadn't found anyone who they thought was good enough and fit in to the overall vibe of the shop. The tattoo parlor didn't just have customers from Alina, but citizens from the outlying county and as far away as Durango came to the shop. Their reputation for having top-notched tattoo artists was known throughout the southwestern part of Colorado.

"Looks like we'll be hustling our asses in about another hour." Skull looked at the wall clock that was surrounded by framed pictures of tattooed men and women. The clock read eleven: soon people would be leaving the bars. "I hope I don't have to kick anyone's ass tonight. We don't have time for that shit." Skull guzzled the root beer.

Goldie nodded. The Road Captain for the Night Rebels usually loved a good fight, but not when he was working and needed to concentrate on what the hell he was doing. Many people staggered in, drunk and loud, demanding to have a tattoo or a piercing. The policy was to turn them away. Sometimes they had to get tough and throw them out, and there was always someone who thought he could fight them. It really got under Goldie's skin.

"Hey, guys," Kelly said as she walked through the door. She was one of the club girls for the Night Rebels MC, and she usually was the one who offered to help out at the club's businesses if they needed a backup.

"Hey. You're the receptionist for the next three hours." Goldie moved aside as she squeezed in behind the counter, rubbing her behind against him. "You owe me. I was right in the middle of getting real cozy with one of the Fallen Slayers. He was cute too."

The Fallen Slayers MC was a club the Night Rebels were friendly with. They lived about an hour away in Silverado and would come to the club's weekend parties. Once in a while, the Night Rebels would go to Silverado to shoot some pool with them or hang at one of their parties.

"You guys need anything else?" Paco asked.

Goldie smiled. "No. You anxious to get back to the party? How's the citizen turnout tonight?"

"Fucking awesome." Paco lifted his eyebrows.

"Damn. We need to be there." Skull came out from behind the counter and sank down onto one of the black leather couches against the wall.

"They'll still be there when we get off," Goldie said.

Paco nodded. "If you don't need anything else, I'm outta here."

Goldie lifted his chin. "Catch you later, dude."

Two guys walked in and approached the counter. "We'd like to get a tattoo," the taller one said to Kelly.

She turned to Goldie. "You available?"

He eyed the two guys. "How old are you?"

The shorter one turned red and looked at the floor, but the tall one said, "Eighteen."

"Bullshit. You guys don't even look sixteen. Show me some ID."

"I left my license at home," the tall one said; the short one kept staring at the floor.

"No ID, no tattoo. Pretty simple."

The tall one shifted his weight from one foot to another. "We heard you guys were cool here. That this was owned by the Night Rebels."

"It is owned by the Night Rebels and we're cool as fuck. I still need to see your IDs. If you're eighteen, you'll go back to one of the rooms. It you don't have any IDs then you'll have to come back when you do."

"But we have the money and are ready—"

Goldie held up his hands. "Now you're just pissing me off, kid. I'm not negotiating with you. I'm telling you that you're not getting a fucking tattoo without any ID telling me you're eighteen. So hit the pavement."

The shorter teenager moved away from the counter. "Let's go, Tyler."

"We'll just go to Bent Needles." Tyler glared at Goldie.

"Do whatever you want, but you're not getting tatted in this shop."

"I'm not going there. My cousin went there and got a massive infection on his leg. Let's just go home. My mom will be pissed if I'm late again tonight." The shorter guy moved toward the door.

"Just shut the fuck up, Brandon." Tyler clenched his fists and stormed out. Goldie, Skull, and Kelly laughed.

"I'm so glad I'm not a teenager anymore. Those years were hell," Kelly said as she wiggled on the stool.

"You're not kidding," Skull said as he glanced at the door at two men who'd come in.

Soon Skull was in one of the rooms with one guy and Goldie was with the other. Thankful that his customer wanted a simple design, Goldie stood up and stretched forty-five minutes later while the man slipped on his shirt. "Remember to keep the bandage on until the morning. No sun for at least three weeks. Follow everything on this sheet of paper and you should be good. It you have problems or questions, give us a call." He handed the aftercare list to the customer and walked out of the room. The man paid Kelly and handed twenty to Goldie. "Appreciate it, man." The man nodded and walked out.

"Skull's still working on his guy. I've gotta pee." Kelly slid off the stool and scratched Goldie's back with her fingernails. "I like your muscles. They make me horny." She winked at him and leaned into him. "You wanna fool around?"

Her body was soft against him, and the scent of orange blossom invaded his nostrils. He wasn't fond of overbearing fragrances and many of the club girls bathed themselves in it. He stepped back. "I thought you had to pee."

"I do. Just thinking about when I get back." She squirmed in place then rushed to the bathroom at the end of the hall.

He watched her go. Normally he'd be all over it, but tonight he wasn't feeling it. He was restless and had been for a couple of months. What he was restless about he couldn't say, he just wanted something different from what he had. Of course, he had his pick of women, and he was the first to admit unabashedly that he was a player. What could he say? He loved women—all types of women. But for the past couple of months, he hadn't felt that energized when he'd been screwing the club girls. It'd begun to seem routine.

He half-sat on the stool and pulled out a copy of *Easyriders* and thumbed through it. As he was reading an article in the magazine, the door opened and loud giggling filled his ears. He looked up and saw three women, but the one in the middle made his blood pump. She kept covering her full pink lips with her hand as if to suppress her snigger. Her chestnut hair had blonde streaks in it as though the sun had kissed it, and it cascaded past her shoulders which were bare. Raising her eyes, she looked at him. Her eyes were seriously blue—field of cornflower, summer desert sky at noon. Perfect. Her hand dropped down to her side and her lips parted. Goldie watched every movement, wishing he could slip his tongue into her mouth for a quick taste.

"I really had to go." Kelly's voice broke through the intensity of the moment. The woman turned away, and her friend whispered something to her. A peal of laughter erupted from them. Kelly came behind the counter and he stood away from the stool. She settled herself onto it.

"Can I help you ladies?" he said. *I hope the she wants a clit piercing. I bet her pussy is as pink as her mouth.*

The two women next to her shoved her forward saying, "She wants a tattoo." They laughed. She shooed their hands away from her and shook her head. She looked at him again.

He groaned inwardly and his cock stirred as she skimmed the tip of her tongue over the contours of her upper lips, lips that were made for sinning. "Is it a yes or no?" He threw her the smile that melted most women's panties. She shrugged. "Have you been thinking about this for a while or did you have a couple of drinks and come over here?"

Laughter burst from all three of them and it made him grin more. *She's fucking sweet.* Kelly tapped her fingers on the counter. "Do you want a tat or not?" The women quieted down.

Anxious not to break their jovial mood, he turned to Kelly. "I'll handle this." She rolled her eyes then looked down at the magazine Goldie had on the counter.

"Hay's been thinking about it for a while. That's all she talks about," the dark-haired woman said.

"Especially when she's had a couple of white Russians," the other woman chimed in. That made them start laughing again.

Goldie moved in front of the counter. "Are you drunk?" His voice was low and gravelly.

She darted her eyes to his and their gazes locked on each other. The laughing hyenas, Kelly's aggravated sighs, the whir of the needles all faded out, and it was like there was nothing in the room but him and her. Heat stirred within him as his hungry gaze devoured the sight of her rounded hips and long shapely legs. Her cheeks burned brightly as she shifted in place.

"So are you?" he asked.

"Am I what?" she breathed.

His eyes climbed slowly from her pretty-sandaled feet to her bright red face. "Drunk?"

"Hay's not drunk, but we are," the dark-haired woman said in-between sniggers.

"So, Hay's getting the tattoo?" He locked gazes with her again. She nodded. "Where do you want it?"

"On her butt." Her friends giggled.

He raised his eyebrows. "Your friends seems to be doing all the talking. Is that where you want it?"

"Uh…yeah. I've been thinking about it for a while now. I'm also not drunk. I've had a couple of drinks but I'm good."

"Do you know what design you want?"

She nodded. "It's nothing too big or anything." She pointed to Kelly whose head was buried in the magazine. "Is she the one who's going to do the tattoo?"

He shook his head. "She's the receptionist. I'm going to do it." She gasped as her hand covered her pretty mouth. He chuckled. "You seem to have a problem with that."

"Oh, go on, Hay. I'm sure he's seen a lot of asses before. It's like a doctor. After a while asses and boobs all look alike." Her blonde-haired friend pushed her forward a bit.

"Stop it, Claudia. You and Rory are starting to get on my nerves."

*Mine too.* "You're not going to find a woman artist in Alina, or the county for that matter. If you go to a bigger city you'll find them there." *I bet she has a gorgeous ass.*

"Is it like Claudia said? I mean, you must do a ton of these. It's probably like no big deal."

He pressed his lips and ran his eyes over her face. "Yeah. I do a ton of these, but it's up to you. I don't want you to feel uncomfortable."

Snickering, she threw her shoulders back. "What the hell. Let's do it."

A celebration complete with horns and streamers broke out inside him. "Yeah. What the hell. Follow me."

# Other Books by Chiah Wilder

## Insurgent MC Series:

**Hawk's Property: Insurgents Motorcycle Club Book 1**
**Jax's Dilemma: Insurgents Motorcycle Club Book 2**
**Chas's Fervor: Insurgents Motorcycle Club Book 3**
**Axe's Fall: Insurgents Motorcycle Club Book 4**
**Banger's Ride: Insurgents Motorcycle Club Book 5**
**Jerry's Passion: Insurgents Motorcycle Club Book 6**
**Throttle's Seduction: Insurgents Motorcycle Club Book 7**
**Rock's Redemption: Insurgents Motorcycle Club Book 8**
**An Insurgent's Wedding: Insurgents Motorcycle Club Book 9**
**Insurgents MC Romance Series: Insurgents Motorcycle Club
Box Set (Books 1 – 4)**

## Night Rebels MC Series:

### STEEL
### MUERTO

Find all my books at: amazon.com/author/chiahwilder

I love hearing from my readers. You can email me at
chiahwilder@gmail.com.

Sign up for my newsletter to receive a FREE Novella, updates on new
books, special sales, free short stories, and ARC opportunities at
http://eepurl.com/bACCL1.

Visit me on facebook at
www.facebook.com/Chiah-Wilder-1625397261063989

Printed in Great Britain
by Amazon

19888353R20169